COMMODORE PERRY'S MINSTREL SHOW

COMMODORE PERRY'S

James A. Michener Fiction Series
James Magnuson, editor

MINSTREL SHOW

A Novel

BY RICHARD WILEY

UNIVERSITY OF TEXAS PRESS *Austin*

Requests for permission to reproduce material from this work should be sent to:
Permissions, University of Texas Press, P.O. Box 7819, Austin, TX 78713-7819.
www.utexas.edu/utpress/about/bpermission.html

∞ The paper used in this book meets the minimum requirements of ANSI/NISO
Z39.48-1992 (R1997) (Permanence of Paper).

LIBRARY OF CONGRESS CATALOGING-IN-PUBLICATION DATA

Wiley, Richard.
  Commodore Perry's minstrel show : a novel / by Richard Wiley. — 1st ed.
    p.   cm. — (James A. Michener fiction series)
  ISBN-13: 978-0-292-71470-0 (alk. paper)
  ISBN-10: 0-292-71470-X (alk. paper)
    1. Minstrels—Fiction. 2. Americans—Japan—Fiction. 3. United States Naval
Expedition to Japan (1852–1854)—Fiction. 4. Japan—Social life and customs—
1600–1868—Fiction. I. Title.
  PS3573.I433C66 2007
  813'.54—DC22   2006101821

For Pilar and Morgan

of whom I am most proud

Contents

PART THREE: SHIMODA

Cast of Characters

Ueno, Lord Abe's aide and enemy of the Okubo family

Lord Tokugawa Nariaki of Mito, a "collateral" lord of great influence,
Lord Abe's nemesis. No one from a "collateral" clan may ascend
to the position of Shogun.

Tokugawa *Keiki,* Lord Tokugawa's seventeen-year-old son, loyal friend
of Tsune, and, after the story ends, Japan's last Shogun

Kyuzo, a famous samurai in Lord Tokugawa's employ

Ichiro, a young samurai who comes under the influence of Kyuzo

Numbers 75 and 111, two members of Ueno's *ronin* samurai army,
hired by lottery

Momo and Manzo, cleaners of toilets

Who can be wise, amazed, temperate, and furious,
loyal and neutral, in a moment?   —*Macbeth*

"IT'S LIKE A CITY. Like more than one. It's like little cities near each other with nothing in between 'em but the dark," said Ned.

"There's water in between them," Ace pointed out, "and all manner of fish just under the surface, easy to catch. I do believe a man could scoop them up with his hands if he was quick enough. If you want to get a dinghy we could row out and give it a try right now."

Ned leaned way over the ship's railing and looked down, his face clouding up. "We'd get throttled twice for a trick like that," he said. "First by the fleet's high muckamucks and then by the Japanese. Neither one of 'em want us goin' where they can't keep an eye on us, Ace. How many times have we been told?"

He leaned out farther still, staring down at the black and silent sea. "I do wonder if they're strange tastin' though, them fish I can't quite see. It's another world under the ocean, Ace. Another world in Japan, too. Another world pretty much everywhere we ain't been."

Ace put his hands on Ned's shoulders, drawing him back until both his feet were firmly planted on the ship's planks once again. Both men stood at the port railing of the *Pohatan,* the flagship of the East India fleet, commanded by Commodore Matthew Perry. Seaward and across a short expanse of bay they could see the low-burning lanterns of the *Susquehanna* and the *Lexington,* two of the "little cities" Ned had been talking about. There were dots of liquid light from other American vessels, too, farther down the inlet, bobbing yellow like rays of fallen stars tangled up on buoys.

"Yessir, like houses across a dark prairie," Ned said, "like little homes away from home. It gives me the urge to get back where I belong, Ace. I hope we ain't here too long. There's surely another blue-eyed woman, waitin' somewhere to meet me."

He would not have been able to say it this way, but what Ned was after with the images he was making was an apt enough metaphor for Ace to want to pound into a lyric later on. Ned thought Ace had the rarest of gifts when it came to music, while Ace thought of music as a path to something else, to a calling that he couldn't quite hear yet. And when he only nodded, lost in those thoughts, Ned yawned and went below, for the wind was high by then and it was cold.

ONCE HE WAS FINALLY ALONE Ace held his right fist up, blocking out the lights from the *Susquehanna* and the *Lexington,* then extended the top two fingers of that fist, to block out the wan half moon, as well. He had, indeed, thought to write a song about this armada of American sailors, strung out across a vast and lonely world, some of them true naval men, some adventurers or solitary wanderers like himself. But the images Ned had made were obstacles to his imagination, not a help to it, so he soon gave up. He crossed to the ship's landward side, where the quality of light was duller, where dark Japan offered up images of its own. Now he could see parts of a village and more lights moving in the forested hills, as if men on horseback were carrying lanterns. Now again, in the dimmest possible way, quite as if a finger had scratched it on the velvet curtain of the night, he believed he could also see the paper doors of a farmhouse, mournful and low, a whole family of farmers sleeping behind them. Or perhaps awake and staring back at him, curiosity about the coming world pouring from their narrow eyes.

At eleven o'clock, sounded out in high-pitched eighth notes on the ship's triangle, Ace went astern to read in a book of essays that he prized above anything else and had brought on deck with him. But he found instead a group of sailors, sitting and listening to one of their number sing "Buford Holden," a ballad Ace had written for this current minstrel show they were about to perform for the Japanese. The sailor had a decent voice, and knew the lyrics well enough, but in other ways he got the song all wrong. "Buford Holden" was a freed slave who, while heading north on a railroad train, imagined the glory of the cities he would see, and how grandly he would be welcomed when he arrived in the free states. When Ace sang the song it was ironic, abolitionist to its

core, but the sailor seemed to miss the point entirely, lauding instead
the natural beauty of the American landscape.

So though Ace was intent on reading, he started singing along
behind the sailor, to try and correct the misconception of the song.

> Oh, what I'll find there I don't know,
> Wide boulevards? Big houses, all in a row?
> Or maybe I'll find myself on Commerce Street,
> Where the bosses will shake my hand.
> "Glad to have you, Buford," they'll say . . .

As he sang Ace could see Buford Holden's face reflected in the window of that northbound train.

"*Philadelphia!*" sang the sailor, quickly abdicating the main part to Ace. He became, instead, the conductor, passing through the third-class car, a man who by then had called out the names of so many cities that Buford had grown confused, forgetting even those he had previously memorized. Ace provided the litany of towns.

> Philadelphia, Pennsylvania? Philadelphia, New York?
> I used to know them all by heart so why not now?
> Baltimore, Ohio? Boston, Maine? New Bedford,
> That one I know!
> New Bedford's in Connecticut!
> Wide boulevards? Big houses, all in a row!

"Buford Holden" was a long song, a melodrama, really, that followed Buford into the heart of the same northern ambivalence that Ace had always felt. But there were several possible stopping places in the song and tonight, with his book still beckoning, Ace chose this one. The plaintive quality of his tenor voice left its own imprint on both the sailor and the night.

Ace went to the rail again, to calm himself before reading, but in the quiet that followed something caught his attention from shore. It wasn't singing, yet it had the depth and clarity of a good human voice.

"London, England! Paris, France!" it said. And after a while. *"Dutch, Amsterdam!"*

Far from growing calmer, Ace's heart swelled. So he sent his own voice back across the water in a kind of offering. *"Oh what I'll find there I don't know. Wide boulevards! Big houses, all in a row!"*

The sailor came in behind him, a half a second late and harmonizing with his eyes closed.

PART ONE
EDO

1. | *Dutch Learning*

"A GOVERNMENT ORCHESTRA . . . They've brought a bronze orchestra with a group of government musicians on board."

"They don't call it an orchestra," said Manjiro, patiently. "An orchestra must have stringed instruments that one plucks as one does a *shamisen* or *koto*. Also, what you see glowing in the sun isn't bronze, Einosuke, but brass. Think how heavy bronze would be. And no one, not even the Americans, could get it to shine that way."

"Brass. Bronze. What possible difference could it make? It wouldn't surprise me if these braggarts made their instruments out of solid gold. But I swear, Manjiro, I don't know how you remember such trivialities. What do you think we should do now, send out a barge full of *shaku-hachi* players to sail around them and educate their ears?"

"Their ears are educated, my brother," Manjiro said. "It's called 'Dutch Learning,' you know that. Don't make the mistake of underestimating these Americans. Their ears are educated, but in an entirely different way."

Manjiro, the younger of Lord Okubo of Odawara's two remaining sons—a firstborn had died some years ago—smiled at his older brother to cover the didactic nature of the speech he had made, but Einosuke was irritated and did not return the smile. He didn't need instruction from a brother who had spent the last five years of his life holed up in a Buddhist temple studying barbarian ways, from a brother who had surpassed him in the eyes of his government simply because he could speak a barbarian tongue. They had been arguing forever about "Dutch Learning," which to them meant anything that had not originated in China or Japan, but recently their arguments had grown harsher. Einosuke believed Manjiro to be in favor of everything foreign, disdainful of anything traditionally Japanese, and sometimes, though Einosuke's arguments always equaled Manjiro's in energy and skill, he imagined himself and his opinions as artifacts heaped upon a wagon, his brother the horse that would pull that wagon to the refuge depository! Harmony, Shinto rituals, the purity and beauty of the Japanese race itself—who knew what his brother might want to jeopardize next, or what foreign novelty he might embrace?

"Please, Manjiro, do me the favor of standing here silently for a moment and just looking at these ships, enjoying the day," he finally said. "I heard this morning that the points of the treaty are nearly ironed out. That means that you and Lord Abe will be boarding one of these vessels soon, forced to smile into foreign faces and listen to that bronze band. So why not give us a minute of peace, as a favor to your older brother, before all the real trouble begins?"

Manjiro pursed his lips and nodded. He said the word "brass" again, but was careful to utter it silently, quietly kissing with it the bright March air.

EINOSUKE'S WIFE, who went by the name of Fumiko, was at the seaside also, along with their two daughters and their infant son, Junichiro. Manjiro loved his brother's children, and was devoted to his brother's wife, the eldest child of a chief retainer of the daimyo from Mito, a vastly larger and more powerful clan than that of Einosuke and Manjiro's father, Lord Okubo. Fumiko was well educated for a woman, and he secretly believed she shared his political opinions because they shared the same birthday, she was precisely Manjiro's age. She was beautiful, though the blackened teeth of a married woman, a tradition he disdained above most others, sometimes made her beauty seem distant now, and not only could she expertly use the tools of dignity and decorum, but she had a good sense of humor and fun. She kept Einosuke's heart light when its natural inclination was to sink in his chest, and she had managed to raise his daughters so that, at seventeen and twelve years old, they were good at learning, but had also retained an unbridled sense of childlike delight, even, most of the time, the elder one. Manjiro believed, in fact, that though Einosuke's political opinions were perfectly wrong, he had a perfect family. And now that the baby was born, now that his brother had a son, he could tell that Einosuke believed so, also.

It was cold that morning, but the sun was bright, so Fumiko and the girls walked under umbrellas, as if it were summertime. Fumiko had taken the baby out of his wrap and was letting Keiko, her seventeen-year-old daughter, hold him. It was her younger daughter's job to keep the umbrella positioned over the baby's head so that no direct sunlight shone into his eyes. This younger daughter's name was Masako, and when they reached the two brothers, Keiko was scolding her for doing a bad job.

"Masako is so infuriating!" she told her father and uncle. "She's moving the umbrella on purpose, trying to make him squint and cry so she can say it is my style of holding him, my way of walking that's done it, and carry him herself. She's tricky, father, and so obvious about it. You just wait, our baby brother's eyes will be permanently damaged if Masako has her way!"

Keiko was like her father in that she had a forthright mind and an argumentative style, but spending too much time with Masako often made her forget her age. Of course Masako was guilty of moving the umbrella, everyone knew it, but she very calmly lied. "I am holding this umbrella properly and walking at a steady pace," she said. "Keiko is whimsical lately, she's thinking too much, that's the problem. She stops suddenly and tries to show him the American ships, which is ridiculous since he can't even see the bay. Keiko shouldn't be worried about the ships but should be walking properly and looking at the ground. She cares nothing for our brother's eyes, but only wants to show herself off. She's becoming worldly, father. I can't be the only one who has noticed it, any fool can see the signs."

If it could be avoided no one in the family ever wanted to argue with Masako, who used passion as if it were logic, and threw words around as if they were skipping stones. Masako would never quit, so their mother simply said, "Be quiet girls. At least while we're with your uncle, at least during our remaining time in Edo, let's try to have him think us well behaved. We don't want him to tell the Americans that we squabble all the time."

"Mother's right, Masako," said Keiko, "we mustn't let the truth get out. But wait, maybe we can use you as a weapon against the Americans. If they knew about your squabbling that would put an end to all these negotiations. If they heard about you they would turn their ships around and go home."

Masako handed the umbrella to her mother and squeezed in between her uncle and her father. "Tell her the medical truth, uncle," she said. "Tell her what awful things the sun can do to a baby's eyes."

She took a breath to start again but her father put his arm around her and cupped her chin and jaw. Keiko saw him do it and said, "Part of a father's job is quieting a mouth that will not quiet itself." But speaking again had been a tactical error, and because of it she was forced to hand the baby back to her mother and go stand by her uncle on his other side.

————

IT WAS TRUE that Einosuke and Manjiro had fought over what Japan should do about the Americans, they had argued about politics in general all their lives, but they were close and affectionate brothers in other ways. Einosuke was forty-one, Manjiro thirty-four, and as they strolled away from the shoreline, his daughters' argument somehow made Einosuke remember carrying Manjiro through another sunny spring, just as Keiko had carried his son today. It was in such ways, by honoring the elder daughter with the right to carry her baby brother before the younger one got the privilege, it was through such traditions as these that strong family bonds continued, that parents could give their children the opportunity to experience true responsibility and a sustained sense of joy. Einosuke didn't know what would happen when the Americans came, but he believed with all his heart that the world as they knew it would be irreparably changed, and was bereaved by the additional belief that Manjiro wanted it that way.

Einosuke's house was in a convenient area of Edo, not far from the castle where the Great Council met. For a decade Lord Okubo had leased the house, and last year he had finally bought it and invested in an expansion of its garden and in shoring up its foundation and cracked front wall. The house was still too small, especially now that Junichiro was born, and there were workmen coming daily, repairing the bath and kitchen, even at this most awkward time. Not only that but as soon as the family left for Odawara an entire second wing would be built.

O-bata, their troublesome maid, met them in the entryway. She took the baby and bowed and waited until the adults, Keiko included, had passed into the garden room, before hurriedly pulling Masako aside.

"Well?" she demanded. "Did you see them? Did you see the American ships? The maid next door saw them yesterday and said that carved on the side of each one is the image of a foreigner's face! That can't be true, can it? Tell me, Masako, did you see such a thing?"

"They are big and ugly and stupid," said Masako. "They are dark and looming, all eight of them, and it seems to me that if you tried to make them move they would not go fast. But if they've got faces on their sides, they're not as ugly as the one on the maid next door."

O-bata threw her hands to her mouth but laughter came out anyway, jiggling her breasts and snorting between her fingers, like the steam from one of the foreign ships. Masako was becoming rude these days! "Oh, Masako," she said, "I pity the man who marries you! When the investigators come I hope they don't ask the opinion of the maid next door!" She laughed again, then waited until Masako left before picking up Junichiro and slipping back outside. She was in love with the local fish seller's son, and, even under threat of firing, would not leave the young man alone.

The others had walked through the house, stepping over workmen's tools, to settle into a long tatami room that overlooked the newly finished rock garden in the back. This room was warm in winter yet in summer it was shaded, and when the doors were opened the garden seemed to come up into it, making it a favorite of everyone. It had been Einosuke's idea to add the room first, before any of the other new construction, and his idea, also, that the rock garden below it should be a smaller but otherwise precise replica of the one at Ryoanji Temple in Kyoto. Einosuke had not admitted that he wanted the garden for reasons other than aesthetic ones, but in fact it had been while viewing the original garden that he had finally found the resolve to change his life. Until that day, eighteen years ago now, he had been a carouser and a gambler and a regular visitor to pleasure quarters everywhere.

"It is difficult to judge his speed of travel," Einosuke said, "but I think father will be here sometime tomorrow."

"Father will travel slowly," said Manjiro. "He will bear his colors high."

There was something in that statement that both brothers recognized as true and false at the same time. Lord Okubo would indeed travel slowly, but not so much out of a sense of regal passage as because he abhorred coming to Edo. He was following the Shogun's decree, coming for his year of duty, but he didn't like the expense of it, nor did he want to hurry into the political turmoil that awaited him. Einosuke, on the other hand, was fond of Edo and did not look forward to returning to Odawara, even for the few months it would take to get the Edo house remodeled. He and his family had stayed in Edo for a decade, only occasionally visiting Odawara, and he was miffed that his father insisted upon their return to the countryside. His father had often said that Einosuke should return to Odawara in order to better learn how to run the estates once he became lord, but Einosuke suspected it was merely that his father wanted to be in Edo without him, to deal with the edicts concerning behavior toward foreigners without his counsel.

The brothers looked at each other with rueful smiles. Once again their time alone together had been short. They both knew that their father's arrival would reconfigure things, making their relationship unrecognizable compared to what it was now. Unlike Manjiro's earlier visits, though, which might have been too short but had been harmonious, this time the brothers had shouted and argued bitterly every night. It was for that reason that Fumiko felt it important that there be no arguing on this, the last solitary evening they would have. She believed that harmony at the end of a visit was more important than harmony in its middle. She had instructed her daughters in the matter, but when Masako joined them in the garden room she was still under the influence of O-bata, and her words came out wrong.

"Think of it," she said. "By the time our fat little brother is grown up there will be foreigners everywhere. Even when we move back to Grandpa's castle we will probably have foreigners living right next door."

Manjiro reached up and pulled his niece down next to him as she spoke. Whenever he was around these girls what he longed for most was not intercourse with the outside world but marriage and constancy, a family of his own. He hoped, in fact, that he might quite soon find both. "Your father and I discuss such things only so that we can make them clear," he said.

When Einosuke heard that he knew it was his responsibility, more than his brother's, to regret their long hours of discord. But when he tried to do it, to agree with Manjiro at least that far, he found he couldn't do it well. He admired Manjiro greatly, but at the same moment was angry with him, not because Manjiro held opinions of his own, but because he could not see the need for a united family view. In earlier days, when his role had been subordinate, he would not have dared speak to senior family members the way Manjiro seemed to have no trouble speaking to him now.

"If you are eating in tonight I must send O-bata out to buy fresh fish," Fumiko finally said. "Are you eating in or are you eating out?"

There was a kind of code in this, a reminder delivered from wife to husband, not concerning Manjiro this time, but concerning O-bata, the maid, and the fish seller's son. Fumiko nearly dismissed her earlier but had lately relented, just the night before allowing O-bata to deliver her farewells to the boy in person, before going to Odawara with the family.

"Oh, we must eat in," Einosuke told his wife, "but Manjiro and I will buy the fish ourselves. That way we may speak together without the family spies."

Once outside, however, Einosuke and Manjiro argued about the Americans again, standing next to each other in the frigid night.

They were an hour late for dinner, everyone was upset, and when their father arrived the next day he, too, immediately started arguing, even before he had unpacked his bags.

2. *Oh, What I'll Find There I Don't Know*

THE FIRST SURPRISE was that the deck felt smooth under Manjiro's feet; familiar, like standing on planks of Japanese cypress, in a temple or in a bath or in someone's finely made entryway.

The American sailors stood silent but bug-eyed, oddly dressed and chopstick straight, backs against the far railing, while the Japanese contingent of eleven walked by. For each of the eight great lords a high-ranking American naval officer acted as escort, but for Manjiro and the Dutch-speaking interpreter there was no one, and there was only a mid-level officer for Ueno, Lord Abe's surly and ubiquitous aide, who earlier that afternoon had referred to Manjiro as a "toad." The interpreters were last to go in, so Manjiro took the opportunity to look into the nearby sailors' faces. It was a violation of protocol but impossible not to do so, and it was instructive as well. The American faces were strange—had not his brother always said so?—but they were also well kempt and contained, not like the ruinous and combative face of Ueno.

Below deck, in a hallway brightly lit with lanterns, Manjiro took his place at the front, directly behind Lord Abe and his aide. He bent over, nearly touching the great lord's shoulder with his nose as he tried to make himself small. Lord Abe, however, felt him there and said without turning, "Ah yes, I know your father, don't I? He is in Edo now, is he not? Come up to help cast these barbarians from our land?"

"Yes, sir," said Manjiro, bowing farther down. Lord Abe's short stature often made him do so, so that his physical proximity to the lord might equal his social one.

"You really do speak English, I hope. It's not just hearsay, is it, not just a rumor that got out of hand, but something I can actually count on?"

If asked that question under normal circumstances, say, in a Great Council antechamber or in a riverside geisha house, custom would require Manjiro to answer that his English was poor. But he knew the great lord would have no patience with such self-deprecation now. "I have had the honor of learning it well," he answered, "but I fear there will be words I don't know, idioms, expressions whose meaning cannot be deduced by taking them apart."

"Oh well, there are words I don't know in Japanese," said Lord Abe, moving a hand up as if to push Manjiro's mouth a few inches farther away, "but let me hear you speak this English of yours before we go inside. It will calm my nerves. Say something to this gangling oddity standing here next to me. Don't just greet him, but compliment him. Tell him he's handsome. . . . Let's see, tell him he is handsome and ask him if all Americans are so tall."

Manjiro had prepared for the difficulty of political speech, working hard on vocabulary these past few weeks. He would have been readier to make such trivial comments up on deck, to one of the sailors whose rank was low, but the "gangling oddity" now in question was a dignified-looking man with medals on his uniform and graying hair. And because he had been given the honor of escorting Lord Abe himself into the banquet room, his rank, perforce, could only be high. These cautions came to Manjiro in a split second. Of course he could neither question Lord Abe's choice of phrases, nor allow his own opinions any further rein. Already he had waited too long.

"You are handsome and tall," he told the man. "Lord Abe asks if all Americans are like you."

The officer was startled, but said, "Oh no, nothing like me, most of the time. By that I mean that at six foot three I am particularly tall, so much so that my wife can always spot me in a crowd. As to handsome; handsome is as handsome does, my wife always says."

Manjiro's face fell but he caught it quickly and put it back up. He knew American measurements and had otherwise understood the words well enough, but just as he'd feared, he had little idea what was meant by them when put together that way.

"I think he's speaking in dialect," he told Lord Abe, "but he says that he is unusually tall and that he's got a wife and that his wife is the only one in America who thinks him handsome."

"That's pretty well spoken," said the lord, not to Manjiro but to Ueno, his aide. "I wouldn't mind engaging these tyrants, you know, getting to know them better, if we were on their land instead of ours. But look, we're going in now." He turned back to Manjiro. "Stay beside me and keep your ears open. The official language of these proceedings is Dutch, of course, so I want you to focus on what is spoken casually. If you hear deceit, note it and tell me later. Can you do it, young man?"

Manjiro said he would do his best, and when the banquet-room doors opened, sliding on rollers into the ship's wall, the Japanese lords got the elegant greeting most of them had expected a few minutes earlier on the deck. Though the light in the hallway had been bright, now they were faced with such brilliance that Manjiro thought it was like going outside in the morning and looking directly into the sun. The very plates on the banquet table were gold-rimmed—surely not brass or bronze—the utensils beside them were gold, and shining silver medals so decorated the chests of the waiting officers that they seemed like nothing less than the shimmering bellies of fish in a bowl. Manjiro didn't know whether to think it garish or fine. And he had just glanced at Lord Abe, to see how the great man was taking it, when English came from the mouth of the one man whose uniform was unadorned.

"How long we have waited for this day!" said Commodore Perry, smiling and extending his arms. "You are welcome, gentlemen. Come in, we don't stand on ceremony here! Be casual, stand at ease! This is not a time for protocol!"

The Commodore's exuberance was dulled by the lengthy process of translating his words from English into Dutch and then into Japanese, but Lord Abe waited until the job was done before simply thanking the Commodore on behalf of everyone. There had been posters depicting the threat of foreign attack all over Edo lately, some serious, some comic, and now that Manjiro had his first close-up look at them he marveled at the accuracy with which the artists had caught the angular lines of the American face, the high noses and deep-set eyes; especially those of Commodore Perry.

"Well sit down, ease yourselves, my friends!" said the Commodore. "This, after everything else, is a time to relax, to let our hair down! How hard we've all worked to get even this far!"

As per earlier Japanese instructions there were eight guest chairs, with stools for the interpreters and Lord Abe's aide. Commodore Perry's banquet table seemed inordinately high, as if designed to embarrass the shorter visitors, and roughly formed a horseshoe with Americans sitting along both sides and the Japanese in the middle, closest to the door. Manjiro waited for Lord Abe to balance himself on his chair, then sat down himself, adjusted his *hakama,* whose long skirt was too stiff to tuck around his stool. He stretched, trying to make himself tall. The great lord's aide, the mean-spirited Ueno, sat on Lord Abe's other side and glared at Manjiro, for he was too low to give his usual, biting advice.

Commodore Perry spoke for a long time and seemed to leap after topics of conversation quite as a collector might leap after butterflies. "The weather!" he said. "Is it always so mild here during the early spring? My, my, and the wind is such that it warms an old sailor's heart! I must admit, I expected the north Pacific to blow us around much more than it has. But maybe it's just luck, maybe it won't hold. Is it unusual to have such fine weather this time of year, or do I detect a hint of approaching rain?"

Manjiro hated Dutch. His tutor had disliked it also, comparing it to vocalized lumps of coal, but what he hated most was the way the Great Council used it as a thick and cumbersome tool, an ugly tunnel through which good-sounding English was brought into normal Japanese. Part of what he felt was jealousy, maybe, since his skill was in English, but he also felt that if he were the primary translator there would have been a lively exchange from the beginning—something of the kind that poor Commodore Perry was trying to put forth—not this constipated, thick-tongued, dull concoction of ugliness that the lords were forced to hear now.

"Ah, yes," came Lord Abe's slow reply. "It is no longer winter but nearly cherry blossom time. Is it unseasonable? I think you are right about the coming rain. But we will make you a gift of a few cherry trees before you go home. I mean, of course, if they are fine this year, if we have good trees to offer by the time you leave our shore."

"That would be most kind," the Commodore said, after Lord Abe's words had gone through Dutch and come out constrained. "And let me say something personal. I love the material I see on everyone, the cloth that makes up your extraordinary kimonos. I have written in my diary that we in America can learn a thing or two from you about formal dress, and perhaps about textiles in general."

"I will make you a gift, a gift," Lord Abe repeated, this time about either cloth or kimonos, but even when someone said something simple, as the two leaders tried to do several more times, the translations were slow and, to Manjiro's mind, often slightly wrong as well. Even Manjiro knew that Dutch, because of its neutrality, and because there were some few dozen Japanese who could speak it, had been useful when negotiating the treaty, but here tonight, once the wine was poured and the toasts were given, both sides grew quiet, defeated by the Dutch just as surely as much of the world had once been, finally letting the room's only chatter come from the gold forks and spoons as they came down softly to speak in murmurs to the golden plates.

Though in truth, as much as anything, it was a monument to the Japanese inability to be informal, it seemed to Manjiro that the central part of the meal was over in no time, not only because he had no food himself and had therefore been daydreaming, drifting back to earlier arguments with his brother, but also because when the eight lords saw how quickly the Americans ate they tried to match them, plunging heedlessly forward, stabbing at the great chunks of meat with their forks. They hunted them down, threw them into their mouths, closed their eyes and swallowed and reached their hands out for wine. It was like a comic scene from Kabuki, and though Lord Abe was their leader in everything else, in this speedy eating ritual his physical coordination did not nearly equal his rank. Meat fell into his lap and bright orange lengths of carrot bounced onto the floor beside Manjiro, long and thick as severed American thumbs.

"Everyone's drunk and this thing is impossible to handle," Lord Abe whispered, showing Manjiro his fork. "Hide those damned carrots and sit up high enough to get the waiter's attention. Tell him to pour me more wine. Have you noticed that the Americans serve only themselves after the first cup or two? They serve themselves and not their neighbors! That is the first line of barbarism, don't you think, not tending properly to another man's cup of wine?"

That comment not only meant that Lord Abe himself was getting drunk, but that Manjiro now had to concentrate. And at just that moment, just as he corralled the carrots and swept them out of sight beneath his stool, Commodore Perry stood again and walked around the table to the center of the horseshoe, directly in front of the exhausted and panting lords. This time his voice was less exclamatory, as if all that quick eating had taken some of his energy away, too.

"In America we believe in treating guests properly, in feeding them and making them comfortable," he said, "so tonight there will be no more speechifying, nothing in the way of politics, no more epistles from the president to read, and no more talk from me about this grand and historic moment. Instead, we have arranged a small entertainment, an amateur effort to be sure, but one prepared in earnest, through the sweat and labor of a few good members of our crew."

As he spoke his smile grew wider, and when Lord Abe finally heard the words he, too, tried to smile. He turned to Manjiro and said, "Tell him this in English. Say that a country's true heart can best be judged through the endeavors of its amateurs. Tell him also that in that same spirit of amateurism, even a country's leaders, whether traveling the world or sitting at home, should not be afraid to open their mouths and sing."

Lord Abe was sure of his own good singing voice and pulled Manjiro forward by his sleeve, but Manjiro had only begun to work the phrases into English when Commodore Perry strode back across the room and slapped the wall with his palm, raising a deep and hollow echo. The wall buckled into itself, as the Japanese now saw it was designed to do, and from the widening rectangle came two bizarre-looking creatures, the sight of whom made most of the Japanese lords stand out of their chairs. They were men, these creatures, that much was clear because they were clothed, but otherwise they looked more like Sarutahiko, the monkey god, might look were he to suddenly climb out of a vat of steaming black bean paste. Their faces and arms were covered with the darkest stains and their knees seemed to come up to stab at their chins, while at the same time their hands were busy banging those knees back down. And against this dark tragedy of cindered skin their eyes and the palms of their hands were as white as bleached whale bone. Commodore Perry had called this an entertainment but it seemed to the visitors, even as the creatures grinned and shook their shoulders and pranced into the center of the room, like nothing short of a visitation by messengers from the tar pits of hell.

Music was coming from somewhere, but not until the monkey gods stopped directly in front of Lord Abe did Manjiro understand that their high-stepping dance was connected to that music, that there was a fiendish kind of syncopation going on.

"Mr. Bones?" said one of the monkeys. *"Did you hear the news? I'm goin' north on the railroad train."*

"Why no, Mr. Buford, I didn't know, how'd you do it, I say, how'd you do it? How'd you get away?"

Lord Abe had recovered enough to look wide-eyed at Manjiro, clearly expecting a translation, but all Manjiro could find to mutter was, "The thin one will go north, the other is surprised."

"How'd I get de masta to let me go? Is that what yo askin' Mr. B.? Why, he's dead, that's how. Didn't you know it, I say, didn't you know? He's dead and set me free in his will!"

Now the first monkey sang, *"All aboard, all aboard, train's pullin' out. Sit by the window, I say, sit right now."*

"They are repeating themselves," said a desperate Manjiro. "And the first one is telling the second to sit down."

But as if to call his translation into question, the second one did not sit down. Rather, both monkeys ran around the room again, somehow coming back with big black hoops in their hands, spinning black circles with torn pieces of white cloth hanging loosely down.

"Woo woo, chug chug, woo woo," said the thin one.

Lord Abe stood still, completely captured by the sight. The spinning pieces of cloth allowed him to peer through the nearest wheel as if into some kind of carriage, and into the eyes of the nearest man as well.

"All aboard," the first monkey yelled, and to the whirling confusion they added a kind of bucking back and forth that somehow made them seem to be moving forward though in fact they didn't go anywhere at all. It was an interesting illusion, and when the music suddenly stopped and the monkeys also quit making noise, the nearest one started singing.

"Got my papers in my pocket and I'm headin' north."

His voice was surprisingly good. "Excellent," Lord Abe told his aide, and while the other monkey started whispering, *"Big mistake,"* he continued his song.

Oh, what I'll find there I don't know,
Wide boulevards? Big houses all in a row?
Or maybe I'll find myself on Commerce Street,
Where the bosses will shake my hand,
"Glad to have you, Buford," they'll say.

Now the second monkey alternately whispered, *"Big mistake, no mistake, big mistake, no mistake,"* with such a fine and worried rhythm that Manjiro's face lit up. "He feels unsure!" he said, too loudly. "Unsure about whether to go or stay! And the other man's voice is meant to represent his second thoughts!"

"But this is wonderful," said Lord Abe. "The singing is masterful, the sense of movement convincing and strange."

Philadelphia, Pennsylvania? Philadelphia, New York?
I used to know them all by heart so why not now?
Baltimore, Ohio? Boston, Maine? New Bedford,
That one I know!
New Bedford's in Connecticut!
Wide boulevards? Big houses, all in a row!

At the song's end both monkeys repeated the last line, but with diminishing volume, as the train, moving in place for so long, finally began to move for real, chugging past the astonished lords, around the happy Americans, and back through that hole in the wall. *"Woo woo, chug chug, woo woo,"* they sang, before four white hands from the other side pulled the doors closed.

"Absolutely marvelous!" said Lord Abe, looking around at the other lords. "Was that not astounding? Amateurs indeed! That is the oddest and most wonderful entertainment I have ever seen!"

He had more to say on the matter, an unfolding revelation, Manjiro was sure, on the nature of surprise and the sudden discovery of pure delight, but before he could find the words, before he could begin to collect himself, Commodore Perry rang a small bell, smiled and bowed, and said that the evening was over, that the launches were at ship side, ready to take his guests ashore.

After the transcendent strangeness of the show it seemed an abrupt and dissatisfying ending, but as Manjiro stood behind Lord Abe, and Ueno steadied him with discreetly placed fingers, things were brought into focus again by the introduction of Commodore Perry's last surprise. The eight attendant American officers came forward with gifts, one each for the eight Great Council lords, and the two monkeys, the entertainers, sweating through their blackened faces and smiling like sharks, came back into the room again with similar packages for the interpreters. This was uncalled for, this was not the time for a gift exchange, but when one of the monkeys approached him Manjiro could only extend his hands and let the gift come into them, and bow.

"I got these chocolates for you," said the monkey, "an after-dinner treat." Then he said, "You might not know it from what you heard just now, but ours is an abolitionist show. It's meant to be taken with a healthy dose of irony, and I always worry that it might not be taken that way."

Manjiro did not know what to do. Could he speak English to this man who had been the main monkey, the best singer, without an express order from Lord Abe? He had taken the box because, from the corner of his eye, he saw the Dutch interpreter do likewise, and had quickly noticed, even in his confused state, that the box was not clean. There was a black mark on it, a grease-paint smudge on its side. The monkey saw it too and pulled out a corner of his shirt to dab the smudge away, but for reasons unclear to him Manjiro put the gift behind his back.

"Thank you for your performance," he said. "Your voice . . . Your singing. Lord Abe very much liked the sound."

The monkey seemed about to say more, and then he stared at Manjiro as if expecting more from him, but Manjiro only rushed to find his place behind Lord Abe, where he finally noticed, as the Japanese dignitaries held their gifts in front of them, that the furious aide, Ueno, had got no gift at all.

That pleased him more than it should have, but he managed not to smile.

3. | *Accident upon Accident*

"I PROMISE I will wake you when she comes," Keiko told her sister. "That is my job as elder daughter. Your job is to go to sleep immediately. It's already late so hurry up. Do it and don't pretend! I'm watching you! Go to sleep like you always do, with your mouth wide open and your tongue sticking out."

Only when she was exhausted did Keiko speak like Masako, so as Fumiko listened to her daughter she learned that Keiko was the one who would be asleep in no time. It was, after all, nearly midnight and they had all been up since dawn. Fumiko herself had spent much of the day preparing for the move back to Odawara, not exactly packing, but stepping around the workers and instructing O-bata about which items would go and which would be stored in the closets of the house. And she had spent the rest of her time out in Einosuke's garden, not actually raking it, since that was her husband's only relaxation and greatest joy, but doing the difficult work of preparing the garden for raking, of reaching in among the boulders and snatching away the leaves and debris. There was a stand of deciduous maples in the next-door neighbor's garden, an unruly hybrid that irritated Fumiko because it seemed to lose its foliage all year long. Even now, though it was late March, those soggy leaves were as much a disruption of nature's ways, it seemed to her, as the American ships were of society's.

"I have an idea," she told her daughters, so tired herself that she could barely keep her eyes open. "Why not ask O-bata to bring our bedding downstairs? That way no matter who falls asleep first we will all be sure to awaken when she comes. Remember, your auntie never arrives quietly, no matter what the time of day."

"O-bata is sleeping with the baby," said Masako. "And all the futon are already spread out upstairs. There will be six of us in the eight-mat room, you know, because Aunt Tsune's usual room is now taken over by Grandfather."

Keiko's eyes had closed during Masako's speech. She had slumped back in order to rest her head on the edge of the *tokunoma,* and had rolled onto her side, her hands tucked between her knees. But she was not asleep. She had only escaped into her thoughts, wondering how long her favorite aunt might stay and whether there might be an actual marriage arrangement, an *O-miai,* between Tsune and her Uncle Manjiro. Oh, she wanted it so much! And so, indeed, did her uncle, she could easily tell.

Fumiko watched the rise and fall of Keiko's breasts and the composure of her face, the fine structure of the bones beneath a beauty so deeply born that it refused to leave even when the muscles that held it in place flattened out into a kind of sleep of their own. She sighed and reached over to touch the flower arrangement beyond her daughter's head, to assure herself that it was still steady on its base. This was a new arrangement of bare branches that she had done just yesterday and of which she was inordinately proud. It was a proper representation of how she often felt.

"Masako dear," she whispered, "don't you think you should sleep, too? Auntie may not come for hours and no matter how little sleep you get I'm waking you both up early. You can't skip your lessons tomorrow."

Masako yawned but shook her head. "Not me," she said. "I'm not like Keiko. I can stay up all night long."

Because Tsune and Fumiko's father was Lord Tokugawa's chief retainer, Tsune had been invited to come to Edo from Mito with Lord Tokugawa himself, in order to attend the treaty-signing ceremony which was scheduled for the thirty-first of March. It had been unclear, at first, whether or not Lord Tokugawa would attend, since he was no longer in government yet remained Lord Abe's main competitor—so Tsune's own decision to travel had also come late. She had stayed the first nights in Lord Tokugawa's hunting lodge, way across town, but had sent word that she would come to her sister's house today, in plenty of time for Keiko's dance recital and—somewhat grudgingly?—to be reintroduced to Manjiro. The girls had been waiting since noon but Fumiko knew that her sister was unreliable. She might come tonight or she might come tomorrow. It was even possible, though she would never miss the dance recital, that she might balk at such casual talk of marriage and not come to the house at all.

"I hear her!" shouted Masako, chasing her mother's thoughts away.

She and her mother both jumped up, but were disappointed when the voices that answered their calls were male.

"Oh, it's not Aunt Tsune but Grandpa and Daddy and Uncle Manjiro," said Masako. "I hate it if I'm still awake when they come home."

This final disappointment made her give up her vigil. She bent down and pulled on her sister until Keiko, too, struggled to her feet, rubbing her eyes. And before the men came into the house, both girls had climbed the stairs to bed.

"Welcome," said Fumiko, stepping out to the entryway. She liked her father-in-law, who had arrived two days before, and tried to hide her own disappointment that he was not her sister standing there.

"They were late in breaking up," Einosuke explained. "In times of crisis everyone likes to hear the sound of his own voice."

He was talking about a Great Council meeting that their father could attend but that he and Manjiro could not. Because the brothers had waited in a bar for the meeting to end, Einosuke's face was flushed from drink, but his mood was good. No doubt his father had endorsed his point of view while deploring Manjiro's. Everyone now seemed to think that Japan had no choice but to show a reasonable face, that she should hear the American demands with a polite ear, agree to give shipwrecked American sailors safe harbor, for example, but otherwise ask for a year or two to think about trade, which was the true purpose of the American sojourn, and build up her navy in the meantime. Hardly anyone, save the likes of Manjiro, believed in absolute engagement with the outside world, except with the Dutch who were confined to Nagasaki, and there were not many left, either, who thought that the time was right for outright war. Moderation had won the day, and, far more than drink, moderation was the tonic that calmed Einosuke.

"Ah, my daughter-in-law, I am tired," said Lord Okubo, when Fumiko asked him if he would like some tea and rice. "I never sleep well my first few nights in Edo, and the meeting really was excessively long."

When Fumiko looked at the brothers she could see that they were as tired as she was, as tired as their father. She could have sent them to bed in an instant, but instead she surprised them by asking, "Do you suppose they worry so much about Japan in America? When Americans think of us do you suppose they wring their hands?"

Lord Okubo was ready to climb the stairs, but the unexpected wistfulness of his daughter-in-law's remark, on her mind since she'd made her austere flower arrangement yesterday, stopped his foot in midair. Manjiro thought it was an excellent question, but because he had now become central to everything, he could no longer easily say so. And Einosuke always waited to hear what his father would say.

When Lord Okubo only grunted and continued up to bed, however, Fumiko followed him. She knelt and waited while he stepped behind a screen to prepare himself. She could see his futon in the center of the room, a small pillow at the top of it, one side hard, one side soft, much like her father-in-law himself. When he came back out she bowed until her forehead touched the tatami and the grassy smell of the mats entered her nose. And when she sat up again Lord Okubo, reposed now on the darkened floor, kept her another moment by reciting a favorite poem.

Accident upon
accident, that's what life is,
as it wends its way.

He made no movement after he spoke, but when Fumiko left the room he put a hand up to test the muscles of his jaw. This was his nightly habit, formed to reassure himself of his continued strength as he grew old.

4. *Whitman Sampler*

MANJIRO HAD NOT TOLD anyone about the chocolates, but on an extraordinary whim he brought them out and gave them to Fumiko's sister, Tsune, shortly after her arrival early the next morning.

Manjiro had met this sister twice before, first many years ago at Einosuke and Fumiko's wedding, and once more during a family cherry blossom viewing excursion to Kyoto. They hadn't spoken at the wedding, but in Kyoto they sat together at the edge of the wooden walkway that bordered the rock garden at Ryoanji Temple, while Einosuke sketched it, even then preparing his replica. Tsune was younger than her sister by some half dozen years, but even then it was clear she would become the true family beauty, not only exquisite of face and form, but in possession of a poise and bearing surpassing even those of Fumiko.

Because Manjiro had not known what to do with the chocolates he had hidden them in his father's room, behind a screen and beneath a window that was kept open at night to accommodate Lord Okubo's love of cold air. He had been afraid to speak of the unexpected gift before Tsune arrived, for neither Lord Okubo nor Einosuke had visited a foreign vessel yet, and he knew they would be angry with him for accepting the gift at all. But the presence of Tsune gave him some latitude. Until quite recently everyone had said she was destined to marry high, an opinion that, by bestowing a foreign gift like this, Manjiro, rather than promoting his own vague hopes, oddly seemed to magnify.

"I know you remember our meeting in Kyoto, Manjiro-san," Tsune said. She had taken the chocolate box from him and placed it on the tatami. "I know you remember the occasion, but do you remember our conversation? I do. I remember what we talked about that day, but I think you do not."

In fact Manjiro remembered every second of his time with Tsune, not only what they had said, but that he had hoped against hope that when they got older there might be a marriage arrangement for them.

Einosuke had talked with him about it once or twice several years ago, but with the advancing wealth and stature of Tsune's clan, the possibility had grown slight. So Manjiro's tendency was to dismiss this small resumption of such talk now, wondering only what had changed to once again make him a more likely candidate. That Einosuke had successfully married her sister meant little because Einosuke was Lord Okubo's eldest son and heir.

"We spoke of lots of things," he said, "and I remember them all. What seems ironic now is that for a while we tried to guess what people in foreign countries might be like. I remember that your interest was as keen as my own."

He was ashamed of it, but Manjiro wanted to work the conversation around to his time aboard the foreign ship, so that he might tell Tsune about his private conversation with that strange and black-faced entertainer. And since he had not been able to do it with the chocolates, he was now trying to use the past.

"Ah, then you do remember," she said. "You bragged that you would travel, that you would subdue foreign enemies and one day know the world. I did not believe you then, but how proud we all are now."

Manjiro reddened and looked down. By speaking so directly wasn't she saying that his maneuver had been too obvious, that he was too brazenly asking for the compliment he had received? She gazed at him steadily, and just then Lord Okubo entered the room. Einosuke and Fumiko were with him, O-bata behind them, trying not to trip under the weight of a tea and *sembei* tray. When Einosuke opened the *shoji,* the March air played upon the replica garden as if to further remind the two potential lovers of their conversation at the edge of the original one. The raked lines of gravel and the garden's mauve walls added definition to the moss that clung to each of Einosuke's boulders, both large and small. Manjiro was so taken by the sight, and by the nearness of Tsune, that he failed to notice everyone else focusing on the strange-looking box.

"Manjiro has given me his welcoming gift," Tsune mildly said. "Whatever might it be?"

The box seemed dismal and battered in the good new light, a poor welcoming gift if one didn't know it had come from an American. Both Lord Okubo and Einosuke looked at it with critical eyes. The box had no doubt been quite lovely once, and a close inspection would even now show that it was strongly made. But its edges were turned down, the straight line of its bottom bent up at the midway point, and on the side that was most easily visible to them was that crisp black thumbprint.

"What's in it?" asked Lord Okubo. "Its weird look is not an act of kindness to the eye."

"It's got a smudge," Einosuke said.

Manjiro was stung by their remarks and spoke gravely. "When I was leaving the American ship a man gave this to me. He was one of the singers I told you about. Inside this box are 'chocolates,' an after-dinner sweet."

Even as he spoke the box improved before their eyes. Now they could see that it might as easily be called "old" as "battered," and age became an asset, just as it would be in a box that held an antique tea bowl.

"We didn't know about this!" Lord Okubo said. "Did you report it to anyone at the Shogunate? Did you put it on the list with the gifts man?"

His father's words were stern, but they still contained awe, so before another family argument could begin, Tsune picked the box up and turned it in the chilly air, focusing everyone's attention on the thumbprint.

"What an odd idea," said Lord Okubo. "The Americans place their seal on things by directly touching the inkstone with their hands. Look how clean the mark is, how well practiced, see the ornate articulation of the lines."

Indeed, it was a perfect thumbprint, an accident of the moment, perhaps, but from the point of view now favored by all of the men in the room, it seemed to seal the box, to warn against its opening. When they tried to focus on the way the lines of the thumbprint traversed the box's seam, it made them a little cross-eyed.

"What does chocolate taste like?" Tsune asked. While she'd been holding the box she had noticed not only the thumbprint, but an inlay of satin flowers on its top, one a rose, another perhaps a chrysanthemum. "After all, the design is too busy, don't you think?" she said, and then to everyone's dismay she placed the box back down on the tatami and opened it. It was an extraordinary thing to do. No one else would have done it. A box that came from an American ship was a gift that should be given many times, passed up high. At this early stage of the American presence, in fact, Lord Okubo was of the opinion that no one should consider opening it save the Shogun himself.

"Chocolate is edible, is it not?" she asked. "If it is an after-dinner sweet can I assume it is an edible thing?"

The odor of the chocolate, faint but clear, rode out on the cold air and made them all stare at the individual candies that had appeared. Manjiro did not know it but he had stored the candies well. Because he had kept them directly under his father's window the designs that covered each piece had remained intact and intricate. There were twenty-eight candies, in alternate rows of sixes and fives. Under their ornately carved caps, they were uniformly shaped domes, about the size of mushrooms.

"Look," said Fumiko, who was first to recover from the shock of what her sister had done. "Each piece has an individual design, like *netsuke*. Here I see a leafy pattern, there a cluster of grapes." She didn't touch the candies, but put a finger so close to them that Einosuke thought she had.

"Don't do that!" he hissed. "Let's replace the lid now. Maybe there is something here to salvage."

He only meant that maybe the thumbprint could be realigned, that they might still be able to pass this rare gift along, but he should not have spoken. The gift, after all, now belonged to his sister-in-law. Lord Okubo grumbled and Manjiro stared out at the garden where his brother's boulders were like fifteen large chocolates in a box of their own, but Tsune acted quickly, and saved Einosuke from embarrassment. She had taken a tiny knife from her *obi* a moment before. Her intention had been to cut one of the chocolates into wedges, so that each of them might have a taste, but she changed her intention without changing the movement of her hand.

"As usual Einosuke is right," she said. "But before we close it let me arrange these things so that their designs all point the same way."

She handed the lid to Fumiko, then used the tip of her knife to turn the chocolates until the cluster of grapes on the top of one moved in congress with the filigreed pine needles on another. She made the oval acorns atop the chocolates at the corners of the box look like sentries with fat round guns.

"That's better," she said. "Now it is more pleasing to the eye." She would have closed the box immediately then, but Keiko and Masako came into the room, Keiko struggling under the weight of her fat baby brother.

"What's better?" asked Masako. "Let's see."

The side of the box's lid with the thumbprint on it was facing Fumiko, but the thumbprint on the box's base was not. That misalignment was the only thing that kept her from instantly slamming the lid down. Tsune might be destined to marry higher than she, but unlike the three men in the room, she would not hesitate to interfere. Just as her sister's self-absorption had nearly let her cut one of the chocolates apart, so her second daughter's curiosity would surely send her hand out to mess up the order of the chocolates again, maybe even spilling them onto the floor.

"Stay a little back, dear," she said. "Satisfy your curiosity with your eyes this time."

Because it was unlike her mother to speak abruptly, Masako did as she was told, but Fumiko's words also served to bring Keiko around.

"Okay then, what is it?" she asked. "Here, Masako, take our Jun-chan."

A stream of liquid was drooling from the baby's mouth, and when Masako took him from her sister's arms a fine line of it arched out into the air, falling down across the nearest corner of the chocolate box. It settled over the guardian acorn like a thick strand of spider web.

"*Chikusho,*" said Lord Okubo. "What do we do now?"

"Is it bean paste?" asked Keiko. "If it's bean paste simply give that one to Junichiro. If it's bean paste I don't want any at all."

"It is not bean paste, dear," said Tsune. She still had her knife in her hand but she was looking directly at Manjiro. Her look seemed to say, "Don't you agree that we have no choice now but to eat the piece that the baby has spit on?"

Manjiro had been sitting pretty glumly all this time. He had given the chocolates to Tsune because there was something in it of the flirtation they had had in their youth, and, of course, because he wanted to show off, but the reactions of the others had brought him down. Now, however, Tsune was giving him a chance to find his previous mood and he smiled. "Let's eat it," he said out loud. "After that we can close the whole thing up again, pass it on."

Tsune laughed, and as soon as she heard the easing of tensions, Keiko laughed too, taking her aunt's free arm. Masako, however, who had been struggling under the baby's weight, finally sat him down. She enjoyed mischief more than anyone, but she also had her mother's sense of protocol. "Such a plan will leave a hole in the box," she said, "an empty space at its corner while all the other spaces are full."

The idea really was too frivolous, even Tsune knew it, but how would it be to leave the corner chocolate as it was, covered with baby drool?

"Maybe we could put something in its place," said Lord Okubo, "a piece of fruit or an actual *netsuke,* if we can find one that small."

He began touching his clothing as if he might right then come up with a *netsuke* just the right size, and Junichiro, whom no one was caring for, fell over onto his side. It was then that Tsune stuck the ruined chocolate with her knife, pulling it from the box. The knife was in the chocolate's heart and when she applied a little pressure it split into two equal halves.

"I don't want any," said Masako. "I don't like bean paste, either. On that, at least, I can agree with Keiko."

Tsune quickly cut each of the candy halves into thirds. "Without Masako there are six of us," she said. "Isn't that nice?"

The acorn adorning the top of the chocolate had not broken apart as well as its body had. When the chocolate was initially halved the acorn had been halved too, but now each acorn half affixed itself to a one-sixth piece. The center of the candy was softer and apparently stickier than the candy's outside, for when Tsune held up her knife they could all see bits of the white stuff stuck to the blade. She put the knife in her mouth, letting Manjiro see the sharpness of it against her tongue.

"What does it taste like, Auntie?" asked Keiko. "Tell me, does it truly taste like bean paste?"

Tsune pointed the knife at the ceiling. "Not like bean paste," she said, "nothing like beans at all."

That was enough for Keiko. She took a one-sixth piece of chocolate and popped it into her mouth. It was rude to go first and she only hoped her mother would notice that she had stayed away from the pieces with the acorns. Pretty soon worry about her mother went away, however, when the taste of the candy came over her like a wave.

"It's good," she told her aunt. "It makes me want to close my eyes."

After that Manjiro and Fumiko and Tsune took the other three pieces without the acorns, rolling them around in their mouths. When they were finished Fumiko picked up the two acorn pieces, placing one each in the hands of her husband and father-in-law.

"It's a strange thing," she told them. "I think it's overly sweet. Perhaps one small piece like this is enough."

When Masako heard her mother's words and surprised everyone by starting to cry, her father and grandfather each offered her his piece of candy, Lord Okubo even joking that, though it was all right for the others, until the treaty negotiations were done, he felt it best that he stay clear of anything that might be construed as foreign trade.

"Please, Ma-chan," he said, "eat mine."

Masako took the candy from her grandfather and ate it before her mother could intervene. And since her father still had his hand open, she took his piece, too, broke the acorn off its top and pushed it into Junichiro's still drooly mouth. The baby looked surprised. He closed his mouth and flapped his arms and fell over on the tatami one more time. "Now we've all had some," Masako said, and though that wasn't quite true, Lord Okubo and Einosuke both felt satisfied.

As for the candy itself, none who had eaten it had liked it very much. They had all lied. Maybe they thought that to tell the truth would be a reflection on Manjiro, who, so far as they knew, was the only man in Japan to have thus far received a personal gift from America.

Keiko stood up and stepped down onto the pathway that surrounded her father's rock garden. She bent without looking and picked up a small stone.

"Here," she said, passing it up to her Aunt Tsune.

The stone was perfect, precisely the size of the candy they had eaten, and when Tsune put it in the box's empty corner its solid calmness seemed to settle the remaining candies down.

Tsune closed the box and turned it in the air, letting everyone see how well the thumbprint realigned. She placed it on her lap, sliding half of it under the folds of her kimono.

They all stood then, as if the morning had suddenly grown too cold. The women left the room first, hopelessly followed by Manjiro. When Keiko stooped to pick up the baby, Masako said it was her turn and began pulling on his arms.

"Stop that," said their grandfather. "Here, I will carry the little boy."

Argument often invaded the household when it came to other things, but when their grandfather spoke both girls still knew enough to obey.

It was only then, after all this time, that Junichiro opened his mouth again. He had been sucking on the chocolate acorn, and, despite what the others thought, enjoying it well. He smiled at his grandfather and his grandfather swung him high, letting another line of thick brown drool come out of his mouth, to swing through the otherwise empty air like a vine.

5. | *Approach of the Outside World*

THE RECENTLY COMPLETED TREATY house sat on a gentle rise of land, at Kanagawa, a quarter of a mile back from the water's edge. It was a simple structure, closed on three sides but open where it faced the sea. Six thick beams supported its roof along the front, yet it had within it only a single large room with a single low table at its center. Unlike the banquet table on the American flagship, this one was not surrounded by chairs, but the walls were hung with scrolls, bold black ink on long white paper, poetry and slogans about casting the barbarians out.

In order to find a good spot Einosuke had insisted that his family, minus his father but including his brother and sister-in-law, arrive earlier than anyone. The interests of most of the Shogun's other guests were elsewhere, however, on the less formal aspects of the American arrival, and the girls were irritated to have to stand for so long. Over the last few hours sailors from the fleet's cargo ships had come ashore to lay a mile of circular railroad track, and now, while people hurried over to watch the arrival of an actual one-quarter-scale railroad train, all the family could do was stand on tiptoe. It was ridiculous and Masako fumed, angry with her father and trying to pull away. Manjiro saw what was happening and offered to take her closer. "Come, my beautiful nieces," he said. "Only comport yourselves well. That strange American beast eats children, I am told."

Masako held her uncle's sleeve but Keiko moved only enough to place herself closer to her Aunt Tsune. She disdained being thought of as a child, even by her favorite uncle, and in any case did not want to appear to be rushing anywhere. The kimono she wore, of yellow silk with white cranes upon it, was too formal for speed, and made to be slowly admired.

But in another moment it became apparent that they had missed their chance to get very near the train, so Manjiro briefly lifted Masako high. She could see a silver engine and a black coal car, a caboose and eight passenger carriages which, rumor had it, they would actually be allowed to ride upon later in the day. The engine, winking at her in the morning sun, had a steam whistle whose shrill voice horrified her and made her ask her uncle to put her back down.

Because Commodore Perry had not yet arrived, the official Japanese contingent had not appeared yet either, but Einosuke nevertheless earnestly searched the crowd, hoping to find his father near the great Lord Abe, so he could point out both men to the girls. When the steam whistle blew again, however, in three measured notes accompanied by three puffs of pure white smoke, the strangely unbrassy sound of military music came to them from the far side of a stand of scrub pine. All could hear the music from wherever they stood, but no one could see its source. It wasn't the same sound that had serenaded them from the bay these last long days, but was rather the strung-out strains of whistles and drums.

Einosuke and Fumiko, the girls and Aunt Tsune, strained their eyes, trying to match a vision with the cacophony, but when Manjiro touched them they all looked back inside the treaty house to find five of the eight lords who'd attended the American banquet, Lord Abe in the middle, already sitting behind the table. It was as inspiring a sight as it would have been if the Shogun himself had come. There was an area directly beside the treaty house that had been roped clear, but now that area, too, was packed with lesser members of the Great Council. To have these lords in attendance but not inside the treaty house seemed an unprecedented public demotion, and while Manjiro bowed toward their father, whom they all could see among the outcasts, Einosuke only stood there, embarrassed and appalled. Just then, however, the whistles and drums grew louder, and when the musicians came coughing into view everyone was united again, watching the approach of the outside world.

"He does know how to make an entrance," Tsune said. "I'll give him that much."

The musicians had burst from the stand of pines with such power and muscle that they made the trees look small. It did not seem likely to Manjiro that the American Commodore could have picked these men for size alone, since the first requirement of musicians, even in America, had to be their ability to perform, but the drummers were as thick of body as young sumo wrestlers, with necks that looked like the beams that held up the treaty house. They played their drums as if they were trying to break into them, and the flute players, too, seemed to want to pry the music out of their instruments as if it were enclosed in jars. Even so, they didn't play badly, and for the first time both brothers understood how directly connected music was to war.

The effect on the Japanese was quite what Commodore Perry must have wanted. The musicians numbered twenty-four and wore red jackets with tight white wigs on their heads, their faces pink as fish bellies, sweating under the cool March sun. Even though they were big men they were trying to march across the sand lightly, like they'd no doubt done while practicing on the deck of one or another of the American vessels, and their feet looked small. The music itself dictated their pace, but as they came closer and the sand got deeper, those in front bogged down. Their movement wasn't slowed, but they had to pick their feet up higher, like horses might, flipping bits of sand into the tightly packed crowd. They marched right into the treaty house, boots twisting sores into the delicate tatami, and the moment they turned, freezing in their positions like dolls, a brass band, which had also been hiding in the little pine forest, burst into a breezy version of "Anacreon in Heaven," the American national song.

"Here comes the man himself I'll bet," said Einosuke, so captured by the moment that he started rubbing the *netsuke* carvings that held together the drawstrings of his various pouches.

The band came the same way the fife and drum corps had, but stopped short of the treaty house, turned and folded into itself, and separated again to form two columns. The anthem finished just as the musicians faced each other, from either side of the newly formed and deathly silent corridor. For two full minutes no one moved or spoke. Even the wind, which had been playing out among the waves all morning, seemed to stop the whitecaps in their cresting while the seconds ticked away. It was like a moment of prayer followed by a drum roll so soft at its beginning that people thought it was only a new wind rising in the pines. But pretty soon the tip of a shaft came out of that sound, the American flag below it, and carrying the shaft in his thin black hands came an actual American Negro.

The Negro's appearance had a strong effect on everyone, but Commodore Perry himself came next, and in such close proximity to his color bearer that people no longer knew where to cast their eyes. Though he wore a uniform that was as dark as the one he'd worn on shipboard, this time it was so festooned with medals and shoulder tassels, that though he was an average-sized man, he appeared now to be small. He walked with an exaggerated swagger and held his left hand up in the air, as if at any moment he might start waving to the crowd. Behind the Commodore came a line of other high-ranking men, but by then no one could concentrate on anyone but Perry. It was like he'd practiced his smallness in order to give himself an indisputable sense of ultimate size.

When the Negro reached the treaty house and turned to hold the colors at an angle under which the Commodore could stride, Lord Abe and the other lords suddenly stood up again. The American officers had fanned out behind Perry with their hands locked behind their backs, while Perry simply waited, his own hands at his sides.

"Good day, gentlemen!" he said, as exuberant as he'd been in his banquet room. "How well we are received! How beautiful everything is! This structure—how magnificent!—built in honor of what this day will bring, seems as solid as, I pray, the friendship between our two countries will turn out to be."

His interpreter commenced putting his words into Dutch but Manjiro translated for Einosuke.

"You are welcome. Please, join us at the table now, let's proceed with dispatch," was Lord Abe's only reply.

There had been so much pomp, so much weight, placed on the American arrival that even these plain words could not break the spell. It was broken, however, for the brothers at least, by having to watch Commodore Perry try to sit down. He spent a long time wedging his knees under the table in order to keep from falling over backwards on the floor. While he turned and twisted the Japanese lords looked away, but once he was settled, now wearing an uncomfortable smile, someone began reading the treaty aloud. Each section was read twice, first in Dutch, then simultaneously in English and Japanese. It was a strange process, cumbersome and noisy, difficult for anyone to understand. Many times one side or the other stopped the reading, but it wasn't so much to clarify a meaning as to simply catch their breath and go on.

In this way the signing of the Kanagawa Treaty of 1854, signaling Japan's emergence from two hundred and fifty years of relative isolation, took three hours and nine minutes by the official American pocket watch, which was presented to Lord Abe after the ceremony was done.

6. | *Tell Him I'm in Mourning!*

"I MIGHT AS WELL have stayed home," said Masako. "I couldn't see a thing, unless you count the backs of heavy kimonos!"

At first she presented her outrage as energetically as always, but now that the boring part of the day was over—all that talking, all those long-winded speeches—she decided that it really might be grand to ride in a circle on the steam train or study the face of a foreigner for a while. When she thought of the train she felt excitement in her spine and imagined the wind in her face, her fingers plugging her ears to keep out the noise. Her mother's expression told her that if she kept on complaining she might very well miss those things, however, and her father's told her that something weighed heavily on his mind. So she closed her mouth and found Keiko, falling back to walk at her older sister's side.

Only a few weeks earlier a treaty with America had been an impossible thing for Einosuke to contemplate, but when he finally spoke to his family on this bright March morning, his desire was not the continued expression of his dismay, but to take defeat with dignity and find reconciliation with his younger brother. He spoke to all of them in a formal manner, but his gaze fell upon Manjiro.

"Because the issue of whether or not to sign this treaty has been decided by its signing," he said, "we will now have some few months, some few weeks at least, before we have to consider the Americans again. Let us try to use that time to put our differences behind us. Wrongly or rightly, if we can go forward with a unified Japan, why can't we do likewise with a unified family?"

He raised his hands to indicate that the weather, at least, agreed with him, and then he put them down.

It was a sweeter gift than the chocolates for the others to hear him speak that way, not only because they knew the truth of his words, but because they knew how supremely difficult it was for Einosuke to say them. Manjiro bowed, Fumiko touched her husband's wrist with approval and affection, and the girls each took one of Aunt Tsune's thin and oddly reluctant arms. Tsune herself remained as she had been, de-tached and contemplative, but she too was moved. She thought the comment contained elements of grace and for the first time in years remembered what she had tried to tell her sister at the time of her wed-ding—that marrying Einosuke was a lucky thing for Fumiko, like catching a firefly whose light flittered into the present darkness from a past era, but burned a noble flame. Fumiko herself had been ambivalent about the marriage, but had grown to care deeply for Einosuke, even before the birth of their first child.

Where previously they had felt only irritation at the crowds, now they all looked around in pleasant amazement. Was it only last week that this land they stood upon had been barren, uninhabited but for the wind and the cold and the scrubby pines? Einosuke smiled when he finished speaking, his heart once again at ease. He looked at the tightly packed throngs both surrounded by and surrounding the whistle and chug of the American steam train and thought that though he would not mount the thing himself, he could not forbid his children to ride.

THE MINSTREL STAGE was strongly built and large, higher and wider than the treaty house, and backed up against the largest stand of pines. When he looked up at the makeshift curtain, which had been stretched by the Japanese carpenters in error, across the back rather than the front of the stage, Manjiro tried to tell the others that they should forget the train for a moment, that here on this stage the strangest and most wonderful entertainment would very soon take place. A sign said that the minstrels were scheduled to perform three shows that night, but thus far all anyone could see were the scarred sides of an upright piano, streaked with sand and salty lines of dried seawater. The girls had just started speaking again, resuming their lobby in favor of the train, when one of the minstrels came out from behind the curtain, carrying the piano stool and wearing a tall brown hat. His face and arms were once again covered with black paint, while his teeth and the whites of his eyes startled and silenced the crowd. When he reached the piano he put the stool down and looked out. It had grown slightly dark by then, but the stage was lit by torches on the tops of bamboo poles.

"Stay awhile folks," said the minstrel. "Come now, gather \'round. This'll be better for your eyes and better for your ears too. . . . Better for every part of you than a ride on that ridiculous monstrosity. It ain't the real thing but we are. And that's a promise from me, Ace Bledsoe, the star of the show."

When he smiled the people nearest him leaned away, most of them afraid. Manjiro could see fear in the eyes of his family members, too, and that made him strangely happy. He wanted to speak English now, to show off. This was the man who had given him the chocolates so shouldn't he acknowledge him, use his years of study to say hello? He had not had a chance to speak English casually since his tutor left Shimoda.

"It is true," he said in English. "This entertainment is fine."

"Who's there?" asked Ace Bledsoe. "Hey! If it's not the same fellow from before!"

He dropped his piano stool and jumped off the stage, coming down like a spider with his arms out. People wanted to run, but at the same time were calmed by Manjiro, captivated by hearing him speak the spidery tongue.

"Howdy do?" said Ace, sticking out his hand. But then he dropped his act, telling Manjiro very quietly, "I've been looking for you. I thought you might show me the town."

Manjiro's intention was to present Einosuke, who had just brought peace to the family in an elegant and generous way, but when he turned to do it, Einosuke surprised him by standing back, and his nieces were already glued to their aunt in the rear, so the person closest to the grinning foreigner was quite suddenly his sister-in-law, Fumiko. She held her ground, but when the man came closer and reached out an oily black hand, she was so completely startled that she stared up at him, her own white face and blackened teeth a mirror image of him. Something passed between them, or more accurately from him to her, and a trembling started deep in her heart which she instantly mistook for fear.

"Pleasure's mine," he said, in his regular voice. "Ace Bledsoe's my name. I hail from the free state of Pennsylvania, not far from New York. We don't cotton to slavery, never mind what you see here tonight."

In part Fumiko could see now how truly opposite they were, the Americans and the Japanese, that it wasn't Manjiro but her husband

and her father-in-law who had been right all along. This man's white teeth might bite her if she didn't run, and his sticky black skin, if she let it touch her, might mark her so badly that she would never again get clean. In larger part, however, she was appalled to understand that she was drawn to this man, that there was a look in his eyes, behind his dark makeup, that she recognized. She tried to concentrate on his lips, which continued to smack out impossible sounds, but his eyes drew her strongly and she simply could not look away.

How ridiculous it was, how outrageous and offensive and horrifying! Only a moment earlier she had been happy, pleased with her husband's speech and to be walking here with her beautiful girls, yet now that she saw this American's face her deepest childhood memories came back to her; that of a mud monster from the depths of Lake Biwa, slime and water dripping off of him, plus that of a gallant and genuine *koibito,* who would one day carry her off and who, she had always told herself, she would instantly recognize.

It was an impossible, a nearly unbearable moment for Fumiko, and before she could do anything about it, before anyone could intercede, she began to cry. Oh, it was humiliating! She tried to stop immediately, of course, but the more she resisted the more her tears flowed. When the American saw them he cocked his head like someone's pet dog, so she slammed her eyes shut, lest he discover for himself her tumultuous state.

Einosuke and Manjiro came to her quickly, though it seemed to Fumiko like an hour had gone by, and when Einosuke touched her she was finally able to break the spell that had so overcome her, by sighing and shaking herself. She opened her eyes again, squinting at the ground, then pulled out a handkerchief. Her tears had already ruined her powdery makeup, streaming down her face like a slug clearing a trail.

"You must tell him something!" she hissed, suddenly furious with the men in her family. "Find some excuse, Einosuke! Tell him I am in mourning. That's it! Hurry now! Tell him some relative has died!"

"But who?" asked her husband. "None of your relatives are even sick just now."

Manjiro, however, put her request into English without taking any more time.

"It is not your countenance that distresses her," he said, "but the face of a favorite aunt who has recently died."

"Sorry to hear it," said Ace, trying to imagine how he could possibly resemble this Japanese woman's aunt. "I've lost family members of my own, so I know it's hard."

Lucky for everyone, the other musician came out just then and glared from the edge of the stage. It was time for the show to begin, past time actually, and the man who was facing Fumiko, throttling and rifting her heart, was late.

He took Fumiko's hand and shook it, then before she could cry again, dropped it and shook everyone else's, one at a time.

7. | *He Didn't Care about the Neighbors Anymore*

WHEN EINOSUKE and Fumiko got home that night they immediately began quarreling in the garden room. They were alone in the downstairs portion of the house—the girls had gone to bed, Aunt Tsune was off with Lord Tokugawa's entourage, and Manjiro and his father had stayed to see the last performance of the minstrel show—but around them Edo was listening.

"I realize I should have shown more strength, that I should not have let that creature see my tears," Fumiko began, "but I was not prepared. No one, least of all you, my husband, told me the foreigners would look the way they did, that they should hold such powerful weapons in the features of their faces!"

The other half of what she had felt she had already begun to dismiss, to attribute to the move to Odawara, to the fact that her period was coming, even to the trouble she'd been having with her maid, the extraordinary difficulties of her life these last few days.

Einosuke was tired and wanted to change his clothes and go out to work in his garden, to rake and smooth the pebbles and extract the latest set of soggy leaves. What he did not want to do was talk about the Americans, and so he replied without consideration. "I was at a loss when you cried," he said. "Luckily Manjiro rescued us."

Fumiko understood as well as anyone that it was a wife's job to soothe the wounded sensibilities of her husband, but this time it had been her sensibilities that had been wounded, she who had broken so horribly into tears, and what she wanted now was to be soothed herself, and to purge forever those untoward thoughts.

"Do you not remember that it was my idea, not Manjiro's, to invent the dying relative?" she asked. "That it was I who, even in my shock, tried to rescue the situation?"

"To claim a recent death might explain your tears," Einosuke told her, "but it also might make us seem harsh for coming to the treaty-signing ceremony so soon after a death in the family. In America I bet there is a proper time of mourning, just like there is in Japan."

Not once in a year did Fumiko's anger vent itself outwardly. That, no doubt, is why Einosuke still didn't see it coming.

"Ah," she slowly said, "so if it is Manjiro's idea you will offer credit but if it is mine you will criticize. It seems to me that a recently dead aunt requires the same consideration no matter whose invention she might be."

"Do you know where we put the rake with the shortest handle?" Einosuke asked. "I can't find it anywhere. I hope you didn't allow O-bata to lend it to that neighbor again. Last time I had to go and ask the man directly before he gave it back."

He had stepped down off the porch and was bending to peer under it, looking among his orderly collection of garden tools. He had spoken quietly because the neighbor in question was sometimes outside at odd hours and could be lurking just across the fence right now. Einosuke imagined him sitting down low, purposefully shaking the base of one or another of his horrid little trees.

The most painful sting often comes from the smallest bee, and Einosuke was hurt just as much as he would have been had Fumiko whacked him with the handle of that missing rake when she said, "You are my husband, but you are a vain and foolish man sometimes."

He remained bent for a moment, staring into the darkness under the porch, but when he stood back up the darkness in his eyes was replaced by fire. "All this trouble, all this talk!" he hissed. "Is it too much to ask that such things be left outside, that they not be so readily ushered into a man's home?"

"At the moment I'm not concerned about what is inside or outside a man's home so much as I am about what is inside or outside the man himself," Fumiko replied. "Speak plainly if you are to hiss at me, don't rely on form."

Fumiko was older than her sister, and not so beautiful, but she had at least as much skill with words. Her own voice had remained calm.

"How can you attack me after such a day!" Einosuke shouted, knowing even as he spoke that if he couldn't find better words to fight with he should opt for silent indignation and continue looking for his rake. He glanced up at the flat side of their house, at the second floor window behind which his children were supposed to be sleeping. He imagined the maid, O-bata, crouched there listening, her eyes as large as plums. Tomorrow, he knew, she would repeat every word he said to the awful neighbor's maids.

Fumiko understood that Einosuke's upward glance was his best argument, but she was too angry to worry about what people thought. "Why was I crying?" she heard herself ask. "You are my husband. If you know me so well, tell me why I did such a thing."

Her words remained steady, but they had come out as loudly as Einosuke's own, so the next thing he did was hurry back inside the room and close the doors.

"Can't we be a little circumspect?" he asked, but her look told him that she expected an answer to her question. She had cried because the foreigner was terrifying and ugly, she had already said that much, yet it could also be something unrelated, like how much work was left for her to do before they left Edo for Odawara. Einosuke busied himself with an arrangement of his *obi* and his *netsuke* and then sat down and poured the waiting tea, but Fumiko was waiting, too, for his reply. He wanted to find the deeper reason for her tears before he once again committed himself by speaking, but however much he thought about it, all he could come up with was the ridiculous notion that she was crying over that made-up aunt who had died.

Fumiko herself was desperately sorry she had asked the question. What did she expect him to say? And why couldn't she deal with this strange abnormality of hers alone?

"The death of an invented relative reminded you that life is short?" he tried. "Strange though it is, it reminded you that you don't have such a long time left with your children and me, not so much time to spend with the living, uninvented, ones?"

What a feeble and stupid thing to say! He knew he would have fared better either to admit his ignorance of why she was crying or simply to slump there awaiting sympathy, like a defeated and puffed-up frog. Now that the words were spoken, however, he stood behind them, brave-ly hoping that exhaustion would get her and she would not go on.

Fumiko sat down and leaned forward, putting her hands around her teacup in order to get hold of herself. Einosuke believed that that was a good sign, for her deepest level of anger would not allow her to touch a cup of tea poured by him.

"Go on," she said, "what else?" She simply couldn't stop herself.

My God, he thought, what else? What else could there be? But softly now he spoke as if he had been sure of his first answer all along. "Not only the children, but our way of life. Whatever will become of our daughters and our baby boy when they learn that men with such ugly faces control the world, roaming it in black ships and stopping wherever they like to force themselves ashore? How can we deal with such barbarians?"

To speak this way had begun as a supreme act of daring, but now he let himself be grave, captured by the words that his own heart so deeply believed. What *would* happen to their children under conditions such as those? Einosuke hadn't forgotten the speech of reconciliation he had only that afternoon made, but tonight he remembered all the reasons he had had for opposing the Americans in the first place, and when he looked at Fumiko now, there were tears in his own eyes.

"Oh, my husband!" Fumiko cried. "Of course I understand that just as my teeth are black and my face is powdered white out of a sense of decorum, so that man's face was made up contrarily, to give us pleasure, not pain. But when he looked at me I saw the future too clearly. Oh, Einosuke, you and your father were right after all! We should have been steadfast from the beginning! That we and the Americans are opposites, that we can never understand each other, was reflected in that man's face tonight! Whatever will happen now? Whatever will become of the life we know?"

Fumiko's voice cracked as she let tears more completely spoil her face than they had earlier, but she also crawled around to Einosuke's side of the table and fell against him, wetting his chin and mouth, sorry for her earlier disloyalty, but satisfied with her lie. And as she wept Einosuke's own posture improved, his own eyes dried. Oh, he had a most wonderful, most perfect wife, a wife who could see into the center of an issue while men, especially the scoundrels in the Great Council, spent their time fighting over semantics, over phrases in a document that would do nothing, in the end, but gain entry into Japan for the outside world as a whole. Oh, why had he not been adamant when he had the chance, why had he not been firm? Never mind that his voice was small, why hadn't he spoken with its full volume anyway, casting his father's lot with the pure isolationists, just as his father, in his deepest heart, also wanted?

Einosuke was ashamed of himself as Fumiko was of herself, though for utterly different reasons. He was ashamed of his calculation, his earlier devotion only to discovering how to soothe his wife. But had he not known the true answer to her question after all, had he not said it right? He knew his wife's heart even without knowing he knew it, and as an expression of his love he threw the doors open again and flung his tea into the night. The gesture was wonderful, and so unexpected that it made Fumiko sit back up. They both saw the tea arch, cut sharply through the reemerged moonlight, and splash against the nearest of Einosuke's boulders, a lighter blemish of darkness trailing along the interceding ground.

"That is what has happened to Japan!" Einosuke cried. "By letting the Americans in we have marked our islands far more deeply than I have marked my stones!"

He didn't care about the neighbors anymore. He pointed out at the remaining dry boulders, unstoppable now. "But look, we are still unblemished in the larger part, and I swear right now that that larger part will forever belong only to our infant son and our two girls, only to the children of Japan. I swear on my ancestors' graves that the foreigners will go no farther than the harbor where they reside at this moment, no farther than Shimoda and Hakodate, those unfortunate and already lost towns!"

Oh, how he thanked his wife for what she had done! She had moved him back to his center again, making his own former resolution return! He was out of breath from the passion of it, and the tea, as it dried and faded on the nearest boulder, was quickly losing its power as metaphor, but when he moved to close the *shoji* again, Fumiko touched his hand. And after that another kind of passion came into his heart.

"Our house is nearly empty, my dear," she whispered. "That's unusual, don't you think? It has not been nearly empty in a good long time."

Of course, of course, this was how she would purge herself, she thought.

"Father and Manjiro will be back soon," Einosuke said, but when he reached around and touched her *obi* he found that she'd already loosened its knot. Einosuke had forever been proud of the solid beauty of his wife, which he knew had at first been aimed at a level of society higher than his own, but when she opened her kimono, shifting her weight to make it slip off her shoulders until it puddled about her on the floor, he let such knowledge go, along with his sense of propriety and discomfiture, of worry over what the neighbors might think were he to make love to his wife with the *shoji* open.

Fumiko's right breast was in the moonlight, her left one still in the dark.

"Your own clothing now looks too warm," she told her husband, "and I will not be cold alone."

Oh, with what happiness Einosuke undid his sash, crawled out of his own stiff clothing, and set aside his favorite little erotic *netsuke* carving. He stood in the shadows and reached down to take Fumiko's outstretched hand. Both of them thought they would closet themselves among the extra futon at the end of the upstairs hallway, or sneak into an unused maid's room near the kitchen, but when they stood close together Einosuke's penis knew no such protocol. Unleashed as it was from the constraints of his clothing, it moved up to touch his wife's abdomen, stiffly knocking twice, like the outstretched beckoning of a small baby's arm. For the briefest instant both of them laughed, but when Fumiko took it in her hand, pushing it down and raising herself up to slide upon it at the same time, Einosuke's knees buckled and both of them fell onto the pile of kimonos on the floor. The parts of their bodies fit together of their own accord, slippery with excitement, but as they cried out, bucking and heaving, they also began to roll. Einosuke started it, thinking it would be beautiful were they to end such grand lovemaking with their torsos on the porch, but alas he confused the speed of their roll with the speed of their motion up and down, giving

Fumiko barely enough time to throw a hand back to grab a kimono, before they tumbled off the porch and into the garden. For some good reason the kimono twisted under them, softening their landing, cushioning the blow.

For a second everything was still, until Fumiko, whose fall had also been broken by Einosuke, said, "Shh. Listen carefully, be quiet before you speak, my love."

Oh, she was fine now! Back to her earlier self. Oh how she loved her husband!

"My dearest one," moaned Einosuke, but Fumiko shushed him again. She pushed herself up just enough to reach back through the open doorway and pull Einosuke's kimono down. She hoped it would hide them, since it was not only larger than hers but also russet, in the darkness surely the same color as the ground.

"I think my gown is ruined," she whispered, putting a hand over his mouth lest he say he didn't think so.

They let another minute pass while they listened for sounds from the next-door neighbor's yard. Einosuke was dismayed by their behavior, sure that they had never before been so noisy. But the outside world seemed to surround them again without much shock or comment, applause coming only from the wind, slight, to be sure, and freezing cold.

"We should go back inside," said Einosuke, and Fumiko asked how she would explain, to the laundryman, how her kimono has been savaged by stones.

"Maybe it's beyond repair," said Einosuke, a hopeful note in his voice. "If that is the case we shall simply have to throw it away."

Considering that this kimono was her favorite it was odd solace, but Fumiko nodded, also hoping so. And then they wrapped themselves in their messed-up gowns, and sat back up on the porch.

"Look at your poor garden," said Fumiko, "not only have we ruined my kimono but we've pretty severely altered the garden's flow."

"We have improved it," Einosuke replied, "by taking it out of perfection for a while."

That was a very fine thing to say, and after he said it they were both not only content, but proud.

It took another fifteen minutes for the feeling to pass, and during that time, as they leaned into each other, snug in the tents they had made, the wind rose and maple leaves blew over the neighbor's fence in bunches, and the moon went to stand behind a cloud. It appeared that the coldness of winter was returning, that the good weather had come only for the treaty signing, and when Einosuke finally said, "Why does he insist on keeping such terrible trees right at the edge of his land?" Fumiko knew his mind was on his raking again, that he'd had enough of imperfection and not only wanted to step out and pick up the leaves, but to fix the damage done by their bodies as well.

She pushed a hand more deeply into the folds of her kimono and wrapped it around that part of him that she had thought of only moments earlier as a small baby's arm. Oh, she was herself again, thank God! Had she known a proper poem she would have recited it, to try to keep the blessed mood for a little while longer, but, alas, the mood was at that instant strained, not by the sound of poetry, but by a rattle and a shaking, a shouting coming from the front door. They both leapt up like burglars, bolted down a narrow hallway and tore up the stairs. They were out of breath and panting, dragging their kimono behind them, but Lord Okubo had come in so angrily that, lucky for them, his voice was the only thing anyone with him could hear.

"I don't care!" he shouted. "As soon as this thing is over you will forget these barbaric languages! I was wrong to have allowed it in the first place. I've been soft! I should not have given you such free rein!"

Lord Okubo was so angry that he might have ordered Manjiro out of the house right then and there, so, ruined or not, Fumiko put her kimono back on and ran down the stairs saying, "What in the world is the trouble? What's going on?"

And that, not the old lord's shouting nor the sounds that had come from the garden before, brought O-bata out of the room across the hall. She was sleepy and disheveled, and didn't seem to notice Einosuke hiding in the closet.

She only went downstairs to ask who wanted tea or if anyone required anything from the kitchen, following her mistress's voice like a dog.

8. | *Don't Get Up on My Account*

THIS IS WHY Lord Okubo was so angry:

Earlier that evening, after the last of the minstrel shows, Manjiro went in search of Ace Bledsoe and found him sitting behind that misplaced curtain at the back of the stage, peering into a hand mirror and swabbing the last of the paint from his face. Manjiro was not searching him out on his own, but had been sent to find both minstrels on Lord Abe's order. Commodore Perry had asked for them, also.

"Forgive me," he said, "but our leaders want you at the treaty house." He was nervous to be alone with the American again, without the artificial intermediary of makeup and a show. Still, he had practiced the sentence and said it well.

"Me?" asked Ace, watching himself speak the word in the mirror he held. "I'm not one of the powers around here, are you sure they don't want someone else?"

He had been looking at his own broad forehead and high cheekbones, wondering what there was about him that had so distressed the woman in Manjiro's group. His English was like it had been when he'd tried to greet Fumiko, also, cleaner and easier for Manjiro to understand, unaffected by the fiery inflections necessary to draw a crowd. And seeing that he was far less ugly, less sharp-featured and more serious than he'd been before, Manjiro wished that Einosuke and Fumiko had not so quickly hurried home. Ace's cheeks were narrow and his eyes, Manjiro could have pointed out, were the same brown color as Fumiko's.

"I am only their messenger," said Manjiro.

Ace got off the stage, retrieved his satchel from somewhere, and followed Manjiro into the clearing. Manjiro was pleased that on this, the occasion of his second private conversation with the man, his English had held up, but at the same time he was disappointed to find the crowd substantially diminished, that far fewer people were there to see them walking together toward the treaty house. The steam engine still chugged in its circle, a slow silver bullet defining the ceremonial space, but that space was now occupied almost entirely by Americans.

"Where is everyone?" asked Ace. "Did your family go home already? For once in my life I was in a mingling mood. Where did all of your countrymen go?"

He had not seemed to Manjiro to be in any kind of mood other than tired and contemplative, but all he said was, "They are sleeping. These days exhaustion is rampant among the Japanese."

He wasn't sure why but he felt ashamed, as if, though the American was speaking normally now, he had let artifice sneak into his reply. To be sure, he didn't want to say that there were edicts and curfews posted everywhere, strictures against interaction with the foreigners, but what he had said sounded arch, and he tried to think of something more genuine.

"I don't like Dutch," he said. "English is the language of the future. Dutch clogs everything up!"

Ace looked at him, thinking to say "London, England! Paris, France!" in order to determine if it might have been Manjiro who had called out from shore the other night. But because most of the people had gone home and their walk between the minstrel stage and the treaty house didn't take long, he didn't respond at all. Though the ground was strewn with the crates and wrappings that had earlier held the American gifts, it otherwise no longer looked like it could have contained such a large crowd. Rather, it appeared desolate again, as if it, like the Japanese people, were prone to exhaustion.

Directly in front of the treaty house stood four guards, two Americans and two Japanese. The Japanese were young samurai, sure and steady in their gaze, but the Americans looked like giants, this time no doubt chosen because they were large. The Americans stood at stiff attention, the Japanese with their legs spread wide. Because the treaty house had an open front, the two men could see directly into it as they approached. Lord Abe and Commodore Perry were sitting behind the table again, alone but for the company of a solitary whiskey bottle, and looking so unhappy in the dim light that had Manjiro not known the treaty was signed, he'd have called it a light in which negotiations had failed.

When Perry saw them, however, he tried to stand, and to recover the earlier booming quality of his voice. "Ah," he said, "Bledsoe, is it? Come in, come in, young man!"

He pushed himself away from the table as he spoke, but his knees were stuck beneath it and he couldn't get up. Lord Abe sat next to him, calm and oblivious, while his Dutch translator and the grim-faced Ueno stood against the back wall.

"Yes sir," said Ace, as he stepped into the treaty house, "Bledsoe, it is. What can I do you for? I sorely hope it's not another song."

This was Ned's way of speaking, not his, but he used it anyway, in an effort to achieve nonchalance. He owed Commodore Perry a lot and, of course, would sing if that was what he wanted.

"Listen, your show was a success, outstanding," said the Commodore, hardly hearing what Ace had said. "It's been the subject of much of our talk. More, actually, than I had hoped."

He gave up the idea of standing and waved the musician over. "And now this man here, I mean Lord Abe, seems to be asking if he can borrow you and your partner for a while. He brings it up every other minute no matter what else I try to talk about. He says he wants you to perform for the congress, for the national assembly or whatever they call it, the House of bloody Lords."

When Manjiro heard Commodore Perry's words he badly wanted to interrupt, to let Lord Abe know that a terrible mistake had been made, but when the Commodore asked, "Where is your partner, anyhow?" instead of speaking he stiffened, suddenly remembering that he was to have brought both minstrels and had brought only one.

"I think he wandered on down to the shore," said Ace. "He thinks there might be fish of a different nature than we've got at home, just lined up on the sand and ready to be picked up."

The Commodore sent a sailor to find him, and then said, "Come help me get up off this infernal floor."

Ace went over to him, but Manjiro stood there, in real shock over what could only be the deepest sort of misunderstanding. There could be no invitation to bring these two minstrels ashore. Not even Lord Abe could do such a thing without a consensus, the approval of the entire Great Council, and perhaps that is why, when two more lords came into the room, Manjiro was slow to grow alert. One of them was his father and the other was Tsune's renowned benefactor and Lord Abe's sometime rival, the man she had traveled to Edo with, Lord Tokugawa. Manjiro knew he was not to do so, that his job was to concentrate on the words alone, but he could not help looking at his father. His father glanced back at him, but far from understanding Manjiro's alarm, his look was one of pride. And when Lord Tokugawa saw that only one thin American was trying to help the Commodore stand, both he and Lord Okubo rushed forward.

"The Japanese way of sitting is impossible if you haven't been doing it since you were five," said Lord Okubo. He thought his comment clever and hoped his son would translate it. He even looked at Manjiro and nodded, but by then Manjiro had moved over beside Lord Abe, determined to straighten things out.

"Thank you, gentlemen," said the slowly standing Perry. "When I get back to my ship I'm going to make this country the gift of a few good chairs."

"Sir," whispered Manjiro, but Lord Abe, who had remained lost in thought all this time, suddenly saw that he was the only one still sitting, and sprang up. And just then the other musician appeared at the door.

"Don't get up on my account," said Ned.

"Ah, good," said Commodore Perry. "You, steward, bring more whiskey from my parcel. We'll all have a drink together while Lord Abe explains his idea. It's an odd one, to be sure, but vets my belief that in this business of countries coming together you never know what to expect, even when the negotiations are done."

Now that he was standing again the Commodore grew more animated, massaging his legs and back. "Pour a liberal measure," he told his cabin boy. "Come, my man, don't delay."

He kept his gaze on Lord Abe until Lord Abe cleared his throat, and, waving away the Dutch interpreter, called Manjiro.

"Tell them what I say," he whispered, "and use my words exactly." He raised his voice again and said: "I think the Japanese people can learn more about your country from true human contact, from a week or two of fine entertainment, for example, than from a year of explanations, a year of treaties written down. Therefore I want to invite these two superb musicians into Edo to perform. After all, if we are to be nations who recognize each other, as the agreement we signed today clearly says we are, what better way to begin than through singing, through some kind of cultural exchange?"

His aide was standing beside him as he spoke, an eerie smile on his face.

It was Manjiro's voice the Americans heard, of course, but he had been concentrating so hard on using Lord Abe's *exact* words, that he had not caught their full meaning until after they were out. When he looked at his father and Lord Tokugawa again, however, he saw a reaction similar to his own. They had gotten everything from Lord Abe's original Japanese and were supporting each other behind Commodore Perry, as apoplectic as stroke victims.

"Your request is unexpected," Commodore Perry said, "and my problem in accommodating it is that these men aren't quite the amateurs I may have hinted at before. They are civilians, I am forced to admit, entertainers that I rescued from some trouble in America and brought along on this sea voyage of ours because I thought their show would please you. Like everyone in the fleet they are under my command, of course, but I can't order them to do a thing like this. Unlike ordinary sailors these men have some amount of free will. I can't order them to visit a country with which we have just now negotiated a treaty. I can't . . ."

He hadn't finished, he was engaged in a tactic, building a plan of his own, but Ace interrupted him by saying, "I accept. It is just what I've been waiting for. I'd love to go."

He had tried to say it casually, but his words came out like he was Daniel Webster himself, making a point from a pulpit.

Manjiro could see Commodore Perry's incredulity and knew at least that here was something the two countries had in common, that, just as it would in Japan, speaking up like that had violated American protocol. "I accept," he said in Japanese. "I would love to go."

"There, you see," said Lord Abe, "if we can put political issues aside, men from one part of the world will want to visit men from another, nothing could be more natural."

He smiled as he spoke and then hurried over to the two disgruntled lords, Manjiro's father and Lord Tokugawa. "Give me a moment here," he whispered, "all is not as it seems. I know what I'm doing and you both know where I stand."

But confusion and discord were everywhere by then. Lord Tokugawa and Lord Okubo stared furiously, the first at Lord Abe, the second at his son, while Commodore Perry kept both cold eyes on the wayward musician, Ace Bledsoe.

"I'm the negotiator here, young man," he finally said, "and I will do the speechifying, if you don't mind."

He then turned his attention to the second musician, Ned Clark, who still stood in the doorway.

"I want you to answer freely," he told him. "Will you undertake traveling into Edo with our impulsive Mr. Bledsoe here, or are you disinclined, *as many men would be,* to leave our American vessels?"

But Ned no more understood the Commodore's message to him, the emphatic nature of *"as many men would be,"* than he would have had it been said in Japanese.

"Go along with Ace on a mystery tour?" he asked. "Suits me fine, your honor. I'm a bit of a homebody, but Ace is always sayin' that goin' where we ain't been before is life's elixir. So I might as well have a sip of it myself."

Only a moment passed while the Commodore stared from one man to the other, but it seemed to both of them like an hour.

"Very well," Commodore Perry finally said, "if you are decided, I will allow it." And then he smiled his coldest smile of all.

After that each man wanted to get away, to go off by himself and think things over, but because of the full glasses of whiskey they couldn't do so. Commodore Perry solved the problem and at the same time gave another lesson in American democracy, or at least in how a man accepts a small defeat gracefully, by taking the tray from his cabin boy and delivering the drinks himself. Eight glasses went one each to the Japanese lords, the two minstrels, Manjiro and the Commodore and Lord Abe's aide. One glass remained untouched and when Lord Abe said it should be left alone, as a tribute to each man's ancestors, everyone, save Manjiro's father, found the ability to smile and bow.

For his part Lord Okubo decided that he could not be a party to such treason no matter how great the lord who organized it. That is why there was nothing for him but, with the perfect backward logic of fathers everywhere, to vent his anger on his son; both in their short ride home and as they burst through the door, almost catching Einosuke and Fumiko making love.

9. | *A Word Overheard Is a Word Forgotten*

WORD OF LORD ABE'S illegal invitation spread, with anger over it building and continuing for days, not only at Einosuke's house, but in the hallways of the Great Council chambers, in the gardens below those hallways, at Lord Tokugawa's Edo hunting lodge where Tsune had spent her first night in Edo, and in tearooms and geisha houses from deep in the heart of the Yoshiwara pleasure district all the way out to the fishermen's brothels not far from the now empty treaty house. Gossip! Gossip! Gossip! All over town people talked of little else.

Inside the Great Council meeting rooms Lord Abe's censure, and even his ouster, were called for—for 250 years no one had invited foreigners into Edo!—but Lord Abe, always impassive, weathered the storm. During the debates, necessary, to be sure, but as predictable as melting winter snow, Manjiro's father swallowed his anger and stayed true to Lord Abe, but it cost him dearly to do so. His dignity and his sense of propriety had once been as strong as Einosuke's, yet tempered, he liked to believe, with Manjiro's streak of independent thought. In other words there was a time when Lord Okubo would have counted himself among those dissenting lords who called for censure, and it irked him to find he could no longer do it, that a certain softness, a lack of the vital energy necessary for political outrage, had invaded his inner core.

But all that was later. On the morning after the invitation was extended, by the Western calendar April 1, 1854, Manjiro, still in trouble with his father, and especially worried that Lord Tokugawa might not see him as a proper marriage candidate for Tsune, got up at dawn and went out into his brother's rock garden to think things over. The cold of the night before had produced a spring freeze, as unexpected as Lord Abe's invitation, so he wrapped himself in a heavy coat and found a fur-lined hat to wear. The hat was a relic from the days of his grandfather, and when he put it on it seemed to calm him, making him wonder what his grandfather would think of Lord Abe's chicanery.

A thin layer of ice had formed on the branches of the neighbor's nearest tree, where it peeked over Einosuke's wall. Its leaves were too heavy to do anything but sag, and as Manjiro smiled at the idea that his brother, at least, would find relief in the unseasonable weather, he suddenly saw Einosuke, standing at the far side of the garden, gray as the dawn.

"My poor brother," he said. "Are you not frozen? Should I bring some tea or a coat?"

To be sure he had been concentrating on the events of last night, but it was extraordinary not to have seen Einosuke earlier. Einosuke's hands were encased in the gloves that went with the hat that Manjiro wore, so it seemed as though both brothers had retreated into the old and better-known world of their grandfather. Einosuke's garden was properly raked again, he had removed the last of the leaves and smoothed away the evidence, the glorious mess he and Fumiko had made of things, even before the first streaks of dawn woke Manjiro.

Einosuke had an ingenious little charcoal brazier which he had salvaged from a broken *kotatsu* the year before. He had put the brazier in a large-mouthed pickle jar and packed the excess area of it with dying coals. From the time of the construction of this new room the brazier had sat on the porch above his garden, always ready with new charcoal. So when Manjiro sat down, Einosuke hurried around the side of the house to the kitchen for fire. With the nation in such turmoil he thought it would be grand, the two sons of Lord Okubo, each in a piece of their grandfather's clothing, sitting around a hot brazier on the newly built porch.

While Manjiro told the story of Lord Abe's invitation, Einosuke grew calm. No one knew better than he the degree of their father's frustrations, or that the importance of their father's opinions, in the eyes of the Great Council, had heretofore been small. For a decade Einosuke's job had been more like that of a secretary than the representative of an influential lord. He knew also, deep in his heart, that men like Lord Abe were solicitous of his father now for two reasons alone: First because Shimoda, the town where the American presence would soon be felt most strongly, was on the Izu Peninsula and thus near his father's jurisdiction; and second, irony of ironies, because the only man anyone could find who spoke English was Manjiro.

Einosuke waited until Manjiro finished his story and then said, "Maybe you know that I have not been called upon to work very hard during my years in Edo. Ours is a small fiefdom, my brother, unimportant and without a strong voice in national issues, especially in times of political calm."

When he'd come outside Manjiro had at first been sorry to find Einosuke there ahead of him, but now he was glad. Einosuke's comment was refreshing in its candor, and so bold that, as with his speech of yesterday, Manjiro knew he was about to hear from a brother he had rarely heard from before.

"It's a trick, you know," Einosuke said of the invitation, "nothing more than part of Lord Abe's design. Such thinking is what makes him our most dominant lord."

"He did ask father and Lord Tokugawa to give him time to explain," Manjiro said, "but more time did not prove enlightening and, as you must have heard when we came in last night, father wasn't pacified."

Einosuke cranked a gloved hand through the air as if manually making his voice low. "I can enlighten you if you like," he said. "I have a story of my own to tell."

Since he had no hat and Manjiro had no gloves, the hands of the younger brother and the head of the elder had slowly come together over the fire, as if they belonged to a single man. "Do not misunderstand. I have done my duty over the years, representing father as well as I could," said Einosuke, "but my opinion was almost never sought and I kept finding myself with extra time. Some days I would stay in the Great Council antechamber sleeping or writing letters or talking with those in the same boat as myself, but other days, I confess it, I would seek variety by strolling the nearby roads, learning the various byways of Edo."

Manjiro tried to speak, to say that anyone might have done likewise, but Einosuke stopped him. "One evening I happened to see Lord Abe walking ahead of me. I was surprised because I thought he was inside the rooms I had just left, but I was also surprised because he was alone, with no accompanying samurai and not even that turnip-headed aide of his, Ueno. So, almost by accident, I followed him. I did so at first, I think, because I supposed it was not Lord Abe after all, and I simply wanted to satisfy my curiosity."

"You didn't greet him?" asked Manjiro. "You didn't wish him good evening on behalf of our father?" Manjiro was unencumbered by fidelity to the past in political ways, but was unfailingly polite, more attached to good deportment than Einosuke.

"I have been in Lord Abe's presence numerous times," Einosuke answered, "but he never remembers me. He knows neither my face nor that we have met before. So if I am to greet him on behalf of father, I first must once again tell him who I am and it infuriates me."

Clouds had come in during the night bringing warmer temperatures, and it had started to rain, but the eave over the porch had so far kept the brothers dry. The rain sliced into the garden away from them, wetting the boulders and Einosuke's newly raked gravel. Inside the house they could hear others rising, a cough from the baby, Junichiro, and Lord Okubo calling for tea, but neither brother wanted interruption.

"Where did Lord Abe go?" Manjiro asked. Because he was hearing a story set in the early evening and Lord Abe was alone, he expected to find that the great man had disguised himself and would presently do something low. So he was quite astonished when his brother said, "He turned down the street of libraries, and into the Bansho Shirabesho."

"The Bansho Shirabesho!" Manjiro's hands had strayed too close to the coals and he jerked them back, turning in order to stick them out under the rain. "You must be mistaken, Einosuke. I have been there. It is not a place Lord Abe would go."

The Bansho Shirabesho was "The Institute for the Investigation of Barbarian Books," a library of sorts, and it was common knowledge that Lord Abe hated the place and wanted nothing so much as to shut it down. It had been established back in 1811 by the Shogun himself, on "know your enemy" grounds, and whenever it was mentioned in Great Council meetings it made the isolationists furious. But in fact it was just one small room, in a building which also housed the Institute for the Investigation of Chinese Herbs and the Institute of Fish. Only one man worked in the Barbarian Library, and the number of translated foreign books he oversaw could be counted on the two brothers' fingers and toes.

"That's what I thought, too," Einosuke confided, "so I followed him inside. The building is oddly built, and I suspected he was merely using it as a shortcut, a way of quickly getting to an opposite street."

"Lord Abe inside the Barbarian Book Room," mused Manjiro. "What do you know!"

"Listen," said Einosuke, "Lord Abe paused by the Institute of Fish man for such a long time that at first I thought he had business with him. I had slipped past him and was standing behind a giant jar of ginseng root, pretending to examine its label. In turn Lord Abe pretended an interest in fish. He spoke casually, picked up a newly published study on the migratory and eating practices of sperm whales, and walked, as if reading it, right into the library! He didn't sign in. He didn't do anything."

"But you can't do that," said Manjiro, "you have to have special passes. It took me forever to get mine."

"The Barbarian Book Room was empty," said Einosuke. "The door was open but the official in charge of it was gone. I waited by the ginseng root until the fish man saw me and asked if he could help. He said he was doing triple duty that day because the other two men were ill."

"And all this time Lord Abe was in there by himself? Could you see him from where you stood?"

"I could see him, but not well. He hadn't closed the door, but there wasn't much light in the room. When I stepped up to the fish man's table I could just see Lord Abe's back. He was bent and examining something."

Manjiro shook his head and said, "When I went there it took a week just to get the proper forms."

"I remembered that," said Einosuke, "and so I thought the fish official was either incompetent or Lord Abe had somehow given him the forms without me noticing. But I could see no evidence of the first in the man's behavior or of the second among the papers that were stacked around him on his dais. It was a mystery, so in order to stay longer without appearing to spy I assumed a level of friendliness I don't usually have, much as Lord Abe had done. But I'm not a good actor, I guess, for the fish man immediately saw through my ruse. What he thought I was after, however, was not a moment of spying on Lord Abe, but information on the sexual properties of the ginseng root."

Manjiro didn't want to draw the attention of those inside the house, but he laughed, his heart growing progressively light. "Ginseng cures impotency, Einosuke," he said. "Did you tell the fish man that your own root had lost its form?"

Einosuke let his thoughts shift back to the night before with Fumiko, but all he said was, "I let him assume what he would. I wasn't aware of it before that visit, but this Chinese Herbs Institute is not purely informational. They also have a selection of ointments and medicines for sale."

"So you bought ginseng in order to cover your ruse? That's expensive. Let me see it. Let's try some now, do you have it in the house?"

"The fish man got down off his dais and, since he didn't know the Chinese herb section well, took a long time looking around. And when he came back he not only carried a dripping wet ginseng root, but a box of ginseng powder, too. We were both shocked by the prices, but he left the powder on the table when he went to put the root away. And while he was gone this second time, Lord Abe came back out of the Barbarian Book Room. I was no longer comfortable with the subterfuge and had decided to greet him properly, but he hardly looked at me and he didn't slow down until he turned to slip into his *geta* at the door."

"What had he been reading?" Manjiro asked. "Did you discover the book's name after he'd gone?"

"I thought I would," said Einosuke, "I thought I might be able to get the fish man to tell me, but when Lord Abe finally looked up I saw that he still had the book in his hand. I was surprised that the book was so small."

"Those books are to be read in the library!" said Manjiro. "And then only when you've got the necessary stamps." His voice grew louder. "Even a member of the Great Council . . . Even the Shogun . . . !"

"At the time I assumed that a member of the Great Council might be able to go there without the proper stamps, but since then I have found that you are right, no one, not even the Shogun, can take a Barbarian Library book home." That the Shogun had no interest in the daily machinations of government, let alone the intellectual curiosity necessary to want to venture into the Barbarian Book Room, the brothers acknowledged with a glance.

The charcoal had burned down but Manjiro no longer noticed the cold. The single time he had visited the Barbarian Book Room he had been sent by his tutor to catalogue the books so his tutor would know which of them came from German, which from English, which from Dutch. Manjiro remembered the experience well. Because it had taken the better part of his stay in Edo to get the approval stamps, he had made a day of it, going to the book room early and not leaving until it closed. It had taken him no time to list the books, such a list, in fact, was given to him by the attendant, so he spent his time reading. He read the first chapter of every book in the library, all forty of them, and then went back to three that had caught his interest and read them in their entirety; two books of scientific inquiry and one of poems. The visit had been a defining moment in his life, reinvigorating his interest in studying English, and making him doubly curious about the outside world as a whole.

"What happened next?" Manjiro asked. "Did you find out where he went or which book he took home?"

"No, the fish man didn't know anything, and it would have taken a long time in the book room just to discover the book's name. I was suspicious and curious by then, and decided to be even more careful than I had before. So when the fish man came back to his desk I bought the ginseng powder and followed Lord Abe out into the night. But, unfortunately, I could no longer find him."

The brothers had grown cold again, what with the rain and the brazier's fire burning down, so when he finished speaking Einosuke opened the *shoji* and they went back inside.

"But what does it mean?" Manjiro asked. "Do you believe Lord Abe is secretly learning about the West, that he isn't an isolationist anymore?"

Manjiro himself could never believe such a thing, even after hearing Einosuke's story and observing Lord Abe's strange behavior the night before, but Einosuke was stopped from answering by the sound of a woman's voice.

"One might just as well ask, 'Do you believe that Japan is not an island anymore?' or 'Do you believe Lord Abe is a woman under his robes?'"

It was Tsune. She had just returned from Lord Tokugawa's hunting lodge and was sitting there staring at a calligraphy that hung at the room's far end.

"I'm sorry," said Einosuke. "This room is for contemplation. We should not have interrupted you with our gossip."

He was angry. He had told Manjiro his story on a whim, without really deciding to do so, and now it seemed possible that everyone in the house might know. Of course he had already told his wife, but what if Tsune told his father, or worse, decided to tell Lord Tokugawa? If that happened Einosuke might be called into the Great Council chambers to explain himself!

"These stamps, Manjiro-san, these permissions one needs to enter the Barbarian Book Room, once you have them how many times are you allowed to go?"

Tsune had turned away from the calligraphy. She now faced the brothers directly but remained on her cushion, knees together beneath her gown.

"Ah," said Manjiro, as much in answer to her continued ease as to her question.

"I am asking because it occurred to me that you, Manjiro-san, might be able to return to the room and by simply asking the attendant for another list, deduce which book is gone."

"It's true, I'm an authorized visitor now," Manjiro said. He gave Einosuke a glance that he hoped apologized for him thinking that Tsune's idea was a good one, but Einosuke now spoke directly to her.

"A word overheard is a word forgotten," he said. "I think that's a useful proverb."

He did not like to be blunt but if Tsune would involve herself so blithely in the affairs of state and if Manjiro could find nothing better to do than agree with her, what else could he do?

"Of course," said Tsune, "you have my promise, Einosuke-san."

When he heard that Einosuke saw, yet again, that Tsune was more beautiful and disarming than his wife and, just at that moment, as if catching him in the thought, his wife came into the room.

"Breakfast is ready," she said. "Did O-bata not call?"

All three of them turned to face her and Manjiro said, "It should be easy. I will go today."

"Go where?" asked Fumiko, but Tsune touched her sister's hand.

"Do we have any ginseng in the house?" she asked. "When the subject came up just now I realized that though I have heard of its powers often, I have never tried it. It might be interesting to see if its effects are as readily available to women as men."

It was a harmless joke, meant to tell Einosuke that she was a reliable sister-in-law, but it titillated Manjiro and entirely perplexed Fumiko.

"Have you done your raking this morning, dear?" she asked her husband. "Did you smooth the gravel below the porch?"

Einosuke assured her that he had, and when the others left the garden room ahead of them he slid his hand along the contours of his wife's back, hoping to let her know that he would like to meet her here later, and mess up the rocks again.

At breakfast Lord Okubo was contrite about the shouting he had done the night before. He apologized to Einosuke and Fumiko, but could manage only a nod to Manjiro.

10. *The Pavilion of Timelessness*

TSUNE WAS KNOWN in Edo society not only because her name had once surfaced on a list of candidates when a previous Shogun needed a wife, or because in recent years she had had two marriage proposals from sons of members of the Great Council and had cut off negotiations with both, but also because of a certain recent and serious indiscretion, word of which had somehow reached Edo. And now that she was back in the capital, now that she had been seen at the treaty-signing ceremonies, people were talking again. What was she up to, this woman with the spotted reputation, this no-longer-quite-so-eligible daughter of the realm? And who was this strange younger brother of her brother-in-law, this usurping young scoundrel, Manjiro?

Such were the public conditions under which the two young people left Einosuke's house the next morning, to search out the Barbarian Book Library. Manjiro had departed first, so was inside the library's main room, in the presence of the official from the Institute of Fish and the previously missing Barbarian Book Room man, when Tsune arrived shortly after him.

"Ah, my husband, I have found you," she said. "I worried I might not."

Manjiro's face darkened. Wasn't that too bold a comment, too risky a joke? There had been no formal talk yet, nor had there been the slightest private word between them concerning marriage. Was she trying to tell him something, or was she merely choosing the most obvious ruse to fool the book room man?

"Here I am," he said.

Her entrance drew the man from the Institute for the Investigation of Chinese Herbs, making him hurry over to join the others. He had not heard the exchange and assumed that whenever a woman came into the building she wanted what he had to offer. Exotic Chinese herbs! The constantly whispered-about promise of female sexual pleasure!

"Good morning, madam," he said, in a slightly lascivious voice. "Allow me to help you find what you want."

The herb official's greatest joy came when he placed his medicines in front of these young wives or geisha, for years earlier he had discovered that if he leaned into the table while explaining their properties, and if he watched the expressions on the women's faces as he did so, the herbs worked far more quickly for him than if he ingested them.

"Please," he said, "there have been so many advances recently, let me give my little talk. There is nothing for you to spend on it except time."

He bowed, in respect for Tsune's station, but he also waved his hands in the air in the way certain merchants had recently found to somehow garner authority. Tsune knew that Manjiro's papers would not allow him to take her, wife or not, into the Barbarian Book Room with him. Her idea had simply been to engage the room's attendant in small talk so that Manjiro could search in peace. She was therefore hesitant to go with the herb man until she saw that the book attendant followed right along behind them, a little like a dog in heat. He, too, had taken up the habit of pressing against the edges of his table while the herb man gave his talk, it seemed, and he left Manjiro fast, saying only, "Read at your leisure, sir, I know you have the verifications. I remember you from before."

So that is how Manjiro was able to mirror Lord Abe's time in the Barbarian Book Room alone. He remembered the room exactly. During the first thirty years of its existence books had been translated and added to the collection regularly, but it had stopped growing a decade ago. Now there were forty strange and wonderful foreign titles, each arranged on its own low table.

He could see in an instant that no book was missing. To speak precisely there were eighty books, for in every case the Japanese translation and the original text lay together, the Japanese version inevitably larger, as if the information contained in each volume had been augmented by its translator, exploded by Japanese grammar and syntax. While Manjiro gazed at the books he thought again of his tutor, an ex-priest and wayward intellectual named Wilhelm Mundt, whom he had rescued from Nagasaki some five years ago, and who had finally been forced to leave

Japan only six months earlier, at the beginning of this current antiforeign furor. His tutor's dream had been to add another book to the collection in this marvelous room. He had completed his work before he left, and it sat in their study in Shimoda, silent in both its languages, waiting for Manjiro to collect it and bring it to this room. Its title was *Faust,* and Manjiro loved a particular line from it that read, *"If ever I lay down in sloth and base inaction, then let that moment be my end."* It was how he hoped to live his life—with that thought as his admonition.

Manjiro glanced back out at the men before going over to the book attendant's table and turning the ledger around. The ledger recorded the names and interests of all visitors to the room, but though it went back more than forty years, it was still only one-third full. He found his own name, with notations next to it telling how long he had stayed and what he had done, and he saw that after him no more than a half dozen people had visited the room. Lord Abe's name was not among them. Now what would he do? He could tell from the quickening pace of the herb official's monologue that his time alone might be short.

Starting on the left side of the room, Manjiro opened each book in the wild hope that he would be able to guess Lord Abe's interest from the title or the first few lines, when suddenly he remembered Einosuke saying that the book Lord Abe took with him had been small, that Lord Abe had held the volume in one hand. He picked up the nearest book and found that he could only carry it comfortably under his arm, so he put it down again and stood in the middle of the room, surveying all of the books, this time forgetting content and paying attention only to size. The largest book, rising off the floor to mid-calf level, was the Christian Bible, and the smallest, which he knew immediately could not be the one, was a volume of sonnets by the English poet William Shakespeare.

Manjiro crossed the room to the only other book that could be taken out of the room in one hand, but before opening it he parted the *shoji* a little, so that he could see the backs of the caretakers again, a dozen feet away. He could also see Tsune, who had drawn her kimono sleeve back and was just then pulling a ginseng root out of a large-mouthed jar. It was a gesture that made his mouth water.

"Show me," she was saying. "Can you cut it a little? I have never seen it before."

Manjiro closed the *shoji* and picked the book up off the floor. The original volume was in Spanish, or perhaps Italian. The Japanese title was *Ooji*, Prince, and it had been written by someone named Niccolò. Manjiro still had the intention of reading a little bit from the book's beginning, to see what he could learn, but the book opened at its middle where a thin sheet of paper fell out. The paper was covered with Japanese words, with lines of expert calligraphy. He was at first indignant, nearly ready to call that lax attendant back into the room and complain. What if the ink on this paper had not been sufficiently dried and had marked the pages of the book with little half circles or parts of a phrase? There were only forty books and each was a treasure, fashioned with grace and care; each a work of art. What was this attendant's job, then, if not to keep the books safe, if not to walk among them looking for such problems as this, to open and close them occasionally so that their unread pages got air?

His anger would have gotten the best of him on another occasion, but in fact the book had not been dirtied and for an instant his new fear was that an actual page had come loose in his hands. Manjiro opened the *shoji* again, an inch or two. How could this be? There was no question that the loose page and the one it marked contained precisely the same words, and there was also no question that they had been written by different hands. Had Lord Abe, then, or someone else, copied the words out and then inexplicably forgot them when he returned the book, or, for some even more unfathomable reason, purposefully left them behind? Manjiro stood against the flow of such thoughts until his eye was caught by the flourish of Tsune's sleeve and he saw that the Chinese ganglion was sliding back through the mouth of its jar. The prurient party was breaking up. He had just put the book back down, in fact, and tucked the loose page up his sleeve, when the barbarian book man came back.

"Tell me," asked Manjiro, "who cares for these volumes? How often does someone dust them, how often does someone clean?"

He had intended to sound merely curious, but had not been able to hide his irritation. The book room man's face was red. "I do, sir," was his reply.

When Manjiro turned back into the room and pointed, both men saw that everything before them was in order. "I meant to ask how often their pages are aired," said Manjiro. "I thought I saw a bit of yellow in the *Sonnets* of Shakespeare just now."

He was still pointing, though he couldn't even remember where the sonnets of Shakespeare resided.

"I assure you, sir, not only do I air the pages of these books, but I actually read them, one after another, over and over again, year after year. I believe it is the act of reading, not the air, that keeps the yellow out."

The man was small, but his voice and bearing were not. He looked directly at Manjiro and began to recite:

Not marble, nor the gilded monuments
Of princes, shall outlive this powerful rhyme;
But you shall shine more brightly in these contents
Than unswept stone, besmeared with sluttish time.

"That's Shakespeare," he said. "Isn't it beautiful? It's meaning comes clearer if you read it more than once or twice."

Manjiro was so taken by the words that he might have stayed, turning back to Shakespeare to read for a while, had he not seen Tsune again, this time at the book room door. "My husband we must go now," she said. Her eyes flashed at him, dimming the book attendant's quote.

It only took another minute for the attendant to stamp Manjiro's papers, and when he reentered the larger room the herb man was in its most distant corner and Tsune was gone. Seeing him standing there so filled Manjiro with fury at how he had used the woman he loved, that his right hand actually touched the shaft of his sword. He would teach the man a lesson he would not soon forget! Never in his life had he known civil servants to be so bold!

But behind his anger Manjiro understood that no one was less likely than Tsune to act as someone's pawn, that far from having been used, it was she who had engineered everything, carefully and well. He might have drawn his sword anyway, or cut the man with words, at least, had that single sheet of paper not slipped out of his kimono sleeve and scratched his arm. He bolted from the library then with such quickness that the cold morning sun hurt his eyes.

"Ah!" he said. "Ouch! It is bright!"

She was sitting in a partially opened palanquin, its bearers below her on the ground. The other palanquin, the one Manjiro had come in, was gone. She told him to get in, and when he was beside her in the crowded space, the soft material of her kimono touching him, she lowered the palanquin's side panels. Such closeness unbalanced Manjiro more than the sharp-edged sun, but he ordered himself to be calm, determined not to push up against her, as, through that surrogate table, those abhorrent custodians had done.

———

NEITHER OF THEM spoke again until they were halfway across Edo and began to hear the bearers' efforts as they ascended a hill.

"But where are we going?" asked Manjiro. "Have you not instructed them to take us home?"

"I have told them to bring us here as a precaution," said Tsune, leaning over to turn the side panel nearest Manjiro up again. "If you have discovered that Lord Abe's activities are suspect, then you might also decide that you need to inform another powerful lord. And if not, then I brought you here because I wanted to show you Lord Tokugawa's beautiful forest and hunting lodge. They are quite exquisite. The lodge is modeled after Nijo Castle in Kyoto, you know, the famous one with the chirping floors."

Lord Tokugawa's hunting lodge? How strange that they should come here instead of home, to bring the news of what they had found to Einosuke. Was he also in trouble with Lord Tokugawa, Manjiro wondered again, for the same reasons he had been in trouble with his father? And was Tsune therefore bringing him here to save their chances of marriage? Manjiro sighed. Was it due to strength or weakness that he could not decide whether or not Tsune had gone too far?

"Are you carrying any coins," she asked him, when they stepped out into a dimmer daylight than the one outside the library, "or shall I fetch some inside?"

Manjiro found a few coppers for the exhausted palanquin men, who had fallen down around them on the ground, and when he returned his purse to his sash the stolen paper touched his arm again. He had no intention of showing it to Lord Tokugawa—on the point of Lord Abe's activities he was sure that Tsune was wrong—but he revealed the paper anyway, smoothing it against his chest.

"I found this," he told her quietly. "I took it from a book in the library."

He had not read the paper yet, and in his mind's eye he saw Tsune sitting beside him, faces touching while they puzzled it out.

"What could you have been thinking?" she said. "Surely you didn't cut it?"

She had turned him up the path to the lodge, but when Manjiro handed her the paper she turned him again, down toward a teahouse at the center of a bamboo grove. She lifted her head from the paper long enough to order tea from the attendant at the door, but even after they entered the building, which had the words "Pavilion of Timelessness" cut onto a sign above its arch, she studied the paper for a long time.

"I don't understand this very well," she finally said.

"I found it tucked inside what I think was Lord Abe's volume," Manjiro said. "Someone had copied it and left it there. It marked an identically worded page."

"Read it to me," Tsune ordered. "It will be clearer, maybe, if you say the words out loud."

So while the tearoom girl poured tea, Manjiro took the paper back and leaned away from Tsune toward the light.

Therefore it is unnecessary for a prince to have all the good qualities I have enumerated, but it is very necessary to appear to have them. And I shall dare to say this also, that to have them and always observe them is injurious, and that to appear to have them is useful; to appear merciful, faithful, humane, religious, upright, and to be so, but with a mind framed that should you require not to be so, you may know how to change to the opposite.

Though he was only half done, Manjiro stopped. It was no doubt philosophy, for he recognized, in it, some of his tutor's argumentative tone, but who could think such a thing, what breed of man would subscribe to such beliefs? If this was American philosophy then maybe he and the others on his side had been wrong about wanting to engage them.

"Does it seem correct to you," asked Tsune, "or does it seem wrong?

And whose thinking does this document represent? Is it the belief of the outside world that a man must pretend to honor but not of necessity have it? Do I understand it correctly or not?"

If Manjiro had learned anything in his years of study with his tutor it was that philosophy was difficult. His tutor would often trap him, sometimes even arguing the opposite of what he believed in order to force Manjiro into thinking well. So he said, "Let me read the rest before we decide." He took a sip of tea, cleared his throat, and read on:

> And you have to understand this, that a prince, especially a new one, cannot observe all those things for which men are esteemed, being often forced, in order to maintain the state, to act contrary to fidelity, friendship, humanity, and religion. Therefore it is necessary for him to have a mind ready to turn itself accordingly as the winds and variations of fortune force it, yet, as I have said above, not to diverge from the good if he can avoid doing so, but, if compelled, then to know how to set about it.

When he finished Manjiro sat there for a long time, the paper on the table next to his hand.

"I am glad we came here instead of returning to Einosuke's house," Tsune finally said. "You will, of course, decide for yourself, Manjiro-san, but I think we have no choice now but to share your strange discovery with Lord Tokugawa."

Lord Tokugawa again! Oh, why did Manjiro feel like a student, his many accomplishments dimming, when confronted with a mind more beautifully housed and of firmer resolve?

"If we show it to him it will be out of our hands," he said.

"On the contrary, showing this document to Lord Tokugawa may be the only way to keep it in our hands," Tsune said. "Do you not see that? Otherwise we will be able to do nothing. Knowledge without power is a weakly burning light."

That she had said he would be allowed to decide for himself made Manjiro calm. He thought about it for a while but soon he asked whether Lord Tokugawa was at home that morning, and, if he was, whether Tsune could arrange an audience.

11. *Where Has My Heart Gone?*

WHEN THEY LEFT the Pavilion of Timelessness it was just after noon and raining. Manjiro carried the smoothed-out sheet of paper inside his kimono, and Tsune carried a *bangasa,* one of those thickly waxed paper umbrellas that seemed permanently stationed by the teahouse door. The bamboo forest was quiet as they walked. The tops of the trees swayed in the rising wind, but the leaves on the pathways were as sodden as the ones from Einosuke's neighbor's yard.

Some of Lord Tokugawa's samurai had come out to practice their skills in the rain and were strutting about in a clearing close to the lodge. A few made passes at each other with bamboo swords, while others exchanged insults in the dialects of fiefdoms that were most often politically opposed to their lord's. They wanted to be ready with words as well as with weapons, on the off chance that interfiefdom warfare should break out.

All Lord Tokugawa's samurai knew Tsune and all, save the older of the two men at the door, had at one time or another fallen into gossiping about her, saying that her father had been lax, that he and Lord Tokugawa should have married her off years earlier. The older man who had not gossiped about her was the famous swordsman Kyuzo, originally from Kyoto and in Lord Tokugawa's employ for just this last half year or so. He had come not only out of respect for the lord, but also because he hoped, as the end of his life approached, to be at the center of the action should there be a war with America. Tsune had not expected to meet him, standing as if on guard duty, and seeing him made her face grow flushed and her feet stumble on the path.

"Will his lordship allow me to present this nobleman?" she asked the younger samurai, and while he went to inform Lord Tokugawa of her arrival, she introduced Manjiro to Kyuzo, who bowed but did not speak, though Lord Okubo's crest, plainly visible on Manjiro's sleeve, seemed to require him to do so. When he came out of his bow the older man examined Manjiro thoroughly, with engaged and honest curiosity. Manjiro felt like one of the three-legged toads that Masako had been finding lately, hopping along in front of their disrepaired home, yet there was no rudeness in Kyuzo's glance, no hostility. Manjiro stared back at him but soon grew comfortable enough to begin thinking about those paragraphs again. Tsune, however, could not bear what was happening and left the men quickly, tripping up into the lodge, to run down the nearest hallway before the "chirping" floors called to her in a strong enough voice to make her slow down. There was a bench in the hallway and she fell upon it, slumping there with none of the presence she had shown in the Pavilion of Timelessness. Her chest heaved and tears gathered in her eyes. She said, "Oh this complicated, mixed-up life of mine!"

Despite the outside world's view of her, Tsune believed her life to be painful and unlucky. She had first met the older Kyuzo just a few months earlier, when he'd arrived in Mito from Kyoto. He had been teaching *kendo* to Lord Tokugawa's younger samurai and reading Confucian doctrine for a fortnight before she truly noticed him. She had heard stories of his earlier exploits, of course, of his great accomplishments with a sword, but because she was by nature dismissive of such tales it was not until she felt a certain lassitude one night, and hoped to confront it by reading *Empty Chestnut,* an old collection of Basho poems, that she came upon the man directly. The room that contained the volume—another library!—was one Lord Tokugawa's samurai rarely entered, so she was surprised not only to find him there, but to discover that he had that very collection before him, *Empty Chestnut,* and was reading it aloud. As usual she had come with her maid, but when she heard Kyuzo's halting voice she left the girl outside.

Kyuzo stopped his recitation when the door opened, but she had already recognized the poem and said, "What I have come for, sir, is that which you hold in your hand."

Kyuzo barked out a laugh, so fearing she had been rude to him she offered a kind of explanation. "I often take a book to my bed chambers and the one you are reading best suits my mood tonight." After that she waited. She would not speak again, nor would she give up the volume. Let him read fighting manuals if he had to read something, or if he wanted to broaden himself let him read one of those ridiculous new popular novels.

Kyuzo seemed to understand that he couldn't beat her by waiting, so when a small amount of time had passed he simply bent to the book again and resumed, as if she were not there, in the same unmodulated voice.

> Tired of Cherry,
> Tired of this whole world,
> I sit facing muddy saké
> And black rice.

Tsune was insulted, but felt that to show her anger would be unseemly and also grant this man what he was after. So since she knew the poem better than he did she strode up to him and spoke its second verse in a far more suitable tone. She hoped it would offend him on several counts, not the least of which because he was old.

> Who could it possibly be,
> Who mourns the passing autumn,
> Careless of the wind
> Rustling his beard?

There was a third stanza, and if he looked down to read it, if he did not immediately close the book and recite it from memory, she would snatch the volume from his hands, declare victory, and march back out the door. She stared at him, but while she waited she began to remember that her maid was shivering on the porch, and in the instant her attention shifted Kyuzo slammed the volume shut with a startling crack. He stepped off the dais to land in front of her quietly, like a ghost from worlds past.

> With frozen water
> That tastes painfully bitter
> A sewer rat relieves in vain
> His parched throat.

At first she wanted to slap him, to make the same noise the closing book had made with the palm of her hand on his face, but his look was quizzical now, not victorious, as if he only hoped he'd said it right, and the voice he had used was so opposed to the despair of the poem that she abruptly lost her anger and started to laugh. Kyuzo puffed up again, letting air whistle out through his mouth.

"What?" he asked. "Why in the world are you laughing?"

"Forgive me," she said. "Your rendition was adequate, I guess, but had I taken it to my bed chambers I think I would have captured a little more of the poet's original intent."

Kyuzo's reply was immediate. "Because my rendition was frivolous or because your bed chambers harbor despair?" His voice, like his stare at Manjiro, did not easily carry insult and Tsune was not offended. Rather she considered the question seriously, succumbing to a long pause.

"'Despair' is too strong for what I always feel. Is there not another word that carries just a bit of it, in the midst of something easier to bear?"

"Loneliness," he said. "Not only another word but a better one. You are entirely too young for despair."

"I'm not too young for it but too strong," Tsune responded. "And while loneliness might feed on strength, despair despairs of it."

They were both quiet for a moment, proud, despite themselves, of the exchange. And then Kyuzo handed her the book and left the reading room by a back door.

That was all, but later in her bed chambers, dressed in gauzy white and sitting before a fickle candle, Tsune couldn't concentrate. The poems had always before served to alleviate her sadness, reinforcing her view that the world's nature was harsh, but on this night she put the volume down and was abstractedly thinking things over when her maid came in with a note, folded and cross-folded, as if by a teenage girl.

Where has my heart gone?
Of late I have wondered.
Did I leave it in Kyoto,
Under a crust of dark winter snow?

Tsune had never before thought of taking a lover so much older than herself, but she bid the maid wait and penned a quick reply and sent it off.

> Under a crust of dark winter snow,
> Or under early autumn rain
> My lover's lonely heart.
> Will it know fulfillment or despair?

It was too enigmatic, she did not know herself whether she was telling him to come or stay away, but she waited beside that fickle candle, until the maid had time to deliver the poem, until Kyuzo had time to read it, until he was either stealing toward her or limp with indecision, hung up, like a younger man would be, on that final question mark.

Was it the midnight wind that blew the candle out, waking her? The question came from the same frame of mind that had let her write the poem, but her eyes snapped open, searching the incredible dark. Kyuzo's thumb and index finger had come down upon the flame, making it hiss in his spittle, and then he was beside her, removing her gown. They didn't move or roll, like Fumiko and Einosuke had done, but seemed to find an unreachable stillness, one inside the other inside the other. And then the coming tremor, like the shivering surface of water in a broad-mouthed jar.

Every night after that when the sun went down and the lamps at Lord Tokugawa's main house closed in upon darkness, they were together. Kyuzo sang to her, his voice deep and haunting, nothing like his recitation of the poem, and she danced the dances she had learned as a girl. They read books aloud, poetry sometimes, but more often erotic tales of how Prince Genji had stolen into countless maidens' rooms, wooing them with words and glances nine hundred years before. They read freely, always after they made love, never before, but they stayed away from *Empty Chestnut,* which they both cherished for bringing them together, but which they both also greatly feared because they no longer understood it, could no longer fathom its despair.

Why such a thing could not go on forever was a question others might have pondered, but neither Tsune nor Kyuzo asked it of themselves. She was an aristocrat and he, by comparison, was nothing much at all. They weathered one fearful storm when two months after the beginning of their affair Tsune turned down another marriage proposal, but that was all. Lord Tokugawa let her know that the next time someone approached them with a good match he would accept on her behalf, whether she liked it or not, after the investigations were done.

Maybe because he was older and had been in love before, Kyuzo was more philosophical about it than Tsune, for, in the end, it was he who insisted that they stop at a moment chosen by them, that they do so out of strength, before the day of the awful ultimatum. He also suggested something that was at first unbearable to Tsune, but that took root over time: that she strike first, that she find her own suitable husband, someone she could respect and admire. And so, very slowly, she had begun to think of her sister's brother-in-law, whom she had not seen in years but would see again soon, when she visited Edo to attend Keiko's dance recital.

And now, while she waited in the hallway, benched like a censured maid, Manjiro and Kyuzo faced each other just inside the main door of Lord Tokugawa's hunting lodge.

12. | *A Fly in the Ointment*

BUT NO MATTER WHAT his mood about her marital status, Lord Tokugawa always received Tsune when she came to visit, and when he heard she was waiting now, he got up from his futon where he'd been pondering Lord Abe's minstrel invitation, and dressed in a casual gown.

On his way out of his rooms he stopped to get Keiki, his son. It had earlier been Tsune's father's hope, and the primary reason why he had not pressed her into some other obligation, that she might one day marry Keiki, but aside from the fact that she was far too old for him, Lord Tokugawa was against the match. Though he loved Tsune like a daughter, he wanted to marry Keiki into one of Japan's "hereditary" families, actually have him adopted into one of them, so that Keiki might someday be Shogun. That, no matter what the political issues of the day, was what Lord Tokugawa constantly worked toward.

Tsune had just got up from her bench and gone back to join Manjiro—Kyuzo had left some moments before—when Keiki came around the corner to say that his father awaited them in his study. Keiki's hair was mussed, his kimono askew—Tsune was like a sister to him, so he didn't feel the need to better his appearance—but when he saw Manjiro and heard her say his name, he gave a hearty laugh and tried to straighten his clothes.

"How splendid to meet the newly famous man!" he said. "Come in, come in, tell me the latest! What's the news? What goes on? What do they really look like, these foreigners?"

Keiki was overweight and energetic and had a ready smile. His exuberance reminded Manjiro of the American Commodore.

"Nothing but sun in the morning, rain in the afternoon," Keiki continued, "and if more cold is on its way it's sure to make the cherry blossoms late this year. I've been hearing recently that there are parts of the world where summer comes in winter or doesn't come at all! Do you suppose that's possible, Manjiro-san? I know we've only just met but if you find the opportunity, ask one of the Americans. Try to get the names of the places that are constantly warm."

The hallway they were walking down was opposite the one Tsune had recently sat in, and was in grave disorder, as if no maid had yet cleaned it from the night before. But its floors "chirped" under their feet again, just like the famous ones in Kyoto. Keiki, who was in bare feet, did his best to make the floors sing louder as they progressed toward Lord Tokugawa, and when they entered the study he said, "Ah, father, we really must rediscipline ourselves. We are rising later every day we are in Edo. Both of us need to try harder, you know."

But while Keiki seemed to have risen from his futon as a beaming sun rises in the sky, all Lord Tokugawa could manage was a nod and a groan. His intelligence was a good deal sharper than his son's, but he couldn't easily find it so early in the day.

Manjiro, nervous and solemn, bowed when Tsune introduced him, pulling the sheet of paper from his sleeve even before he sat down. To meet this great lord in such a private way was as fine an honor as being among the first to visit the American fleet, but the lord seemed only peeved, his eyes still half closed. Manjiro had no idea of the exact time, but he knew that in his life he had never slept so late. This, plus that old warrior Kyuzo's strange attitude toward him, made him try to remember what he was doing there in the first place. His own father, though he admired Lord Tokugawa, had always been firmly pledged to the Shogun, and thus to the Great Council and Lord Abe. What had made Manjiro forget it for a while was the shock of reading the horrible paragraphs with Tsune.

He was on the point of picking up his paper again and making his apologies, when Lord Tokugawa spoke for the first time. "What's that?" he asked. "What do you have there, young man?"

"That is the reason we are troubling you like this at the crack of dawn," said Tsune, her buoyancy regained. "That is the fly in the ointment, the chink in someone's armor that you have searched for for so long."

"It doesn't look like a chink," said Keiki, but his humor was ill timed.

"Don't speak in riddles. Give it here," said Lord Tokugawa.

Manjiro wanted to take a moment to explain, but all he could do was push the paper across the table. Lord Tokugawa read it and handed it to Keiki. "It's Lord Abe's handwriting," he said. "After all these years of sparring with the man I know that much, but what has he written? Is it a novel? I hope not, I don't like it when politicians are of two minds."

Lord Tokugawa was looking at Manjiro, but this was Tsune's domain, and Manjiro was grateful when she spoke, telling the story of what had happened in the Barbarian Book Room, yet careful not to violate her promise to Einosuke.

"I don't trust it very much," said Keiki. "Was Lord Abe really this careless? Are you saying that he went to the trouble of copying a page from a banned book and then left it there for you to find?"

It had at first seemed unlikely to Manjiro, too, but upon reading the paper he had noticed that the brushstrokes on some of the characters were sloppy, one or two of them entirely wrong.

"I think this was a kind of draft," he said. "I think he's in possession of another copy, one with more perfection in the writing."

Lord Tokugawa got to his knees, looming over them. "It is late in the game since the treaty is already signed, but do you think Lord Abe intends to try to use this piece of thinking against the Americans in some way? Do you think that's what was behind his stupid invitation, what he was trying to tell your father and me in the treaty house the other night?"

Manjiro was perplexed. He didn't think anything, and he hadn't the slightest notion what Lord Abe's intentions might be. But while he was wondering how best to answer, Keiki posed a question of his own.

"In the old days if some lord were carrying out a plan against another, if the two lords were, let's say, on the brink of war, what would the second lord's reaction be if the first one were to capture a few of his musicians and refuse to let them go?"

Manjiro could not see how Keiki's question related to the paper, but he was glad to have an easy one to answer. Not only in the old days, but in these current days as well, it would be unlikely that the second lord would care. Musicians were expendable, and so, for that matter, were samurai warriors. Lord Tokugawa, however, seemed to see more relevance in his son's question than did Manjiro.

"Lord Abe's no fool," he said. "Someone read it aloud. Let's try to better understand what we have here."

Keiki was a good reader and was pleased to show off. He took the paper and sat up straight, trying to make the words sound ominous.

> Therefore it is unnecessary for a prince to have all the good qualities I have enumerated, but it is very necessary to appear to have them . . .

When he finished, his listeners were no closer to understanding the thing than they had been previously, no closer to seeing how Lord Abe might use it to his advantage.

"It's intriguing," Lord Tokugawa finally said, "and it's quite like Lord Abe to find his poison in the medicine chest of his enemy. Someone say, in plainer words, the meaning of these paragraphs."

"One must appear to be acting in the common good while using whatever means necessary to achieve one's goal," Tsune said, but Lord Tokugawa ignored her. He had fixed his eyes on Manjiro, asking, "Where do you find the crux of the matter, young man?"

Manjiro didn't want to comment again, since he was remembering his father's loyalty to Lord Abe more clearly with every passing second, but he found himself answering anyway. "I think Lord Abe has not so much devised a plan as a frame of mind," he said. "Previous to reading the book from which these paragraphs came, I think he felt that however loath he was to perform them, his dealings with the Americans had to be honorable. Now maybe he has changed his mind."

Tsune and Keiki sat in silence but Lord Tokugawa was engaged. "Do you think he means harm to the musicians he so brashly decided to invite ashore?"

He was looking at Keiki, but all his son could do was shrug. "Maybe Lord Abe has not yet decided how to act and has invited them so that, when he finally does decide, he'll have someone to act upon."

But Lord Tokugawa rapped his knuckles on the tabletop. "Come,

Keiki, this is Lord Abe we are discussing, not some Confucian scholar! He's less philosophically minded than anyone I know."

That sounded right to Manjiro, too, not only because Lord Tokugawa said so, but because Lord Abe's methods had proven it. Lord Abe was a strong leader precisely because of his predictability, precisely because the other lords knew he was someone who wasn't frivolous, someone they could count on.

All three men felt relieved, glad to properly pigeonhole Lord Abe again, until Tsune said, "If that's the case then why didn't he ask for the Great Council's approval?"

Lord Tokugawa looked at her meanly but she went on. "I am suggesting only that because you do not know what he is up to, rather than guess at it, you should meet with Lord Abe and ask him. After all, our two most powerful lords aren't enemies but allies who speak together often."

"But how am I to know he's up to anything but the desire to hear these minstrels sing?" asked Lord Tokugawa. "Am I to say that it is because you two have brought me this copied page?"

Manjiro and Tsune would have urged against that, but this time it was Keiki who spoke. "Yes, father, just so, only tell him it was delivered to you in confidence. And tell him you knew it was his because his calligraphy is among the finest in the land."

Keiki was cheerful again, insisting it was the best course of action because, while it included only true statements, it would at the same time force Lord Abe either to lie or to tell Lord Tokugawa of his plan.

"Ah, yes," said Tsune, touching Manjiro's fingers under the table, "don't you agree Manjiro-san? Doesn't Keiki's idea have the simple elegance of which you and I have so long been fond?"

She smiled, but could not help wishing for such simplicity in love.

13. Three Tulips in a Boat

IMMEDIATELY AFTER returning home Tsune and Manjiro had to leave again. They knew perfectly well (said Masako) that they were expected to attend Keiko's dance recital, which had been scheduled for months, and was to begin in the entertainment district at four that afternoon. Everyone had waited at the house, but if not for the fact that Keiko's teacher, a retired geisha and dancer of the Fujima school, had already been told how many family members would attend, they would not have done so. Masako was adamant on her sister's behalf. "I'm no admirer of Keiko, but even I understand the meaning of family obligations," she said.

Fumiko was angry, too. It was true that she was exhausted from the difficult family dynamics of having both Manjiro and Tsune with them at the same time, as well as from constantly having to think about this impending trip back to Odawara, but she would have been angry anyway. She could forgive anything in those she loved except thoughtlessness, and though thoughtlessness had been an occasional visitor to Tsune since childhood, she was worried now to see it rubbing off on Manjiro. If he was dedicated to one member of her family over the others it was to Keiko, and this was Keiko's day!

Keiko herself tried not to show her disappointment, but she didn't succeed very well, and once Lord Okubo saw the face of worry through her dance makeup, even he grumbled. Only Einosuke, who had waited all day to hear what had happened at the Barbarian Book Library, was easy on his brother and sister-in-law.

"You know these Edo crowds," he told the others. "Sometimes it is hard to be on time."

Four o'clock was the last hour that it was possible to schedule recitals in the entertainment district, for by six the geisha houses opened to their nighttime customers and the teaching geisha, who were almost always retired, had to be out of sight. It was a common belief among working geisha and their *maiko* apprentices that men did not like to see old faces among the younger ones any more than they liked viewing cherry blossoms the week after the first flush of beauty had spread across the trees. It was too reminiscent of life's brevity, of the walker's shadow passing by him as the sun sets on his walk.

"I wanted to be here to watch the smaller children dance, too," Masako said, when they all stepped out of their palanquins in front of a house called "The Thousand Cranes." She had ridden across Edo with her Aunt Tsune and Keiko, and had lost most of her anger during the ride, but it came back now. The Thousand Cranes sat on the edge of the Sumida River where it wound through Asakusa. It was a part of town she rarely got to see, and the famous street, lined as it was with closed building fronts and mysterious mauve walls, would have supplied her with daydreams for months had she been allowed to walk along it at leisure, as she surely would have had they arrived on time. Even now her eyes were wide as they took in the building and the river behind it and the other guests who milled about in fine kimonos.

"Come," said Tsune, touching Masako but speaking to Keiko, "there is still almost an hour remaining, is there not, before you perform? Let's go in and watch the others, see if we can spot their mistakes."

The schedule was such that during the early morning hours the beginners had performed, then from after lunch the professionals who had studied with the teacher and come back to honor her. In the late afternoon the teacher herself was to dance with an ex-student who was now a famous Kabuki actor, and the final dance was to be by a select group of her best students, with the seventeen-year-old Keiko as the principal dancer.

When Fumiko and O-bata, who held onto the squirming Junichiro, stepped from the second palanquin, the five of them hurried into the geisha house without waiting for the men, who, at the time the women had left the house, had still not found palanquins.

"If anybody misses my dance I will never forgive them," Keiko said, but when she heard the music she followed the others inside.

"Listen, my dear," said her mother, "I can hear the summer rain in the *shamisen*. Can't you hear it, too? Can't you, Masako?"

Because the partitions had been removed to make the room large, they were easily able to join the audience. Keiko's teacher, in a pure white kimono, had just finished her individual dance. Keiko and Masako and Fumiko feigned disappointment at having missed it, but all three had seen it enough in practice and were secretly glad. When the teacher looked their way Fumiko bowed and then sat with her sister and younger daughter while Keiko hurried off to join the other students, all of them sitting together across the room. O-bata had stayed at the back with the baby, standing among a scrubby forest of maids.

The recital was well attended, with most of the children from the morning still there, no doubt because their mothers and fathers wanted to see the famous Kabuki actor, Morita Kan'ya, who was scheduled to dance with the teacher next but had not arrived. As the musicians continued their interlude the teacher suddenly left her spot in the middle of everything, threading the same careful path the five family members had just found when coming into the place. "I hear a palanquin," she said, as she passed Fumiko. "Morita's lateness can only be forgiven if it is he who is inside."

It was a family joke that when Keiko's teacher had been young enough to work as a real geisha even Lord Okubo had been a boy, and now, as Fumiko followed her back out of the building, to apologize for their own lateness, it was not the famous Kabuki actor, but that very same Lord Okubo, who stepped with his sons from the three arriving palanquins.

"We haven't missed it," he announced, "or if we have surely you can do it again."

"Do you know the difference between an actor and a dancer?" the old teacher asked him in a wretched voice. Lord Okubo said he did not, and when Fumiko said that the answer must be that an actor retains the vanity necessary to forget a promised appointment, the teacher bowed her head. "That is correct. He was my student as a boy some forty years ago. When dance was his first love there was no vanity in him, but now . . ." She sighed. "To dance with him today would have been the highlight of my season."

Fumiko believed it was a shame, too, but anger over the earlier lateness of her sister and brother-in-law had used up her store of energy for such things. The teacher might have been forgotten by the famous actor, but she would make it her job to see that Keiko was not forgotten by this teacher in turn. After all, with most of them leaving for Odawara shortly and with everything else in constant turmoil, who knew when her eldest daughter would return to such a study?

"Ah, but the program can be salvaged, can it not?" she asked. "It still has dancers, a final performance, a climax?"

"Yes," said Tsune, who had come back outside, too, "it's a shame he hasn't come but to turn a climax into an anticlimax because of it would be a second shame."

Lord Okubo was embarrassed. He thought the two young women were being too direct with the teacher, too stern, but when he looked past them into the recital hall where Keiko was standing in the wings, the expression on his granddaughter's face made him add his own admonition. "No matter how beautiful a flower is when cut, it will still wilt quickly if it doesn't find some water and a vase," he said. It was uncharacteristic of him, but accompanied as it was by a quick jerking of his head toward the girls, it served to wake the dance teacher up. "Of course," she said. "Oh my! Yes! We must proceed."

There were now a few empty spaces on the floor of the recital hall for the adults. Lord Okubo sat directly in front with Fumiko and Tsune, while Einosuke and Manjiro sat behind them. The teacher whispered to the members of the orchestra, but when she turned to the audience her voice rose, cracking out toward them like a sudden rent in her gown.

"Ladies and gentlemen, students new and old, we will move now to our recital's final dance, 'Three Tulips in a Boat,' on which my most accomplished students have worked so exceptionally hard these past weeks and days."

Lord Okubo grew attentive when the music started and he saw Keiko disappear behind a screen. Three Tulips in a Boat? He hadn't known the name of the dance when he made his earlier aphorism about cut flowers, but now a certain pride in its appropriateness served to make him relax for the first time since his arrival in Edo. If things could still go on like this, if girls could still dance at their recitals, then maybe the American presence did not mean so much, maybe change of the very worst kind was not inevitable.

After the orchestra's opening strains, when one of the musicians sang, *"Three tulips grew down by the river, red, yellow, and white, lips pursed, necks craning toward the sky,"* the screen seemed to depart under its own power, exposing Keiko and two other girls. Keiko was the tallest tulip. Her face was fine and bright, her red kimono the tightly pursed mouth of an unbloomed flower, and she kept a perfectly taut neckline.

"The three tulips grew in a bed of a thousand, but one day a boat came by . . ."

Masako, who had stayed with the other students even after Keiko stepped behind the screen, now went to sit by her uncle. She whispered, "Keiko's tulip has had this idea of leaving the flower bed in her head for ever so long. She can't get rid of it, can't stop wondering what it might be like in the world at large. Look, she is leading the other two tulips astray."

It was true that as the three tulips got closer to the river their lips seemed to un-purse, their mouths part in what Manjiro thought of as a particularly erotic way, but otherwise leaving the tulip bed seemed to do them no immediate harm. People in the audience could see for themselves how wonderful the new wind must feel, how fresh the river water and how tempting it would be to step off the bank, into the calmly bobbing boat. Manjiro was watching the back of Tsune's neck, wishing to place his fingers upon it, but the dancers' delicate movements soon drew his attention again. They seemed to interpret nothing but a safe journey and a safe return. Everything was in favor of it, even the music, which had none of the crescendo that might indicate an approaching storm. When the girls actually took the fateful step, however, showing the audience their legs as they tried to maintain their balance in the boat, the music suddenly changed.

"A wind came up and the three tulips realized that the boat was leaving the shore. They also knew, too late, too late, that their roots had left the soil."

Keiko was the best dancer by far. The other girls were not only followers as tulips, but in the intricate steps of the final root removal as well. Masako told her uncle, "Now they're in for it. There is a danger in leaving your home, you know. There is a lot in this dance that is really perfect for Keiko."

The river got rough so quickly that the members of the audience understood its earlier calmness had been a ruse, a trick perpetrated on the tulips by the evil river god. For a full minute the dancers were yanked around so violently that they seemed about to dance, not only out of the boat, but right out of their kimono. Keiko was especially expert at jerking this way and that, especially practiced at making the outer layers of her gown come undone, so innocently amorous, as if, ready or not, a tulip's breast were about to pop out. The two brothers looked at each other. The children in the audience, all the dancers from the earliest part of the morning, seemed to sit up straight and watch.

"Oh, who will help the tulips once they have left the shore?" asked the singer from the orchestra.

The answer, quite to the delight of everyone, was that one of the tulips, Keiko, of course, would find a way to save them. The other tulips were too terrified to act, but Keiko stepped over the side of the boat, even though it appeared to be too late, not knowing as she did so whether she would meet her death instantly or find the river shallow enough for her to stand upon its bottom and pull the bucking boat to shore.

For another few minutes it was difficult to tell what the outcome would be. Keiko fought for her footing and pushed against the depth and strength of the water and against the other forces of the awful river god. But then, very slowly, she began to make some headway, to pull the other two terrified tulips home. The audience could see them leaning, yearning, pushing their roots toward the lost safety of the tulip bed.

It was a perfectly performed dance, Keiko did better than she'd ever done in practice, but perhaps because it was expressed so well, its ending bothered Masako like it never had before.

"Well fine for the two whose disruption was small," she said. "What will happen to Keiko's tulip, though? She's been very badly roughed up. She is wet and disheveled. What are we supposed to think about her prospects, that she just got up and planted herself back into the dirt as if nothing at all had happened? I don't think so, Uncle. You can't just return to a normal life after a trip like that!"

Masako's questions were good ones, but the rest of the audience got up and went to congratulate the teacher and the dancers, and Manjiro wanted to be among the first to reach Keiko. So he somehow ignored Masako, while at the same time pulling her with him to the front. "Such a tulip!" he said. "Such perfection. My, how your practice has paid off!"

Keiko was still on the floor, exhausted and kneeling where the tulips had finally reached the shore, but she was smiling. The other girls, as Masako had predicted, seemed far less affected by the adventure, and had left with their families immediately after getting out of the boat.

"It's a shame about teacher's duet with what's-his-name," Keiko said, feeling it necessary to deflect the attention from herself, but her grandfather said, "Nonsense." He did not mean, of course, that it was not a shame, but only that he was proud, too, and that not a word should be spoken, not even by Keiko herself, to take away from such a fine performance.

"A dinner!" he said. "Einosuke, Fumiko, invite the dance teacher, too. We must all go out together, to some fine establishment to celebrate!"

Again, since Fumiko had reserved a room at a nearby fish restaurant weeks before, and since there was no question but that the teacher would dine with them, Lord Okubo's bombast was misplaced. The spirit behind it, however, greatly pleased everyone, especially Manjiro. This was the father that both he and his brother remembered from before the rotten seed of the American arrival had been planted in his mind, this was the father-in-law Fumiko had learned to admire when her marriage was new and her children were small. And her grandfather's exuberance so pleased Masako that she forgot, for a while, the nagging questions she had had about the resolution of the dance.

"Get up, Keiko," she said. "Drowned or saved you should straighten your kimono now. Don't show your body so much, we are going to eat, did you not hear? Get up and thank Grandfather before he changes his mind."

Keiko didn't want to straighten her clothes, nor did she want to leave her place on the floor while there was still a chance that someone else would praise her dancing, and she was irritated with Masako for saying she should. From where she sat she could see the entrance of the geisha house, where her teacher was standing again, looking down the road. She could see the lovely *maiko* now, too, the youngest of those working after six o'clock, coming in from outside in twos and threes, turning left and walking down the hall.

Peace and harmony. Calm before the fall.

14. *Under the Falling Wisteria*

OUT AT Lord Tokugawa's hunting lodge the old warrior Kyuzo walked away from the Pavilion of Timelessness, where he had been sitting and thinking about Tsune, and into a small cemetery at the upper edge of the bamboo forest. He was looking at the wooden statues of dead infants with their red bibs on, and trying to return his mind to tranquility by praying at the graves of old and forgotten samurai. The darkness of the earlier evening had stood back a little, acquiescing to the rainy moonlight, but when he put his hands in front of his eyes the moonlight only seemed to heighten their liver spots, to laugh at him, to accent his age. When he touched his face he could feel the sharpness of his cheekbones and the depths of his eye sockets, his very skeleton tired of waiting to come out.

There was a small Buddhist temple outside the cemetery gate, and on his way back to the hunting lodge, Kyuzo threw some coppers into its receptacle, pressed his hands together, and prayed. He was careful to put Tsune and Manjiro out of his mind, to think only of his father, who had died some thirty years before. He pictured his father's face as it had been at the end of his life, haggard, thin, sallow. During his father's last illness Kyuzo had stayed by his side, meditating and talking with him of his life. His father had died in Kyoto, on a straw mat in a small mud house adjacent to Higashi-Honganji Temple. He had spent his entire career in the employ of one lord, but had died masterless, a *ronin*, sure that his life had failed.

Kyuzo had the thought that, at sixty-one, he was now a year older than his father had been on his final day, and when he tried to push that thought away, too, he suddenly heard his father's voice. *"In the rain near Nijo Castle, under the falling wisteria."* He opened his eyes and glanced around, but of course there was no one.

"Under the falling wisteria . . ." He repeated the words, coaxing, hoping the voice would return, but there was only the temple's open doors, the shadow of its Buddha inside. Kyuzo didn't like this temple and rarely prayed here. He thought it too small, the incense favored by its priest too cloying. When he came here he felt more as if he had wandered into a cake shop than into a sacred place, but he stayed and prayed for some few minutes more before walking out to the farthest edge of the hill.

"What is it?" he asked. "What more can I do? What are you telling me? How should I behave?"

Four questions, the last one identical to that which he had posed to his father on the night of his death, and the same question he asked himself in prayers always. He felt some shame that this time his heart was less pure, that this time Tsune resided in a corner of it, but he listened through the rain, and, to his surprise, the voice did come again, giving him the same message. *"In the rain near Nijo Castle, under the falling wisteria."*

Kyuzo looked at the sky and could see that in the west now the spring storm was beginning to clear. He said aloud, "A man's first loyalty should lie with his master's wishes." He said it because he knew it was close to his father's heart, but at the same time he knew that his father's time had passed, or was passing quickly, at least. He turned and sighed. "In the rain near Nijo Castle, under the falling wisteria . . ." The phrase had the pleasing resonance of a mantra, something not so much to be dissected as chanted. He knew Lord Tokugawa's hunting lodge was modelled after Nijo Castle. Was that the connection then, the thread between his life now and the one his father seemed to be asking him to rejoin?

As Kyuzo walked back through the bamboo forest he let his mind return to Tsune and Manjiro, whom she had brought today for his approval. He had only stared at the young man, hardly speaking, and then had walked for hours, and come here, to this cemetery.

"In the rain near Nijo Castle, under the falling wisteria."

Kyuzo decided that it was, after all, a message, not a mantra. And that its meaning would come clear to him over time.

15. The Experiment of America

THOUGH THEY had never been in it together, the room they now shared was one Lord Abe and Lord Tokugawa had each used before. It was higher than the room it looked down upon and better appointed, with a comfortable dais and actual spy holes in the floor, through which they could see everything. They were in that same entertainment district where Keiko's dance recital had taken place only twenty-four hours earlier, in another geisha house not far from the Thousand Cranes. It was an odd meeting, not because the two men rarely met socially, but because they were not in the presence of other lords; only the two of them, accompanied by Lord Abe's aide, that mean-looking samurai Ueno, by his English interpreter, Manjiro, and, on Lord Tokugawa's side, by Keiki, his befuddled son and the heir to his political aspirations.

The room below them was interesting because it contained the two recently arrived Americans, content, it seemed, but as yet ungreeted by anyone but apprentice geisha. They weren't doing much, the Americans, only taking sips of saké and waiting, but the irregular shapes of their bodies, their weird faces, and the way their fingers moved across the table like hairy spiders' legs, provided an eerie fascination for Lord Tokugawa, who could not refrain from leaning down to peek through one of the spy holes.

"I confess I am still at a loss," he told Lord Abe. "I have read what you copied from the foreign book and I know you see within it some good idea, but after watching these men I can't imagine what that good idea could be. They are curious to look at, that's for sure, but they are also as innocent and as powerless as the palanquin bearers who brought me here tonight. The American Commodore won't give a damn for the loss of them, I know that as well as I know my own name."

"Listen," said Lord Abe, "according to both the American constitution and that loud-mouthed Commodore the rights of low born men are equal to the rights of lords. It may sound absurd to you, but rather than repeatedly looking at them, why not take a moment to try to grasp the idea? *Low born men with the rights of lords.* Now put that together with what those paragraphs I copied advocate. Doesn't it exercise your mind?"

It did not, and Lord Tokugawa said so. "Perry won't care what happens to them," he reiterated. "He brought them along as an entertainment. I'll venture he might even make us a gift of them if we asked him nicely."

Despite himself he bent to take another look through the nearest spy hole, and thought what a fine gift they would be. One of the Americans had broken a chopstick in half, and was dancing around with it protruding from his nose.

"Tell me clearly then, what can be done with these men that would confound a treaty which is already signed?" he asked. "In wanting to rid our country of these foreigners we are all allies."

"That's true," said Lord Abe, "but what does it mean to say such a thing? Since Perry's first visit last autumn, when America made its initial thuggish demands for trade, have we prepared ourselves in even the simplest ways? No, we have not. We've done nothing but sit on our thumbs, lost in rhetoric and worry, everyone wanting to hear the sound of his own voice lamenting things."

Lord Abe bent to look at the two men again, too, trying to forget that it was he who had led the Great Council to its indecision, but Lord Tokugawa only sighed.

"Yes, yes, I know that is true," he said, "and I understand how frustrating it has been for you. But I still don't see what you are going to do with them now, after the fact of the treaty signing. I've grown slow in my old age, I admit it, sir, but answer me that, as clearly as you can. Is there something I have missed?"

Manjiro listened with his head bowed. To hear the two leaders speak like this, directly, equally, without the crippling corset of form, was something he had never in his life encountered, and he wished with all his heart that his beloved brother, Einosuke, could be there to witness it beside him. But this did not sound like the same Lord Abe he had heard earlier, the Lord Abe who had said "gangling oddity" about the American officer on shipboard. Then he had seemed strong while now he seemed to be grasping at straws.

"Listen," said Lord Abe, "have you ever been to the Barbarian Book Library? Have you ever read a single foreign volume anywhere, a single translation from a language other than from Chinese?"

Lord Tokugawa answered peevishly. "You know very well I've read Dutch shipbuilding manuals! The Great Council might have sat on its thumbs, but whose idea was it to build a fleet of warships last summer? Who suggested maybe even buying an entire fleet from the Dutch?"

"All right, so you've read a few manuals," Lord Abe allowed, "but what I'm asking now is something entirely new. You have read manuals but have you read thought? Other than the copy which you somehow managed to get your hands on yesterday, have you ever read a word about what these people say they believe?"

Instead of answering quickly, Lord Tokugawa poured himself more saké and drank it down. He didn't like intellectuals and he didn't like Lord Abe, he remembered that now. If there were shipbuilding manuals to read then fine, but he would not be drawn into Western philosophy.

"I don't mean to be insulting," said Lord Abe, bowing into the silence that had transpired, "but please, if not to investigate this thing I have started, what are you doing here this evening, why have you bothered to call me out?"

He spoke calmly, but lest Lord Tokugawa answer him again with silence, he turned and posed a question to Manjiro. "You, young interpreter, you've been to this foreign library, have you not? Isn't that where you learned the barbarian tongue?"

"It is not, sir, but I have been there," said Manjiro.

"And have you read all the books? There are only forty or so."

Manjiro said he had read a few, but otherwise had only browsed.

"Well if that's the case then I have read more than you," Lord Abe told him. "For I have not only read the book everyone's so bothered about tonight, but every other book, as well. Have you read the American constitution? It's there, you know."

Manjiro said he hadn't.

Shifting his glance back to Lord Tokugawa, Lord Abe said, "Then I wish I had copied that, too. I can't quote from it, but it says in part the same thing that Perry is always lecturing us about, that however insignificant his station, no matter whether he is landed or even whether he has a surname, each man has the same basic rights as any other. It says so in their constitution, sir, how can I emphasize that point strongly enough? Can't you grasp how such a belief might cripple a country?"

"My tutor sometimes called it 'the experiment of America,'" said Manjiro.

He froze after he spoke, surprised and ashamed of himself. What had propelled him to add his voice, and what had propelled him to mention his tutor? It was true that he and his tutor used to spend time discussing such things, but to draw attention to it during these capricious days. This was as big a mistake as showing Lord Tokugawa the paragraphs in the first place.

But Lord Abe only said, "Hmm. 'The experiment of America,' what an interesting phrase. The Americans love this idea and push it everywhere they go. I think they are zealots who want to preach, to convince others of the worth of their beliefs, even more than they want trade. It is like the time of the missionaries all over again, but instead of Jesus Christ, the devil in the middle of everything is 'American Democracy'!"

The others were beginning to see the workings of Lord Abe's mind and, as if instructed to, all bent back down to take another look through the spy holes. The minstrels had moved from their table. The one with the chopsticks in his nose was dancing around the apprentice geisha, all of whom were laughing and covering their mouths.

Lord Tokugawa sat back up and frowned. "All right," he said, "let me see if I understand you correctly. The Americans hold one ridiculous idea and this philosopher you've discovered holds another. The American idea, which you have just now outlined, is ridiculous because it's obvious beyond measure that men are not equal—all men, oddly enough, should be able to see that equally well—and the other idea is ridiculous since, precisely because of this inequality, a ruler has an obligation to look out for the welfare of his peasants and such. And you intend for these ideas to come into contact with each other and somehow explode. Am I right so far?"

"Yes," said Lord Abe, "but to argue the validity of the ideas is nowhere near the point I am trying to make . . ."

For a moment he seemed about to say more, but instead turned to Manjiro again. "Young man, do you understand what I am coming

to? You have read some of those books at least, and you have been in
the American presence nearly as much as I, so perhaps you can examine
our discussion with a neutral mind."

Manjiro knew he had brought this on himself, that had he not
spoken once he would not be obliged to do so again, but he answered
calmly. "I think the Americans are sincere in their ideas," he said, "but
even so I believe Lord Abe is now conducting an experiment of his own
which is in two parts. The first consisted of observing Perry's reaction
when he invited such low-born men ashore. If he saw that Commodore
Perry was insulted by the invitation he would understand that all this
talk of equality among men was hollow. But if he was not insulted, as
indeed, he wasn't, then Lord Abe thought he might discover some new
leverage with which to negotiate."

"Yes," said Lord Tokugawa, "but what leverage? And how can we
use it against them at this late date? The treaty is signed!"

To Manjiro's relief Lord Abe held up a hand, stopping his reply.
He pointed at Ueno, his stark-faced aide. "What if we have to arrest
these men while they are here?" asked Ueno.

Lord Tokugawa scoffed, "These are singers we're talking about,
street musicians of the simplest kind, like chin-don-ya. *Chin chin chin,
bong bong bong.* All they do is make noise. Men aren't necessarily criminals, you know, just because they are low-born."

"Of course not," said Lord Abe, "but put aside the improbability
for a minute. What if they did commit a crime?"

"Then we would inform Commodore Perry and go on from there,"
said Keiki, irked that someone like Ueno had spoken before him. "And
once confronted with the evidence he would agree to some apt punishment. It isn't a difficult problem. There is no conflict where there is
evidence and there is law."

"What if we had no evidence?" Lord Abe wanted to know.

"Please," said Lord Tokugawa. "What if, what if . . . How about
this? What if we enclosed them in pickle jars? What if we kill them right
now and say that they grew lonely for America and thrust those broken
chopsticks all the way up their noses and into their brains?"

"Then we would have nothing to bargain with," said Ueno, "no
living commoners, no pawns."

Lord Tokugawa looked at his son and then, briefly, down into one of the spy holes again. When he sat back up he said, "I want to thank you for your explanation, but I think I need to go home now. It's no doubt the inflexibility of my mind that keeps me from understanding all of this. Perhaps if I sleep on it my brain will adjust."

"Wait, Father," said Keiki, "I think there's something moving in the center of this fog."

The remark was unexpected, and at its heart so rude that Lord Tokugawa, who was halfway to his feet, sat back down. He had been worried about Keiki of late, about his son's ability to stand up to the real rulers of the world, men such as Lord Abe, and he didn't want to miss a chance to hear him argue.

Keiki was glaring at Ueno, but the aide simply said, "What do you mean by fog?"

"By 'fog,' I mean 'fog.'" said Keiki. "As a word it's clear, it is only as a thing that it is not."

He thought that was cleverly phrased but Ueno only put his hands on the table, lightly touching his fingertips together. "How would you like me to be clear?" he asked.

Because Keiki believed that the only thing clear thus far was the stupefying fact that Lord Abe had no idea what he would do with the musicians he had invited, he was surprised at the ease with which Ueno fell into the trap he had set. But at the same time he was disappointed. It was rare that he got to argue in front of his father and he found himself wanting more of a challenge.

"We all know why Lord Abe extended his invitation," he said. "He did so because he wanted to discover how the American Commodore would react. But the clarity I want is both simpler and more difficult. Since they are not about to commit a crime, what do you propose to do now?"

Ueno's thin lips moved up but his eyes weren't smiling. "I have the words but I fear you're unready to hear them," he said.

Keiki barked out a laugh. "I know I look unready for many things," he said, "but if I look unready for words I've got to do something about my appearance."

"Very well," said Ueno, "what if the crime they are not about to commit were high? A crime with an element of surprising heinousness to it?"

Keiki took a drink from his saké cup. His father peered at him avidly, with the bright eyes of a hunting falcon, while Manjiro kept his own eyes closed, his mind awash with the sense of coming trouble.

"Whether high or low, whether heinous or trivial, without evidence Commodore Perry would discount it," said Keiki.

"Of course he would!" shouted Lord Tokugawa. "What are you talking about?"

"If the crime were high," Ueno continued, "if the crime were serious enough, then forget about the American Commodore. If the crime were high our own laws, *Japanese laws,* would dictate that the perpetrators be killed or put in jail for a very long time."

Keiki laughed again though he didn't want to. "So that's your plan? To simply make up some crime, imprison them, and then tell the Americans an outright lie?"

"Why not?" asked Lord Abe, looking straight at Lord Tokugawa. "If we did that, if we were arbitrary, even capricious and clumsy in our accusations, then our very bumbling would trigger Perry's desire to get them back. He would deal with a real crime fairly, you are right about that, but if he believed the charges were unfair, then his inborn sense of that unfairness will override everything else. The American idea of equality, don't you see, provides for no other outcome."

The room was so still that they could hear the faint sounds of singing from the room below. Lord Tokugawa's mouth was open, while Manjiro's mind was awash with a terrible guilt. He had brought this on himself! He was to blame for everything and must do something to make it right. But what?

"This is so shameful!" whispered Keiki. "These men will have done nothing, but you are suggesting that we, Japan's rulers, accuse them anyway? We will have broken the laws of behavior, violated the Bushido . . . We won't have acted like lords."

That was the crux of the matter for Manjiro, too, for beyond all of his ambition, beyond, even, his growing love for Tsune, he had a deeply held belief in Japanese honor and could never be a party to such a plan. But Lord Abe simply said, "Come now, the Bushido isn't sullied by such an action because the Bushido doesn't come into play with foreigners. And this idea doesn't come from us anyway, but from those portentous paragraphs that some barbarian thinker wrote three hundred years ago. That's the beauty of it, don't you see? We'll poison them with their own ideas, drown them in water from their own murky well."

There were more questions that might have been asked but everyone remained quiet, waiting for Lord Tokugawa, whose own deep silence these last few minutes had given him the floor. "Help me stand," he told Keiki. "As I get older I find it difficult to remain sitting for so long. In that, I guess, I am like the American Commodore."

Keiki went around behind his father, but before he got there, Lord Tokugawa had stood alone. He was facing Lord Abe, his complexion as ashen as Manjiro's. "For years I have advocated a buildup of our defenses," he said. "When I was military advisor to the government I always argued for it. Because of the weakness of the Shogunate, I have even gone along with our stupid policy of trying to put the Americans off with schemes and excuses, of trying to buy more time with the ridiculous concept of 'perpetual negotiations.' But, my dear Lord Abe, as far as schemes go, does it not shame you to have dug so deeply only to come up with this one?"

Lord Abe was stung but he held his tongue, rage trapped and growing within his reddening face. Yet when Lord Tokugawa stepped toward the door and Keiki opened it for him, everyone, including Lord Abe, scrambled to follow him down to the building's first floor. There were geisha down there, waiting with food and musical instruments. They had expected that once the meeting was over the lords would join the foreigners, but Lord Tokugawa hurried past them, not speaking, not even pausing when he got to the front door.

The night was mild, the rain of the last few days gone west. But when Lord Tokugawa and Keiki got into their palanquins and departed, without so much as a farewell bow, there was so much brooding in the geisha house doorway that Lord Abe had to speak twice before Manjiro finally understood that the words were directed at him.

"Do you know the Shogun's guesthouses," he asked, "those older ones further down the Sumida River, the ones not in use anymore?"

"Yessir," whispered Manjiro.

"Then take these Americans there. Make them comfortable, feed them and give them saké if they want it, but otherwise say nothing."

Manjiro could not bring himself to answer, so outraged was he by Lord Abe's plan, his behavior—by how severely his greatness was diminished. But Lord Abe was stung by far more lofty slights than Manjiro's and didn't notice. He only turned, barked a fiery order at the tight-lipped Ueno, and frightened the waiting geisha down the hall.

Thus it was that everyone involved, whether traveling across Edo or standing numbly at that open doorway, was cold-eyed or determined or lost or emphatic, burning with one kind of rage or another.

Everyone, that is, but the two American minstrels, who continued to play like bear cubs, singing and dancing in their cell.

16. *Rumors*

DURING THOSE TRYING DAYS even ordinary rumors could spread across Edo more swiftly than fire among its wooden buildings, but the rumor of the rift between Lord Abe and Lord Tokugawa, and the subsequent disappearance of the American musicians, was a seven-headed monster with each head talking in fine full voice. On his way to the palace with his father the next morning Einosuke heard it several times. He was told that the Americans had run from a geisha house and were hiding in the entertainment district; that they were escapees from a harsh America and seeking political asylum; and that they were already dead, their heads spiked on lantern tops, planted at the front of that circular American train. Merchants all over Edo heard they were loose and killing merchants; palanquin bearers, that they were small of frame and short, dressed in women's clothing and murdering palanquin bearers; and samurai, that they were well-trained warriors.

Closer to the seat of government, inside the chambers of the Great Council, in the Edo offices of the Imperial Chamberlain, and in the living quarters of the Shogun himself, the location of the missing Americans was less on people's minds than the situation that had developed between the two great lords. In those places one story had it that Lord Tokugawa had laughed in Lord Abe's face, another that he had refused to hear Lord Abe out at all, and a third that Lord Abe's mean-spirited aide would soon fight a duel with Keiki, Lord Tokugawa's unready son and heir. Oh gossip, how it spreads across the world, irrespective of customs or cultures!

Lord Okubo and Einosuke searched for Manjiro in the hallways and antechambers of the Great Council, for they knew he had been present at the geisha house meeting everyone was talking about and would be able to tell them what had truly taken place. But though they looked everywhere for him, they could not find Manjiro. He wasn't with the Dutch-speaking interpreters in the corner, and he wasn't with those junior aides who stood outside of Lord Abe's inner chamber door. Lord Okubo thought he might find Manjiro in the commissary, though it seemed too early for lunch, and Einosuke searched the castle grounds, through its gardens and around its ponds. Both men still felt the renewed family bonding that Keiko's dance recital had brought them, and very much needed Manjiro.

It was unusual for Lord Okubo to grow anxious at rumors, but when he met Einosuke again, later, he put a hand on his eldest son's shoulder. They sat down on a couple of cushions in a side hallway, from which they could see that the door to Lord Abe's private chambers remained closed, that no one left or entered except the dislikable Ueno.

"I'm going to stop him, ask after Manjiro when next he comes out," Einosuke announced, but when Ueno did come out again, more than half an hour later, he was moving so fast that stopping him became an impossibility. Aides and servants and even some lords had to leap out of his way. Lord Okubo urged Einosuke on, telling him to catch up in a hurry, and soon Einosuke was chasing Ueno down the hall.

For his part Lord Okubo got up and walked along the short hallway, approaching Lord Abe's door, where Lord Abe's secretary, an even older man than Lord Okubo, sat on a high dais and admitted no one, whether lord or petitioner, without an appointment. But when he saw Lord Okubo he straightened up and bowed. "A most unhappy morning, sir," he said. "Please, go right inside."

Lord Okubo looked around the anteroom, but there was no one present to witness the man's unusually accommodating behavior.

The first room of Lord Abe's inner chamber was small. There were two rooms past it, neither of which Lord Okubo had ever been in before, but every time he saw this first room he got the feeling that it was too plain, not befitting the leader of the Great Council. The tatami hadn't been changed since before Lord Okubo's last visit to Edo, and the *shoji* on the windows, which overlooked the castle's prettiest garden, was stained in places and had numerous holes.

Lord Abe was not present in this outer room so Lord Okubo opened the *shoji* and looked down at the garden. Now that the rain had stopped it was possible to see spring's delicate approach, if not in the buds on the cherry trees just yet, at least in the light step people used when walking, and the beginning color of the crocuses. All seemed peaceful and quiet. He could even see the orange flash of a carp's back on the surface of the nearest pond.

"I am glad you were able to come so quickly," Lord Abe said behind him. "That, at least, is a good sign. Maybe we can stop it all right now and say that it never truly began."

Mystified, Lord Okubo turned around. He had not been summoned, he had only stopped in on his own, but when he saw how pale the great lord was, how his hands shook and his lips trembled, he said, "Sir? Is something the matter? Is there someone I should call?"

He meant that ancient secretary, or perhaps the castle physician, but when Lord Abe heard him he let out a bitter laugh, regaining some of his control. He stepped around Lord Okubo so that he was closest to the open window. "Is that your eldest son down there with Ueno?" he asked, pointing out. "Did he come with you today? I had suspected he might not, that he might be in league with the despicable Manjiro."

No one had been down there a moment earlier, but indeed, Einosuke was now standing at the edge of the pond, head bowed toward Ueno, who was throwing his hands about and berating him so loudly that the two lords, though they could not deduce their meaning, could hear the sense of insult in the words.

"In league, sir?" asked Lord Okubo, "Einosuke 'in league' with Manjiro?" He could not bring himself to believe that he had actually heard the word "despicable."

Lord Abe turned away from the window and then back toward it and then toward Lord Okubo. He was perplexed, unsure whether to believe or disbelieve what seemed to be Lord Okubo's ignorance of what Manjiro had done, when suddenly a cloud came over Lord Okubo's face, forcing his eyes closed. It stopped him for such a long moment that when he once again opened his eyes he felt dizzy, and touched Lord Abe's arm with such clumsy disorder that it was the great lord, not Lord Okubo, who rushed to the door of his office for help.

When Lord Abe came back Lord Okubo said, "These rumors . . ." but he had to stop again, leaning against the windowsill. He drank some of the tea Lord Abe had brought him and put the cup down. "Where is Manjiro?" he asked. "And what do you think he has done?"

He turned to look into the garden again, but there was no longer anyone there, and the instant Lord Abe said, "Your son . . ." the doors flew open and in rushed Ueno and Einosuke, agitated and shouting at each other.

"In this man's family treachery runs deep," Ueno began, but Lord Abe told him to shut up and Lord Okubo shoved Ueno aside to look at Einosuke. "We have a problem," he said. "It seems your brother has kidnapped the American musicians in a misguided attempt to keep them from harm."

His tone was instructive, as was his touch down low on Einosuke's hand, and when Einosuke said, "Yes Father, I know," his voice, whatever it might have been earlier, was once again normal.

When Ueno tried to speak Lord Abe once more silenced him, and when Einosuke and his father left his chambers Lord Abe not only kept Ueno from sending for the palace soldiers, but followed them into the long outer hallway, to stand in silence, bowing and watching them go.

Later Einosuke would remember Lord Abe's bow and blame it for the sense he had during much of the rest of the day that things might not be so bad.

And he would also blame that bow for making him unready, for making it nearly impossible for him to believe it when, by late the next afternoon, his father resigned from the Great Council in shame, and decided to return to Odawara with what remained of his family.

17. *Fine Mornin', Ain't It?*

NED AWOKE FIRST, climbed from his blankets in the Pavilion of Timelessness, and stepped out to breathe the cold crisp air. It was true he hadn't really wanted to come ashore, had done it only for Ace, to soothe his friend's desire for adventure, but now that he was there he found the bamboo grove beautiful, with its trees at uniform distances, and when he noticed the side wall of Lord Tokugawa's hunting lodge, his immediate thought was to get a closer look at it, give a warm welcome to whoever might be inside.

As he reached back through the paper doors for his shoes and seaman's jacket, Ned looked at Ace, asleep with his mouth open, next to the Japanese man who had brought them here, a guy that he'd decided to think of as "Mangy," because it was as close to his real name as he could get. Mangy's topknot was loose and creeping down the side of his head like a slug, but both men looked peaceful in their slumber. If there was one thing Ned knew about Ace, however, it was that peace was as foreign to him as a hairdo like Mangy's, and search as he might, he wasn't going to find it by hooking up with strangers in Japan. No sir, that they should have stayed at home was as clear to Ned as the bamboo trees in front of him as he looked out the door.

Still, they were here now and he'd done enough standing still on shipboard, so he pulled on his shoes, stepped off the porch and made his way through the bamboo quickly, by gripping the tree trunks and swinging on them—*allemande left, allemande right*—as if he were at a square dance. And soon he found himself standing on a bare stretch of hard ground next to the side of the lodge. In one direction its wall jetted down to meet the forest again, but in the other it seemed to grow higher, as if yielding more standing room to a man inside. So he walked that way and when he stepped around the corner saw the mouth to a corridor that led to a sun-bright courtyard. He could hear someone caterwauling in there—singing would be a kind word for it—but he could also hear wind chimes, a high-pitched and pleasant ringing, not unlike the ship's triangle.

Ned felt his unshaven face and worked his mouth, briefly thinking that he should pass the courtyard by, just circle the building and go
back to wake Ace. When the man stopped singing, however, and barked
out a phlegmy cough, he stepped inside the corridor and reached into
his jacket pocket to retrieve a small harmonica. And when the cough
came again he blew softly, copying the cough perfectly, finding its pitch
on the first try. The cougher heard it and stopped, while Ned pressed
himself against the wall and grinned mischievously. A moment passed,
and when another cough came, he gave it a quieter echo.

"*Chikusho,*" said Keiki in the courtyard.

Ned would have left then, satisfied that he had a good story to
tell, but a shadow fell across the ground before him, followed so quickly by its maker that he could only press himself closer to the wall. The
man was naked except for a loincloth, and had hair flying everywhere.
He was so comic-looking that Ned might have laughed, except for the
fact that he was carrying a large and unsheathed sword.

The man glanced into the corridor but couldn't see Ned, and when
he went some distance farther and coughed again, a random spasm this
time, like five or six dog barks, Ned put the harmonica to his lips and
woofed out the same sound.

"*Baka yaroo!*" hissed Keiki, nudging his sword in among a nearby
chorus of wide-mouthed barrels.

Ned was quiet the next time he coughed, and also the time after
that, but when he went back to the porch to resume his washing, Ned
played a series of notes up high, extending the joke.

This time Keiki left his sword alone and moved around the courtyard in the opposite direction, carrying only a rolled-up towel. He finally understood there was a trickster in the area and hoped that
maybe it was one of his father's maids, that this might be an inventive
prelude to her coming to his rooms that night.

"*Hora!*" he said, looking in somewhere and snapping his towel.

It was funny, a good game, but the new direction he had chosen
gave Ned nowhere to hide, and when Keiki suddenly saw him he froze,
one end of his towel held firmly in his right hand while his left pulled
the other end back, making it look like a thick white arrow in an invis-
ible bow. From Keiki's point of view it was horrifying, for the man's
long nose, his flat face and the turned-up collar of his coat all combined

to give the impression of a great standing rat who might at any second fall down on all four legs and charge.

"Ahra, kowai!" he shouted. He dropped his towel and reached to the waistband of his loincloth for his absent sword.

"Fine mornin', ain't it?" said Ned. "Didn't mean to give you a start."

Keiki's mouth was so wide that his next cough came out hollow.

"Me and Ace are camped out yonder in that freezin' cold building. Come in late with Mangy. I hope like hell you know him. Nervous fellow? Talks English pretty well?"

He stepped out of the shadows and smiled.

"But you are one of the barbarians!" said Keiki. "One of the men we spied upon in the geisha house last night! How is this possible? What? How . . . ? Did my father . . . ? Did you . . . ? This doesn't make any sense at all!"

He picked up his towel and shoved the corner of it into his mouth, and that made Ned laugh.

"Ned Clark's my name," he said. "What might yours be?"

"Hold it. Please, don't move," said Keiki. "I'll get my father. Who else? What kind of trouble?" He let a laugh fall from his mouth and said, "I see you standing here but everything I know tells me it's impossible. This doesn't make any sense at all!"

"Don't you want to get yourself dressed?" asked Ned. "I mean, ain't you cold?"

He pointed down at Keiki's body. "I ain't never seen a country so full of folks what like to strut around with their naked butts a-showin'. I spied some others doin' it from shipboard with the master's glass. Paradin' around the seashore like nymphs on a weekend holiday."

"Oh, yes!" said Keiki. "What a way to greet someone. And look at the poor condition of my hair!"

He hurried back to the porch and while he snatched up his clothing Ned took a look around the courtyard. There was more order here, among the barrels and piles of lumber, than he had ever seen anywhere before. The lumber constructed something beautiful, even in its stacking, and on top of each barrel were precisely cut lids with well-crafted handles. Ned admired orderliness, to one day lead an orderly life himself was his desire, and he smiled again, pleased with what he saw. Even the way Keiki's wash water came from the well at the side, trickling from a split of bamboo and into his pail, made Ned think he'd made the right decision after all, not only coming ashore with Ace, but venturing out alone this morning to explore things, also.

He nodded at the trickling water. "Bein' it's handy do you mind if I wash, too?" he asked. "There's fresh water for naught but drinking on them ships. A man gets used to his own body odor, but any fool knows it don't afford him a good first impression when he's meeting new folks."

Despite himself, despite his great surprise and the fact that he knew he had to wake his father, Keiki laughed again. He liked this man, whose narrow eyes and sharp features no longer resembled a rat. There was a charming quality about him, something open. What's more, he believed he understood the gist of what he'd said just now.

"Of course," he answered, "help yourself, I'll go get more towels."

So Ned stripped to his waist and started splashing himself, and Keiki put his kimono back down. It was a funny situation, and both men laughed, trying, without saying so, to imitate the sound of the falling water, the rudiments of the game that had started it all.

That is how they were discovered some thirty minutes later, when Lord Tokugawa and Kyuzo, the old warrior, came out the back door. Keiki was sitting on one side of the barrel, Ned on the other. Both men were naked and had commenced to naming body parts.

Though it might not seem like it, it was an important beginning, for though Lord Tokugawa nearly fainted and Kyuzo drew his sword, Keiki believed a genuine connection had been made.

And later, when Tsune was awakened and a disconsolate and raw-eyed Manjiro brought Ace from the Pavilion of Timelessness, Keiki began to remember that favorite old folk hero of his, that story book wonder and savior of the downtrodden, Kambei.

And that gave him a great idea concerning how they would play havoc with Lord Abe.

18. *Commodore Perry's Anxiety*

OUT IN HIS STATEROOM on the *Pohatan,* Commodore Perry wrote letters to the President of the United States and to his friends in the upper echelons of the American navy, and to his wife. When he met with various Japanese contingents it was in order to prepare for his departure to Shimoda, one of the two port cities that were officially opened to Americans by the Kanagawa Treaty of 1854. He was anxious to visit Shimoda and anxious, after that, to sail for home.

He heard nothing of the minstrels, thought of them rarely, and asked after them only once. He was told that they were busy traveling and assumed, by that, that they were doing no harm after all, and having a good time.

PART TWO
ODAWARA

19. *Everything Wrong Everywhere*

BECAUSE OF THE VAST FORESTS of pines, much of the open land around Odawara Castle wasn't visible from its narrow windows, not even from those on its top floor. There were indeed large expanses of meadow, and rice and soybean fields, and even a few small villages where Lord Okubo's peasants lived, but the continuous canopy of trees revealed almost nothing, only, here and there, a slight dip in its prominence, a line of lime-green color distinguishing new growth from old.

From the windows on the castle's north and west sides one could see the parade grounds directly below, and a dried-out ditch which once had been a moat, and beyond the gate one could also see a road leading down the hill to Odawara township. But from the east and the south windows, over the forest top, there was only the Pacific Ocean, whitecaps flashing in the afternoon sun, as if they too had heard the awful story of the family's ruin, coming faster than runners could carry it, down the maritime shipping routes from Edo. Majiro had taken the Americans, acted on his own, defied the leaders of the Great Council! "Oh, oh, oh!" said the waves.

The family had been in Odawara for three days and still things weren't calm. That was the refrain that stuck in Masako's head, worrying her as she walked across the grounds, hoping, though she usually thrived on it, to free herself from the constant sound of bickering for a while. Masako looked back at the castle before ducking into the forest, sneaking onto a favorite old path of hers from past visits. As recently as last year she had been forbidden to take this path because down one of its forks there was a dangerous marsh, so she glanced back again, to make sure she hadn't been followed. A big boulder sat at the edge of the marsh, and she intended to sit upon it until the sun went down, to watch the marsh's frothy stillness, and figure things out.

Even though Masako had taken this path many times, however, she could not remember how far the marsh was from the forest entrance except by the way the trees, no matter what the time of day, at first made everything dark and then made everything lighter again. She always hurried through the darkest part, keeping her mind off the subject of animals, and when she could finally smell the stagnant water, she slowed and tried to walk silently. Her goal was to arrive at the marsh without interrupting the chorus of croaking frogs that sang their hearts out when no people were around. But no matter how quiet she was, she never achieved her goal.

This day, however, probably because she'd been away for so long, the frogs were less guarded. She got past the place where they usually stopped croaking, even though she was bigger and more awkward now. She even reached the spot where she could first glimpse that boulder, the place where its massive grayness looked like nothing so much as the shoulders and buttocks of a huge sumo wrestler, crouched down and relieving himself, defecating directly into the marsh. Masako loved the look of him so much that once or twice she had nearly brought Keiko here just to show him off. He was perfect. There was even an elongated piece of darker rock that seemed to jut from the center of his enormous buttocks, a thick and healthy-looking bit of stony waste forever falling into the water.

When Masako laughed at the image the frogs stopped singing and the marsh grew quiet, as if all eyes were on the sumo wrestler to see if he would ever complete the movement of his bowels. But even when she climbed upon his back, putting her foot on the falling excrement to help her up, he remained oblivious to everything. And Masako believed that that, even more than his looks, was the central reason that she loved him so much. Unlike the real people in her life, he wasn't so quick to judge.

Masako had two main worries, but once she was settled on her boulder she tried to breathe easily and notice the beauty of the place, before turning her thoughts to them. Someone had been here while she'd been gone, she saw that immediately, to cut away the moss that always before had grown everywhere, thick as whale blubber.

Masako looked back along the path she had just traversed, and off toward each of the other paths that opened onto the marsh, before she let her right hand drift up to touch her lower lip and pull it out.

This was her first worry, that her lower lip was getting fatter, and even though she knew it was a trivial thing to worry about with all this current family trouble, she fretted over it constantly. And she pulled on it so often that she feared she was causing the trouble herself. There were other things too, changes in other parts of her body, that her mother and Aunt Tsune, and even Keiko, had warned her about.

Masako sighed and leaned back against her sumo wrestler's neck. She could fit her entire upper body along that neck, which now sloped more than any real neck would, and from her reclined position she could see the bamboo supports and partially submerged gates that lined the marsh at its edges. Once she had seen her grandfather's workmen putting those supports in, and another time she had seen them repairing one of the gates, but when she asked her grandfather what purpose the fence served he had said only that he thought he'd told her not to go there anymore. She was afraid, after that, to bring it up with her mother or father, but when she finally asked Keiko she was surprised by Keiko's good answer. Keiko had told her that the marsh was meant to contribute to the natural beauty of the castle grounds, and that as often as once or twice a year their grandfather had workmen go in there to maintain it. She said that a marsh was most beautiful when it reached a state between the freshness and vigor of an ordinary pond, and the rotting stagnancy of a swamp. In a pond there was beauty yet there was no sense of life passing, and in a swamp there was ugliness and all kinds of death and dangers, but in a marsh everything was in balance and their grandfather's workmen did things that maintained that balance because nature would not.

Keiko, of all people, had told her that. It was one of the few times, in recent years, that the two of them had spoken without fighting, and as she pulled at her lower lip Masako somehow reflected back upon Keiko's answer and began to think that it not only fit the marsh, but herself as well. She had been like a pond and now was changing, all too quickly passing by her marshness and turning into a stinking swamp.

Masako took a breath and looked at the sky and tried to find animal shapes in the clouds. Once she had seen a sumo wrestler up there that seemed an exact copy of the one she lay upon. That had been marvelous and she tried to see something like it again, but in a minute she understood that today she would not find anything so lovely. And though she still worried, she was tired, also, of pulling on her lip and making it sore. Everything was wrong everywhere, Masako decided, and so the bravest thing she could do would be to sit here for another long time and face it. But unfortunately she didn't know the facts of what was going on. At first she thought it was only that her mother and father were angry about having Grandfather return to Odawara with them, but then she noticed that they all got furious whenever she mentioned Manjiro. And, except for the fact that no one wanted to talk about the marriage arrangement anymore, she did not know why her mother always had to be so wretched. Unless it was something else, something she had no idea of. Oh, she hated being so ignorant, and being so little respected by the others that no matter what was happening she was always the last to be told.

She sighed and then thought of Keiko, who, she had to admit, seemed a bit more lively than the others, probably because she was still proud of herself for doing so well at the dance recital. But even Keiko, though she didn't cry and carry on like their mother, would only walk around the castle or along the edge of the forest. She wouldn't talk to Masako frankly and she wouldn't play their usual games, and when Masako taunted her by carrying Junichiro precariously she refused to rage and storm. It was unlike Keiko not to rise to such bait, even if Keiko now thought of herself as grown.

It was a circle, this kind of difficult thinking, and she grew tired of making no progress, of coming to no conclusions no matter how hard she thought. She put her hands up and pointed her eight fingers and two thumbs at a cloud that did not seem to be passing by as quickly as the others. It seemed heavier around its abdomen, this cloud, and looked like a rabbit or perhaps like O-bata would have looked like if she hadn't been forced to stay away from that fish seller's son! Masako smiled at the idea and closed her eyes and opened her own mouth. It was nice lying on her sumo wrestler, and pretty soon she was asleep with her arms down by her sides, and quite as if they knew from her breathing that her presence was no longer a threat, the frogs opened their mouths again and croaked.

20. | *Saved from the Realm of Absolute Calamity*

AH, BUT INSIDE ODAWARA CASTLE, things were far more serious than Masako wanted to believe. It was true enough that they had all come down from Edo in a state of shock over what Manjiro had done, true also that they stayed that way during these three days, going about their business without speaking, crouched inside their own disappointment, but even when they came back to themselves they still couldn't speak his name. When first they tried, over breakfast on the fourth morning, Einosuke and Fumiko found it clogged their throats, making them so rude to each other that they ended up fighting as they had not fought since the night of the treaty signing ceremony. It was horrible, and Keiko, who overheard everything, ran out of the castle with her brother in her arms, in search of Masako, who was impossible to find.

And what made things even worse for Fumiko was that at Odawara Castle there were servants and attendants everywhere. Oh, how she missed the privacy of her Edo house with its unfinished rooms and clutter! After her fight with Einosuke she sought refuge on the castle's fourth floor and then on its fifth, as high as she could go without flying into space, but each time she believed she'd found a sanctuary where she could decide for herself the level of calamity in what Manjiro had done, or try, once again, to purge the foreigner from her thoughts, she was forced to leave it again when some maid came in to sweep the tatami or inspect the walls for mold. Once she dug into a packing crate in search of her *ikebana* tools, hoping she might cover the awful feeling she had by arranging flowers, only to discover that two of her favorite Bizen vases were broken.

"O-bata!" she screamed, but O-bata was five floors below, asleep in a room off the kitchen, her own loneliness to contend with—no more fish-seller's son—her head stuck beneath a pillow.

———

EVERY BIT AS ANGRY as Fumiko but even less capable of finding a solution, Einosuke ran outside when he saw Keiko at the edge of the forest, carelessly carrying Junichiro.

"Hey!" he shouted. "Be careful, won't you?" But Keiko ignored him, and when he turned back toward the castle he, too, saw a packing crate from Edo, with the words "Garden tools" written on its side. Einosuke was luckier than his wife had been, though, for when he tore open the crate he found everything he needed, not only his shovels and various rakes, but also coats and hats and watering cans. As he looked at them he let himself forget why he'd come outside in the first place, and rummaged around, trying to find his favorite three-pronged digger. There was a good spot of land near the castle wall, he thought, and a better one off toward the forest where he could now see Keiko walking more carefully with the baby. He had his rock garden's measurements locked in his memory, so why not build another one? He took a moment to find his measuring stick and his rope, before walking over to calculate the slope of the land with his expert eye.

"Keiko, I need your help," he called. "Come here, won't you? Bring Junichiro over and lend me a hand for a while."

He used a kinder voice than he'd used a moment earlier, and looked up and smiled, but Keiko was careful to keep her back to him, lest he see the way her tears were wetting her baby brother's clothes.

"Did you call me, Father?" she managed to ask, but her voice, like her whole inner spirit, was strangled.

"Yes, I think what I'll do is rebuild my rock garden on this patch of unused ground," said Einosuke. "Don't you think that would be nice?"

When she walked toward her father she turned Junichiro in order to keep the sun out of his eyes. She most certainly did not think it would be nice, when everyone was torn with shame and anger. What a stupid idea and how like her father to think a new rock garden would solve anything at all! Rock gardens! She let the words take the form of curses in her head, but she kept her thoughts to herself.

"I'll drive the stakes and measure the distances," he said, "you tie this rope around them and follow me. Be mindful to keep the rope taut, and put your brother down, it won't hurt him to get dirty for a while."

Junichiro waved his arms, as if celebrating this return of civility, and though Keiko looked to make sure her mother wasn't watching from a high-up castle window, in a moment she did come closer, to do as she was told.

"You don't remember the original garden, do you, Keiko?" her father asked. "Let me see, how old must you have been when last we visited Kyoto?"

Because of her father's kind smile, Keiko smiled too, wanting to apologize to him for her earlier irritation, even though he hadn't known about it. But she remembered the visit to Kyoto clearly and would have told him so at any other time. She had been seven or eight and had sat on her Uncle Manjiro's lap whenever he would allow it. She remembered most clearly that she liked to keep her head wedged under his chin while he talked with her Aunt Tsune, both of them dangling their legs over the garden's walkway, letting their feet swing out. It renewed her heartache to think of such things and she sighed.

Einosuke, in the meantime, had taken up his hammer and a single sharp stake, and then, for a full five minutes, seemed to focus all his attention on the chosen space. His eyes turned inward and his mouth moved as if engaged in a calculation. Keiko allowed herself to be caught up in it too, for a minute, persuading herself that to work on such a garden would provide just the necessary regimen to defeat all those other horrible thoughts.

But when her father raised his hand and pointed his hammer, her sense of sadness returned. There would be no marriage now, she suddenly understood, between the two people she loved most in the world, no chance for such a splendid happiness for her aunt and uncle. Tears came to Keiko's eyes again and when her father spoke again she let out a cry.

"Yes," he said mildly, "that will do."

Once more he hadn't noticed her tears, but only bent to pound the first of his stubborn stakes in the ground.

———

THE FAMILY'S SHOCK over Manjiro's behavior was so great, really so overwhelming, that in an odd way it had saved them from the realm of absolute calamity. That is, had Manjiro done something less distressing, had he found some way to discredit them less completely, they might have acted sooner, done more to make up for it, to clear the family name. But as it was the enormity of what he had done seemed to be keeping the sharpest pain away, letting them do little save argue and plan gardens and cry. Such was the principle, at least, that worked for all of them except Lord Okubo.

Fumiko didn't know it, but as she sat trying not to think that the man who had most bothered her piece of mind since she was a girl was now in the country somewhere, under the protection of her own brother-in-law, Lord Okubo was in a room not far from the one in which she had sequestered herself. It was a secret room, built to hide the family's ancestors from marauders, a windowless room in the fifth floor's center, surrounded by walls that were plain and heavy. Lord Okubo had gone in there on the morning after their arrival, but had sealed the room again and stayed away from it, hoping that time and deeper thought would provide him with a better solution than the one that room provided.

But deeper thought eluded him and time only made his first impulse seem inevitable, so on the morning of this fourth day he opened the room again and quietly slipped inside.

The room was gold, fitted with golden cushions and with gold-colored panels painted by Lord Okubo's father, a lighthearted man who did not like simplicity, even in a sanctuary. There were gold futon in the room's closet, a golden altar with sweet-smelling incense ready to light, as well as selected remembrances of past Lords Okubo, bits of poetry by the current Lord's great-grandfather, a silk-threaded fan favored by some other past Odawara Castle master, and an old gold ring worn by yet another.

When Lord Okubo closed the door behind him he lit the candle that sat on the floor and used it to light an old oil lamp that, judging from the way its flame danced in the stilted air, was surprised by what it had to illuminate. From a drawer he took a heavy wooden case, placed it lightly on the altar and then sat down and prayed.

The knives in the case were golden too, but the whetting stone next to them was black, making Lord Okubo smile, glad for a break in the color. He had not seen these knives in a dozen years, but chose the shortest one because he thought he remembered his father telling him that though they were a set, it had a better blade. When he picked it up he was surprised by its lightness, but did not test the blade against his thumb. Rather, he put the knife in front of him, on a small white pillow, and reached back into the case for the whetting stone. He waited for his calmness to return and then picked up the knife again and sharpened it.

Lord Okubo hadn't thought whether or not to leave a suicide note until he put the whetting stone back in the case and saw its similarity to an inkstone. He would not leave a note, he decided, not only because he could think of nothing to say, save more recriminations of Manjiro, but also because he did not want to leave the room again, to steal back down the stairs for paper and brushes. As it was he wondered how long it might be before Einosuke, the unfortunate heir to all his troubles, would think to look for him up here. He knew that when he did not appear for dinner Einosuke would know what had happened, but he couldn't be sure how many years it had been since he'd shown his son this room and he worried that he might have forgotten it. It had been a family tradition for a century that the only people privy to the room's existence be the current lord and his heir, yet Lord Okubo decided that he could not chance the greater dishonor of having his body rot undiscovered. So he walked across the room again and cracked open the door. It would still likely be Einosuke who found him, but now, at least, someone was sure to see the surprising new fissure in the otherwise seamless wall.

When he sat back down Lord Okubo loosened his *obi* and pulled open his kimono, baring his chest and belly to the tepid air. He didn't like to think of the pain but it was important to do a good job, to be thorough, at least, in his departure, so he pressed his abdomen here and there, searching for a soft spot. It wasn't that he was firm of muscle but that, over the last few years, he had noticed the appearance of certain tumors, rigid knots of fiber under the skin, and he worried that the blade, whatever its sharpness, might pass through them only with difficulty. There was one such knot just above his groin on the left. He wanted to make two incisions, one across his lower belly from left to right, and a second, vertical cut, from below his navel moving upward. He would die proudly, he decided, if he could do that much.

Lord Okubo washed himself along the lines of the imagined knife thrusts with one of two rolled towels he had thought to bring along. The feeling of the cloth on his skin was pleasant, somehow reminiscent of his earliest youth when his mother used to bathe him, so he said a prayer to his mother, who he knew would be sincerely grieving now. After that he unrolled the cloth and let it travel down to scrub his genitals so they would be clean if he fell over in a way that left him unsightly and exposed.

The second towel was for the just-honed knife blade, and he took it up only after folding and setting aside the first one. With the second towel in one hand and the knife in the other he could feel a slight deepening of his breath, and an increase in his pulse rate, but otherwise he remained determined and calm. He searched himself for fear but found little. Well, some, perhaps, for the pain involved, but none concerning what would come to him in the afterlife.

Lord Okubo squared himself on the cushion and opened his left hand and drew the knife blade across the towel, a gentle second honing. He noticed that a long rectangle of soft light had come into the room through the door he had opened, settling itself upon a corner of the altar and the wall behind it. Also, there now seemed to be less pressure in the room, as if it breathed, for once, with the rest of the castle. And where before the room had been soundproof, now he could hear voices, even distinguish, if he turned his mind to it, one voice from another.

Ah, but enough. Lord Okubo had found the necessary courage to do what he had to do, yet he did not think that courage would wait for him to sate his curiosity, even though someone was certainly shouting. He took the index finger of his left hand and pushed it into his abdomen just to the inside of his left hip bone. He closed his right fist around the knife's handle and crossed his body with it until the knife's point came down and replaced his finger. In order to be successful the whole thing, the first cut and the second one also, should take no longer than a few quick seconds, and he decided to occupy his mind with counting those seconds away, plunging the knife into himself at number one and so on, until he could count no more. He took a breath, let the faces of his children and grandchildren flow down a kind of river in the center of his mind, and then, just as his lips formed the first number, he heard Fumiko's voice echoing loudly through the outside halls. Had he not cracked the door he wouldn't have heard her at all.

"There is a runner!" she cried. "A message! My sister is coming with news! We can expect her tonight!"

News? thought Lord Okubo.

His right fist was shaking, the tip of his knife making little nicks in his flesh, nibbling at it like the sharp tooth of a hungry dog, but instead of speaking the number and ending his life, Lord Okubo willed his fist to ease away again, to open up and release the knife so that he could use that hand to cup his ear and better hear what Fumiko said. News of any kind must mean news of Manjiro.

Lord Okubo got up and hurried over to the door to close it, lest the castle's biggest secret be relinquished without the central prize of his golden corpse inside. He returned the knife to its box, next to its unhoned sister, and adjusted the whetting stone so that the box's lid would close. He blew out the lamp and crossed the room to put away the knives and before he reopened the door he blew out the candle.

Oh, his heart was lighter than it had been.

"What news? What news?" he said.

21. | *"Kambei"*

MASAKO HEARD the crier, too, but stayed in the forest until the activity of her aunt's arrival let her slip out of hiding, joining the others unnoticed. Tsune's entourage was small, just the one palanquin with her inside of it, a couple of attending samurai and six exhausted bearers, the last of those who had relayed her down from Edo. When they came under the castle gate Lord Okubo received the samurai greeting, in the name of Lord Tokugawa, while Fumiko and Keiko rushed over to the palanquin to help Tsune get out.

"Are you well my sister?" asked Fumiko. "Was the trip not overly tiring?"

To Masako her aunt looked both well and rested, while her mother and Keiko looked awful, as if they were the ones who'd endured the horrible ride.

"I'm fine but am I welcome?" Tsune answered. "I would have come straight down yesterday had I been sure."

Fumiko opened her mouth and closed it again, while Einosuke looked away, back toward the thin perimeter of the new garden he had started. Lord Okubo waited until a servant took Tsune's samurai off to feed them before their return journey, but once they were alone he asked the question that was on everyone's mind. "What word have you of Manjiro?"

It was so direct, so much without the usual delays, that it made Tsune pause. The lord, however, had not put his suicide on hold merely to pay attention to form. Already such vacillation had done irreparable harm.

"I have some news, my lord," said Tsune. "I wish I knew everything but Edo is in confusion now. So many opinions to listen to. People are taking sides."

"Let's have some tea," he said, "or if it's late enough for dinner let's have that. Tell me everything slowly if you must, but you must tell me everything."

Inside the castle O-bata was waiting to lead the bearer of Tsune's trunk up to the family quarters, but Lord Okubo impatiently ordered tea brought to a main room on the first floor. None of them liked this room, which was typically reserved for audiences with petitioners and representatives from Edo, but at the lord's insistence they arranged themselves on cushions on the floor.

"Now," he said, "speak clearly. Don't worry about Edo's confusion, so long as it is not your own."

Tsune understood she would not be allowed a respite, but rested her lips against the rim of her teacup, taking a short one anyway, while deciding how to proceed with the story she had to tell.

"First, there has been a surprise of sorts, a groundswell of support for Manjiro among merchants, and, to some degree, among the peasant class," she said. "There is a division of opinion among court ladies and lower-ranking bureaucrats, and even among some members of the Great Council. The gist of their talk is that Lord Abe went too far, that he should not have brought the foreigners ashore without a consensus. They are charging him with arrogance, calling for his censure once again, and, as the story of what Manjiro did leaks out, some people are beginning to see his motives as selfless, based upon the old ideas of moral integrity and right action. They are casting him as a hero, and Keiki, always the clever one, has ordered some very inventive posters made depicting Manjiro as someone like the Kambei of old. The posters are everywhere in Edo, the absolute talk of the town."

She turned to her sister. "You remember the Kambei stories, don't you? We used to hear of his daring exploits when we were children."

Lord Okubo stared at her uncomprehendingly, and Fumiko leaned her weight against Keiko, unable to grasp what she had been told. Only Einosuke answered, and he barked out a terrible laugh.

"Kambei!" he said. "Oh, that's just wonderful! I don't know much anymore, but I don't think what we need just now is another titillation, another such as Kambei with irresponsible Manjiro at its center! Keiki started such a thing, you say?"

No one was entirely sure whether he had ever truly lived or not, but Kambei was indeed a famous folk hero, a *ronin* or masterless samurai from the sixteenth century, a man of great character and forbearance, who gave up everything in order to fight for the peasantry of a particular village, against a gang of bandits. There were drawings of Kambei in children's books, occasional references to him in Great Council speeches, and he was the hero of several Kabuki plays.

"Not so fast," Lord Okubo told Einosuke. He could feel the scratches that the knife blade had made on his belly and adjusted himself on his cushion, to make himself more comfortable. Tsune was sitting in that direction, so he appeared to be focusing entirely on her, and scolding his elder son for his outburst.

"Tell us what else you know, my dear," he said.

"At first I was incredulous, too," said Tsune. "You will perhaps remember that on the evening that the American musicians came ashore, on the night Lord Abe and Lord Tokugawa had their now infamous meeting at that geisha house, I was not at home with you, but had gone to spend the evening with Keiki, who had said he might leave Edo early. When I got to the hunting lodge, however, Keiki wasn't there for he had accompanied his father."

Tsune looked at Lord Okubo steadily, but felt her own duplicity. It was true enough that Keiki had mentioned leaving Edo early, but she had not expected to find him at the hunting lodge that night. Rather, she had gone there expressly to see her former lover, Kyuzo, and to discover what he had thought of Manjiro.

"Because it was too late to travel back across Edo I stayed at the hunting lodge that night," she continued. "I was tired from all the recent intrigue and slept soundly in one of the inner rooms, completely unaware of what might be happening outside. I didn't hear Lord Tokugawa and Keiki return from the geisha house, nor, several hours after that, did I know of the arrival of Manjiro and the two Americans musicians, out in the bamboo grove, at Lord Tokugawa's Pavilion of Timelessness."

"So that's what happened!" said Lord Okubo, slapping his knee. "Instead of following Lord Abe's orders, Manjiro took the Americans to Lord Tokugawa. Not to his actual hunting lodge, which would put Lord Tokugawa in an awkward position, but to the pavilion in its garden."

"Yes," said Tsune. "It is I who introduced Manjiro to the Pavilion of Timelessness, I'm afraid. I remember telling him that I felt it to be detached from Lord Tokugawa's aura of power, that I liked it because it had a kind of separate integrity. I'm sure he thought that if he remained only there, then welcome or not, Lord Tokugawa's name would not be sullied."

When Einosuke heard that he scoffed even more emphatically than he had the first time. "Are you saying that Manjiro took the Americans on a whim, on the spur of the moment, all on his own, and not because Lord Tokugawa instructed him to do so earlier that evening? Are you saying that upon leaving the geisha house my brother knew only that he would disobey Lord Abe, but otherwise had no idea what he would do with the two musicians?"

The truth was that Manjiro had not known even that much, Einosuke understood it even as he spoke. It was quite like Manjiro and it made him angry all over again.

"They arrived late but got up early," Tsune said. "I was finally awakened by the extreme commotion."

As Lord Okubo listened he was glad he hadn't killed himself but doubly sure he would have to do it all again later on. Kambei indeed! Einosuke was right about that, how ridiculous! Kambei was a military strategist of the first order and in each of the stories about him one thing was always certain; however great the odds against him, however impossible his task, long before he made his move, Kambei had a plan.

Lord Okubo looked at Einosuke and then at Tsune. "It isn't every day that a man wakes up to find foreigners in his teahouse," he said. "Lord Tokugawa must have been surprised."

Tsune bowed in acknowledgment of that surprise, though it was she who'd had the most of it. It had been her intention to get up early that day and ask Lord Tokugawa to proceed with the marriage arrangements concerning herself and Manjiro. She had prepared for it the night before, talking the whole thing over with Kyuzo. Imagine her amazement, then, when she found the four of them—Keiki, Lord Tokugawa, Kyuzo and Manjiro himself—all sitting together in the courtyard in the morning.

"How was Manjiro's demeanor?" Fumiko asked. "Was he excited or calm, glum or cheerful? Did he seem beside himself or was he resolute and thoughtful? What was the demeanor of the American who made me cry that day? Was he worried for his life, or calm?"

Fumiko believed that in the end the answer to the first of her questions would be important to both her husband and father-in-law, so she persisted though both men clearly disliked the interruption now. She was chagrined to understand that she had asked the last of her questions for herself.

"Manjiro was quite calm," said her sister, "and he answered Lord Tokugawa's inquiries with the utmost seriousness. I have always admired Manjiro, as you know, but he was at his best that morning. I don't mean to belabor the point, but he was gallant and Kambei truly did come to mind."

Tsune let her voice drop, feeling something move inside her when she listened to the words she herself was uttering. She had resolved to marry Manjiro for reasons that still seemed sound—because she might as well have him if she couldn't have Kyuzo—but now, as she described his conduct, another reason came to her, unbidden yet fully realized. She could be happy with Manjiro. She could love him with the largeness of her heart, not merely with her mind and her sense of practicality. She looked at the others and began to cry.

"We know you are tired," said Lord Okubo, "but you can't stop now. We have waited, knowing nothing, for four long days. Skip to the end if you must, but tell us how things sit with my youngest son now? What's going to happen next and how is he going to survive the scandal?"

"What he intends to do is simple," Tsune said. "Perry knows nothing of what has happened to his musicians and, indeed, has just set sail for Shimoda. Manjiro intends to do a similar sailing, only overland, with his own unfortunate cargo. And once in Shimoda he will return the Americans to the fleet from which they came. That's all, but to that end he is intractable."

"Oh, who taught him to act like this?" Einosuke moaned.

Tsune glanced at him and then looked down. "There is more, my brother-in-law," she said. "It's difficult to tell, but I think you should hear it all."

"We know Lord Abe's opinion only too well," said Einosuke.

"Yes," she asked, "but do you know his henchman, the shadowy character who always seems to stand by his side?"

Einosuke and his father both nodded as the specter of Ueno appeared in their minds. Lord Okubo, who resided above Ueno in the circle of power, thought him humorless and dull, while Einosuke remembered the violent verbal attack on him recently in the castle garden.

"Well it is he," said Tsune, "with a group of masterless hirelings, who is going after Manjiro. He has pretended to resign his post with Lord Abe because the Great Council, unlikely as it may seem, really has censured the lord at least insofar as to not let him use the Shogun's troops. So while Lord Abe fights his political battles, Ueno has formed a small private army, with revenge and punishment as his primary goals. They are currently scouring Edo, tearing down Keiki's Kambei posters as they find them. There is little doubt that they will soon come down here, however, toward Odawara and Shimoda."

They were quiet again. It hadn't occurred to any of them that Lord Abe might actually send soldiers after Manjiro, and it hadn't occurred to them, either, that Manjiro would try to return the Americans to Perry in Shimoda. Nor, of course, had they thought that the Great Council would find the courage to take Lord Abe to task. It did occur to more than one of them that if Manjiro had only waited, if caprice had not once more alighted on his shoulder, Lord Abe's demotion might have made it possible to return the Americans to their ships right there in Edo Bay, with no harm done to anyone.

"We have to do something to help him," said Keiko. It was the first time she had spoken since her aunt arrived.

"We do, indeed, my dear," said Tsune, "and luckily there is already someone with him who can help greatly. His name is Kyuzo. He was in Lord Tokugawa's employ until yesterday but resigned his post in earnest, so that his actions would not cast a bad light on Lord Tokugawa. He has made it his business to act as Manjiro's protector, to see that he succeeds in his endeavors, and that he stays safe."

It made her heart ache to say such things but she kept her voice even, unencumbered by the tumult of her emotions. She had promised Kyuzo she would say less than she had already said. His face came to her mind's eye, but she sent it away.

The dirt of the long trip insisted itself upon her then, riding up out of her pores to streak across her body. She squeezed her nieces' hands and leaned against her sister until they got the message and stood up.

They would not all bathe, but they would leave the men alone. The girls would prepare their aunt's bath and sit around its edges, watching her and thinking things over, before the strangeness of everything caught up with Tsune and she asked to be alone.

22. | *Angelface*

EINOSUKE WAS RIGHT about Manjiro. He had indeed taken the Americans to the Pavilion of Timelessness on the night after the geisha house meeting entirely on a whim—because he could no longer stand Lord Abe's duplicity, the dishonorable nature of his plan. And Tsune was right, too, in telling the others that now that he had acted he was intractable. But as to Manjiro himself, oh how he wished he hadn't acted at all! Oh how he wished he could undo everything, rolling his life back to when he lived in Shimoda with his tutor and worried only about his studies and the ordinary loneliness that played upon him during countless lonely nights! What did he care what happened to these Americans, whether Perry got them or Ueno jailed them or even cut their heads off, if he, in the meantime, lost his father's goodwill, his brother's respect and friendship, and maybe even the chance to marry the only woman he had ever loved? Oh, he had acted without thinking what his actions would mean in the long run! And damnable Keiki was turning him into a hero for it, too, in these ridiculous posters that were beginning to appear everywhere, even on the back roads!

For their part the two Americans didn't react in a uniform way to the news that they had been falsely invited ashore, but when they were finally made to understand that their lives were in danger, that rogue swordsmen hunted them, and that Manjiro was trying to return them to their fleet at great risk to himself, Ned, at least, grew serious and helpful, putting on the monk's clothing that his new friend Keiki had given them (in exchange for his harmonica). He remembered that he could act as well as sing, and took to acting like a Buddhist monk. Coming ashore for a day or two had been okay with him, since it had gotten him away from those rank-smelling sailors and unending card games, but now he was ready to go back. So he walked out of Edo wordlessly, hair and eyes hidden under a sloping hat, and each night he waited in the darkness while Kyuzo, who was also with them, hurried off to some nearby village for food and drink. He put his trust in Mangy, and thought about home.

For Ace, however, all of this was an entirely different matter, and though he acted like Ned did during their daytime walking, he was convinced that he was where he should be, that the itch he'd been feeling his whole life long was about to be scratched by Japan.

For three days they made good progress, but on the fourth exhaustion caught up with them, and as they sat rubbing their feet by the side of some stream, the tongues they had held during the day began to waggle. And to make matters worse, Kyuzo sat beside them like a curious owl, and insisted on having everything translated for him.

"I figure it this way," Ned said, when Ace expressed surprise that no one had tried to talk to them as they walked along. "People here don't much cotton to religious folks, they ain't drawn to 'em like we all are at home."

"Not everyone cottons to religious folks at home," said Ace.

"What?" asked Kyuzo. "What did he say?"

Manjiro's thoughts were awash with what his own fate might be, and he was continually fighting off showing disgust for all three of his traveling companions. What he really wanted to say was, "To hell with monks and to hell with you, see how my life is ruined?" In actual fact, however, all he did was drink from a bottle of saké that Kyuzo had purchased in a nearby village, sometimes translating properly, sometimes not, while Ace told them the story of his life, of growing up in the forests of Pennsylvania.

This is how the story went:

As a boy Ace had loved the forests. He had trapped and hunted in them often with his father, and by the age of nine had learned their pathways and clearings far better than he'd learned the workings of his own young mind. He knew how to make a rabbit snare from the leafy branches of a willow tree, how to turn hemlock bark and river mud into a salve for cuts and bruises, and he could recognize vast varieties of mushrooms, the deadly from the delicious, no matter how insignificant the differences.

Soon after Ace's thirteenth birthday his father was killed in the forest behind their house, mauled by a thin and sickly bear who at first

had appeared to be dead herself, lying among the springtime wildflowers. Ace's mother had always disliked the forests and after his father's
death moved the family—herself and Ace and his little sister, June—to
Philadelphia, where she quickly found work putting up preserves in a
building that June insisted on calling "The Apricot Factory." Ace was at
first inconsolable with the move—he missed the forests desperately and
he missed his father more, but in Philadelphia something unexpected
occurred. They were living in a room near the city's central market, in
the same building that housed "The Apricot Factory." In some of that
building's upper floors there was a music school, and when spring came
and the weather grew mild, Ace and June would often wait on the stairs
for their mother to finish work, and pass the time by listening to the
music school students singing and playing various instruments. Most of
the students were women, with one boy among them, not much older
than Ace, and by the end of a single day of listening to him, Ace made
June laugh by ascending the steps until he was staring in the school
window, all the while singing along, his mouth a perfect zero and a
perfect imitation of the music teacher's surprise.

The school gave Ace a scholarship. He became the teacher's pro-
tégé, the pride of everyone, and worked so hard and well that by the
time he turned sixteen he had not only gained a reputation as the best
young tenor in Philadelphia, but had begun building a name for himself,
the tendrils of which stretched off toward the more demanding singing
world of New York. Ace's life seemed set, and he began to believe that
his father's death and the subsequent loss of his beloved forest served
the unknown purposes of fate, of God's mysterious plan for him.

But then, on a cold March morning in 1847, the building that
housed the music school burned down, razed by a fire that started in a
bucket of burning apricot pits, something someone had lit on purpose
in order to keep warm.

There were dozens of advertisements, bills and posters, nailed
along the panels next to the building's front door, but the only one
untouched by the fire's savage tongue, the only one unsinged even at its
edges, announced the coming auditions for a traveling minstrel show.
Before that day Ace had had no interest in minstrel shows. He had never
even seen one. But this was no ordinary show and Ace came to believe

that the poster advertising it had not been saved from the flames for ordinary reasons. The show was called "Colonel Morgan's Dark and Mighty Abolitionists," and its single purpose, so said the ad, was to "help eradicate the abomination of slavery in these United States."

Ace passed his audition and during the first of his almost seven years with Colonel Morgan, studied the issue of slavery until a vehement opposition to it was born in his heart. He came to believe that slavery was not only a great enough evil to bring down the United States, but anathema to God himself, and that the true purpose of his life, the single reason he had been taken from the forests and given his wonderful singing voice, was to fight against it. So he not only sang in the shows, but began to write them as well.

Then one clear fall evening, during a midnight show in Boston, Colonel Morgan was killed by an up-from-the-South slave owner who stood out of the audience, shouted a string of curses, and cocked and fired his gun. The slave owner tried to shoot others, too, but his pistol jammed and Ace and Ned, who was also in the show, jumped down from the stage, lyrics still leaking from their mouths, to wrestle with the man until the pistol unjammed, clefting Ace's chin with a passing bullet that wedged into the slave owner's brain.

As it happened Commodore Perry, himself an abolitionist, was in the audience that night, sitting two rows behind the slave owner. The Commodore had missed most of the show because he had been preoccupied, busy considering what aspects of American culture he might take as entertainment for the Imperial Court of Japan.

But though he missed the show, he didn't miss the shootings, and when Ace and Ned stood out of all that smoke it was he who used his naval rank to escort them out of there.

When they arrived in Japan Ace didn't know anymore whether his life was to be led as an outcast, whether he'd been born merely to kill some no-account slave owner, or whether God had got him through all his troubles so that he could serve some higher purpose, the essence of which, he now felt certain, would one day soon, quite miraculously, unfold.

THAT WAS ACE'S STORY, or at least the version of it that Manjiro translated for Kyuzo, and it had a surprising effect on Manjiro, making him think about his own fate in more stable ways than those which had infected his mind on the first three days after their departure from Edo. It was nevertheless Ned, not Ace, who caused his thinking to take an even more radical turn, forcing him to consider stopping at his father's castle, to see if there wasn't some action he could take to salvage his ruined life.

He had gone to stand away from the Americans after Ace's story, letting Kyuzo and Ace work out a rudimentary way of communicating without him, and was absently writing Tsune's name in the dirt with a stick when Ned came up to ask what he'd written down.

"It is the name of a woman," Manjiro said, "the name of my . . ."

He paused trying to think of what word to use.

"The name of your sweetie?" Ned offered. "Your beloved? Your wife? I had me a wife once. How about writin' her name down, Mangy? It don't matter 'bout her real name, I always called her 'Angelface.'"

Manjiro knew both halves of the name, but like the idiomatic expressions he had run across on shipboard, when put together like that they didn't make much sense. What kind of language was this he had been studying, that could allow such untenable combinations? Angelface! He should have studied German. He should have studied Dutch!

"'Angel,' like on high," Ned prodded, "like one of them lovelies that sings in the celestial chorus. And after that just regular old 'face,' like the gloomy one you're lookin' at me with this very moment. It means she's pretty, Mangy, though she run off first chance she got and divorced me soon as she could." Something loosened its grip on Manjiro when he heard those words and he said them to himself several times over, in order to make sure of their meaning. *She run off the first chance she got, divorced me as soon as she could.* If a foreigner, if such an obviously unschooled fellow as this one in particular, could smile and find lightness in his step even after such cruel treatment at the hands of his actual wife, why couldn't Manjiro stop wallowing in this newfound self-pity, why could he not, at least in some small part, get ahold of himself?

"Angel is '*Tenshi*,'" he explained, writing it out in the dirt next to Tsune's name. "And in Japanese 'face' is *kao*. Like this."

Ned bent down to frown at the roughly written characters, but then stood back up and started to laugh. "Well, 'cow' sure enough suits her," he said.

For reasons unfathomable to him this little joke—perhaps the first he had ever truly understood between these two languages of his—moved Manjiro as much as Ace's entire story had, making him resolve to cast the ignoble grumblings that he'd been wallowing in out of his heart and to stop by his father's castle. He would face his father and he would face Einosuke, too, before continuing on to Shimoda. He would try to explain himself and win their support. Who knew, maybe he could get a semblance of his old life back? And if he couldn't, if his capricious action had burned the bridge he had so longingly built toward Tsune and a life of study, then maybe he could garner a little bit of Ned Clark's spirit, his unadorned acceptance of whatever came his way.

"Well, cow sure enough suits her."

Manjiro looked at Ned again and smiled.

23. | *Hired for a Bad Cause*

THEY WEREN'T REALLY very far from Odawara—they had to pass it by to get to Shimoda—so on their fifth morning out of Edo, when Manjiro saw a stranger on horseback on the road in front of them, he told the Americans to hide in the nearby trees, lest it be one of his father's soldiers. Kyuzo wasn't with them, because he had gone into the nearest village for information and supplies.

When the Americans were gone he rubbed his shaved pate—his hair, topknot and all, had been left on the floor of the Pavilion of Timelessness, snipped from his head by Tsune so he could pass as a monk—and took a drink from a ceramic saké bottle that they had filled with water before breaking camp that morning. By the time he put the bottle back down the rider had closed the distance between them and was waving his arms, to tell him to stay where he was. The rider was a samurai, but not one of his father's soldiers. His horse was old and unimpressive but the man himself was young. He seemed to want to make the horse prance, to cover the distance between them with a certain bearing, and when the horse wouldn't do it he put on a frustrated smile. "A man's beast should not also be his burden," he said as he dismounted. He looked at the monk before him carefully, not to determine whether or not he was one of the escaped foreigners, but to see if he appreciated the cleverness of his comment.

"Good morning," Manjiro said.

"Is it?" asked the samurai. "Tell me, monk, what's good about this morning in particular, as opposed to, say, yesterday's morning or tomorrow's?"

"There is only a little breeze," Manjiro answered, "and it's getting warm."

"I like it when it's hot and I like it when it's cold but I don't appreciate these in-between days," said the samurai. "They seem indecisive, and remind me that there's too much indecisiveness in men as well."

He laughed, but stopped when Manjiro didn't join him. He knew he was taking advantage, but riding along alone these last few days had made him anxious for camaraderie.

"Don't monks like anything?" he asked, his bombast suddenly gone. "I know you don't like women or drink, but aren't you even fond of playful language, a repartee, a friendly exchange on the road?" He saw the saké bottle and said, "Wait a second, perhaps I spoke too fast."

"It's only water," Manjiro told him, "I get thirsty during the day."

The samurai took the bottle, uncorked it, put it to his lips and tipped it back and drank. When he returned it to Manjiro he said, "It's almost empty. Why is that, so early in the day?"

Manjiro could see that this young man had eyes that didn't carry the weight of too much disappointment. He could also plainly see that he rarely talked with so much authority. "I filled it only partly," he answered. "So it would be easier to carry."

"But if it's that kind of ease you want, why not carry water in your belly," asked the samurai, "and refill it when you come to a stream?"

Manjiro turned the bottle in his hands, wondering what was keeping Kyuzo in that village. He was learning nothing from this exchange, yet one wrong word might give him away.

"Some men like saké," he admitted. "Never mind their vows."

"Ah ha," said the samurai. "I thought that might be the case."

He was pleased with Manjiro's confession. He'd seen something odd in Manjiro, perceived some secret, and was glad to discover it was an ordinary human weakness, like dependence on drink. He turned to bring his horse around, ready to remount, when something else occurred to him.

"Where do you get the money for saké?" he asked. "And in such an expensive bottle? When a man begs for food he can expect that if he fails at one house he'll succeed at another, but do people have sympathy for a monk with a vice?"

Manjiro glanced at the bottle's bottom, as if looking for the answer, and said, "In some there is a readiness to see a man fall."

"What is your name?" the samurai asked. "When you knock on people's doors, who do you say is calling?"

"I am only a wayward monk," said Manjiro. "I never say my name out loud."

"Well my name is Ichiro," said the samurai, "and you cannot

deceive me. I can see that you are a man of rare intelligence. I can also see that you are still young, not much older than me in fact, and I'll tell you something I believe. Japan will change greatly in our lifetimes. There are good chances coming, and not just for aristocrats and samurai, but for peasants and merchants and even for monks like yourself. My advice to you is to seize this chance when it comes, be ready for it, my fine fellow. You are smart enough and young enough to lead a better life than you have led thus far."

He paused and added ruefully, "And so, of course, am I."

Manjiro stared at the ground, both in order to make the samurai think he was ashamed and to defeat the urge he had to glance toward the trees where the Americans were hiding. And that made the samurai not only take pity on him, but also take his bottle. "As a first step toward strength I'll leave you empty-handed," he said. Then he swung onto his horse again and galloped up the road.

Manjiro stayed where he was until he could no longer hear the sounds of Ichiro's departure. He had been impressed with the young man, had liked him despite the fact that he was no doubt working for Ueno, whom Kyuzo had discovered the night before was after them. Of course he knew that samurai were like other men and thus visited by numerous imperfections, but meeting the young man had shown him something he had never before thought of: that in these days when a man could wander for years with no lord to whom he might attach his loyalty, and with so little money that he might as well be a monk as a warrior, he could just as easily be hired for a bad cause as a good one. It was the second insight he had had in two days, however disconnected it was from what he'd learned from Ace Bledsoe and Ned Clark.

He lifted his eyes and looked back down the road the samurai had just come up, and there was Kyuzo, too late for anything, limping along.

24. *Whoa, Nellie*

KYUZO WAS NOT ONLY limping, as he walked along the road toward Manjiro, but simultaneously using the tip of his short sword to try to dig a deep sliver from his palm. It wasn't working very well. "I can't get at it because my hand keeps shaking," he said. "Here, you give it a try."

When he extended his sword toward Manjiro however, the hand in question didn't seem to shake in the slightest. The Americans were with them again, both had their hats off, and were staring at the sliver like they were trying to read Kyuzo's palm.

"I should have brought my sewing kit," Kyuzo said, "or at the very least a needle. An old man gets lazy, that's a lesson I've learned these last few days on the road."

The sliver had been driven into his palm at a forty-five-degree angle, falling away from its surface like the body of a carp does from the surface of a pond. "I hurt my toe, too," Kyuzo explained. "I was walking on an overgrown path, looking at the mountain view, and caught it on a protruding root."

He lifted his left foot up so that all three men could see his red and swollen big toe. His toenail was wrenched loose, gaping at them like the sprung lid of a soybean jar. Manjiro had taken the blade and was bringing it to the sliver cautiously when Ace, seeing the clumsiness of the approach, sighed.

"Oh, please, give me that thing," he said, "I'll go cut a proper needle." And without waiting he grabbed the sword and plunged across the stream into the forest.

Kyuzo and Manjiro looked at each other, both thinking that maybe the sword, plus one of the Americans, was gone for good, when Ace came splashing back again with a length of dried bamboo in one hand and an entire young bamboo sapling in the other. He used Kyuzo's knife to slice the dried wood into finely beveled spikes.

"Close your hand a bit now and maybe look down yonder," he said. "The trick to this technique lies in not using any one needle for too long."

Ace had Ned hold the extra needles he had cut, then carefully dug a trough around the sliver, flicking bits of stringy flesh away. He used two more needles to hook the sliver's end, pulling steadily until the head came out, then he pressed down around it with his thumbs, bent to grasp it with his teeth, and pulled the sliver out. It was a full inch long and still as sharp as the unused needles he had cut.

"That was well done!" said Kyuzo. "It was artful! Did your father teach you that or do all Americans know how to do such things?"

He showed his hand to Manjiro, pointing at the hole in it as if it were a medal, but by then Ace was busy with the bamboo sapling. He used Kyuzo's knife to strip it of its outer skin, making lengths of fibrous bandage, laying them across Ned's arm, while he knelt to examine Kyuzo's toe. It was in far worse condition than his hand, with a distance as long as the sliver's length between the end of the nail and the toe it was supposed to cover.

"You really ought to rest after this," he told Kyuzo. "No more walking until it heals up."

While Manjiro translated, Ace took the longest of the strips he had made and tied a hangman's noose in the end of it, lowering it over the wounded toe, slowly working it down as if over a condemned man's head. He then yanked on it with one hand and pushed on his noose with the other, lest there be more resistance than he expected. He held on tight when Kyuzo first tried to get away, then held on tighter still when he attempted to reach for his sword. Kyuzo would have killed Ace quickly had he got it, but instead both his hands flew to his temples and he howled a howl not heard in those parts since the extinction of the howler monkey. He jumped into the air two or three times, landed hard on his good right foot and sat down.

"Whoa, Nellie," said Ned, but Kyuzo was up again in an instant, bellowing his outrage into the forest. Ace, however, only took a second bandage from Ned's outstretched arm and knelt in the dirt, catching Kyuzo's instep, and guiding his foot until it rested along his own left thigh. There was a bit of new blood around the replaced nail, but otherwise it was once again properly aligned in the bed of his toe. When he loosened the first bandage Kyuzo felt an echo of the earlier pain, but in a minute his toe was so completely wrapped in strips of bamboo that it looked like something to eat, like a delicacy one might find in a cake shop. He bent and grabbed his ankle and pulled his wounded foot up, until it hovered under his nose. His kimono split, exposing his other leg, which was thin and straight, like a crane's at the edge of a pond. He worked his fingers in beside the bandage, and between each of his other toes, his grounded leg like a fence post.

It was in this way, through the utterance of a wayward wife's pet name from one, and the issuance of this good medical treatment from the other, that the two Japanese finally began to think of the Americans as individual men, and not as merely cargo on its way to Shimoda.

And a short time after that, when they came down out of the foothills that led into Odawara proper, Kyuzo was in the lead again and hardly limping at all.

25. | *Come to Me, My Dear, Come*

MEANWHILE IN THE CASTLE above Odawara Fumiko fell asleep on the tatami of the room she shared with Einosuke and had a very disturbing dream. She was at a wedding and dressed so formally that at first she thought she was the bride. She could feel the stiff material of her kimono, heavy against her shoulders, could hear the complaining rustle of it when she walked, and could see an old Shinto priest out of the corner of a thickly powdered eye. It was worrisome, since in the dream as in life she was already married, but presently a bride and groom stepped into the picture before her, followed by a dozen attendants and flanked by rows of formally dressed aristocrats. They were somewhere in the mountains, with storm clouds threatening and banks of impending fog, but the priest performed the ritual as if everyone were enveloped in quiet and calm.

Though she couldn't see the bride and groom very well, Fumiko knew that this was the wedding she had worked toward for years, constantly pressing for with both her sister and Manjiro, as well as Lord Okubo. She felt her breasts swell with gladness and her eyes grow moist, and she looked about for Keiko and Masako, so that she could bring them into the folds of her pleasure, share with them the success that they all three hoped for. She walked forward, to better see the looks upon those two wedded faces, but as she did so the stiffness of her kimono departed. Now she was wearing the sheerest of sleeping gowns and instead of treading upon a mountain path she was inside an inn facing a series of delicate doors. She was the bride again, she knew it for she could hear her husband singing out, *"Come to me, my dear, come."* Each time she opened a door she thought she would find him, but the pattern of rooms was unending and she was always disappointed.

"Call again," she whispered, "let me hear the direction I should go."

Why he was singing she had no idea, but she found it slightly bothersome.

"This door," sang the voice, *"open this one,"* but she couldn't tell which of the doors he was talking about. So instead of opening more doors she did a strange thing, very much unlike her. She untied her sash, letting her gown fall away until she was naked in the hall. She had never acted so rashly, not even in the garden with Einosuke that night. She had never been so excited, either, or feared less what those in the neighboring rooms might think about it.

"Why not open it from the inside?" she suggested. "Why not come out and find me if I am such a prize?"

When she spoke a door to her right opened to reveal her American standing just as she was, naked, his own bed clothes folded behind him on a futon. There was nothing fearsome about him, he was handsome and smiling, his Japanese was perfect and his body stood out toward her.

Fumiko's desire overwhelmed her even in her dream. She felt it first in her thighs and then, like the pleasant component of a mild fever, it surged through her torso. She remembered she was married, she even remembered her daughters and her infant son, but she went to him with no hesitation and felt the boundaries of their bodies mingle until everything turned into a growing circle of heat with an achy kind of longing at its middle. She had the sensation of *hanabi,* of colors falling silently earthward after a series of beautiful explosions.

"My love!" she whispered, wondering, as she said it, if she ought to try to say his American name.

She was not finished, not in the least desirous of awakening, but someone was knocking on the door, someone else was lost in that hallway and calling out, "Hello? Hello?"

Fumiko squeezed her eyes tightly closed, and would have put her fingers in her ears to block out the voice, were her fingers not engaged elsewhere. It was her husband who called her, she knew it was Einosuke, but when the door opened again and a hand tapped lightly on her shoulder, there did not seem to be any outrage or anger in it, only her husband's voice saying, "Get up and come properly to bed. If you sleep here all night you'll be sore all over tomorrow."

She didn't want to do it but Fumiko opened her eyes.

"Really, my dear," said Einosuke, "our beds are waiting for us. Why don't we retire?"

In her husband's smile there was no knowledge of her betrayal, but Fumiko closed her eyes again anyway, willing herself to reenter that other world so the betrayal could go on.

To her profound relief he was there again immediately and she fell against him, even as her husband took her elbow, gently pulling her off the floor.

26. *I Guess There's Hooligans Every Damned Where*

THEY ENTERED ODAWARA to a change in the weather. A cold April wind came off the Pacific, with cargo ships from Edo banking and hovering in the lee of the promontory.

At the town's edge Manjiro, still optimistic, still bolstered by his renewed spirits, took the Americans in one direction while Kyuzo went another. His job was as it had been in the villages along the way—to discover what he could of Ueno and the soldiers who chased them, to hear what news he could about what went on in Edo. He was to meet them later in a field by the castle, before Manjiro went in to show his face to his father and brother.

In earlier centuries the castle's walls were all that kept its occupants protected from marauders, but those walls had succumbed to fire during the rule of Manjiro's great-grandfather and now the castle simply sat there, approachable from a dozen directions, though there were only two official roads. Manjiro decided they would cut through the thickest part of the forest, coming past Masako's marsh, to a clearing where he and Einosuke had often played as boys. There were tall grass and fresh water in that clearing, and he could watch the castle through the foliage, think about how to make his approach while they waited for Kyuzo.

When they stepped out onto a street of low brothels and drinking houses, most of which were closed until summer, the Americans were walking, as per Manjiro's instructions, in a single line some twenty feet behind him and twenty feet apart, as well. But because he'd been thinking about how he should greet his father, and about whether it would be his father or Einosuke who was angrier at him, Manjiro hadn't been paying attention, and before he could come back to himself someone spoke.

"Are you following me monk, or are you only looking to fill your saké bottle in the cheapest part of town?"

It was, of course, the young samurai who had questioned him on the road that morning. Manjiro turned to see that only one of the Americans was visible, had thus far come into this street behind him.

He spoke loudly, so the second one might know not to show himself. "Alas, as you know I no longer have my bottle," he said. "All I am doing is passing by."

The samurai—Manjiro remembered that Ichiro was his name—sat atop a closed water barrel outside a ramshackle bar, the only one on the street that was open. Beside him was another barrel with its cover off. The clouds had parted and the moon was reflected in the surface of this second barrel's water. When the samurai noticed that there were two monks now, he called the second one forward, waving at him with an empty flagon.

"Do either of you know the old song about the monk and his mate?" he asked.

The American, whichever he was, had seen that the safest thing to do was to stand next to Manjiro with his hat still on and his head down. When the samurai touched the surface of the water in the barrel beside him, the image of the moon shook and he began to sing his song.

> Oh where are we walking?
> said the monk to his mate.
> Oh where are we walking
> in the mountains so late?
>
> We are walking to cover
> the distance to God,
> the distance to God.

"I learned that song as a boy but I don't like it much anymore," he said. "Though I still think the second monk's answer is splendid, all the first monk does is ask the same question again, 'Oh where are we walking in the mountains so late?' If I were the second monk I'd have said, 'Get away from me fool! From now on I'm walking alone.'"

He laughed and got down from his barrel, then sighed and got back on it again, deflated. "Ah, what's the use of talking to you?" he said. "When I get older I may choose a religious path myself, but I won't lose my spirit like you two obviously have. And that, Mr. Drink-weak monk, is a promise."

Manjiro bowed, hoping they might continue on their way, but as he touched the sleeve of the man beside him, a shout came from inside the bar and two more samurai staggered out. "Here you are!" one of them yelled. "Sitting like a dummy outside." When he saw the two monks standing there he covered his mouth.

Manjiro noticed that the third man, the one who had not yet spoken, was older than the other two, and he hoped he might issue an order for them to act properly, to go about their business and leave the monks alone. The older man, however, only pushed Ichiro off his perch and sat there himself, tipping sideways into the center of that adjacent barrel, soaking his arm and shoulder. His companion laughed again and the reflection of the moon disappeared from the surface of the water.

"Go on, laugh!" the older man roared, righting himself and standing again and stumbling back against the nearest wall of the bar. Manjiro thought he saw a chance to get away amid the confusion, and he nudged the American. But then he made another inexplicable error, larger, even, than letting the samurai see them there in the first place.

"Just walk slowly," he whispered in English, at the precise instant that all three samurai grew silent.

"Whoa!" said the loud one. "Were those words you said just now, or were you only farting?"

Manjiro took his hat off. "I told him not to hurry," he said.

The older samurai stood away from the wall he'd crashed into and the loud one pulled out his long sword and flicked the second monk's hat off. Ned Clark's hair fell across his forehead, framing startled blue eyes and a decidedly foreign face.

"Well I'll be picked and damned!" the older man said.

Behind him, to the left of the bar, a path lined with bamboo poles led to an outhouse. Balanced on top of the nearest pole was a small clay teacup.

"He looks like the devil himself," said the younger one. "And he stinks worse than that rotten outhouse back there."

"Who are you, then?" Ichiro asked Manjiro. "A monk who speaks English or the people's new hero, the latter-day Kambei of those posters we keep finding everywhere?"

He spoke politely, but the older man said he wanted to go find Ueno and report. Let him know who they had captured.

"Hold on a second, Grandpa, let's think this through first," said the younger man. He put his long sword away but pulled out his short one. "Is this not an enemy we've caught here? Is he not the first actual enemy any of us have ever seen in our decrepit and pitiful lives? Before we call Ueno I think we should exercise our right as captors. Let's mark him like they used to in the real Kambei's days. Let's cut off his nose."

Indeed, there were many famous stories concerning nose-cutting, about how, for example, Hoshimaru snuck into the camp of the great general Norishige and took his nose while he slept. Such stories were at least as old as those which heralded Kambei, but they had to do with good swordsmanship and deserved humiliation, not with the low level of bullying this man was talking about.

"Cutting his nose would be easy," said the older man. "Look at the size of the target."

Ned's body had started to shake and his knees were about to buckle, so Manjiro put a hand on his shoulder to calm him and spoke directly to Ichiro. "It's unbecoming of you to play on this man's fear," he said, "and pointless, too, because he doesn't understand the language."

The other young samurai chose that moment, however, to touch Ned's nose with the flat of his blade. It was cold, and so close to his right eye that Ned leapt up. "Lord almighty," he said, coming down so hard that the teacup tumbled off the top of that nearby bamboo pole.

"*Sha-sha-sha,*" said the older samurai, dancing in a little circle. "*Bosa, bosa, baka waka.*"

Manjiro understood that Ichiro was embarrassed by this display, and was about to ask him to intercede, when the loud young samurai told the older one to go back into the bar for some soy sauce and mustard.

"I want to paint the target so I get only his nose," he said. "If he keeps an unmutilated face, we will have acted like the samurai of old."

"You haven't the vaguest notion of the samurai of old," Manjiro said. "How about handing me a sword, see how you fare against a worthy opponent?"

Ichiro nodded. "That's sounds like Kambei all right," he said, but the older man had found the soy sauce and mustard by simply reaching into the bar and taking them off the nearest table. He mixed them together then turned to Ned in the waning moonlight.

"Well fine then," said Ned, "there's hooligans every damned where,

I guess. If you wanta be stupid your whole lives long, it's no sweat off my backside. You don't know 'bout me, but I can eat a dozen peppers in a heat wave without it even waterin' my eyes. So go ahead and do your damnedest with that concoction you dunderheaded rascals. See if I care."

He then actually opened his mouth, ready to prove what he'd claimed.

The older man put the soy sauce dish on the top of the pole from which the teacup had recently fallen. "Now don't move," he said, "I'm going to start at the tip and work my way back." He painted quickly, with the thumb and index finger of his right hand, and when he finished Ned's nose looked as black as it did in his minstrel makeup.

"Good job," said the younger man, but Ned, finally understanding that something meaner was afoot than just pouring hot sauce down his throat, jumped away as he spoke, darted past the distressed Ichiro, and back up the road the way they'd come. He was so fast that they'd never have caught him, but just before he disappeared around the corner another samurai stepped out and stopped him, catching him by his robes.

"Gentlemen, please," said Kyuzo, "take your pleasure a bit more quietly. And find a worthier target than this poor fellow."

"Who's that?" asked the older samurai.

"It's only me," said Kyuzo, "invigorated by the evening air."

He had Ace with him and brought both Americans back to stand next to Manjiro. "My name is Kyuzo, until recently in service to Lord Tokugawa of Mito," he said. "Can we not settle this amicably and then retire? It's late and I, at least, cannot put up with insufficient sleep nearly so well as you younger men seem able to anymore."

The younger man's short sword still gleamed in the air, but there was something different in his manner now, and Manjiro saw that Ichiro, too, had stood back in order to allow room for his sword to clear his belt. Only the older man remained nervous. He rocked on the balls of his feet and licked his fingers and smoothed back his hair.

Such behavior in a man his age disgusted Kyuzo and he touched his sword, a tactical error. All three men scowled at him and the older one said, "You've got one and we've got the other. That's one prize each, so why don't you be on your way. We'll settle the issue of this one ourselves."

"Very well," said Kyuzo, "but whatever happens you mustn't pretend. Now that you have painted it you must really cut his nose off, for only that will show a man like Ueno that you have discharged your duties seriously. If you bring him a man with a painted nose that still sits on his face he will know that you are frivolous men."

It was a bold thing to say but it came from an accurate observation and the younger drunk flinched. "Oh come on!" he said. "In these difficult days what samurai doesn't have the right to engage in a little fun?"

"In that case simply go back inside this bar and engage in your fun alone," said Kyuzo. "And no one will even know that we met like this tonight."

He tried to maintain a level voice, with no opinion in it. He believed the older samurai would do as he suggested, and even the young leader seemed undecided, but there was too much shame in it for Ichiro.

"No, sir," he said.

Kyuzo nodded again, and looked at Manjiro. To find a man of honor in an otherwise dishonorable band made things vastly more complicated, for it embarrassed the other young samurai so much that he made a noise in his throat, called up a ball of phlegm, and spit it between Kyuzo's legs. The phlegm, round and greenish-yellow, was the most impressive thing about the man thus far.

Kyuzo nodded again, sighed a little bit, and knelt down to examine the phlegm. He threw enough dirt on it to cover its color, slipped his short sword beneath it, and stood back up. He pushed it out toward the offending man. It shone there like a delicacy on a shiny narrow plate. "Put this back," he said.

The younger man's eyes moved from the phlegm to the faces of the two Americans. Put it back? Surely he wasn't suggesting what he thought he was. "We have laws," he said.

As he spoke, however, the older man's mouth fell open, as if understanding for the first time just how far they had fallen. "You mustn't take such ridicule," he told his younger colleague.

"Ah," said Kyuzo, "you're in luck, a volunteer."

He turned and flipped his sword toward the older man, rotating its blade and stopping abruptly, an inch in front of his face. The man's eyes bulged out and his mouth opened even further and the phlegm flew directly inside. "Ahg, arr," he said, as it lodged itself halfway down his throat.

There was a second of frozen astonishment and Kyuzo used it well. He turned his short sword back on the younger man, tucked it under his chin and danced him high up onto his toes. Ichiro charged him, but too quickly, and Kyuzo pulled the dancing man between them so that Ichiro's sword went into his thigh. The older man was clutching his throat and thrashing around, searching for something to drink, so Manjiro got that bowl of soy sauce and mustard from on top of the pole.

"Here," he said, "this might help."

Kyuzo released the wounded man, and when he fell, Ichiro, lest he cut him more deeply, had to drop his sword.

"Let's stop now," Kyuzo said. "And reconsider everything from the beginning." He was speaking only to Ichiro and he used the highest forms of speech. He had seen good swordsmanship in Ichiro's thrust, hands that were as quick as his own used to be, and a steadiness that could not be taught. He smiled at Ichiro, but the older man flung the soy sauce away and wrenched open the door of the bar, in search of water. When he was gone the wounded one hissed, "Why are you waiting? This old man has no skill!" His own sword was stuck beneath him, making it useless unless he stood up.

Ichiro did not know what to do. If he drew his short sword he would either kill Kyuzo or be killed by him, he understood that well enough, but what should he do, where did the right path lie? He was still thinking about it when the older samurai came back out of the bar. His legs were still shaky but his embarrassment had steadied the steel of his blade.

Kyuzo knew he had acted rashly with the phlegm and was sorry. He had seen too many men embittered at the ends of their lives to want to have a part in helping this one meet his ancestors, and he put his sword away. "I know how you feel," he said, "but over the years we masterless men have had far worse things shoved down our throats."

Those were the truest words he could find, and he bowed, hoping they would suffice as an apology.

The older man didn't respond, yet his eyes did turn briefly inward, as if gazing upon an earlier part of his life. Perhaps that is why his attack was surer than Kyuzo expected. It made him jump and turn in a wide circle, his dash for safety momentarily erasing the taste of the phlegm from the other man's mouth. Manjiro pulled Ace and Ned back from the line of battle, and with the same quickness he'd used to put it there, Ichiro snatched his sword from his fallen comrade's thigh. When the older man attacked again Kyuzo deflected his blade. He knew how to fight this man, but, like Ichiro with his question of honor, he did not so clearly know what was right. Should he keep on deflecting his thrusts or simply strike his own blade home?

It must have taken a great deal of effort, but while everyone else's attention was thusly focused, the wounded samurai got to his feet and, with his own sword finally drawn, hobbled toward the fighters. Kyuzo knew that if Ichiro joined the battle, too, he would be in trouble, but Ichiro was so lost in thought that he seemed hardly able to take in the fact that there had been a change in the equation. Kyuzo expected the younger man's attack to coincide with the next by the older one, and had just decided to kill them both when, instead of running toward him, the younger man lunged at Manjiro and the Americans.

"Watch out!" Kyuzo cried, but though Ace and Manjiro jumped back, the samurai's blade came down over the unmoving Ned's forehead and, precisely along the lines that had been painted there, perfectly severed his nose.

To those Japanese who had seen them firsthand, the worst feature of the American face was its pronounced and ugly nose, but infinitely worse was to suddenly see a face without one. Manjiro screamed and Ichiro threw his hands up over his eyes, and Kyuzo and the old man he was fighting both gasped like geisha. For his part, however, Ned just stood there, his eyes growing larger and his cheeks widening out, like all of his features were painted on a plate.

Nothing would have made the old samurai stop fighting Kyuzo save the fact that this wild sight left him retching and bent over, an evening's worth of cheap saké, and the phlegm, too, dislodged from his belly. The young samurai's intention was also thwarted, for though he intended to kill the others after cutting Ned, his success in the first part of his plan so surprised him that he abandoned the second, pausing just long enough to lift Ned's nose out of the dirt, before turning and limping away. And in a minute the old man wiped the vomit from his mouth and followed him.

Ichiro stayed where he was, fixed in mortification, until Ned slumped into Manjiro's waiting arms. And that pitiful sight was what decided him, severing, as clearly as Ned's nose had been, his ties to those two fleeing men and his loyalty to Ueno.

"Young Kambei," he said. "Go into the bar for some towels."

In another situation his words would have been improper, for Manjiro's station was far above his own, but as it was Manjiro and Kyuzo both hurried into the bar, and came back out again with rags pulled from a bucket of cold water. Ichiro took one and folded it and tried to show it to Ned, who looked up at him and said, "I don't feel no pain."

Ichiro worked the towel beneath Ned's fingers and he and Kyuzo each took an elbow, pulling Ned up. They followed Manjiro and Ace out of the bar street, then cut between two buildings and onto the forest path at the bottom of the hill, carrying Ned up a switchback trail.

At a clearing near the castle they stopped to rest, subduing their heavy breathing, until only Ned could be heard above the whisper of the wind that had come up.

He was freely crying by then, and kneeling before the others with his eyes open, staring over his own laced fingers and the lumpy mound of towel.

27. | *Twenty Questions*

TSUNE AND HER NIECES had not gone to bed early that night and were in a first floor room playing word games. Masako was "it" and had chosen a word that began with a certain Chinese character containing seven brushstrokes which, when put together with another seven-stroke character, depicted an embarrassing situation. Tsune and Keiko were irritated by the vagueness of Masako's hints but were asking questions anyway, for if they failed to guess the word in twenty tries they would have to take their hair down and walk out onto the castle grounds under the chilly April rain that had just come up. That was the punishment Masako had endured when she lost the last game, and she still looked bedraggled.

A scratching sound had been coming from outside the castle for quite a while and Masako said it was made by the ghost of the first Lord Okubo, who, everyone knew, sometimes haunted the family during rainstorms. The first Lord Okubo had died, legend had it, during the longest drought in Japanese history, and therefore liked to walk around the castle with his head turned up and his mouth open. Masako reminded Keiko that they had seen him once when they were younger, and that he was not likely to remove Keiko from the list of those he would haunt simply because she now considered herself an adult.

"He wouldn't bother us in normal weather," she admitted, "but he'll find you and scare that haughty attitude of yours out of you if you're out tonight."

Keiko and Tsune were exchanging glances. They had only one remaining guess in the current game and what they were telling each other was that they would accuse Masako of cheating if they guessed wrong. They would say her hints were misleading or that the word didn't have enough of the sense of embarrassment to it, or simply that it was time for bed. In any event both of them had decided not to go outside in the rain.

"But what is that scratching?" Tsune asked. "Really, there isn't a tree, is there, that could reach this high up the castle wall? I think you should go look, Masako. Perhaps the first Lord Okubo's ghost is standing on stilts at the window with the answer to your question, and if that's the case it would be fruitless for Keiko or me to go for we wouldn't know whether his answer was right or wrong."

"I'm not stupid, Auntie," Masako said, but the issue of the scratching had taken hold of her imagination. So while the others pretended to discuss what her word might be, she walked to the edge of the room to listen. The windows on the castle's upper floors were only wide enough to shoot an arrow out of, but in a recent remodeling some of those on this first floor had been widened to provide a better view and better ventilation. When Masako opened this one, however, she discovered that it was still shuttered from the outside. They had all arrived in such a deep depression over Manjiro that no one had thought to properly air the place out.

"I'm not stupid, but I am tired of waiting for you two," she said, "so I think I will go out for just a second. And when I come back I'll want your last guess with no excuses. Don't say I'm cheating or I'll scream and wake up everyone."

The castle had wide hallways on the first floor and when Masako stepped out of the room Tsune and Keiko jumped up like cats to follow her. If they could catch her walking far enough away from the main door they might sneak after her and hide, yelling like the first Lord Okubo's ghost when she came back past them. Keiko knew that normally she had to be careful with tricks at this time of night, but with her aunt in on it, even in their state of grief, she was prepared to be more daring than normal.

Masako had gone quickly through the hallway because she was afraid of its echo. She unbolted the main door and took an umbrella and stepped into waiting *geta*. And just as her aunt and sister hoped she might, she left the door open, oblivious to the wind and rain that came inside. As soon as she walked down the stone staircase and around the bend of the castle wall, Tsune and Keiko took the single remaining umbrella and followed her, smiling like devils and leaning into each other.

"We shouldn't frighten her too severely," warned Keiko. "It won't be worth it if we wake Grandfather up."

When Masako got to the first set of shutters, which were more than thirty feet above her, she was no longer sure that they were the right ones. And in any case there was nothing next to the shutters that could make such a scratching noise, so she soon walked on.

"Oh, first Lord Okubo, are you haunting us now?" she called, on the off chance that she had been followed.

Tsune and Keiko stifled their giggles, and pressed themselves against the wall.

But the next set of shutters was such a long way off that before Masako got halfway to them, she turned back. She stopped and listened, to see if she could still hear the scratching, and what she heard instead was an actual human voice.

"Do not be frightened, Masako," it said.

"Ayai!" she gasped, leaping and dropping her umbrella.

It was a man's voice, so not a trick played on her by her aunt or sister. At least that's what she thought until her aunt and sister suddenly appeared behind her, themselves surprised to see her stopped, halfway between the two sets of windows, her umbrella pitching toward them like a pinwheel. Tsune expertly caught it up.

"You devils!" Masako cried, but the man's voice said, "Please, all of you, listen. Do not shout again and do not run away. This is an emergency!"

"Who's there?" asked Keiko. "Who have you got with you, Masako?" But Tsune passed both umbrellas over to her elder niece, stepped out into the rain and said most seriously, "Is that you, Manjiro?"

He was in the very clearing that Einosuke had chosen for his garden, standing within its thin rope cordon. Tsune pulled the bottom of her kimono up, and stepped over the string. She touched Manjiro's arm and held his gaze until the moonlight came into his eyes, telling her he was unharmed.

"Where are they?" she whispered. "Has something gone wrong?"

"There has been an accident," said Manjiro. "One of them is bleeding in the marsh."

To him it seemed a terrible thing to have to say, an admission of defeat that reflected back to all the other mistakes he had made. But he spoke without emotion, trying to remember how much better off he was than Ned.

"We need bandages and medicine and blankets. We need a doctor and we need fire, something with which to cauterize a most horrific wound. We need food and changes of clothing for five . . ."

The girls had come forward but stayed on the other side of the cordon.

"I want to talk to Einosuke if he'll allow it," Manjiro said. He turned as he spoke, as if expecting Ueno's soldiers to come riding up the main road from town. But nothing was visible anywhere save the rain and the darkness through which it fell.

"It would be better if you brought them here, easier than for us to try to carry everything down to the marsh," said Tsune. "And leave Einosuke alone for the moment. Why don't you speak directly to your father?"

Tsune knew as well as Manjiro did that in the end Einosuke would help him, but she also knew that he would do so only after using precious time, to brood and think things over. And she had seen a change in Lord Okubo since her arrival from Edo, some fundamental alteration in his perception.

"My father is a repeater of edicts," Manjiro said, surprised by his own returning bitterness. He looked beyond Tsune at his nieces but did not apologize.

"Yes, well, I have often thought so of all such lords," said Tsune. "But why don't you try him anyway? I have an intuition."

Manjiro well remembered their visit to the Barbarian Book Room and to the Pavilion of Timelessness, how she had jeopardized their chance for a happy marriage with her intuition before. Still, though only a moment earlier he would not have considered waking his father for anything, because the words suggesting it had come from Tsune's precious mouth, it now seemed entirely right.

"He is no doubt sleeping," he said.

"He is but I will wake him," said Tsune. "You, in the meantime, bring your companions to the stable and the girls will set about finding what you need."

She turned and said, "Won't you girls?" and her nieces nodded.

So it was that, though they had gone outside in search of frivolous games, all three women reentered the castle with a new and serious purpose. Masako said she knew where they kept the medical supplies, and Keiko that in a room on the castle's third floor there were endless stacks of old kimono. Both girls hurried off, lest the frightful task of waking their grandfather somehow fall to them instead of Tsune.

When they were gone Tsune walked up the flights of castle stairs slowly, not out of fear but out of wondering how it would be to see Kyuzo and Manjiro together again.

At the top of each flight she stopped and looked through the narrow window slits at the rain and the far off ocean with its broad expanse of darkness. On its surface she thought she could see ships, perhaps the Americans passing on their way to Shimoda, and directly below her, at the entrance to the stables, she saw more clearly the figures of five men.

After that she went faster up the stairs, choosing correctly, without having seen it before, Lord Okubo's room.

Allergic to Pain

THOUGH LORD OKUBO hadn't heard any of the outside goings-on, he was not asleep, for the cuts he had made on his abdomen were inflamed, itching like the nervous rash that had plagued him as a child. He was, in fact, sitting by a candle in a loincloth, examining those cuts, when Tsune came in and told him her news.

He dressed and followed her out into the hall, several times glancing over to make sure the door to that golden inner room was closed. On the ground floor he woke a guard, sending him for the castle physician, and when he passed down the long stone stairway he thought of the late night rain as a pleasant accompaniment to the unexpected cheerfulness that rose from his bosom the moment Tsune mentioned Manjiro's name. It was extraordinary, for wasn't it only yesterday that he had been so ashamed of that name that he'd nearly taken his life? Yet now he hurried across the castle grounds to do what he could to help. Tsune's intuition, it seemed, had been right.

Lord Okubo pushed open the stable doors with the kind of authority he had not felt in years, as if the spirit of Kambei had somehow alighted, not so much upon Manjiro, as on himself.

"What misfortune befalls you this time?" he asked, but Manjiro was in the background and what he saw before him was difficult. Three strangers, two poorly dressed warriors and one of the foreign musicians, stood beside a sight both strange and humbling, touching and repulsive at the same time. The second foreigner reclined on a bed of hay, his legs bent under him like those of a newly born foal. He had uncovered his wound only seconds earlier, relinquishing, as a kind of first experiment, the pressure of the towel. When he heard Lord Okubo's voice he said, "It still don't hurt at all. I seem to be allergic to pain."

Indeed, the serious bleeding had stopped, leaving only a slow bubble coming from the middle of his face, like one might find on the surface of a stew pot on a low boil. Lord Okubo came closer, and when he put his hand out the foreigner took it, pulling him down next to him in the straw. Tsune knelt too, peering at Ned with sympathetic eyes, and when the castle physician came hurrying in, only a minute behind them, Manjiro stepped out of the darkness. The physician was as old as Lord Okubo and had feared his liege had had a heart attack or a stroke. He didn't hesitate, though, when he saw Ned's face.

"Someone light a fire," he said, "and someone else bring the detached appendage. The wound looks clean, so maybe if we hold it in place long enough it will remember its allegiance and grow back."

Lord Okubo glanced at Manjiro but now his eyes were hesitant. His son was harder to look at than the foreigner's ravaged face.

"Alas, the nose is gone," said Kyuzo, "taken, as a prize, I'm sorry to say, by the villain who cut it off."

"Well, then, has someone seen to the clearing of his air passages, to extracting the blood and mucus so he won't drown?"

No one had seen to anything and when Kyuzo said so, the physician reached out to turn Ned's face in the dim light.

In the corner of the stable farthest from the horses Ichiro had found a small pit and started a fire. And when he came back the physician gave him several tools to sterilize: a steel prong, old and dark from repeated bluings, two long knives, and something that looked like a pair of garden scissors. When Ned said, "What's the use of them devices?" Lord Okubo listened with all his heart, as if he, and not his son, could interpret the foreign tongue.

"First I need to know what blockage there is," the physician explained. "After that I'll clear the nostrils, if we can call them that now, and then I'll cut away the bits of excess flesh. Finally, I want to sear the entire wound, and douse it with my healing powder."

"Will it hurt?" Lord Okubo asked. "Should we hold him down like we would a wounded pig or a foaling mare?"

"Well, at least he's got to keep his head still," the physician said.

Ned's head was anything but still, as he turned it between the physician and Lord Okubo, but when the physician approached him again he did seem to try to cooperate. He closed his mouth, which had been gulping at the stable's stale air, and even found the courage to blow a little of the carnage from the front of his face, like a whale.

"Good job," said the physician. "Now don't move young man, let me see what's left inside to take away."

There was an oil lamp by the door, which Kyuzo picked up and held as close to Ned as he dared. In the meantime Ichiro had brought the sterilized tools back from the fire, setting them quietly on a blue ceramic plate, the last of the items pulled from the physician's bundle. When the physician touched him Ned clenched his jaw, but the man's touch was light. He removed whatever blockage there was with easy, graceful movements, then picked up the scissors from the plate.

All this time Tsune had stayed behind Lord Okubo, steadily watching everything, but when Masako called her, from just outside the stable door, she nearly fell forward onto the old lord's back. She didn't want to leave again, for the presence of her lover and her prospective husband really did seem to keep her in balance, and she hoped the guards would have enough sense to keep the girls away. But despite her hope the stable door opened and the heads of both her nieces appeared in it, one above the other, their eyes as bright as candles. They had gained a clear view of Ned, who said, "This ain't no carnival show."

The girls were quiet for such a long time that Tsune thought their reactions might be like the American's pain, and simply not come. But when she stood to get the clothing they had brought, both girls finally did open their mouths, leaking out a sound that rose in two falsetto screeches, reaching a horrible crescendo, like barn owls fighting over the remains of a field mouse. Ned flinched when he heard them, and tried to jump up. Ace and Kyuzo were strong enough to keep him from standing, but they couldn't make his head stay still, so Ichiro fell upon him, too, locking his arms around his forehead and throat. Tears sprung from Ned's eyes and the hole in his face began to bleed again and he looked wildly about. The two girls ran back out of the stables, but their screams had so unhinged the physician that he was now afraid to use that smoldering prong. First he feared it was too hot, then he couldn't find the steadiness of hand to burn the wounded part of the Ned's face without burning the rest of it. On his first approach he touched Ned's cheek. On his second he burned one of Ichiro's arms.

"Give me that thing!" said Lord Okubo. "What kind of way is that to act in a crisis? Put your hands in your lap and tell me what to do, we mustn't be defeated by the fears of a couple of girls!"

The strength of the old lord's command not only worked to good effect on the physician, but on everyone else as well. The physician sat down, Ace and Kyuzo held Ned more calmly, and when Ichiro loosened his grip on his forehead Ned stopped thrashing, once more understanding that the best thing he could do for himself was hold still.

"Now tell me how to proceed," said Lord Okubo. "And you, Manjiro, make yourself useful by speaking English. Soothe this wretched fellow."

It was the first time he had spoken to his son since Keiko's dance recital.

"Without blocking his nostrils, burn everything lightly," said the physician. "Let the prong rest on each bloody place for a second and then move on."

Lord Okubo held up the instrument, showing it very deliberately to Ned. "It isn't as bad as it looks," he said.

"That's my father speaking now," said Manjiro. "He will touch your wound only once, in order to make the bleeding slow down."

Maybe Ned had forgotten about Manjiro's English, for as soon as he heard it he jumped again, and looked away, toward the stable's far wall. But when he turned his face back again it came against the side of Lord Okubo's prong. There was a hissing sound, slight, as promised, like meat when it first hits a pan. And as quickly as that the prong was gone.

"Good," said the physician, "that's a third of it already."

"That didn't hurt either," said Ned, and Lord Okubo burned him twice more.

"Now the cleanser," said the physician. "In that bottle next to you. Dab the wound with it and try not to push anything back into those blow holes."

There was the kind of muslin cotton wrap that women used under their kimono encircling the bottle, and the physician tore a piece of it and doused it with the liquid when the lord didn't see where he'd pointed. "Hold it on there gently," he said. "Dab it like a geisha might, when reapplying makeup at a party."

Lord Okubo tried to do as he was told but Ned defeated the idea of dabbing by resting his entire face against the old lord's hands. So it looked to everyone like he had his nose back and was crying into a towel.

OUTSIDE THE STABLE most of Lord Okubo's guards were awake by then and milling about. Tsune was with them, she had gone out to tend to the girls and had not wanted to interrupt things by going back inside, but the girls had not only run across the grounds and reentered the castle, they had gone up the main inside stairs, as well. Einosuke and Fumiko had been sleeping on the top floor, but a minute after the girls awakened them Tsune saw lanterns burning in their window, and then she saw Einosuke and Fumiko looking out. Both of their faces were easy to read. Einosuke's looked pained that he had not been consulted immediately upon his brother's arrival, and Fumiko's looked wild, almost wanton, like she'd been having some horrible dream and was having trouble waking up to reality.

When the doors to the stable opened again some five minutes later, Lord Okubo emerged first, in magnificent slow form, the wounded American by his side. He was not much taller than Lord Okubo, but people could now see that he was leaner and more muscular, and that he walked with a litheness most often present in animals. That he was maimed was as plain as the rain that wet them. That he was foreign, however, in the light of that maiming, did not seem to occur to anyone.

29. | *Einosuke's Anger*

INDEED, Tsune had been right. Einosuke was deeply angered by his father's change of heart toward Manjiro, and stunned by the fact that he had not been consulted the moment his brother and the others arrived at the castle. And so to spite them all he got up at dawn the next morning and, without greeting Manjiro or asking a single question about the foreigners, threw himself into working on his garden. That is why he was the first to get news, brought by a runner from Keiki in Edo, that the Great Council had in fact removed Lord Abe—for the moment, at least—from all dealings with the Americans. It was a situation that was aided greatly, Keiki's note strongly hinted, by the advent and wide distribution of his now famous Kambei posters. A man by the name of Lord Hayashi had been put in charge of any remaining talks with Commodore Perry, and Manjiro could therefore continue on to Shimoda with the musicians or return them to Edo, whichever he wished. Lord Abe's dislikable aide, Ueno, though probably still unaware of the altered political climate, would soon be ordered to disband his illegal army and go on about his private business, no more threat to anyone.

Einosuke did his best to dismiss the importance of the news and rode on horseback to the edge of the sea, where, with an unerring eye and profound concentration, he selected the necessary boulders for his garden. But then he sat down on one of them to brood and think things over. Now it seemed his brother could return the Americans to their vessels freely—never mind that one of them had lost his nose!—even strut around as a hero of the realm, if he had that much bombast in him. It made Einosuke both glad and furious to contemplate such a thing, glad because it meant his father's resignation from the Great Council would not be accepted, that his family could return to Edo when their house was done with few remaining clouds of disgrace, but furious because, just as he'd done innumerable times since childhood, irresponsible Manjiro had bumbled into prominence while he, Einosuke, had worked behind the scenes without the slightest accolade from anyone.

———

ON THE SECOND MORNING after Manjiro's arrival, when talk of Lord Abe's demotion was everywhere, all over the castle and surrounding town, Einosuke was up and off at dawn yet again, before anyone could speak his name. This time he traveled to a mountain village known for the production of superior sand and gravel. He found just the grade of pebble he wanted for his garden—each one about one-eighth the size of those American chocolates—and paid the village elders the asking price on the condition that the loading and delivery of his purchase take place that day. When the elders agreed and offered him tea, he accepted, and when the tea was gone he asked for lunch and a quiet place to take a nap.

In this way, though he could not control his anger, he stayed away from Odawara Castle two days running, until late at night.

30. | *Japan's Conundrum*

MEANWHILE, from the rooms they had been given in the row of buildings that stretched out beside the castle's gate, Kyuzo and Ichiro, the recent defector, could watch Einosuke at work on his new garden, with Keiko walking around its perimeter, relief over her uncle's amazing good fortune everywhere on her face and in her pace. Ichiro tried not to stare at Keiko, to whom he was drawn, and instead hefted a pot full of tea. Kyuzo had had enough to drink but nodded anyway when offered more, holding out his cup.

"It is good to rest," he said. "The other night's fighting was harder on me than I like to admit. I still enjoy the idea of fighting, but my body doesn't seem to want to cooperate."

Kyuzo counted Ichiro's defection as his doing, but even though the entire situation now seemed disarmed, he was having trouble finding a way to talk about it. He wanted to make the young man feel welcome, but he also needed to gain a better understanding of why Ichiro had so readily changed sides. It was an unusual act and very modern. Kyuzo himself would not have done it, even if some other great man had been able to show him that the path he had chosen was wrong.

"Resting and waiting," mused Ichiro, who wanted the same discussion. "We enjoy the first but dislike the second, yet often have a great deal of trouble telling them apart."

Kyuzo appreciated that observation and laughed. "Now we are doing the first," he said, "but if we continue for much longer it will be the second."

Ichiro drank his tea boldly, as if it were saké, and poured himself more. Kyuzo had noticed a similar tendency in him when they'd been fighting, and he let his own expression turn serious.

"How old are you, Ichiro," he asked, "and what's your story? Where did you come from, where did you gain your skill with a sword, and what will you do now that this current interesting conflict is over?"

Ichiro said he was twenty-one, born in the year of the snake, and that he'd learned how to fight in the far northern part of the country, on the coast of Ezo, from his father.

"Ezo," said Kyuzo. "Then you have come a very long way, indeed. But why did you leave a beautiful place like Ezo, may I ask?"

"My father urged me to go lest I turn the skills I had learned to some less honorable occupation," the younger man said. "As to what I will do in the future, he hoped that I might find some sort of trade."

Kyuzo nodded. "No work and your father's blessings. A nation of warriors really does have a difficult time of it when there is peace for too long. That's why we should have gone to war with America in the first place, not so much to defeat them as to keep up our skills. What does a unified country want with a warrior class and what does a warrior class do in a country that is unified? That is Japan's conundrum, the paradox in the way things are now. A trade, you say?"

"I know I'm young," said Ichiro, "but I have noticed that we often do things simply because we are able. And we continue to do them even when they become outdated or unnecessary. That's why it's so easy for a warrior to turn criminal, because the skills, on the surface at least, are the same."

When Kyuzo looked at this young man he wanted to give him his own views, in some poetic metaphor, on the matter of intransigence, which was really what they were talking about. He saw himself some forty years earlier and was both glad of his advancing age and despairing of what the next forty years would bring to others. What Ichiro said was true, of course, there was an aspect of the ridiculous in studying *kendo* and the other martial arts, in keeping oneself constantly ready for the kind of warfare that had died out centuries ago. He satisfied himself with sighing in recognition of that truth, however, before finally asking what he most wanted to know.

"Why did you come with us, Ichiro? Why did you abandon Ueno? Don't get me wrong, I wanted you to do it, I hoped that you would, but if it had been me I think my sense of duty would have made me stick it out where I was. Give me your reasons in words I can understand, so I can stop playing with it in my mind."

To ask such a question made Kyuzo feel contemptible, for to

welcome a young man and then immediately suspect his motivations seemed small-minded. But the idea that a samurai could do such a thing, never mind the reasons, and never mind, also, that the conflict seemed over now, went against all of his instincts. He was glad to see that Ichiro did not wait long before answering.

"As you know, because of the Great Council's initial censure of Lord Abe, Ueno's force could not be made up of government samurai. But he easily found great numbers of soldiers anyway. He found some of us at Nihonbashi and others, like me, at the Sumida River ferry landing in Asakusa. He wanted only twenty men but he could have had two hundred, so numerous were those who were willing to work for anyone with cash to pay them for their swords."

Kyuzo's question wasn't satisfactorily answered but he kept disappointment at bay by shaking the now empty teapot and looked off toward the castle, as if he expected to see a maid coming toward them with more. There was, in fact, someone emerging from the castle, but it wasn't a maid.

"So he hired us by lottery as a way, I guess, of entertaining himself," Ichiro continued. "He gave us each a number and we drew lots. He took us irrespective of our abilities or the good or bad qualities of our characters, not even asking our names or, as you have just done, sir, caring where we came from. I was Number 24 in the beginning and continued to be Number 24 until the other unfortunate night. Had he hired Ichiro then Ichiro would have given him his life, never mind whether the cause for which he gave it was right or wrong, but Number 24 felt no such compunction. Even now I don't think he knows that Number 24 has defected, unless he was informed of it by those two nefarious others, Numbers 111 and 75."

Ichiro laughed, relieved to have spoken, and then grimly smiled, for now Kyuzo was more than satisfied. While it appalled him to hear such a story—samurai hired by number!—at the same time it gave him a sharper sense of Ueno and made him doubly glad that the conflict was over, for a man who hired samurai by lots would not care how many he buried that way.

"Well, here we will call you Ichiro," he told the young man. He might have said more, he might have stood with Ichiro, pacing him through the movements of his too-quick sword thrust from the other night, but Tsune herself had come out of the castle, and she walked across the grounds calling his name.

"We are summoned to Lord Okubo's chambers," she said, "to hear him speak on the matter of the foreigner's injuries and on what he has decided that Manjiro should do now."

She kept any hint of irony out of her voice, and for his part Kyuzo tried to look at her as if she were someone else coming to get him, one of Lord Okubo's granddaughters, perhaps, betrothed and unavailable, or even truly a maid. When he stood Ichiro stood also, not because he thought he was included in Lord Okubo's summons, but because his name had been returned to him, and with it a renewed sense of protocol.

Tsune turned back toward the castle before Kyuzo got to her, and Ichiro watched them until they reached the stone stairs. He then strolled off toward that half-made garden.

He was young and pretended that he had been called too, not by Tsune but by Keiko.

31. *An Earlier Walker than His Uncle*

THOUGH THE OTHERS were pleased, even somewhat giddy, with how things had turned out, Einosuke was not so quick to forgive his brother. He skipped his father's meeting on the subject entirely—an unprecedented act of protest in itself—and the following morning, the third after Ned Clark's wounding, went out to his garden early again, with Masako this time, who ran from the castle to help him when she saw him getting his rakes. She stepped on top of Keiko's cordon, rubbing it into the ground with both her feet. She had faith that she could end her father's grouchiness better than anyone else.

"I think we will need a wall," she told her father, "to give our new garden the necessary privacy. Then we can come inside of it and be as gloomy as we want and no one will even notice. We can pout and rage in here, then rake everything nicely again before we come out. How would that be, Father?"

It was raining again and a group of laborers from the pebble village were slumped nearby, using their empty A-frames for umbrellas. Einosuke gave his younger daughter a grim-faced smile, but went on with his work, would not be drawn in by her teasing, so Masako gave up, and did what she liked best to do anyway. She sat down next to the laborers to ask if they had seen any three-legged frogs. She loved talking to anyone about nature's aberrations, and workers were more observant than lords.

———

ABOUT AN HOUR LATER, when his garden site was leveled, the problems of drainage corrected, and Einosuke was instructing the laborers concerning the last remaining unpebbled corner, Lord Okubo, Manjiro, Kyuzo, Ichiro, and the wounded American minstrel all came riding around the side of the castle, heading for a village of artisans, to the shop of someone named Denzaimon, a well-known prosthetics maker. It was Lord Okubo's idea, announced at the meeting Einosuke hadn't attended, that when Ned was finally returned to his ship, there should be some small evidence, at least, that they had done what they could to repair the irreparable damage. The village was only a thirty-minute trip up the lowest mountain road, but the American was ensconced in a palanquin, while the others surrounded it on horseback. Tsune and Keiko were going, too, in open sedan chairs, so the whole event might double as a family outing, a reunion of sorts. They were dressed demurely with their heads covered and holding fans below their eyes, the two beautiful women, and looked across the courtyard at their solitary brother-in-law and father. The other American would stay at the castle, so that if there was trouble on the road, one of them, at least, would not be put in the way of Ueno's sword.

Einosuke, tired and sweating among the laborers, leaned on his rake in order to watch them pass. The evening before he had had a short conversation with his father, in which Lord Okubo had repeated what he'd told the others at the meeting, that he was moved to pity by the thought of a man, even an unknowable foreigner, having to live his life without a nose. He thanked Einosuke for his long years of service in Edo, told him he understood the nature of his work in the garden, and also that he was satisfied with Einosuke's preparation, the much harder work he had done, to get ready to succeed him as the fiefdom's lord. They would both, he let it be known, find a way of properly admonishing Manjiro once the Americans were actually back on their ships and the trouble was truly over. Manjiro's engagement to Tsune, it now appeared, would be announced soon, also, in a letter from Lord Tokugawa.

At just about the time that Fumiko, herself struggling under all these family upheavals but also under the secret weight she bore, came from the castle with tea for Einosuke and Masako, the gate opened and the party moved out. Manjiro, however, sorely sorry for Einosuke's continued distance from him, waited until everyone else was gone and then dismounted and walked toward his brother. Einosuke knew that he could not stay angry forever, that some kind of mending was in order—that, of course, had been the point his father was trying to make last night—but he couldn't keep the pain he felt from showing in his eyes. Manjiro had survived this incredible folly of his, as always, through the good auspices of others and through pure dumb luck. And so when Manjiro said good morning he barely nodded.

"We won't be gone long," Manjiro said. "Father thinks if we try to fix the unfixable, the mendable things will take care of themselves."

He looked at his brother keenly, hoping for some sign.

"I am told more rain will come by midday," Einosuke said.

Fumiko had brought only two teacups, and as she filled one for each of the brothers she was reminded of the political arguments they had had before their father came to Edo, how easy that all seemed now, and how long ago. She touched her husband's sleeve so that he might try, at least, not to start another argument.

"I've made such grave mistakes," Manjiro said. "I know I have been thoughtless, Einosuke, that I am an unworthy brother and son. I hope you can believe that I will be more serious as a married man."

He disliked having to say such words with Tsune, quite miraculously, at the center of them. Einosuke, however, seemed to accept the words for what they were, and replied with this small offering. "You have been wrong, but unworthiness is not in your character. And I wish upon you a marriage that will do for you what mine has done for me."

"A more cautious approach from here on out," said Manjiro. "I know that is the lesson you have been trying to teach me since I was a boy."

But Einosuke waved further conversation away. That Manjiro would never learn what he had been trying to teach him was the lesson Einosuke, himself, had learned too well. "Others can see the honor in what you did," he said. "To others you have become like Kambei. I am not unhappy to see that our father is among them."

"I hold your good opinion above those of others," Manjiro answered, "even Father's."

But then he strode off toward the open gate, and got back on his horse, fearing he had said too much.

———

BECAUSE THE OTHERS were gone and the great weight of the family's shame had been so suddenly and unexpectedly lifted, Fumiko meant to work beside her husband for the rest of the day, as she had often done in Edo. By doing so she expected to reinvest herself as a dutiful and single-minded wife. What was a dream, after all, but the random wanderings of an undisciplined mind? And what dreamer, when she awoke, did anything but get on with her ordinary life? A child might be forgiven her desire for romantic love, but not a mother of three, some eighteen years after her *miai,* her arranged and successful marriage.

But Einosuke, his mood somewhat better but still not entirely assuaged by what Manjiro had said, told Fumiko that he didn't want her working with him, that they couldn't act so expansively in Odawara, and that she should return to the castle where she belonged. At first she was hurt and intended to go to her room to sulk—how dare he continue to pout so obstinately when the need for it was gone?—but soon she realized that it was that kind of reaction that exhausted her more than anything else. So she decided that she would forget her selfish husband and called out for O-bata instead. And by noon the entire castle staff was flinging wide the doors to unused rooms, cleaning everywhere, futon sticking out of the windows like dozens of severed tongues. It was good to be busy, to hear the slap of sticks against those futon, and to see dust rising in the rainy morning like the sighs of relief they had all, save Einosuke, expelled the night before. The guards at the gate felt it, and so did Masako, whom her father had finally chased away, too, and so did Ace Bledsoe, who was wandering the castle's lower floor and grounds, wondering what the day might bring him, and longing for someone to talk to.

As the hours passed Einosuke sped up his work to conform to the sounds of the work from the castle, and made such good progress with his final raking that he decided to place just one large boulder in the garden, as his own symbol of better times to come. The one he chose wasn't nearly the largest boulder, but was important to the garden's strict asymmetry, and he wanted to be able to see it there, providing stability, when he brought Fumiko out that evening to show her.

When he called the workers and went to retrieve the boulder from its place at the forest's edge, however, he was surprised to find that a fissure had appeared, thick as the line of a closed eye, over most of its near side. At the beach there were more like this one, others that conformed to the necessary look and size, but he had been sure of his decision and had brought home only one. Now what would he do? He couldn't have a broken boulder outside the castle of a slowly repairing family, so he called his workers, deciding to go to the beach for a replacement while there was still sufficient light. If he didn't go now he would have to go in the morning, when everyone was back from the prosthetist's village.

"Quickly then," he told the workers. "If we hurry we can be back in an hour."

While the workers, trying not to grumble, moved off to get their nets and poles, Einosuke went to the castle's side door and called for Fumiko. He didn't want to enter the castle because of his filthy clothes, but though he called repeatedly, his wife didn't answer. As he turned to look elsewhere for her, however, he found both Fumiko and Masako standing nearby and broadly smiling, Junichiro between them, his stubby legs firmly planted on the ground. And a few feet beyond them stood the remaining American, unseen by the women and shyly watching.

When the baby saw his father he pulled his arms from the grasps of both his sister and mother, staggered forward, then turned and staggered back. He took a step in one direction, a step in another, stopped to gain his balance, then took two more. There had been evidence that he might soon stand by himself when Einosuke and Fumiko played with him at night, but little hint of early walking, and Einosuke knelt, delighted when his son plunged into his open arms.

"What's this?" he laughed, his heart finally freed from the last of the recent trouble. "What power are we unleashing on this poor country of ours?"

"He did it inside, too," Masako cried, "but not nearly so well."

In truth she had been irritated earlier, at not having been allowed to go with Keiko to get the foreigner's new nose, but oh how happy she was now. Think what she would have to goad Keiko with when the party returned that night. Junichiro walking! What better sign could there be that they were about to reenter normal life?

"He really is precocious," Fumiko said. "We're going to ask his grandpa if he took his first steps earlier than his father or his Uncle Manjiro."

When she turned to point at the gate through which that grandpa had gone, she saw Ace Bledsoe standing there, smiling at the universal treat of having been allowed to see a baby's first walking. Masako bowed to him, and Einosuke did, too, then pulled Junichiro up against his dirty chest.

"He's an earlier walker than his uncle," he told his wife. "I can tell you that right now. I remember Manjiro's first steps better than Father, for he, too, walked into my arms."

It was as precious a memory to him as watching his son's steps just now, and a few wayward tears washed the dirt from his eyes. Fumiko, however, stood looking at the American. He was not fearsome as he'd been at the treaty-signing ceremony, nor was he particularly handsome, if you stayed away from his eyes. He was just a man, younger than she was, probably, who might very well have a wife and children of his own waiting for him. Oh, she had been so foolish! Of course the way to disarm this anxiety—no, she must not be coy—the way to disarm this *attraction* was to face the man squarely, talk to him in some personal way, and by so doing take away his strangeness, take away his draw. And that, she decided, was what she would do, as soon as the chance presented itself.

Einosuke let the squirming Junichiro fall back into the waiting arms of Masako. He smiled at his wife and said that though he was going to the beach for another boulder, he would be quick about it, and when he returned they would spend the evening together, just the four of them, eating and talking and finally celebrating the fact that, though it had seemed impossible only a day ago, things would now be fine. He thought that perhaps they might even include the American, though he kept that part to himself. Until he got back, until he decided if he was capable of such a thing.

The laborers had assembled at the gate but Einosuke decided that instead of walking with them he would take a horse to the beach. That way he could choose his boulder and be ready when they arrived, and return to those he loved. Lord Okubo's fiefdom was cash poor but rich in horses, so though many of them had been taken that morning, Einosuke was still able to select a good one. He had often argued with his father in favor of selling most of the horses, in order to pay their bills, but as he rode under the castle gate now he was glad he had lost the argument. To be poor in Edo and rich in Odawara, it seemed, would continue to be the state of things for a while.

By this late hour most of the vendors who set up shop in front of the castle each morning were gone. But as always there were *ronin* standing idly by, talking and getting ready for another cold night. As Einosuke passed them he made the horse go faster, until he had passed his laborers, too—men who did not look forward to the work that was in store for them, and seemed to be trudging along.

32. | *Extra Circumspect From Now On*

STRANGE FORCES were at work in Fumiko, but she remembered her decision, and though she had not expected to fulfill it this quickly, considered it a solemn promise to herself. So once Masako and Junichiro were safely inside the castle she summoned her courage and sought out Ace Bledsoe, who was easy enough to find. He had gone around to the sunny side of the castle and was sitting on a stool with a book in his hands, reading aloud in the spidery tongue.

Ace noticed her mid-sentence and stood up. He was holding a book of essays by Ralph Waldo Emerson, given to him by Colonel Morgan when he'd first joined the Mighty Abolitionists. At first he hadn't understood the essays, but recently, especially during the sea voyage, he had committed parts of one of them to memory. He had not, in fact, been reading, but reciting it when Fumiko came upon him. *"To believe your own thought, to believe what is true for you in your private heart is true for all men,—that is genius. Speak your latent conviction, and it shall be the universal sense, for the inmost in due time becomes the outmost,—and our first thought it rendered back to us by the trumpets of the Last Judgment."*

He thought it was both beautiful and true, and was trying to make it his code, the way he intended to live his life from then on. He had the feeling that if he could speak his "latent conviction" to the woman who approached him now, she would speak her own back to him.

"I appreciate what you all did for Ned the other night," he said. "Not everyone would take in a wounded stranger."

"Shall we walk together a minute?" Fumiko asked him. "Shall we remove ourselves to the forest, so I can speak to you honestly, without a visitation from Masako? She's inquisitive and if she sees us she will defeat my purpose before I even start."

She gave him a demure smile and gestured toward the path that led to Masako's marsh. She had watched only his mouth as she spoke to him, and was satisfied to find that her heart did not flip over in her chest. Yes, she'd been right, he was a normal man, fervent, perhaps, and kind, but as men often were at moments like this, utterly unaware of what she'd been feeling, of how he had ruined her peace of mind. She smiled again, surer now that she would free herself, once their little walk was done.

Ace moved along behind her, pleased with the effort she was making. It was the first time anyone other than Manjiro, and Kyuzo a little bit, had tried to talk to him since Ned's injury. It hadn't been bad, though, being left alone. Today, especially, he was glad to have some time away from Ned, whose constant harping on the fact that he wasn't feeling any pain had been driving Ace to distraction.

He thought he'd better try to hold up his end of the conversation.

"I always thought Ned talked too much," he said. "I'll bet he's doing it again with your menfolk or with the carpenter they took him to visit. I'll bet he's telling them how he wished he had a nicer partner than me, or someone a little less serious, at least. He says I spend too much time worrying about my life, and in actual fact I'm not easy to get along with. I'd like to remedy that."

That was not what he'd meant to say and he was surprised. How could he remedy such a thing?

"There was a wonderful old teahouse down this way once," Fumiko told him. "When I first married Einosuke we used to come here and sit, to try to get to know each other. I hardly remember it now, but at the time I was deeply disappointed, really in pain, for though he seemed a decent enough man I didn't want to be married to him. I was such a sentimental girl. I cried myself to sleep almost every night, once I heard him snoring. I just did not feel he was a *jibun no ki no atta hito,* a kindred spirit with myself. Does that sound selfish to you? Did you know your wife before you married her? Are marriages arranged in America as they are here in Japan?"

It took her breath away to say such things, to tell this unvarnished truth and ask such pointed questions. She had never done it before out loud, not even with Tsune. She had spoken slowly, though of course she knew he wouldn't understand, and she had watched him as she spoke, determined to get everything finished, even at the expense of looking into his eyes. Her own eyes were moist and her lips were dry.

Ace nodded when he was sure she was finished. He had recognized it as something deeply felt and said, "I've a little confession to make about Ned. I used to like to go fishing when we were both holed up on Colonel Morgan's farm, practicing for some new show. There was this nice little stream running through his place, but I really only went there for self-communion, you know, to get away from everyone and think about how my life was going and such. I even talked aloud to myself so taking Ned with me was out of the question."

He smiled and Fumiko thought, "Can sounds such as those truly make up a language?"

What she said, however, was, "I suppose it is really too much to ask, even in America, that a man recognize the woman he marries for herself, for what she is and what she feels, and not merely as an extension of himself. I suppose it is too much to ask that he *see* her." She paused, embarrassed. "I hope you won't think it horrible of me to talk this way. I hope you will understand that Einosuke is really a most wonderful husband in every other way. It's just that he rarely penetrates my heart."

The heart he rarely penetrated was in her throat.

"So I used to try to trick him," said Ace, laughing a little and raising his eyebrows. "Sometimes I'd say I was going off to write a song, and other times I'd lie down in Colonel Morgan's barn and pretend to be napping, all in search of solitude, you know, all in search of time alone. Ned was suspicious, I think, but sooner or later he'd get interested in something else and I could sneak off. Hell, there was only the one stream, so nothing would have been easier than finding me. I used to think he was stupid, but of course that wasn't the case. Ned had his own kind of dignity. I guess that's why I'm saying all this now."

Fumiko looked at him. She had stopped thinking about Einosuke. What she wanted to do was touch this man, to break the spell her dream still held over her by putting her hand on his face. And so she did it, even before he stopped talking. She reached up and touched his cheek with the middle three fingers of her right hand, letting them slide from his eye socket to the corner of his now unmoving mouth. It was at once the bravest and the most provocative thing she had ever done.

She kept her fingers there for the merest seconds, though it seemed far longer. And when she finally released him Ace nearly fell. He bent toward the ground, steadied himself, then picked up a twig and pre- tended that that had been his intention all along. He stood again and passed the twig between his fingers like a coin. It was a trick his father had taught him, that he hadn't tried to do in years. She watched as it wove itself around his knuckles, then took it from him and placed it out of sight, inside her kimono.

"I will go back before you," she said. "We must, of course, be extra circumspect from now on."

She put her hand on his, kept it there until she'd moved a half a step toward the castle, then let it go and held her palm out, so he might know what she meant.

Ace watched her walking back over an entire bed of twigs, the brothers and sisters of the one she had taken from him.

Little bits of nature, one indistinguishable from another, all of them spread about.

33. | *Behold Your Defeated Lord*

HORSES MIGHT HAVE BEEN plentiful in Lord Okubo's stables, but they were rare among masterless samurai, for if a man had a horse but no employment, it wouldn't be long before he would either have to sell his horse to provide for his sustenance, or risk having it stolen. Unlike acreage or outbuildings a horse was a moveable commodity.

Among the *ronin* Ueno had hired, however, there were two with horses, given them as a reward for cutting off Ned Clark's nose, and they, plus the very man who had hired them, sat atop those horses watching Einosuke leave the castle. Number 75, the older of the two *ronin*, had been masterless for twenty years and, when not drunk on cheap liquor, was adjusted to his status. The younger man, however, Number 111, had been out of work for less than a year, and had not in the least come to terms with the fact that he did not wear the crest of a clan anymore.

The beach that ran along the coast was not too distant from Odawara Castle, but neither was it easily approachable. Only a few paths wide enough for horses led to it, and these necessitated riding either north or south, then doubling back through underbrush. For this reason Einosuke's laborers, who were able to walk more directly, arrived at the site only a few minutes after him. It was raining again but the boulders were always wet anyway, pounded twice a day by the sea.

As a child, in that distant time before Manjiro was born, Einosuke had had another brother, only a few years older than himself. This brother's name had been Toshiro, and he had seemed to Einosuke to be a young god, able to run like the wind and strong enough to move these boulders around like they were made of papier-mâché. Had he lived Toshiro would have been the next Lord Okubo, and though when the torch of ascension fell to him Einosuke had not shrunk from its flame, he had always known in his heart that it was Toshiro, not he, who could have lifted the clan into national prominence. In Einosuke's memory Toshiro had everything; both Manjiro's curiosity and spirit and his own good discipline, his everyday seriousness of mind. Just as Masako liked to play at the castle's marsh now, it had been Toshiro's greatest joy to play among these boulders, and every time Einosuke returned to the place he felt his elder brother's presence.

Einosuke had dismounted and looked at the head laborer, now, who walked behind him waiting to hear which boulder they would have to dig out. He remembered that when his father came to him one night to tell him Toshiro had died, of something so simple as a fever, he did not believe his father, and there were ways in which he did not believe him still. When their mother died a few years later, giving birth to Manjiro, he had had no trouble knowing that was true, but his mother had been weak like himself while Toshiro had been invincible, like no one else he had ever known.

Einosuke found the boulder he wanted and peered at it, looking for fissures and unseemly angles. He stood on it and jumped and felt the boulder take his weight, just as an ambushed Toshiro used to do when Einosuke jumped upon his shoulders.

"This one," he told the head laborer. "Unless we find that its buried part is ugly, we'll take it home."

A voice behind him said, "Yes, it is the buried part we must always watch out for."

Einosuke turned around to stare at Ueno. He recognized him immediately but asked, "Who travels on this rocky piece of our shoreline?"

"I'm not traveling but have come to seek you out," said Ueno. "We followed you down here from the castle. We haven't been very quiet, you should have heard us coming before now."

The waves were crashing about him and Einosuke had been awash in thought, but he decided not to say so. His laborers were standing close together by then, Numbers 75 and 111 herding them like dogs. He decided to be magnanimous, not to taunt Ueno with the still surprising fact that Lord Abe had been deposed and that he and his ridiculous private army were of no use to anyone anymore. But the words that came out of his mouth were taunting anyway.

"We have always given transit rights to everyone," he said, "so be on your way. Go and lick your wounds somewhere else."

"You are the heir to the fiefdom, are you not?" asked Ueno. "You spoke with the haughtiness of one, at least, in the Great Council garden on the day that your brother's treachery came clear to us all. Do you remember when we met below Lord Abe's window?"

Einosuke's memories of Toshiro were still so strong that he wanted to say that he wasn't the heir, but instead he said, "I remember that you were rude, sir. While I, at least, have the status of family, you are a usurper, a servant who mistakes his lord's position for his own. And though Lord Abe has fallen, you still haven't found a civil tongue."

It was not until Ueno came closer, ignoring the insult, that Einosuke finally saw that he carried something in a teacup. It was difficult to determine what it was because he wrapped it top and bottom with his hands.

"What do you have there?" Einosuke asked. "Are you selling some family treasure? How much do you want for it?"

It had been fairly common in past years for desperate men to approach the sons of lords with something semiprecious, and he knew that to pretend that Ueno was doing it now would be a grievous insult. But he couldn't help himself. He saw Ueno's face harden, yet he lifted the lid to the teacup and held its contents out. Ned Clark's nose bobbed in a pool of stinking yellow liquid, so pungent that Einosuke's eyes watered and his own nostrils flared.

"We have cared for it well and would like to make amends by returning it," Ueno said. "Maybe it's still possible to put it back where it belongs."

The nose was as wrinkled as a prune, and as injurious to the eye as a gangrenous toe. Oh where was Einosuke's sought-after magnanimity? All he had to do was be half as civil as Ueno was trying to be and he could mend something that might otherwise stay torn for decades into the future. And he would be able to tell his father and brother about it when they returned from the prosthetist's village.

"Why come to me?" he asked, mitigating his tone. "You've obviously been watching the castle. Why didn't you simply follow my father? He would have welcomed its return more than I."

Those were good questions but Ueno didn't answer them. Instead he pushed the nose closer, like one child showing another a dead mouse. It was a move that angered Einosuke not only because of its impertinence, but because of the truly horrible smell. He drew his head back and, quite without planning to, slapped the bottom of Ueno's outstretched hand, sending the teacup high into the air. The putrid liquid spilled into the rain and the nose flew out of the cup to dive, like a seabird, into the ocean.

"Hey!" Ueno yelled. He started to reach for his sword, then called one of his hirelings, who dashed into the freezing water and began frantically splashing around.

"Not there," said Einosuke, "a little to your left and farther out."

The nose was still visible, and when the samurai looked where Einosuke pointed he had no trouble retrieving it. "Salt won't hurt it," said Einosuke. "I'll bet it's a more effective preservative than that offensive brine."

Einosuke was a better swordsman than he appeared to be, better than either his father or Manjiro, and he knew the chief laborer would run for help if a fight really started. So he pulled his sword out slowly, watching as the rain hit its blade. Number 111 was soaked and embarrassed but stomped across the rocks to the flung-away teacup. He put the nose inside it again and sat it down on the top of the very boulder Einosuke had intended taking home. Ueno, meanwhile, brought his sword from its scabbard with greater deliberation than that used by Einosuke.

"I came here today to mend things," he said. "It had seemed to me before I met you that the time for petty insults had passed."

Einosuke let his eyes move back to the laborers who were huddled, more like ducks than dogs now, their leader missing from the front. Good, he thought, he's gone for help. He backed up, edging toward the water. He would teach this man a lesson and tell his father about it when the party returned to the castle that night.

"A lord's advantage isn't only with words," he said, "but in having excellent fighting instructors."

Even as he spoke he knew he should stop, that one neutral word, just a syllable of civility, would disarm the situation. Where Ueno was concerned, however, he had no civility, and he cocked his sword above his head. What he'd said about his fighting instructors was a blunder, though, for it made Ueno come at him with more care than he might otherwise have shown. He stepped up and stopped, stepped up and stopped, balanced and searching for the right moment.

Einosuke heard a cough and when he glanced toward the laborers again he saw his older brother, Toshiro, sitting atop the boulder he had chosen, right beside that teacup. He attacked Ueno when Toshiro nodded, running at him and bringing his sword down fast, glancing it off Ueno's blade and narrowly missing his shoulder. Ueno stumbled sideways and, in order to keep from falling, stuck his sword in the sand. Einosuke laughed and took the position Ueno had held before. He could see the laborers easily now but Toshiro was gone from the boulder.

Ueno closed the distance between them carefully, cocking his sword as Einosuke had earlier. He led with his right leg, but at the last instant backed off a half-step and sliced his sword quickly under Einosuke's, in and back out again, dragging it across Einosuke's left thigh. Einosuke's sword hit the sand and he took his hand off its grip in order to touch the wound he'd been given. It was a long and shallow slice, a wan and enigmatic smile, with blood overflowing its lower lip. He grasped his sword with both hands, put his weight on his uninjured leg and charged, but Ueno deflected his thrusts and turned to watch Einosuke stumble past him, down toward the water again.

"While a samurai is practicing *kendo,* young lords are drinking saké," he said, "while a samurai perfects his riding, young lords . . ."

But his mind was slower than his sword and before he could find the proper analogy Einosuke attacked again, cutting Ueno's belt and nicking his abdomen. The belt fell partly to the ground, where it caught on his leggings. In order to free it Ueno had to pull his short sword out, and at just that moment Einosuke hit his buttocks with a swift sword slap.

The stretch of ground on which they stood had narrowed as the tide came closer. Einosuke knew that had Ueno not shown up they would have had the boulder freed by then and he would be on his way home to his family. He considered yelling instructions to his laborers, telling them to start work even while the fight went on. Both men, however, would have been better served by fighting single-mindedly, and not by trying to think up insults or give instructions; that was a lesson Ueno seemed to learn more quickly than Einosuke. He moved to take the upper part of the beach again, backing Einosuke toward the water.

Einosuke could feel the sand give way beneath his feet, and he looked down at its change of color. If he moved to his right Ueno moved with him, and he could not so easily go left, without widening the bloody smile in his thigh.

Ueno's next assault was so slow at its beginning that Einosuke wanted to run at him. But his left leg complained, and when he put his weight on his right leg, his heel sunk into the sand. And then Ueno's speed increased, his sword held parallel to the tide. He knocked Einosuke's blade away twice, down and then down again, and came in above it with the short sword he had rescued from his belt, cutting both of Einosuke's biceps in a single powerful stroke. Einosuke's arms began to fall in front of him, quite as if they belonged to someone else, and as Ueno prepared to make a proper final thrust, there was Toshiro again, standing in the surf to Einosuke's right.

"Where have you been?" asked Einosuke. "Can't you do something to help me?"

Ueno's last maneuver was textbook, as if he had a practice dummy before him, and not a living, breathing man. He brought his sword from its highest position, poised with its tip pricking the sky, then let it speed through the air horizontally, passing through Einosuke's neck without slowing down, or as if there had been only the slightest turbulence against it, like an unexpected gust of wind from the bay. Einosuke saw the blade pass through Toshiro on its way to him, cutting his brother in half, and he felt it, too, the way it hit him so abruptly, like that irritating slap he had previously given Ueno on his buttocks.

Ueno completed his move by dropping both swords and catching Einosuke's head in midair, grabbing it by its topknot. His face was wild as he swung around toward the laborers, shouting, "Behold your defeated lord!" But the laborers could behold very little from their prone and terrified positions on the ground.

Ueno retrieved his swords and walked across the sand, Einosuke's head bouncing down low against his thigh, and when he looked toward the horses and those other horrified riders, he shouted, "Come to me! Do not make me walk!"

But, in fact, he did walk, to swagger among the laborers, dripping blood from Einosuke's head upon each one.

When the younger of his hirelings, Number III, got closer to him,

Ueno gave him Einosuke's head, lest his own horse grow frightened and run, but once he was mounted he took it back again, and twirled it by its topknot, so the others could get a look at his prize. He watched them closely, searching for fear, and then handed the head to Number 75.

"Keep this for me," he said, then he rode into the forest by himself.

For his part the older man gave the head a gentle touch, clasping Einosuke's cheeks like one might clasp the cheeks of a child. He brought the head up so he could look directly into its eyes, and whispered, "I have lived for more than sixty years but I didn't know what my fate would be until today."

He trotted to a spot where he could reach into his satchel and take out his grooming implements and begin recombing Einosuke's hair. It was a proper gesture, a respectful one, his hope being that someone might do as much for him, that someone might take a few moments to make him look presentable too, in the unhappy days to come.

34. | *We Can't Have This*

TOO MUCH TIME had passed, and as the tide came in Einosuke's body began to move in such a way that the laborers, even in their terror, feared it might get loose from the fragile grasp of the sand, slide under the water's rough blanket, and be gone. Their leader should have been back by then with castle guards, but since he was not, one man, and then a second, found sticks from the edge of the forest and pressed them against Einosuke's clothing, their eyes nearly closed against the sight of the headless man. They weren't pleased with themselves but they held on and hollered, using their muscles against the tide.

And that was what the castle guards saw when they came running behind the chief laborer, some ten minutes after Ueno and his samurai had gone.

"What have you found?" one of them barked, and the chief laborer let out a relieved sigh, thinking the fight had ended well and the laborers, in the meantime, had discovered some dead creature, perhaps a sea lion, for dead sea lions had washed up along this beach before.

But when the laborers saw the guards and fell on their faces, moaning and crying, the guards, in turn, noticed the Okubo family crest on the sea lion's shoulder, and then the viscera that had launched themselves from the creature's stomach, unfurling out of its neck like enemy flags, and they fell too, next to their subordinates in the sand. It took a full five minutes for them to stand again, to pull out their swords and thrash about screaming for vengeance, and another ten before they found the necessary courage to pull poor Einosuke out of the apathetic and steadily advancing tide. One of the guards walked down the beach and brought back Einosuke's horse which, inexplicably, had not run away, another covered his neck with a laborer's shirt and lifted him up across the horse's saddle, and in an hour they had walked him through the forest, around the southern-loop road to the castle gate.

Inside the castle, still quite stunned from her moment alone with Ace, Fumiko was directing the cleaners on the second floor when she heard the arrival commotion. Her first thought, oddly enough, was that maybe Ueno had come, in hopes of cutting his losses, and she should send a runner for Einosuke. Her second thought was to find Masako, so the girl wouldn't climb upon the gate, look down at the horrible man, and get in everyone's way.

Fumiko came downstairs in a hurry, but there were no guards at the door, and no Masako in any of the first floor rooms where she most often liked to play. From the top of the outside stone stairway she could normally see the gate well, but so many people had run over there now that she could tell only that the gate was open and that a party of riders had come inside. She didn't like that. She did not want strangers given access to the castle when none of the men was at home, so though she was dressed for work and not for greetings, she went across the intervening ground to investigate. Surely it wasn't Ueno; only some interloper, some quasi-aristocrat, smoothly talking his way inside.

Masako had twice been to her marsh that day, both before and after her mother and Ace, but when the ruckus began she was close to the gate, standing outside one of the castle's side doors with Junichiro, trying to make him do his walking trick over and over. She waited a moment, sure, at first, that what she was doing was more interesting than whatever else might be going on, but when others ran past her she finally picked her brother up and hurried after them, coming into the rear of the crowd just at the time her mother got there.

"Good," said Fumiko, "stay beside me. I'm not putting up with nonsense from anyone."

She looked toward the side of the castle for Ace, but the stool he had formerly sat upon was empty. Had he gone to his room to think things over, then, or followed that drifting bit of sunlight, around to the castle's back? She wondered what he was thinking, and wanted to see his face.

There was so much noise, were so many shrieks and unwieldy voices, that Fumiko thought a fight had broken out, that maybe, after all, the guards were trying to do their jobs. Many of those in the crowd were turning now to look at her, but Fumiko misread their expressions, thinking they were asking her to settle the argument.

"Let me through, then," she said. "We can't have this. When the masters are gone we want this gate closed, is that so hard to understand?" She could hear the curtness in her voice but didn't care.

"We can't have this," Masako told Junichiro.

The crowd held for a moment, then parted despite itself. Fumiko could see the top of the gate now, the place where the guards usually stood, but there were no guards there to yell at. The first sense she had that she was wrong about what was happening did not come until Masako pulled her back a little and told her so.

"Someone's injured, Mama," she said. "I can see his feet, he's slumped across a horse."

From her lower position Masako could indeed see two feet wrapped together, but little more than that. She wasn't as interested in seeing someone who was already hurt as she would have been in watching an actual fight, but Fumiko's reaction was just the opposite. What injured person could force the gates of Odawara Castle so easily open? She imagined again that it might be Ueno, humbled first by Lord Abe's demise and again by some crippling road accident. "Let me through," she said. "Stand aside."

But the crowd didn't want to part and did so only stubbornly. She saw the horse's muzzle first, and then those tied-together feet, and then a hand flung back against the nearest leg as if it were trying to scratch something. That hand, she suddenly knew, did not belong to Ueno.

"Go back, my dear," she told her daughter. "Take your brother and get out of here right now. Go back inside the castle and close the door."

"Why?" asked Masako, but her mother said, "Don't ask questions. Go to our private quarters. Do so quickly and do not turn around."

Fumiko could hear herself as if from a distance. She knew she had found the proper tone of voice to make Masako obey, but she did not know how long she could maintain it. Masako might go only partway back and then turn to ask another question, and if that happened Fumiko didn't think she could find the power, again, to make her daughter keep going. For the moment, however, she only stood there, her back toward the horse.

"Come on, baby brother," Masako said, "if we're not wanted here let's go practice our walking somewhere else."

Fumiko could feel the crowd's silence, a breathless kind of thing that would go on forever if she didn't turn around. But she commanded herself to wait until Masako was at the base of the stairs, until she had carried her brother up those stairs and stepped inside the castle and softly closed the door. And when she finally did turn around it was only through divining a strength that she had always known she had, but had never used before.

"Get back," she said calmly. "Stand back away from there now."

The crowd moved like her daughter had, heads down and grudgingly. Only the guard who led the horse stayed close to her. She looked at that hand again and then stepped up to touch it, actually reaching under it to draw her fingernails across its palm. That the hand was cold did not surprise her, but she had to close her eyes in order to release it, and find the courage to walk around to the other side of the horse. She didn't let herself imagine anything, not what had happened, not whether he had slipped and fallen on the boulder or whether the boulder had plunged from its net and crushed his skull. She did not let herself imagine the look in Einosuke's eyes.

The crowd had stepped out to form a crescent, its back to the castle, so when Fumiko went around to face the end of the world as she knew it, she was alone. At first, however, she could not make out what she saw, could not understand the sight before her. She even felt relief, for a second, as if there had been some hideous mistake. It was odd because even as she fell, even as she clutched the horse's riggings, to keep herself from going all the way down, the thought stayed with her that if this was not Einosuke, then the bile in her mouth, her locked-up jaw, and the streaming flow of her saliva were all unnecessary, all wrong. She screamed but stopped the sound immediately and whipped her head sideways so that an arc of her saliva wet the horse and laced her husband's clothing, like Junichiro's had the chocolate not so very long ago. She reached out and pulled Einosuke's short sword from his belt and pressed it against the soft flesh under her chin and felt the tip go in and would have driven it all the way home had not the horse jumped, in its own renewed terror, turning her and letting her see Masako's headlong rush back down the castle stairs, screaming bloody murder with Junichiro in her arms.

"*MOTHER!*"

Fumiko dropped the blade and ran toward her running daughter, both of them screaming now. Her arms tore her *obi* off and pulled at the sides of her kimono, flinging them out, as if trying to make wings of them, as if trying to turn her kimono into a cape with which she could block her daughter's view of this absolute horror. She felt the wind of her running and saw the ground surge upward and the castle swirl above her and crash down upon them both.

"AIAIAI!"

Mother and daughter came together with such force that Junichiro popped out of Masako's grasp and tottered off by himself, going toward his father and the horse and the crowd. The laborers fell on their faces again, beating the ground around them with fists like hail, and the guards marched around. "Revenge!" they screamed. "War against the enemies of Odawara!"

Those words moved everyone else, but it was the vision of Junichiro staring at the covered neck of his dead and headless father that made Fumiko jump up again, finding herself. She ran back and scooped him up like an eagle might a kitten and clutched him to her and spun around, drops of blood from her own wounded chin surprising and quieting him by spilling into his mouth. And when she got to Masako again she picked her up too, tucked her under her other arm and staggered off with both her children, raging madly back toward the castle.

It was the end of the world as she knew it, it was true, but as soon as the door closed behind them Fumiko knelt and looked at Masako. "Go and wash," she said. "And change your clothes and find someone to take your brother. Where is O-bata? If you see her send her to me. And tell the guards to keep the American away. We cannot see him now."

She hardly knew what she was saying and knew less what might await her in the weeks and months to come, but her intention, as soon as she was alone, was to write a note to Lord Okubo, calling him home. When O-bata came she would send her for a runner, and then she would have Einosuke brought inside the castle and kneel beside him, in a vigil that would last until her own life left her body, and all thoughts save those of him were once and forever washed away.

She stood and started walking and was surprised when her movement was encumbered by Masako, who had not done anything she'd been told to do but clung to her mother, her mouth wide and silent, tears flowing like rivers from her eyes.

So Fumiko knelt again then, and held her daughter, until so much darkness descended that they couldn't see each other. No one interrupted them, no one came from the upper floors of the castle or from outside.

And though they surely wanted to, no one asked what should be done with the waiting corpse of their husband and father, of Lord Okubo's eldest son and heir, of Einosuke, Manjiro's difficult and beloved older brother.

35. | *Is It Easier to Go or Be Left Behind?*

THE NOTE WAS ON a single sheet of crumpled paper. Fumiko's calligraphy wasn't elegant like Lord Abe's. It had, in fact, so much shock in it that her characters ran down the page like words escaping a fire.

She sent the note by runner, after all, and while she waited she tried to think of nothing save its progress, and then, when she felt sure it was in Lord Okubo's hands, she occupied her mind by trying to decide whether it was better to give tragic news or to receive it, whether the sharper pain involved opening such a note, or if the purest agony resided in writing the words down in the first place.

As she thought about it she also watched Masako, who had taken a sleeping potion and lay at her feet, like the corpse of her father, which had finally been brought into the castle and resided in the next room, the one in which they had first heard news of Manjiro from Tsune. Fumiko had bathed and insisted that Masako bathe, too, and now, like two of death's brides, they were dressed in fresh kimono.

There happened to be a collection of ancient battle implements at the far side of the room where Einosuke rested, an entire shelf of helmets and lances and swords. Fumiko's intention had been, when earlier she went into that room alone, to place one of the helmets where her husband's head had been, and then to kneel and speak her farewells through its faceplate, asking his forgiveness for her recent betrayal. But when she got close enough to do it, she saw that her husband had been laid out well, his hands folded across his middle, his bare feet side by side. So instead of kneeling at the top of his body, she was drawn to his hands again, as she had been outside. There, on the one closest to her, she could see the odd angle that his little finger always seemed to want to take, caused by a childhood injury, and there, all across that same hand's back, stood a random line of emerging liver spots, which Einosuke used to insist represented the arguments and troubles he had had, over the years, with Manjiro. There was no facility in these hands, nothing of the living one that scorched her memory now, with its fine and foreign dexterity.

When she touched his nearest forearm it was warmer than she thought it would be, and when she closed her eyes and walked her fingers along his lower body she could feel his presence growing. His legs seemed solid to her, not stiff but muscular, and when she bent to kiss his feet the room became infused with the distinct and pleasant odor of flowers.

Fumiko was meditating, praying, searching for the strength to move up again, to properly fix that helmet at the top of her husband's shoulders, when she felt herself transported out of this death room and placed before the open *shoji* above their newly built garden room, back in their house in Edo. The garden was littered with leaves from their neighbor's tree and Einosuke was before her, bending and standing, bending and standing, throwing the leaves back over the wall.

"It would have been an unending battle," he said.

He showed her wet leaves but she knew he was speaking of everything in life. All that had gone between them, all they had left unsaid.

"Is it easier to go or to be left behind?" she asked her husband.

"It is easier to go, of course," he said. "That's what I have always done, is it not, put the greater part of the burden on you? I was lucky to have had such good children, such a fine and understanding wife."

"I have not understood much," Fumiko admitted. "All this newness, all these recent alterations. I should not have been born on time's cusp like this, but would have better done my duty had I lived a century ago, when our country was insulated. Is that not true for both of us?"

It wasn't nearly so true for Fumiko as it had been for Einosuke, but he nodded, agreeing, taking his way of seeing things from her one last time.

That was all. He seemed about to speak again, but the clarity of her vision faded and when she opened her eyes she was back in his death room, everything but the scent of flowers gone.

So she closed her eyes again and let the flowers guide her.

She put the helmet where her husband's head had been and went to sit beside her sleeping daughter.

36. *Incense or Prosthetics*

AT HIS WORKSHOP, which was housed in an old incense factory at the edge of another of the Izu Peninsula's ubiquitous streams, Denzaimon the prosthetics artisan had been showing examples of his work to Lord Okubo's assembled entourage. He talked for a while about its intricacies and then opened dozens of boxes and drawers, exposing a series of prototypes. In one there were ears, larger than life but so perfectly rendered that light showed through their delicate membranes, and in another there were feet, this time done in miniature, as if for Chinese women or children. He opened a third box to show them hands, with various lengths of blanched-wood forearms, and in others they saw teeth and eyes, fingers and toes. He found examples from everywhere and put them on the table, as if laying out an abstract human form. But there were no noses. He had carved only two in his life and they were sniffing out the world—who knew where?—on living human faces.

Outside the workshop, when they finally left poor Ned alone with Denzaimon, Lord Okubo walked away from the group, in order to relieve himself in the stream at the back of the building. He stood at its edge, and when he undid his clothing he could not help noticing that his own slight wounds, those minor cuts and scratches he had recently made in his abdomen, were already healing well. That was the nature of things, he supposed, they would often get better if you left them alone. And though he didn't believe that Ned would grow another nose, he wished now that they'd been satisfied with the precautions they had taken in the stables, with guarding against infection and clearing those two incredible blow holes. As he tied up his pants again, he even had the thought that incense, after all, probably provided a greater overall social good than prosthetics. If one had to make such a choice.

In front of the workshop Tsune and Manjiro were standing together with their fingers touching while Keiko and Ichiro strolled and chatted timidly nearby, when Fumiko's exhausted runner arrived in the village. He called out Lord Okubo's name first, and then Manjiro's.

Lord Okubo had just come to join the others, so it was Manjiro who took the message and opened it, somehow thinking it would be further evidence of a mending, perhaps a word of kindness from Einosuke.

The note was on a single sheet of paper and crumpled in a way that reminded both Manjiro and Tsune, who continued to touch his arm as he read it, of that other sheet of paper, the one with Lord Abe's offending paragraphs on it. Fumiko's hand wasn't elegant like Lord Abe's, her characters, in fact, had so much shock in them that they shook and wandered down the page, but their message was more powerful than anyone's philosophy.

"Einosuke monstrously killed. Come back to the castle with your swords out!"

Manjiro moaned and his knees weakened, and Tsune saw her sister's face quite clearly, her calligraphy brush held out in front of her like a dagger. She grasped Manjiro's arm, to keep them both from falling, but when a curious Keiko came over to read what had arrived Tsune regained herself enough to push her roughly back again, surprising her niece.

"Auntie, my goodness," said Keiko, embarrassed and glancing at Ichiro. She considered herself an adult now, and would not be treated like Masako.

It was only when Tsune cried out, "Oh evil world, leave this child alone!" that Kyuzo, who had been standing a few yards off watching both the young couples, came forward and took the paper from Manjiro and read its message aloud. "Einosuke monstrously murdered. Come back to the castle with your swords out."

He read so quietly that it took a second for Keiko's irritation to freeze on her face, and shatter and fall.

Lord Okubo took the note from Kyuzo and folded it and slipped it into his kimono until its sharp corners poked against his healing abdomen.

"Prepare our horses," he told Kyuzo. "We will go back to the castle, but will keep our swords sheathed for a while."

Kyuzo bowed and when he moved to follow the old lord's order he pulled Ichiro with him, not because he needed help, but lest the younger man make the mistake of trying to approach Keiko.

Lord Okubo himself was chilled by the news of Einosuke's death, but otherwise oddly distant from it, though at the same time he knew that when the pain finally did arrive it would be his constant companion for the rest of his life. He began doing calculations, trying to remember how long it had been since he'd raised a sword in anger, while Manjiro knelt in front of him, piteously crying, blaming himself. When Lord Okubo put a hand on his head, however, it was not so much to console Manjiro as to steady himself, to keep from joining his sole remaining son on the ground.

"Not yet, not yet," said a voice within him. "Now is the time to act."

"Come," he told the others. "We mustn't leave Fumiko alone."

When the horses were assembled the men left quickly, and when the workshop doors opened a short time later, and Denzaimon and Ned came out, they were greeted only by a cloud of dust and a grieving aunt standing beside a grieving daughter, and a bunch of bearers, ready to take them off again in the waiting palanquins and sedan chairs.

———

THE NOSE DENZAIMON had made for Ned came more from the carver's imagination than from any of the measurements he had taken. Still, it was a fine nose, the length of it derived from his sense of Americans, its shape from one of the most beloved Kabuki characters of the era. He would continue his work on a more precise product; he saw no reason, in fact, why Ned shouldn't have several more noses at his disposal, for use on various occasions. But for now there had only been time to make this one, from selected scraps of quality Japanese cypress, and glue it to the end of a long stick.

The nose was not designed to touch Ned's face. He was to peer from behind it delicately, which he did now for those who awaited him, like a court lady might from behind a fan.

37. | *Irony Provides Relief*

"TAKE A LETTER," said Lord Okubo, in a loud voice.

His scribe was surprised for it was five o'clock the following morning and Lord Okubo himself had awakened him. But he dressed quickly and brought his brushes to the castle office, where he hurriedly ground his inkstones. Manjiro was there, too, waiting with his head bowed, but Lord Okubo only spoke to him to ask, "Do you still have those paragraphs you told me about, the ones which encourage deceit, the ones Lord Abe so stealthily copied down?"

The paragraphs had been pestering Manjiro, certain words and phrases from them running through his mind ever since the arrival of Fumiko's note in the village, so he was surprised.

"Tsune had them last, I think," he said, but he really had no idea where the copied page had gone.

The scribe had his brush ready, with clean paper on the table before him, but Lord Okubo kept his eyes on Manjiro. He knew his son was beset with the idea of killing himself, that were he to speak harshly to him now he might leave the room and pitch himself from the roof of the castle. He knew it and was of two minds; first understanding that he had but one remaining son in this world, and should do what he could to keep him alive, and second that they both ought to do it, that he really should take Manjiro into that secret room, and show him its pair of waiting knives.

Lord Okubo turned to face the castle wall, not speaking for some minutes, and when he turned back again he looked only at the scribe. "This letter is addressed to Lord Abe's erstwhile aide, Ueno," he said. "Stop me if I go too quickly, we have to get it right."

He walked to the room's window and looked out at the dark forest, suddenly remembering Masako's marsh and the odd fact that, since he'd ordered its gates repaired a year ago, he had not been there to inspect them. He started dictating without a salutation:

"I believe that things have gone too far concerning the Americans," he said. "I also believe that no one, not Lord Abe in the beginning, nor any of the members of the Great Council, not your worthy self, nor even my pitiable and recalcitrant son, Manjiro, could have foreseen how far they would go. Indeed, if anyone should have done so it was I . . ."

He paused when he heard Manjiro's breath catch behind him, but continued without looking around.

"Though my mistakes weigh heavily on my heart, however, confessing them is not the purpose of this letter. Its purpose, rather, is to propose that we work toward the return of the Americans to their ships without further embarrassment to anyone. The government needs that to happen, I do not, that is the truth of the matter as it stands now.

"Therefore I will be traveling to Shimoda soon, where I will deliver the Americans to some representative of the realm, just as you will, at that same instant, deliver to me my eldest son's severed head, as well as the man or men who murdered him."

Lord Okubo stopped again, shocked at the sound of his own voice. He asked the scribe to read back what he had written. Except for the words "your worthy self" in the first paragraph, however, he thought the whole thing read well enough. He had the scribe remove those words and went on:

"I propose we meet four days hence and a day or two after Commodore Perry's arrival in that rainy and overburdened town. I did not choose Shimoda because of the American arrival, but because it is close and I am too overburdened, with grief and rage, not to take ease where I can find it."

When he stopped this second time Lord Okubo was wounded anew by the visions his words brought into focus. He drank some cold tea and stared at the scribe but could not go on. Rather, he saw Einosuke as a young boy leaning over his books in the castle; as a young and serious man, awaiting his father in the Great Council corridor. He had been strong when receiving the heinous news, but to actually speak the words, to put it all down on paper—this was more than the old lord could bear.

As the silence extended, from one minute to three and then longer, and as the first dead streaks of dawn came up through the rain, it was

Manjiro, therefore, not Lord Okubo, who braved his own unending sorrow, cleared his throat, and spoke a few lines to finish the letter:

"We can no longer be held responsible for the safety of the two Americans, if Einosuke's murderers, as well as his missing part, are not delivered to us," he said. "The details of everything can be worked out later, by a personal meeting if necessary, but preferably by runner."

Manjiro closed the letter with a high degree of formality, then waited until his father came back to himself, found his seal on the scribe's table, and applied it to the paper.

So it was that while once Lord Abe threatened the foreigners' lives, now it was they who were doing it, this pitiable father and son. Oddly, it was that very irony that seemed to provide some measure of relief, giving both men the will to go and rest for a few hours; to agree without speaking about it that, for these next few days at least, they would put their despair aside, stay alive in the world, and concentrate on that sweetest of all man's follies: Revenge.

38. | *A Fetish without Many Followers*

THE FISH SELLER'S SON back in Edo had had a missing thumb. That was why O-bata had been drawn to him.

Before his accident if O-bata had thought of him at all it was as a gross kind of fellow, overly leering and loud, but when she saw him after his accident he was quiet, sitting on a stool in front of his father's empty stall.

"What's the matter with you?" she had asked him. "Are you closed?"

He looked up and slowly pulled the hand with the missing thumb into the air between them. His thumb was gone, not just to its first or second joint, but all the way to his wrist, and it still bore the craggy redness of something sore. He was in a foul mood, lonely and depressed, and meant to send O-bata running by showing her his scars. But instead of being repulsed, she was moved to a surprising sympathy by his misfortune. She knew it was abnormal, a fetish without many followers, but a fair amount of ardor rose within her as soon as she saw it.

And when she felt that ardor rise again, upon being assigned the job of caring for the two Americans, while the family was embroiled in its tragedy, she did not deny it. Rather, as she watched Ned's new wooden nose sway in front of her one evening—Ace had gone for a walk in the woods, working out his own sense of how he ought to behave from then on—she let him see her in her bath *yukata,* her body still wet and her hair undone. Her nipples showed right through the fabric, as if she didn't have a fabric on. She spoke to him, saying, "Everyone's sad. My mistress and her daughters will never be the same again, and the baby will never know his father. Don't you think there is too much misfortune in this world of ours?"

"It don't hurt a bit," said Ned. "As I was tryin' to tell Mangy before all this new bad stuff happened, I keep waitin' for the pain, but it just won't come."

He took one hand off the stick to which his new nose was glued and pointed behind it, at the spot O-bata was drawn to, and when she came over to touch his ruined face he let his prosthesis fall.

"What's this?" he asked. "Some newfangled kind of Japanese hospitality?"

O-bata took him into her room and closed the door. "I like my men wounded," she said. "Don't ask me why."

She smiled, for in truth she had hardly ever spoken to a man before, let alone uttered anything so provocative. But she seemed to know that with Ned she could say whatever she pleased because he didn't understand. Unlike Fumiko with Ace, she had no sense of intuition, not much sense that they understood each other, at all. She only knew that Ned was someone who would let her talk. Maybe that's what she'd been waiting for.

"*Hana*," she told him, rubbing the nose on the end of his stick. "*Hana* is what you don't have anymore."

"Angelface," said Ned. "I forget the word for 'angel,' but face is '*cow*.' You got the '*cow*' of an angel, just like my old wife."

And with that, though a thick cloud of mourning filled all the other rooms of the castle, there was a small amount of light in the maids' quarters, a pinprick for Ned, a shaft for O-bata.

Ace understood and stayed away from them, walking and thinking about Fumiko.

He felt an abiding sympathy for Ned, who, he remembered, had only come ashore to please him, while he, Ace, had known in his bones that everything he'd done so far had led him here, that his life's true purpose resided on these shores.

He touched his face where Fumiko had touched it, and even closed his eyes, but try as he might he could not recapture the look she had had when she'd left him, and had no idea what she felt about things now that her husband was dead.

He thought about it and thought about it, and walked so quietly through the forest that the frogs didn't stop singing when he arrived at the marsh.

Or even when he climbed upon Masako's sumo wrestler to think some more.

PART THREE
SHIMODA

39. | *Keiki and the Planting,*
| *Ueno and the River Trout*

MORE THAN A WEEK went by—eight days—before Lord Okubo opened the gate of Odawara Castle again, passing through it with his hurt and angry family, and during that time most of the one thousand or so houses in Shimoda, at the end of the Izu Peninsula, were conscripted by Edo government officials. Regular residents had to use either single rooms at the backs of their homes, or go out of town altogether, into the surrounding villages.

Shimoda's official buildings and Buddhist temples were also taken over as various headquarters. Its two main streets, which curved around the bay, had been made up festively, as if the arrival of the American fleet were something to be celebrated, but because the Americans would soon be free to roam those streets, something they had not been allowed to do in Edo, there was a good deal of consternation behind the façade. Would they act wildly, slurping saké and staggering when they walked, like unruly *ronin,* or would they be even more frightening than that, trudging slowly and chanting behind the forbidden sign of Christianity? Shimoda, along with Hakodate farther south, was to be an open port, but what would it mean, in terms of daily life, when such a thing became a reality?

This was the atmosphere into which Keiki came, down from Edo and into the fray. Tsune had written him faithfully, describing each of the incidents that befell the Okubo family, and he had come to Shimoda not only to help stop further fighting—it was he who had invented the clever Kambei posters, after all, plunging Manjiro into heroic national prominence—but also to deliver the letter from his father, at long last proposing marriage between Tsune and Manjiro. His father and he both believed that rage was most easily battled with love, and wanted, at any cost, to prevent more strife between the Okubo clan and Ueno. Things in Edo were healing now, and should heal down here, among these outcast family members, as well.

It was true that the treaty had been signed, but there were still details to be hammered out, and Ryosenji Temple had been chosen as the official meeting place of the new contingent of Japanese negotiators and Commodore Perry's soon-to-arrive party of rain-soaked naval officers. It was there that Keiki had reserved rooms, and there, also, where he was to meet the family's emissary—Kyuzo of all people—who would receive his father's letter in the name of the grieving Lord Okubo.

Keiki arrived at the temple without fanfare and was shown to his rooms in the back. He hung up his spare kimono and arranged his father's letter on a writing table, but he didn't like the darkness of the room and soon stepped out to its surrounding walkway again, to sit in a little patch of sunlight and think about everything once more.

As he did so he absently watched one of the temple's old monks, oblivious to the machinations of the outside world, preparing his spring-time vegetable garden. The monk bent and spiked his hoe into the dirt, dragging it along its furrow, the sleeve of his *yukata* tied back with strands of hemp rope. The temple's soil, Keiki knew, was like Japan itself, far too old for delicate vegetables, far too ready to surrender to the encroaching loam. But this year's early rain seemed to have made the monk determined to succeed with tomatoes, for resting in the shade near where Keiki sat were two dozen crack-bottomed teacups, each holding a sprouted tomato plant, ten inches tall. It was a pleasant thing for Keiki to see and he smiled. Here was the optimism that he wished he could instill in everyone, from his father back in Edo, to the members of the Great Council, even to the grief-stricken Okubos. And if he ever gained a position of power this was what he would insist upon. What a good idea it was—planting with the fullness of one's heart, even in the face of poor soil!

When his garden was ready and the monk retrieved his tomato sprouts he did not acknowledge Keiki, but Keiki, brimming by then with positive thoughts, acknowledged and startled him, by jumping down off the walkway and offering to help with the planting. He followed the monk back to the garden and knelt beside him and picked up a trowel. Work was more important than thought, he thought, action a better tonic than moroseness! That was another lesson he would impart, if he ever gained power in Japan.

The monk had a cheap bottle of saké on the ground next to him, and each time he dug a hole for a tomato plant he poured a little in, as a kind of blessing. Keiki soon usurped the job of taking a plant from its crack-bottomed teacup and sliding it into the hole on top of the saké, and he did so with such exuberance that the monk finally relented a little, accepting him. It did surprise Keiki when the monk took a sip of the saké, and handed him the bottle, but the planting went quickly anyway; a trowel full of dirt out, a drop of saké in, a sprouted tomato placed into the ground, and two men drinking from the bottle.

After twenty-four such sips, Keiki gained a new appreciation for the darkness of his rooms and went back inside to nap. He knew nothing, of course, of Manjiro's earlier drunk-monk imitation on the road outside of Odawara, or that Ned Clark's nose had also resided in a teacup.

And even if he had known it would not have made an impression on him, for Keiki wasn't a believer in omens.

————

MEANWHILE, HOWEVER, at an inn not very far away and afflicted with a deep belief in omens, Ueno reread the letter he had received from Lord Okubo, and severely berated himself for having entrusted Einosuke's head to those two nameless *ronin,* the idiots who had procured Ned's nose. Now where was it? Now how would he get it back?

Choosing his samurai by lot had been a stupid idea in the first place, for a third of them had gotten lost in mountains, while others, like Ichiro, had defected, and still more had succumbed to laziness and drink. He had sent the last group remaining loyal to him after the two, but had little hope that they would be successful. He was confident that Lord Okubo had no idea that he, Ueno, was personally responsible for Einosuke's death—in his experience peasants could rarely tell one samurai from another—but that, too, had been an unfortunate mistake, a bad omen.

The inn where Ueno stayed was next to the tiny Hiraname River, and as he walked in its summer *mikan* orchard he not only carried Lord Okubo's letter, but also a few of Keiki's "Kambei" posters, brought to him the night before by an aide. At the edge of the orchard was a Shinto shrine, and when Ueno came under the cover of its arch, to escape the beginnings of another storm, he unrolled the posters. They were disquieting things and had infuriated Lord Abe, but he couldn't help thinking they were masterfully done. The first depicted Manjiro putting the Americans into palanquins with small U.S. flags on their sides, Lord Abe in the background wringing his hands. *"Just when we need him, here comes Kambei, again,"* the script beside it read.

The next three posters were equally irritating, with Manjiro the hero of their actions, but the last one showed Ueno himself, cowering like a peasant before an angry Lord Abe, while Manjiro and the two Americans danced away from them in monk's robes. The caption had Ueno looking pitifully up at Lord Abe and saying, *"I guess the experiment of America has failed."*

And now Lord Abe had been censured and he, Ueno, had been left to clear up the mess on his own. In that way he felt a sort of affinity with Manjiro—the players continuing to act after the play was over and the directors had gone home. That is what he had wanted to tell Einosuke at the beach that day. That is what he would have told him had he not been so rude. And now what he needed most of all was a change of luck, a good omen.

Ueno rolled the posters up again, threw them into a nearby puddle, then turned to walk along the evenly spaced rows of the *mikan* orchard. Rain had soaked his back and shoulders as he'd been standing there, so he paced the entire length of the orchard as fast as he could, in an effort to rid himself of the frustration he felt.

On the orchard's far side was the bank of the Hiraname River, particularly narrow where it ran past the inn, and on a whim Ueno decided to wade across it, to do it immediately, to defeat this little river as he soon would those other remaining actors in this drama they were continuing to effect. If he could do that successfully, maybe his luck would change.

He slipped off his *geta*, set them on a rock, and stepped into the water's flow. He knew the river would be icy cold, the shock of it, in fact, was what he wanted most, but he had not expected it to be so powerful, and he nearly fell over. He put his hands onto a protruding rock but when he righted himself his feet were far apart and he no longer looked elegant. Rather, he looked like a crab on the shore, and that is how he moved to the river's middle, determined but ungainly, where he found a place to stand again, on the top of a forked tree branch, lodged amongst the stones.

Ueno was soaked and freezing and furious, but did not look toward the inn, did not succumb to his desire to see if his clumsy efforts had been observed by anyone. Instead, he stared into the water as it back-eddied below him, looking deep into the gray-blue darkness for a sign. He could see his toes, curled around the blond forks of wood, and there, below them, something else. Yes, yes, he could also suddenly see the back of a brown river trout, its gill-quiver hardly visible above the slow and stabilizing movement of its tail.

Ueno pulled his short sword from its soaked and ruined scabbard and sent it into the river, not stopping until most of its shiny blade had yielded to the dullness of the water. This gave him true pleasure and now he did look up, not to see who might be watching him, but to glance along the rows of orderly *mikan* trees, along the tight-lipped scrutiny of that orchard. This was his sign. It was not oneness with nature that made man what he was, but dominance and power over it, that was the unlearned lesson, the central failure exhibited by so many of his contemporaries, by these weak and hapless lords: Lord Abe! Lord Tokugawa! Every last one. If only he could spear this trout he would be sure of his place, his victory in the coming negotiations!

He lowered his blade a few more centimeters, until it came directly over the dorsal fin of the trout. He knew, of course, that he would have just one chance, but that knowledge made his breathing easier, wiped the perennial grimace from his face, and maximized his control. He moved his blade closer, then stabbed without warning, plunging it down to a point far beyond the trout's head, ten centimeters into the riverbed, his hands and arms frothing the water, his voice cracking like a gunshot through the air.

"Dekita! Dekita! I got it! I got it!"

The trout's body was pinned so well that when Ueno stood up and pointed his blade at the brooding and unimpressed sky, it slid all the way down to his hand guard, with thin red lines of blood making other little rivers across the back of his arms. Yes! Yes! One at a time, this is how he would get them, this was how he would seek his own revenge, not on the Americans, particularly, but on all these Japanese weaklings who had not stayed the course! Oh what a game it was, the samurai's purest motivation alive again, victory for the sake of victory alone!

If only he had troops he knew by name, and could rely on.

40. The Wind and Intransigence

UNLIKE KEIKI, who had come down from Edo in a large and excellent navel vessel, Kyuzo, accompanied by his new apprentice, Ichiro, had traveled to Shimoda in a terrible open boat and ridden ashore in a barge with a dozen bedraggled and penniless samurai. There were other boats by the hundreds on the bay around them, small ones and large ones crowded with curious onlookers. The American fleet stood three hundred feet off shore, anchored with a majesty more likely to be attached to a visiting city—Ned's image had been right!—than to any of the ships the Japanese were used to seeing.

Before leaving Odawara Kyuzo had had a short meeting with Lord Okubo, and an even shorter one with his beloved Tsune. Lord Okubo had told him that at all costs he must appear business-like, even cordial, to Ueno should he find him. He should do nothing to exact revenge in the Okubo family name, but only look about smartly and collect information that might be helpful to them in the coming fight. And Tsune had told him that he should go immediately to Ryosenji Temple, find Keiki and retrieve that marriage proposal, which might, she believed, still solve everything.

It was late afternoon when they arrived, and men with government crests on their robes chatted and laughed, going in and out of bars and greeting each other far more cordially than they ever would have done in Edo.

"It's a throwback to the old days," Kyuzo said. "Would you look at these guys? They act like everyone in Japan is fully employed, like nothing's changed since the days of Tokugawa Ieyasu."

They had left the waterfront and were standing at the intersection of two streets, under brightly colored banners. The same wind that had battered their boat on its way down from Odawara was snapping the banners, making sounds like small-calibre pistol shots. Both men were hungry and would not have refused a few cups of saké to settle their stomachs, but Ichiro's hair had come undone during the voyage and he wanted to step in somewhere first and have it combed, so he wouldn't have to greet Keiki looking bad. His hair was thick and full, with no part of his head shaved, as was the fashion. Kyuzo's hair, by contrast, had thinned over the years, yet somehow rode the wind as if it were sculpted out of stone. He cuffed Ichiro's cheek and said, "I don't know why we have such difficult styles. When you first saw the Americans did you not notice the efficient shortness of their hair? That's what I will do if I survive this current trouble. Wear an American hair style!"

Ichiro laughed but kept his eye out for a barber's sign and, luckily enough, found one before Kyuzo could locate a noodle shop. "It will only take a minute," he said.

Kyuzo, who for some reason counted barbering among the merchant endeavors he did not quite approve of, nodded but said he would wait outside. The wind wasn't pushing him anymore, yet across the street he noticed others struggling along one way or another, either leaning into it or trying to keep it from making them run. He saw that he was standing in the lee of two low walls, in a lull like a ship sometimes finds in the trough of a wave. When he put his hand up he could feel his fingers reenter the wind and begin to wiggle of their own accord, like his father's had during the last few days of his life. He pulled his hand down to make his fingers stop and up again to make them wiggle, down and up twice more. He nodded, as if some previously muddled thought had finally come clear, something he had intended to tell Ichiro during their talk at Odawara Castle, and opened the door to the barbershop.

"Listen, Ichiro," he said, "there is little we can do about anything. I may be able to defeat you because I am a better swordsman, just as you may be able to cut down another, but that means nothing because the scale we are using, the scope of our thinking, is too small. Let me try to cut this wind out here and it will simply blow against the sharpness of my sword and go around. These fools walking across the street are helpless because they don't have a wall."

Ichiro wasn't alone in the barbershop. Two mid-level bureaucrats were there too, and he was just then sitting down to get his hair combed. Kyuzo's face in the doorway, the poor condition of his clothing, plus the outright oddness of his comment, all served to make the others wary.

No one spoke, however, until the barber asked him to close the door.

"Come in if you like," he said, "but that wind you mentioned is capricious and might decide to blow dirt into my store."

The bureaucrats laughed nervously for they knew from experience that masterless samurai could be as capricious as any wind, and they saw no crests on Kyuzo's clothing that would indicate his attachment to anyone.

"I'm making a serious point," Kyuzo said, but he did come in and close the door. The barber had Ichiro's hair out of its ties and hanging down to his shoulders. The barber was about to tell him that combing it without first giving it a much-needed wash was a waste of time, but Kyuzo's entrance made him forget to say it.

The bureaucrats, both of whom had finished, were simply hanging around. They had come into the barbershop because they were expected to perform official duties first thing in the morning, and they were a little drunk, having just departed a party. One of the bureaucrats lived in Shimoda and was in charge of rice taxation on local peasants, while the other, who was his cousin, had the duty of vetting that taxation on behalf of the Shogunate. The happy coincidence of their employment meant that they were able to meet whenever the vetting cousin came from Edo. A second happy coincidence was that this time they would have the pleasure of observing the official arrival of the Americans.

What they should have done was simply excuse themselves and go home, but something he heard in the barber's tone when telling Kyuzo to close his door emboldened the bureaucrat from Edo, who, as too often happened, had been looking for a way to show off his superior sophistication to his cousin. He was wearing a sword, this Edo man, but in his case it was strictly ornamental. He put a hand on his cousin's arm, to properly get his attention, before walking straight up to Kyuzo.

"A man should speak sensibly," he said, "and what you said just now made no sense at all."

He used a rude form of speech, but Kyuzo was trying to hold onto his point about the wind and didn't hear it.

"Wait a minute," he answered, gesturing vaguely toward the bureaucrat, "I want to remember what I was going to say to this young man."

The bureaucrat looked over his shoulder, made a face at everyone, and said, "Maybe you were going to offer to cut his hair with your sword."

It was a boorish kind of comment, embarrassing to his cousin and not very clever as an insult, and he had used rude speech a second time, no doubt because he had gotten away with it in the first place. He looked at his cousin as if to say, "See how times have changed? We often act with such impunity in Edo."

Ichiro sat up and the barber stepped back out of his way, but the bureaucrat's voice was no more than an irritating fly buzz to Kyuzo, who, though he had lost a little speed over the years, still had excellent powers of concentration.

"Ichiro," he said. "Can you imagine cutting the wind with your sword? You cannot imagine, can you, that such a thing could possibly have any value?"

He looked up to hear Ichiro's answer, but the bureaucrat stood between them.

"I can imagine cutting wind with my ass," he said. "Can you imagine that?"

"What?" Kyuzo asked. "I beg your pardon?"

Even then, however, he was not so much offended as surprised. He had tried to look nondescript in order to do the work Lord Okubo had assigned him, but he glanced down at himself to see if maybe his bad dress and generally humble appearance were even worse than he thought. His kimono was brown and without markings, his leggings dirty and wet, yet otherwise he did not think he looked so disgraceful as to spawn words of outright insult.

"Say it again, sir," he told the bureaucrat, "I'm not sure I heard you right."

He spoke politely and with his forehead furrowed, as if he really did believe the fault could only reside with himself.

The Shimoda cousin took a step forward and bowed. "It was just a poor joke, sir," he said, "a play on words that didn't quite work out."

Had Kyuzo known the men were cousins, one local and the other an Edo-ite, he might have deduced everything and stepped aside. And even as it was he remembered that he was supposed to be circumspect, that his and Ichiro's mission to gather information would not be furthered by a public fight. But the more he looked into the Edo bureaucrat's eyes, the less inclined he was to pretend it had all been a misunderstanding.

"Please . . ." the barber started to say, but everyone knew the next move was Kyuzo's.

"I was thinking about man's true weakness in the face of the larger elements," he told his opponent. "The wind was my example but it could as easily have been earth or fire or water. Or it might have been something more intrinsically human like love for a beautiful woman or intransigence. Anyway, however obvious my observation might be to an established man like yourself, I wanted to point out to Ichiro here, while he is still young enough to care for such things, just how insubstantial we are in the face of real power."

His voice was soft and his words had the odd quality of acceding to and enjoining the Edo bureaucrat at the same time. That is, the man could take it as an explanation or a lesson, the first if he was dead-hearted enough to believe his bluster had cowed Kyuzo, the second if beneath his outer layers of laziness and fat there was still something uncontaminated. Either way Kyuzo seemed to have avoided what he could not allow: an escalation of the argument.

Everyone saw it except the Edo bureaucrat. Ichiro watched with earnest eyes and the barber nodded, and the Shimoda cousin tried to prompt their leaving by rattling the barbershop door. He even said, "I used to think that everyone wanted success. That each man, whatever his station, wanted to be looked up to by some, while at the same time having a larger pool of others to look down upon. But I don't believe I think so anymore."

Kyuzo bowed at this, and gave the man a smile. The Edo man, however, seemed not only not to have heard his cousin, but to be on the edge of another insult. He opened his mouth with a quickness, at least, that usually meant unthoughtful words would fall out. But then he closed it again and his features seemed to alter.

"Did you say intransigence?" he asked Kyuzo. "Surely you don't believe that such things as intransigence are part of nature?"

Kyuzo nodded. "Societies have natures, and if men make them up then men do, also. A man's nature is as difficult to change, sometimes, as the flow of any river."

Now the Shimoda cousin grasped the bureaucrat's arm, and when he felt it he finally understood that in the eyes of this cousin intransigence was one of his great faults. And suddenly, quite as if he'd been caught by a shopkeeper sucking an unpurchased sweet, he felt sorry for it. It wasn't the first time he had felt this way, too much drink often made him maudlin, but he could not remember when such feelings had struck him simply by listening to the words of some badly dressed stranger, some nameless old man. And, oh yes, the words of his cousin, as well.

"Let's go, Kiku," he told his cousin. "Let's go back to your house."

His voice was defeated, but his cousin was delighted by it and bowed his thanks to Kyuzo. Kiku! Chrysanthemum! It was the first time the Edo cousin had called him by his childhood nickname in a decade and a half.

When they were gone the barber turned back to Ichiro's hair, which was in tangles and had to be wetted and combed out again before it could be put into its topknot. So Kyuzo followed the men out into the street to stand between those two walls again and watch them go. Kiku's arm was across his cousin's shoulder and both men bent forward, though the wind had lessened and another drizzly rain had begun.

The nearby businesses were shutting down, their outside lanterns dimmed, but the bars and noodle shops were thriving. Kyuzo could hear doors opening and closing, laughter modulated by it like the waves on the beach below. It was the beginning of an evening of storytelling and gaiety. "The American ships are here," he heard someone say, "like giant black boulders, right out there in the harbor!"

He thought of the lines given him in Edo recently by his dead father's ghost, *"In the rain near Nijo Castle, under the falling wisteria,"* and suddenly he wanted to take part in the festivities, to have one last joyous evening among strangers, before the trouble started again and those lines came home to roost.

And so, with that in mind, and with a sense of magnanimity as well, he took the barber's lantern from its place by the door, killed its flame with his fingers, and went back inside to hurry Ichiro along.

"The bars are filling fast," he said, "let's go. The three of us. Now is not a time to think about class. Men of various backgrounds must learn to get along!"

The barber smiled at that, said he knew the best bars in Shimoda, not only those with the prettiest geisha, but also with the best singers, and Ichiro was happy for he believed what Kyuzo, in his deepest heart, even though he had just paid lip service to it, did not; that something had to change in this ridiculous and unnecessary warrior class to which they both belonged. Maybe by turning samurai into merchants and businessmen, by making them innkeepers and traders, scholars and shipping executives, builders and scientists and yes, even barbers, maybe by giving up something that had been begging to be given up for more than two hundred years, they could still somehow save their country from these invaders!

Maybe so. For the moment, however, all such a mood accomplished was a night of happy revelry, the result of which was that they fell into drunken slumber at the barber's house, and didn't arrive at the temple where Keiki awaited them, himself hung over from the cheap planting wine, until the middle of the following afternoon.

41. *Hide This in Your Wagon*

CLEANERS CAME OUT at sunrise the next morning, brooms pulling debris from its hiding places, fingers digging bits of sodden-colored papers from between the cobblestones, peasants taking advantage of the lull in the rain to silently move up the town's narrow and empty roads.

Oh, it had been a party! Drunks and geisha had warbled until just a couple of hours prior to that sunrise, plunging wildly into stories of better times and staggering outside to hurl insults at Perry's ships with their sleeping cargo of foreign invaders. A cadre of *ronin* had burst from one geisha bar and tried to commandeer a fishing boat, ready to sail out and board the nearest American vessel, while in another a member of Lord Hayashi's new official negotiating team had torn a geisha's clothing from her, in an attempt to dramatize what the Americans would likely do, once they came ashore. He'd exposed himself, the story went, saying, "Look at this, will you look at this? Unlike an American penis it properly fits that purse of yours. Let me show you. Let me show you right now!"

On the port road itself, in front of a shrine built years earlier to honor sailors lost in a memorable storm, the last of Ueno's lottery-chosen *ronin* slept in rumpled clothing—it was they who had tried to commandeer the fishing boat—and on a bar street near them a honey-bucket man walked the narrow pathways, trying not to slop the buckets of human waste that were draped across his shoulders. This man had two sons who waited for him at his wagon, having already finished with the bars and geisha houses assigned to them. His elder son, Manzo, was tending to business, carefully weaving together freshly cut boughs of sappy pine, while his younger son, Momo, swaggered around pretending to be the "Kambei" on the posters they kept seeing, swatting the air with a bamboo stick, as if it were a real sword. The elder son was happy with his lot in life and looked for a peasant girl to marry, while the younger sorely wished that he, too, could be a real samurai, sick with sleep and drink from the previous night's debauchery.

"Who knows what I might do if I had the chance?" he kept asking his brother. "And why must heredity always determine things? Are the sons of fishermen truly born to be fishermen, the sons of farmers to be farmers, and are we born to slog this shit around all of our lives? I don't think so, Manzo. I don't think so at all!"

He would have been happy to know that such luminary gentlemen as Kyuzo and Ichiro had been having those same liberal (and drunken) thoughts only a few hours earlier.

He swung his stick again, perilously close to his brother's head.

"Father won't like it if you wake up these geisha," Manzo told him. "And you won't like it if some hung-over samurai comes out and slaps you around. I remember how you whimpered and mewed the last time that happened, Momo. And if you hit me with your stick I'll make you whimper myself."

"Ah Manzo, you have no imagination, and no ambition, either, that's your problem. If I were a warrior I could wake up any geisha I chose, simply by sliding in beside her, warming her futon!"

"Be quiet, Momo," said Manzo, "I mean it now. Look what your nonsense has brought us! Look there, at the bottom of the road!"

Momo followed his brother's hand when it held a pine bough up, and sure enough, two actual samurai had come into the street at its lower end, as if summoned by his bravado. They were badly dressed men and rode on the backs of two awful-looking horses, a large pickle jar tied to the first horse's flank with strands of thick hemp rope.

"Here comes real trouble, Momo," Manzo said. "Just act busy. What are they doing here so early? Oh, what bad luck!"

Momo hid his stick in their wagon and bent as if inspecting the wagon's wheel, trying to control his fear. Manzo, on the other hand, continued with the weaving of his boughs, looked up at the approaching riders, and smiled.

"Hey dung men, what's your secret? How do you keep the flies away?" called one of the filthy samurai. He had ridden up close to the two brothers, pointed at their wagon, and then at his pickle jar, where swarms of iridescent flies carved geometric figures in the wet morning air. The men had the stench of evil upon them. Manzo recognized it by the ease with which it cut through the shit smell.

"We do it with these," he politely said, holding up one of his nicely woven pine boughs.

The samurai who'd spoken was younger and a good deal more frightening than the other one. He stared at the brothers hard, as if trying to discern some insult, a small bit of drool at the corners of his mouth. But his next words were directed at his companion.

"You should have kept things clean," he hissed. "You should have washed it like I told you! Washed it and sealed its lid every night!"

A small bit of urine wet Momo's thigh, but the older man merely waved his companion's words away, like he'd no doubt waved away the flies, and climbed down off his horse. "I should have stayed away from the likes of you, from the outset," he said.

He looked at Manzo, his voice full of resignation. "Bring me a few of those good-smelling boughs, then. Come on lad, be quick about it."

Manzo hurried to oblige but when Momo saw their father emerging from the pathway between the two geisha houses he swallowed his fear, stood up and spoke deliberately, as if he were just then finishing a long explanation.

"Sappy pine will keep flies away," he brightly said, "but only after you scrub your jar with citrus oil. Flies don't like citrus, even fruit flies don't."

As he spoke he looked to gauge his father's reaction to his fine instructive tone, but when he saw a thin white hand opening the upstairs window of the nearest geisha house his heart turned a somersault, never mind that danger stalked them all. A geisha was looking out at them—looking out at him!—and though she no doubt wished they would be quiet, Momo loved her instantly, and doubled his hatred for the fact that these stinking men could go and drink with her, while he, in this lifetime at least, could not. All he could ever really do, he understood bitterly, was piss his pants and swat the fetid air with his stick!

"I can do it for you if you like," said his brother, bowing down before the men. "I have just now woven these new boughs."

The older samurai held up a hand and the younger one began to tell him to stay where he was, but Manzo, dulled to the danger as usual, had already stepped beside the pickle jar. Flies lined the jar's lip and the tails and rumps of both the horses and were in the hair of the two men.

Momo thought the flies looked like humble and begging petitioners outside a castle, while Manzo saw them as elegant, like an emergency meeting of metallic-blue lords.

Their father had stopped when he saw the two samurai, but came forward quickly now, worried that Momo's unruly mouth had once more got him in trouble.

"I'm sure he didn't mean it like it sounded," he told the two men. Last week's pine boughs were stretched over his shoulders, where they worked to soften the strain of the overflowing buckets.

"What will you do with all the shit you've collected?" the younger samurai asked him. "Sell it to a farmer, or spread it on a field of your own?"

It was an ignorant question—what honey-bucket man had a field of his own?—but the father only said, "We sell it to a merchant who sells it again to farmers, passing it on."

He emptied the buckets into his wagon, careful to ensure that no bits of waste splashed the horrid samurai's already wasted clothes. Then he bowed as low as he could, peeking to assure himself that Momo's head was also down.

"Merchants again!" croaked the younger man. "Isn't that always the problem? Usurping merchants everywhere, even in the shit business! We ought to kill every one of them!"

He raised his voice for a second but then stepped closer to the father, becoming conspiratorial. "You men provide a service and so does the farmer who buys this crap, don't get me wrong," he said. "But tell me old man, what does the merchant do save build obstacles between the two of you, and while he's at it build himself a fine new house?"

As he spoke the older samurai, though he'd finally let Manzo spread fresh pine boughs across the backs of both horses, was having no luck at all getting the flies to leave their pickle jar alone. The boughs, of course, were meant for after cleaning, as a kind of garnish, not for when shit caked everything in sight like hard tofu. That was what Momo had been trying to tell him.

Momo expected the younger samurai to go on about the evils of the merchant class a while longer, but instead he returned to the horses to swat at the flies again and otherwise rummage around. In the window above them the geisha was now singing the refrain of a popular love song— *"I waited for him till my well ran dry, until the nearby fields grew fallow"*—while across the street someone else splashed water from a bucket and mopped another bar's floor. Momo, of course, was convinced that the geisha was singing for him alone. He loved this street with all his heart and, though he would never have admitted it to anyone, had formed the habit of reciting the names of its bars: *"Bizen-ya, Kado, Yamago-ya, Kanzan, Jittoku, Miki, Edo-ya,"* as he scooped the shit from their outhouses.

He recited them now, inside his head, to the rhythm of the song of the geisha, until the younger samurai came back with a fist full of coins.

"We want to buy all this shit," he said. "We'll take it off your hands right now."

"What?" said the older samurai, but the younger one turned on him, in a hissing rejoinder that soon turned into a shout. "You've seen for yourself that nothing else will cover the smell! What rots, rots! That is why we have flies and worms!"

He glanced back at Momo's father and said in a quieter voice, "We'll need the loan of your wagon, also."

The father knew by their weight that the coins he'd been given were sufficient, so he told Momo to go with the men, and bring the wagon back when they'd found their field and the fertilizing was done. Manzo was disappointed that he had not been chosen to go, since everyone knew he was the more responsible son, but he hid it by saying, "That's good shit you're buying, sirs. Everyone loves the shit from a geisha house."

It wasn't only Momo who could say something clever. He could, too!

Despite its awkward look and sloppy, heavy contents, the wagon could be pulled by one man if he were skilled. Manzo was the best puller in the family, followed closely by their father, while Momo was one of the worst pullers in all of Shimoda. So when Momo stepped into the wagon's thick hemp halter, Manzo forgot his jealousy, stopped trying to think of clever things to say, and helped his brother center himself. It wouldn't do for Momo to bring embarrassment to the family, no matter how decrepit the men who had purchased the load.

When Momo was ready Manzo and his father pushed from the sides until the wagon gave a beginning lurch, while Momo remembered to keep his head bent, watching his feet to make sure they were set wide apart. Up the road he went, away from his father and brother and out of the sight of the geisha, who, in any case, had stopped singing and closed her window again some moments earlier.

Momo could hear the samurai behind him, the younger one walking, the older one tense on his horse, when it quite suddenly came to him, as if in a final lyric from that geisha, that there was more to be careful of here than just spilling shit or the pace and gait he chose. His father had told him to come back *as soon as the fertilizing of their field was done,* but these men were no more likely to have a field that needed fertilizing than he was! No sir, they were outlaws of some kind, that's what they were, and their contraband was hidden inside that pickle jar! And if that were true then this, at long last, was the opportunity he'd been waiting for, the chance to break loose from the pitiful peasant shackles that were ruining his days and enslaving his entire life. He had to be brave, that was all there was to it. He couldn't piss his pants again. He had to find the courage he was always bragging about right now.

Momo headed out the way they always did, not stopping until he reached a spot at the edge of town where some two dozen other honey-bucket wagons waited, full and unattended, for the merchant who would later pick them up. "Kambei, the catcher of criminals!" he thought, and imagined himself depicted on a poster.

To cover his growing nervousness Momo sang the second line of the geisha's song, in a loud and quivering voice: *"Until the petals fell from all my pretty flowers and the freezing mountain streams grew murky . . ."*

"Shhh," said the younger samurai, bringing the pickle jar forward. "Be quiet! Stop that horrible noise and take this from me now, my strong young lad. Submerge it in your wagon. I don't want to dirty my clothes."

Momo had slipped out of his halter and turned to face the man, flexing his jaw and trying as hard as he could to cast his fear aside. The pickle jar was heavier than he thought it would be but he pulled it against his chest and smiled, allowing the flies to track their dirty feet across his lips and nose.

The older samurai was slow at getting off his horse and took a piece of material from his pack to cover his mouth before coming forward. He also carried one of Manzo's newly woven pine boughs, and waved it in the air. This told Momo as plainly as words ever could that the smell he'd lived with all his life had become his best advantage. So he stuck his tongue out for extra effect, allowing a couple of flies to land upon it, dancing in the wetness that they found.

The older man coughed and gagged a little bit, but the younger one confided in Momo. "It's only a trick we are playing on a friend. Just lower the jar down into the shit now, that's a good boy, hide it well until we're ready for it."

"There are a lot of wagons here," the older man told him. "If we're ever to find it again we'll have to leave a mark."

Though it was an easy order to carry out, Momo bought himself time by pretending that it wasn't. He strained under the weight of the jar and bumped the wagon, staining his forearms with the little waves of waste that came lapping over its side.

"Just place it in the wagon," said the older man. "Slip it under the surface till we don't see it anymore."

Momo grinned, then lifted the jar up much higher than was necessary and fairly threw it into the center of the wagon, as if it were a heavy stone. Shit splashed everywhere, over the ground around them and onto the heads and shoulders of all three men. Strains of it flew even into the mouths of both the samurai, and while they were spitting and wiping themselves and shouting, leaning over and vomiting onto the ground, Momo stood up straight and ran, not singing this time, but chanting his memorized litany of bar names: *"Bizen-ya, Kado, Yamagoya, Kanzan, Jittoku, Miki, Edo-ya . . ."* until he heard them pull their swords from the scabbards, remount their horses and give chase.

Who knew what he thought he might achieve by such a tactic when, not ten seconds earlier, running seemed to be the thing he most wanted to avoid?

———

WITHOUT THEIR WAGON and with time to spare before they were due at home, Manzo and his father had walked toward the port to take a look at the American ships while it was still early enough for their presence not to bother anyone. It had been Manzo's idea to do such a thing, convincing his reluctant father, because he wanted to have a story of his own to tell when Momo got back and they all sat down to breakfast later on. They had had to slip past that sleeping contingent of Ueno's drunk soldiers to stand at the town's bulkhead, and were now looking out at the ships and the swelling high tide. The weather had held but the offshore clouds were worrisome, frowning at them in a good imitation of Manzo's father.

"Don't fret so much, Papa," Manzo said, but he couldn't help adding, "You know if me and Momo could gather the shit from those ships we could go into business for ourselves and you could retire."

He counted eight ships and had heard that within them were more than a thousand men, filling their bellies daily, and flushing all that potential profit into the bay. No ambition? Who did Momo think he was?

His father nodded, but was so accustomed to Manzo's ramblings that he hadn't really listened very well. Rather, he had been musing on what had happened earlier and said, "You know, the more I think about it the more I worry that I should not have let your brother go with those men. We all knew perfectly well they were masterless, I must be getting old."

He spoke softly, and glanced at the closer, sleeping samurai, to make sure he hadn't awakened them. He looked out at the ships again, touching Manzo's shoulder.

"So much change is taxing," he said. "Our way of life will be over before we know it."

But though soldiers might sleep through such nearby peasant chatter, even drunks like the ones Ueno had hired woke quickly to the sounds of horses' hooves, and the *slap-slap-slap* of a barefooted runner. Manzo and his father heard it too, but didn't look to see what was making the clatter until half of Ueno's soldiers were standing, belching and sheltering their eyes. It was Momo, of course, the furious and filthy riders almost upon him.

"Damn you, peasant scum," one of them yelled, but by then Ueno's men had recognized their prey.

"Well, well," said their leader, "what do you know?" and as Manzo stood out in the road, ready to roll under the hooves of horses if he had to, to save his brother, the soldiers pulled their swords and spread themselves out, like the floats on a net.

"Hurry up Momo!" screamed the father, and he grabbed Manzo's sleeve saying, "Let's go this way!"

The beach bulkhead was high, but the father jumped upon it with ease, pulling Manzo up beside him as if he were a child. "Now let him see us," he ordered. "Wave your hands, Manzo! The tide is in, so let's get ready to dive."

"Over here Momo!" bellowed Manzo.

His voice rose above those of the others like rolls of rumbling thunder, but twice more it seemed the riders would catch Momo, killing him with easy swings of their swords.

"Momo! Momo!" their father yelled.

It was difficult to tell whether the riders saw Ueno's men or not, so intent were they on running Momo down, but Momo saw them, and darted past their waiting swords like a bait fish, to leap over the bulkhead and into the frothing sea, in the arms of his brother and father.

"Swim for your lives!" screamed Manzo, but in a moment they were wading away, in only about three feet of water, while behind them they could hear shouts of joy.

"Tie their hands, men! That's right, bind them up! What do you know? We've actually caught them, just as the master ordered! What in the world do you know?"

The leader had placards, which, through all these recent days of searching, he had somehow remembered to keep on his horse, and when the captives were sufficiently bound he placed one on each of them.

"75" and "111," the placards said.

As they moved out of town toward the inn where Ueno stayed, it didn't seem to matter to anyone that the placards were reversed, each on the wrong man's neck.

42. | *The Omen of the Crows*

FOR LORD OKUBO'S ENTOURAGE—with the notable exception of Ned and O-bata—things were getting worse, not better, by the time they arrived in Shimoda later that same morning. During the eight days since Einosuke's death they had found that they were unable to easily speak to each other or eat together, unable to do anything save follow the Buddhist prescripts concerning Einosuke's burial, fall into the bottomless pits of their broken hearts, and prepare their swords for battle. From the moment after Lord Okubo put his seal on his note to Ueno, in fact, he and Manjiro had found it difficult even to bear the sight of each other's faces. Manjiro continued to blame himself, in long and crazy prayers to his ancestors, and Lord Okubo, in order to avoid another trip to his secret room until revenge was done, blamed Manjiro, also, and took to having rambling conversations with his two already dead sons, Toshiro and Einosuke, alone at the beach where Einosuke had lost his head.

Generally speaking the women fared better, for they could deal with the men, if not very well with each other. Fumiko, for example, would allow herself to be summoned by her father-in-law, but she would broach no contact with Tsune, except through the door of the room that she shared with Masako and Junichiro. All she could manage was to care for her infant son, placing him before her on the tatami and trying to teach him to speak by repeating the word she most wanted him to utter first, and to remember forever: *"Tochan, tochan, tochan.* Daddy, daddy, daddy. Father, father, father."

"Say it!" she commanded, and when he wouldn't do it she said it herself, trading two syllables for four, and crying them out the window into the rain: *"Einosuke! Einosuke! Einosuke!"* Oh, how could she have been such a despicable wife?

As for Keiko, she stayed outside from dawn until the guards called midnight each day, pacing the perimeter of her father's half-formed garden in her mourning clothes. She liked the feeling of the fabric against her skin and soon began dancing to the song in her head, *"Three tulips grow down by the river, red, yellow, and white. . . . Three tulips grew in a bed of a thousand, then one day a boat came by . . ."* Oh sadness! Oh sorrow!

Though they had drifted back a little toward civility by the time they arrived at the Kanaya Inn, up the Inozawa River from Shimoda, they were each still clinging to the ruin of their lives by the fringes of an unraveling madness, with revenge the medicine that kept them each alive.

———

THAT IS HOW THINGS stood when Keiki, Kyuzo, and Ichiro, burdened by three horrid hangovers, but enlivened with the news of Einosuke's murderers' capture, which was all over town, came upon Lord Okubo in the inn's side garden late on the afternoon of the family's arrival.

"Where is Manjiro?" asked Keiki. "Where is young Kambei of the posters?"

Keiki held the misplaced belief that news of the capture, combined with his father's betrothal note, would mend just about everything, while Kyuzo, who had been given the note when he and Ichiro awakened Keiki a few hours earlier, wanted to put it on hold for a while and immediately discuss a battle strategy with Lord Okubo.

The old lord, however, was not alone in the garden. Keiko and Masako were with him, their stricken faces cast toward the ground. So the men had to pause, adjusting their ill-timed sense that things would now go well. No one, in fact, even bothered to answer Keiki's question, save Junichiro, who wobbled out from between his sisters, peered up into Keiki's face, then turned and laughed and ran back toward Masako.

"He gets tired so easily," she said. "Once I wouldn't let him stop walking for an hour and a half."

She said it as if it were a confession. She seemed to have no idea to whom she was addressing her comments, and Lord Okubo, too, disheveled and unbathed, only turned toward Kyuzo and croaked, "They wouldn't stay in Odawara when I asked them to. All of our women insisted on coming here, even Fumiko. And these two won't stay away from me now."

He had a teacup in his hands and when he gestured toward his granddaughters tea spilled out of it. A litter of skinny white kittens had just come from beneath a nearby shrub, but they ran back under it when the tea landed on the path.

"Show everyone to their rooms," Lord Okubo told Keiki, whom he had mistaken for the innkeeper. "And you, Kyuzo, tell me what you've discovered of our enemy."

He tried to stop squinting but his head shook on his neck. He put one hand upon his forehead, the other one up to tell Kyuzo to wait until Keiki and his grandchildren, and Ichiro too, had gone inside. For his part, though, Keiki was disappointed at his reception; his father's representative was usually treated more civilly, but he wanted to find Tsune anyway, so he could get some medicine for his headache, and begin to feel at home.

"Ueno is settled at a nearby inn," Kyuzo said when they were alone. "We heard that he caught the renegades this morning."

"We heard it, too," said Lord Okubo. "A runner has come to say he will bring them here tonight. Do I look unready for battle? I think I look unready. Maybe I should rest again and bathe."

At the nearest end of the garden there was a bench under a trellis, where Kyuzo led Lord Okubo so they could both sit down. Lord Okubo put his teacup in the dirt between his feet and bent forward to peer into the small amount of tea that remained. Kyuzo thought they would sit there like that for a good long moment, that like himself, Lord Okubo believed in the silent communion of men before discussing the details of a battle, so he was a little bit startled when Lord Okubo spoke.

"You are strong, Kyuzo, a famous warrior, but do you think you could go on living after the death of a son? Tell me honestly, I don't want platitudes. Do you have that kind of strength? Most men do not."

He didn't look at Kyuzo but kept trying to find his reflection in his cup.

Kyuzo sat forward, too, in order to gaze at his still-painful toe, its foreign-made wrapping still somehow clinging to it.

"I have enough trouble going on living even as it is," he said. He regretted the answer immediately and began again. "It's true that I am strong, I guess, if you define the word narrowly, but my kind of strength is so old-fashioned that during these times of rampant change it begins to seem a great deal more like weakness."

He was thinking of his talk on intransigence the previous evening, but decided not to mention it to Lord Okubo.

Two large crows flew into the garden, landing in a tree about halfway between the men and the reemerged kittens. Lord Okubo nodded and said, "Change is the real issue, isn't it? If a man lives long enough he is sure to lose everyone, so maybe it's a kind of false grief, to overly mourn the passing of a son."

Kyuzo loved a philosophical discussion as much as anyone. He knew Confucian doctrine and Zen parables, and had memorized dozens of poems, but when he looked at this wounded old man he understood that this was not a time for philosophy.

"Those crows," he said, "do you know why they have come?"

When he spoke the crows seemed to turn on their perches, looking at him out of crooked heads, just like Lord Okubo.

"To pluck at the carrion like all thieving scavengers!" shouted the lord. "To reap those benefits which should rightly go to others!"

His answer made him furious again, and he hissed at the unperturbed crows.

"Often so," Kyuzo calmly admitted, "but that is not why they are here just now. They have come, as creatures will, because of the easy pickings. Soon they will fall out of that tree and snatch up one of those kittens."

He pointed up the path and gave a dark chuckle. "It is nature turned on its head, for most of the time cats eat birds, that's why I think it's interesting."

Kyuzo truly did feel sympathy for Lord Okubo. He believed that having a son and losing him was a far worse fate to suffer than his own sad circumstance of never having been a father. So he decided to stop talking about the crows and wait for Manjiro to join them, before turning to what their posture ought to be against Ueno that night. He looked when he heard the doors opening behind them, as if his thoughts might have brought out Manjiro, but it was only a couple of maids, carrying futon.

Lord Okubo spoke quietly, repeating his refrain about needing to rest and bathe. "What you see before you will subside, I think, if I can only sleep for a few hours. During this last week I've done nothing at night save wander the halls of my castle. And I've spent my days like the man who suddenly discovers that his country is an island, and stands at the edge of the promontory, blaming the ocean."

He did not take his eyes off the crows as he spoke, but his words sounded somewhat sane again and relieved Kyuzo, who turned to dig into the bottom of his satchel.

"I don't often mention this," he whispered, "but fighting insomnia has been the longest-running battle of my life. I always carry a number of excellent potions. Take one."

He turned back toward the lord and opened a folded paper, revealing two large mounds of white powder, neatly separated by a thin bamboo divider.

"Either will work," he said, "and they have never failed to make me sleep when I take a small amount of both."

The smaller of the crows was eyeing them, while the larger had fallen to the ground about ten feet away from the kittens. Kyuzo kept a steady hand while Lord Okubo reached down to get his teacup. He surprised Kyuzo greatly, however, by pouring all of his powder into the remaining half-inch of tea, swirling it twice, and drinking it down. Had there been time, Kyuzo would have told him that on each side of his bamboo divider there was a three-night supply, but as it was he kept quiet.

Lord Okubo wiped his mouth and stood, silently advancing on the crows, the teacup tucked into the palm of his hand like a stone. The crow that remained in the tree watched him curiously, but the other one began advancing on the unwary kittens, every bit as single-minded as Lord Okubo. Kyuzo got up and slipped his short sword from its scabbard. They could both hear the maids behind them, beating the futon.

"You take the high one," said the lord, "I'll get the impudent little bastard on the ground."

Absurd as it was, both men felt that this was an ominous moment, a rehearsal for the evening to come, and full of portent. The odds were against them now, just as they probably would be tonight, and trickery played a role.

Lord Okubo walked away, careful to rotate his teacup in a manner that would make the crow in the tree continue to watch it, while Kyuzo judged the branch on which it sat to be about eight feet off the ground. The other crow had chosen an angle that mirrored Lord Okubo's, and, with an equal amount of nonchalance, advanced upon the kittens, all the time looking somewhere else.

Kyuzo knew the key was in the treed crow. His plan was to appear to be passing beneath the tree and then to fling his sword upward, aiming at its feet. In his youth he had performed similar tricks, in games with other samurai, but now he not only worried about his diminished speed, but also about the available arc in his progressively arthritic shoulder. Had young Ichiro stayed outside, he grimly realized, he would have served Lord Okubo's purposes far better. Kyuzo kept his eyes on the lord, hoping for a signal, but when the inn's doors opened again and Keiki came back out, he acted on his own, leaping toward the tree and flinging his sword upward with such vigor that he nearly released it into the sky. He jumped higher than he had in two decades, turned his sword in midair, and sped it along the barren tree branch toward the crow. The crow's beak fell open, but it sprang into flight an instant too late, and paid a price for its slowness, by leaving its legs and feet behind. They clung to the branch for a second, then swung around in opposite directions to dangle and fall like a fortune-teller's sticks, landing with implicit softness on the ground.

The second crow, still watching everything, easily dodged the teacup, which Lord Okubo had thrown at the instant of Kyuzo's attack, but Keiki's gasp, and subsequent dash into the yard, so confused the second crow that it lost its sense of the best escape route. It couldn't fly straight up because there were branches above its head, so it hopped and then flew toward the kittens in the grass. Lord Okubo chased it, fearful beyond reason that it might still grab a kitten as it passed, when the mother cat, whom no one had noticed, leapt from nowhere, extended her long front claws, and pulled the ascending crow back down. She tore into it quickly, breaking its neck with her jaws and tearing its nearest wing in half.

Lord Okubo stopped and looked about him, first at Keiki, then at Kyuzo, who had come down badly and reinjured his toe, but when Keiki took his arm and walked him over to the dead crow he felt little exultation, little save those triple doses of two sleeping powders, which were pulsing through his bloodstream by then, like six tired men in a boat.

"It will be fine," he told Lord Tokugawa's son. "After all it will be Ueno, not us, who will succumb." He yawned and asked, "Is our appointment not set for six o'clock?"

"It is, sir," said Keiki, who had heard as much inside.

This was the beginning of a speech he had prepared about his willingness to do anything in his power to help, but Lord Okubo, who still thought he was the innkeeper, stopped him.

"Six is too early," he said. "Wake me at six, but send a runner to reschedule. Make our appointment for eight and, come to think of it, do not awaken me until seven."

Keiki might have set the record straight, saying that he was not the innkeeper, but a cautionary glance from Kyuzo made him hold his tongue. Lord Okubo still looked horrible, red-eyed and unbathed, but otherwise it was as if he had been exorcised, saved from his continued downward spiral for another moment, at least, by their surprising victory over the crows.

"What do you think is the proper order," he asked Keiki, "to bathe before sleeping or to sleep before taking one's bath? I had a running argument about that question, years ago, with my wife."

"Bathe before sleeping," Keiki said, taking the old lord's arm. "It is the only way you can truly enjoy both."

As they walked past Kyuzo, however, who was on the bench again rewrapping his toe, Lord Okubo said, "I think I will sleep first, and rid myself of this stench when I wake up."

When they were gone Kyuzo stood and slapped the dust from his clothing and tried to find the crow's legs on the ground. He believed in omens and, though he was as happy with the victory over the crows as Lord Okubo, felt sure that he would be able to read a further hidden message in the way the legs had configured themselves.

The legs were easy to find, but when he bent to examine them he saw that they looked like nothing so much as the scattered twigs that surrounded them, the feet at their ends already atrophied, toes curled up like withered leaves, with no message in them at all.

He didn't like that and stood again, ready to join the others. But to satisfy himself that the storm, at least, would not return for a while, he glanced up at the late afternoon sky. And there he saw that first crow again, wings spread wide, staring down at him and circling, now and forever trapped in flight. Never mind the feet and legs, here was his message, his omen: that soon those circling about him, winding more deeply into anger and grief and revenge, were going to have to find a way to land.

Who knew whether there was more truth in this omen of the crows, or in Ueno's experience with the river trout?

43. *I Have Not, Particularly, Saved Myself*

"DO YOU KNOW the Bunraku puppet story *Shinju, ten no Ami-jima?*" Tsune asked Manjiro. "The one where the lovers die at the end, lying head to toe on the floor of the forest? You must remember it. The woman's hair is spread out like a fan."

They were in an upstairs room of the inn, where they had been since their arrival, unavailable even to someone like Keiki, and two doors away from the now soundly sleeping Lord Okubo. There was a low table between them, empty but for two upside down teacups. Tsune was in earnest and had mentioned the famous double suicide drama because implicit in her question was an offer. Manjiro, however, was put off by it. He knew Keiki was in the inn, knew they must both go speak with him sooner or later, but more than that, did she think she could cajole him by this tactic, make him reconsider the manner in which he would fulfill his obligations, by threatening to join him in his death? His love for her had blinded him before, but no longer.

"That was a play," he said, "and the players only puppets. There wasn't any real blood, and no danger, I think, to the lives of the puppeteers."

Tsune, herself a puppeteer of inordinate capabilities, had insisted after a week of silent suffering that she be allowed to hear directly from him whatever he had to say concerning her own culpability in the death of his brother. That was why she had come to his room and now, as she tried to delve into the deepest intentions of his heart, he was cold toward her.

She placed her fingers upon the nearest teacup and said, "Of course you know that responsibility for Einosuke's death rests first with those who killed him."

"Yes," he answered, "and they will pay first. Soon, if we are lucky."

"But who will pay second, Manjiro?" she asked. "And who will pay third and fourth? Who will go on paying? Don't you understand that that, ultimately, is the more important question?"

That Tsune grieved for Einosuke, that she had poured that grief into daily letters to Keiki and entreaties for an earlier audience with Manjiro, was clear to all who wished to see it, but Manjiro could no longer count himself among that number. Yet neither, in the innermost chambers of his heart, did he blame her very much—if that's what she thought she was wrong. He blamed himself; for his caprice, for his multitude of mistakes, his terminal and interminable weakness.

"No," he finally said, "I think who pays second is of little importance . . ."

He gave her a regretful smile but found it impossible to say more. That he had always loved her he would make clear, he decided, in his suicide note.

"Please, Manjiro, think about how it will sit with others when this revenge of yours is done. Have you thought about what your father might do? Or your nieces and nephew, or my poor sister, your bereft and noble sister-in-law? Have you thought how things might be with her a year or two from now?"

Indeed he had, and concerning his father, though he wouldn't say it, he felt there was no longer any danger of him ending his life prematurely, before his inevitable descent into senility and old age. At the moment of his father's discovery that he, Manjiro, had defied Lord Abe and taken the Americans out of Edo, there had been such a danger, but now he believed it had passed. So far as his nieces were concerned he thought that time would heal them, and he had particularly considered the ironic fact that Junichiro, the toddling next Lord Okubo, would not remember his father or his ineffectual uncle at all.

"I do worry about Fumiko," he admitted, "for she is the best person I know. But in the end I think she will find solace in her children, in her coming grandchildren, and in remembering the good husband she once had."

Tsune shook her head, finally moving her hand from the overturned teacup to his arm. "She will not find solace in them, Manjiro, that is not the word you want, but will understand her responsibility to all of those you have mentioned, and see that responsibility to its end. She will find new strength. She will surprise you by how well she regains herself."

Manjiro pursed his lips but would not be drawn into further discussions of Fumiko, the thought of whom still moved him to a greater despair than he could handle. He profoundly understood his own responsibility and was resolved to see it through, yet he also remembered Tsune's great facility with reason and argument. If she was telling him that Fumiko would soon be focused upon her children once again, that was right and proper. But he didn't want her telling him anything about himself.

He remained silent, at first thinking only how he might greet Keiki, apologize to both of the Americans for appearing to have turned on them, then go off, alone, to prepare himself, when her hand upon his arm began to move and stroke, an unfair strategy to use against one who had adored her since he was a boy. That a man at the end of his life should be buoyed by something beyond physical desire was as clear to him as the indisputable fact that Einosuke's death had been his fault, yet despite that clarity, and despite his sense of shame, he could feel his ardor rising.

Tsune felt it too, and deftly made it the subject of their talk.

"How I had hoped there might be something permanent between us," she said. "Lord Tokugawa hoped so, too, you know, that was the real reason I took you to his hunting lodge that day, so that he could see for himself how fine you are. Those paragraphs were my excuse, that's certainly true, but their bearer was the target. When all this trouble began he was about to write a letter to your father, and Keiki, I have reason to believe, has brought a similar letter now. Oh, Manjiro! If we can only look upon Einosuke's death as the act of unruly criminals and go on."

Manjiro had one hand free that he let fall upon hers, which had not ceased stroking his arm. She turned her hand over and, grasping his wrist, pulled him slightly toward her. She only meant to speak again, to save his life through unending stealthy argument, but this time the words she spoke were not the ones she had chosen. "I am not a virgin," she said. "Lord Tokugawa's letter will admit as much, I'm sure, but I have not, particularly, saved myself."

There was a pause, a fleeting sense of things reordered, before, though her pull remained slight, he came to her as if it were insistent. She used her free arm, first to brace herself against the tatami, then to encircle his neck, thus, as she had always been able to do with words, both resisting him and pulling him down upon her at the same time.

Manjiro thought to protest as entirely too unbearable that his heart's greatest wish should be granted only now, when the last bits of sand leaked from his hourglass, and he did try to rise above it for a moment, like a phoenix from the ashes. But when he opened his mouth to speak, all such thoughts were gone, leaving only the singular idea that there was no sight more beautiful on this failing earth than that of Tsune's legs, bent at the knees and turning darkness into light, coming through the seams of her kimono and slowly parting.

Sex and grief! Oh, it was strange! What could they possibly have in common?

———

LIKE A PHOENIX from the ashes? He had learned the myth from his tutor, but was he capable of such a foreign leaning on this, the last day of his life?

She was both the most modern, the freest of women, and at the same time a throwback to another era, to the days of Prince Genji, when courtiers visited noblewomen at night or delivered, through diaphanous curtains, poems inscribed upon fans.

> Come a bit nearer please.
> That you might know.
> Whose was the evening face
> So dim in the twilight.

Such were the lines that Manjiro remembered, the lines that seemed to capture Tsune for him as he sat watching her sleep, some ninety minutes later. He had dressed again and was about to leave to find Keiki. He had continued his fast from food, at least, and had ordered his swords resharpened. He'd intended to spend these last few hours before Ueno's arrival in seclusion and meditation, but instead all he truly wanted to do was sit where he was and watch Tsune. He reached out to pull her blanket into place, a universal gesture, but even if he survived this night he was too weak a man, he finally knew, to ever survive a life with Tsune as his wife. That it was she who had fueled his dreams when his studies forged a path through Western thought, he had always considered ironic, but now he understood that she could find her way in uncharted lands far better than he, that she might one day lie like this, sated and sleeping beside a Shogun, or even a conqueror, who in turn would sit in the muddle of his manliness, unaware that he was the one who had been unalterably conquered.

Manjiro wanted to extract himself, to expel her with a great loud sigh, reciting the names of the great men from whom he had learned—Tu Fu, Murasaki, Bashó, Shakespeare, Goethe, even Niccolò—but none could find a seat at the center of his thoughts so long as Tsune's bare shoulder refused the enticement of her covers.

He could laugh at himself, for this one moment free of that inevitable tide-pull, but he could not perform the simple act of going to speak with Keiki, without also knowing that if blood still pumped through his veins by morning, it would pump for Tsune alone.

44. | *Life Is Short. Fall in Love*

THOUGH SHE'D BEEN SITTING at the edge of a first floor garden room, absently watching the arrival of Keiki and Kyuzo and the young man whose eyes rarely left Keiko—and watching, also, her father-in-law's eccentric battle with the crows—as darkness descended upon the inn Fumiko suddenly stood and shook herself out of her listlessness, and went out into the hallway, to try and find relief by giving away little bits of Einosuke, a few of his personal belongings.

The floorboards felt good beneath her feet, smooth, like the passage of her life had been before the American arrival had sent them all to hell. He was down the hall from her now, that man whose face she had touched, whose cheek she had found herself touching at the instant of her good and loyal husband's beheading. Einosuke had been fighting for his life, with her and their children no doubt at the center of his thoughts, while she had allowed herself to loiter in some childhood fantasy, loaning her heart out to the strangest kind of stranger. And she would have pursued it, too! She would have continued! Had she not told him *we must be extra circumspect from now on?* Had she really spoken such words, or had she only thought them? She wondered if he knew what turmoil he had caused, how dramatically his arrival had altered everything for everyone. She would have asked him had she been able, she would have said in English, "Have you any idea what damage you have done?"

Ah, but it wasn't his fault, she knew whose fault it was! In all likelihood he'd been indifferent to her, even unaware of her existence before she made him walk along that forest path, before she lifted her horrid eyes to him and found enough deceit in her soul to push her hand out and touch him, and say the words she said! Oh, she could not stop thinking of how these same three fingers that she held in front of her now had reached up and felt the foreigner's blood pulsing beneath his skin just as some rogue's vile blade had severed Einosuke's head from his body, letting his own precious blood seep into the shoreline's dark sand. Oh, how hard her heart was, how hard and how cold, how much like the steel of that rogue's blade itself!

Fumiko stepped past the door to Ace's room, thinking to find a knife and cut her offending fingers from her hand and leave them there as a ghastly souvenir, but in fact the fingers of both her hands were holding things, objects that had once belonged to Einosuke, so she passed by Ace's room with her breath trapped inside of her and stopped instead at the room that caged O-bata and Ned. She hadn't the strength to question why she had so readily delivered her maid into the hands of this second American, when regret concerning her own despicable actions raged inside of her, and she didn't knock, lest the man next door hear it and come out to look at her. Rather she slid the door open unbidden and pushed that package of ginseng powder inside, the one Einosuke had bought from the Chinese herb man on the day he followed Lord Abe. If it had some power to increase the sexual appetite why not let it be for her already wanton maid, lest her already wanton self eat it all and die in the throes of her licentiousness?

She closed the door again and released the breath she'd been holding, and went upstairs as quickly as she could, trying to think of others, to dismiss her horrible self. In Lord Okubo's room, beside her father-in-law's snoring head, she placed one of Einosuke's earliest diaries, with poems of love and filial piety. Her husband's constancy was evident in them, his unity of purpose and mind. When the old man awakened and picked up the volume, it mattered not where he opened it, for Einosuke's devotion to him would fall out of any page.

She stopped at Manjiro's room last, not because she had little to give him, but because, almost as much as she feared seeing Ace, she feared seeing her sister, whom she knew to be in there, extolling Manjiro, courting him, warping his sense of everything until it matched her own. Oh, she and Tsune were born of the same rift fabric, formed from the same static mud, that was something she had denied for far too long! Her sister was more honest than she, though, for Tsune, at least, embraced her inborn selfishness, wrapping herself around it as if it were a mark of beauty and not a horrid scar.

Fumiko would have slipped her offerings inside this door, too, just like she had downstairs, but Manjiro flung the door open as she was kneeling before it, heading for the inn's shrine to say his prayers. He was surprised to see her and stood there speechless for a moment, before he asked, "Where is Keiki? I understand he has arrived."

"I believe he is downstairs," said Fumiko, her voice a hoarse whisper. "Perhaps he is taking advantage of this inn's famous bath." She had not truly spoken, she realized, since before they left Odawara, twelve hours earlier.

Manjiro was chagrined to have met his sister-in-law, for he was no more interested in intercourse with family members than she was. He would have left her as fast as she wanted to leave him, in fact, had Tsune's voice not come from inside the room, calling like a sorceress. "Won't you pause a moment, Fumiko? And let me ask a question?"

"I am only delivering gifts," Fumiko mumbled, "so he won't be forgotten so quickly as he otherwise might be."

To hear herself say such a thing made the gesture itself seem self-serving, and once more she tried to retreat. She would throw the gifts into the nearby river, and throw herself in after them!

"Please," said Tsune, in a calm and kind voice. "I've just been asking Manjiro something that neither of us can answer, but I know you can. Come in, my dear, sit beside me for a moment."

That Tsune was unclothed and huddled beneath a light blanket, behind the fully dressed Manjiro, did not bother Fumiko nearly so much as the prospect of once again being asked to have an opinion on anything at all. Let the fornicators take over the earth, she thought, the fornicators and the foreigners and those who could go blithely on. She felt her sorrow returning, and would have denied her sister's request by simply turning and going back down the stairs, had not Tsune, as had always been her practice about everything, gone ahead and asked her question without waiting for Fumiko's response.

"What would Einosuke's attitude have been were he about to avenge the murder of his own older brother? How would he have acted? What would he have done?"

Fumiko was stunned by Tsune's crudeness, by such a casual invocation of Einosuke's name, and the questions, all three of them, hit her like blows. If Tsune remembered that there had, in fact, been an older brother—Toshiro was his name—it didn't show in the manner in which she spoke. She only leaned against Manjiro, who had sat down beside her again, beautiful and naked and hoping for answers that would save him from the blows he intended, once he succeeded in dispatching Ueno, to rain upon himself.

"I only wanted to leave these trifles," murmured Fumiko. "There is nothing here of consequence, just an old comb he liked and this erotic little *netsuke* carving he sometimes got pleasure from wearing."

She let her hand open to release the gifts but only the comb fell out. The *netsuke* stuck to those three offending fingers, shaking slightly in her palm. She felt consumed with hopelessness coming here like this, but Manjiro cried when he saw the carving, for a time, at least, regaining himself. The *netsuke* depicted two lovers falling off an animal, some mythical bear or lion, their robes parted and their body parts stuck together, and continuing their coitus through a fine midair contortion. Einosuke, normally the most decorous of men, used to wear the little carving on the drawstrings of his pouch, hanging under his jacket, while he waited for an audience at the castle.

"He loved this so much!" Manjiro cried, energy surging back into his voice. "When he wore it he used to say he felt weighted down, for once in his life, by frivolity."

Fumiko let Manjiro pull the carving from her palm. She smiled. "It is true he had a frivolous side," she found herself saying. "He not only loved this carving, but was fonder of the act it depicts than you might imagine."

She looked at her sister as if to say that that, at least, was something Einosuke and Tsune had in common. She tried to put her own act in perspective. It was only a touch, after all, just three fingers gracing the contours of a face.

"I remember it, too," said Tsune. "But not from his drawstring. I remember it sat atop a box in a shop in Kyoto, displayed with great pride. Do you recall that day, Fumiko? The girls were still young. We were on a cherry blossom viewing trip and we had all had too much saké."

"Of course I recall it," said Fumiko. "That was when I bought it for him. That day or the very next morning."

"I will wear it tonight!" said Manjiro. "It is the best way I can think of to represent my brother's spirit while avenging his death!"

He spoke as if he had suddenly found the key to something, but since they all knew that by far the larger part of Einosuke's spirit had been somber it was a strange thing to say. Nevertheless, it served to lighten Fumiko's heart more than anything else had since her husband's death. Until that moment she had hoped to escape this room and the tyranny of her sister's cheerfulness as soon as possible, but now she picked up the comb again. It was made of wood but soft and broad at its base, with two dozen finely carved teeth, each perhaps five inches long.

"He used this less often than he might have," she said, "because he feared it would break." She bent the teeth of the comb and let them go, bent them and let them go, watching them spring back into place.

"One of my husband's blind spots was that he sometimes saw only the surfaces of things," she said, "believing strength was weakness and weakness strength."

Was that what had caused her to do what she'd done? Was that what had kept her separate from him all these years? She recognized that she had heard Kyuzo say something similar, not two hours earlier, when listening to him talking to Lord Okubo in the garden, and she had the thought that there were probably only a few real ideas in the world, and that they floated through the air like pollen.

Tsune took the comb and placed it next to the carving. The carving had a high sheen to it, an almost brilliant look, while the comb was dull, with a delicate inlaid pattern cutting easily through the wood. "Each serves its function," Tsune said. "And we should remember to be both soft and hard, to use all of the weapons at our disposal when we meet our enemy tonight. And let us hope that we are survived by more than artifacts in the morning."

There was a moment of reflection, while the sisters breathed evenly and Manjiro stared at them both, steeling himself again in his determination not to talk about survival, his own or anyone else's. They could all hear Lord Okubo coughing down the hall.

"Everything begins when he wakes up," said Fumiko. "There must be a start to these last difficulties which lie before us, if there is ever to be an end."

She stood to leave after that, but turned at the door, come back to herself enough by then to ask a question of her own.

"Did my husband have a way with words? I've been thinking of telling his daughters that he had a kind of eloquence about him, but perhaps he didn't, perhaps I am wrong."

She wanted to quote something Einosuke had said to her, to give them a way to judge, but in the end she could not come up with a single example and left before they could reply. She escaped down the hall and down the stairs, not stopping until she saw Keiko in front of her room, the constant patina of her sorrow making her look old.

And with that she did suddenly remember something of Einosuke's, not what he had said to her, but something he had written many years ago. It was a song lyric, of all things, scribbled after a night's hard drinking, and left for her to find on her pillow when she awoke:

Life is short,
fall in love, dear maiden,
While your lips are still red,
And before you are cold,
For there will be no tomorrow.

Life is short,
fall in love, dear maiden,
While your hair is still black,
And before your heart withers,
For today will not come again.

Was there eloquence in such lyrics? Could they be the gift she could give that might help her daughters now? Would her American recognize the sadness of them were she able to translate them for him, singing them into his ear?

Fumiko had made up a melody to which she sometimes put the words when she was alone in the Edo house, and she sang it as she descended the stairs now, deeply startling herself.

45. | *Strength and Flexibility*

THUS FAR, though a hint of yesterday's rain had returned, only a slight breeze connected the rooms of the inn. Nevertheless there may have been some sorcery in it, for while Fumiko sang her song on the stairway and Manjiro and Tsune examined the comb and carving upstairs, in their room outside the bath, with only the kitchen noises to guide them, Ned and O-bata tumbled about in a solemn imitation of the scene that the little *netsuke* carving depicted, for the third time since their arrival late that morning.

When Manjiro turned the *netsuke* to see, for example, how the carved woman's left leg so easily circled the carved man's neck while her right leg somehow also wrapped his thigh, O-bata pulled Ned into her with just such strength and flexibility. Ned's body, like that of the man in the carving, was perfectly rigid, save for one radically bent knee, and a foot which held O-bata's hips against him, long toes tapping lightly at her buttocks.

In the room upstairs there was silence now, and an energized stillness as Tsune and Manjiro listened to Fumiko's song, while in the room below, Ned's eyes, dark and round as plums upon a plate, searched O-bata's, his prosthesis resting on the table by their side.

Sex and grief. Oh, it was strange! What could they possibly have in common?

It was a question that Fumiko had been fearful of asking herself all along.

46. | *I Am Taking You Home*

IT WAS THEIR BEST and newest wagon, used for collecting human waste, to be sure, but exclusively from geisha houses, and for less than a month, all told. Manzo's job had been to clean it thoroughly, which he did three times, finally climbing all the way inside the wagon, to pluck away any last bits of debris with his fingers and rub the walls with lily petals. His seriousness and concentration were unrelenting. He lined its bottom with eucalyptus boughs, and decorated its exterior in a lighthearted but dignified way, with sprigs of various wildflowers from a hillside near their village, and a plethora of ancient Buddhist funeral flags, which he'd begged off an equally ancient monk at the nearby temple.

As for the pickle jar itself, when they'd first pulled it from its brown and liquid hiding place they had been sure it would contain something deeply and objectively valuable, like jewels or money or an outlawed foreign spice, and Manzo and Momo had immediately engaged in an argument as to whether or not to return it to its owner even before they tried to open it. "We should, we shouldn't. We must, we mustn't." They pushed and pulled at the question like loggers felling a giant forest pine, each emphatic in his opposition to the other's point of view. Until, that is, their father, in his wisdom, said, "First we will open it, then we will decide what to do."

Manzo worried that again their father would simply side with Momo, who, though clumsy with his fighting stick, was better with the weapon of words, but he nevertheless kicked at the jar while Momo threw rocks at it, following his father's instructions like the loyal son he was. They kept it up for fifteen minutes, then for thirty, but though the jar was cracked and leaking putrid fluid, the lid was so secure and it was otherwise so toughly made that they finally had to roll it into their shed and hit the sides of it with mallets. And only when that, too, did not readily work did Manzo judge it proper to say, "All right father, here's what I think. It is a sign that we should leave it as it is, if it doesn't come apart on the very next hit."

When he saw his father nod in acquiescence he gave the jar that hit himself, a roundhouse slam with a broken wagon axle. He hit it as hard as he could so his father wouldn't think he was shirking, and the pickle jar exploded, with shards of it slapping against the walls of their shed and the putrid liquid covering all three of them. They spit and stomped, yelling and gagging with their hands on their knees, but what was even worse was that the shed was built on a hill, with its open door on the downward side, and when Einosuke's head got free of the jar it rolled out that door and down the path toward their house and the forest and streams beyond it. It rolled with an energy that seemed to come from within, bounding over hillocks and dodging wagons and extra buckets, even dancing around the edges of their well, like a wagon on two wheels. It seemed to be rolling with both determination and malice, as if it was headed back to avenge itself, until it suddenly came to an abrupt and terrifying halt, not against a wall or a tree, but where nothing at all was in its way, atop their mother's vegetable garden. It spun for a second like it was trying to dig a hole, then turned so it was facing them, gasping once like it was out of breath.

The father and his sons saw all of this from the doorway of their shed, locked together in a fused collapse, like a statue of exhausted warriors after battle. But they pulled themselves apart and pulled themselves together, and approached the head cautiously, one at a time, their mallets at the ready, lest it begin to move again and attack them.

Einosuke's head was preserved fairly well, but with several thick tangles of hair hanging over his bleached-out eyes, and an expression on his face that equaled their own, save for the fact that Manzo and Momo were crying as they approached it, as they let the knowledge of what had just rolled out of their shed roll over them. But because he had seen Einosuke before, and because the story of his death had sped down the peninsula faster than those Kambei posters, the father knew immediately who was facing them and what it might mean to them in the long run. So he sent his sons away, telling them to go and practice acting like men, and sat in front of Einosuke for a very long time, looking at his face and thinking what to do about it. He had seen the way the head had a mind of its own, and he knew there was a message in it. But what that message was took him hours to decide.

———

THAT AFTERNOON the father built an entire outhouse floor, complete with a hole in its center and wood planks aligned to perfection, and nailed it to the top of their best wagon, which he had ordered Manzo to prepare. The wildflowers and Buddhist funeral flags had been Manzo's idea, the suggestion that Manzo should clean the inside of the wagon, too, had come from Momo.

Though the pickle jar had broken badly, most of its bottom third still formed a solid bowl, which the father filled with clean garden dirt and pushed down into the outhouse-floor hole. It fit there remarkably well, and after placing Einosuke's head on top of it, facing the wagon's front, he spent another hour straightening and combing Einosuke's hair, much as the older of the two outlaws had done. He thought it was a dignified and reasonable idea to take Einosuke back to Lord Okubo like this, for it now seemed as if he were hiding in the wagon and peeking out through its hole. That his eyes were missing was a problem that the father tried to solve by placing radishes in their sockets, and then removing them in favor of mushrooms, and then removing them in favor of nothing at all. The hard reality of a horrible death could not be softened with vegetables. That, at least, he was finally sure of.

During all these difficult preparations it had not been Momo's job to do anything save stop his crying, calm his shaking limbs, and clean himself at least as well as Manzo had cleaned their wagon, in a nearby creek. And once he was clean he was to dress in a set of armor, complete with an ancient bow and a single well-made arrow, that had been taken from a dead samurai's body two generation earlier by his great-grandfather. It would be his responsibility to actually return this piece of his son to Lord Okubo, and he had to look the part of a dignified pallbearer. In choosing Momo for this job, the father had recognized his younger son's desire to get out of the business they were in, and thought it might give him a nudge.

When everything was finally ready the father found an old sloping hat and used it to cover Einosuke's head, so as they made their way toward the inn in which the Okubo family was staying they would not draw a crowd. The idea of such a dignified passing was somewhat hindered, however, by Momo's incessant questions.

"Should I knock first and explain what I've brought," he asked, "or should I pull the wagon up to the inn and leave it there to be discovered after I'm gone?"

The latter had been his father's idea, the former his own, so he was addressing his brother, who was sweating as he pulled the wagon, alone in the halter at its front. Momo kept wrenching his samurai suit around so it fit him better, and moving his old bow and arrow from one hand to the other. He didn't have a sheaf for the arrow, and once or twice poked Manzo in the buttocks with it, causing the wagon to lurch. Their father walked pensively nearby, for the first time wondering if the entire venture might not be a mistake.

"Do you simply want to give it back or do you want credit for it?" asked Manzo.

He tried to speak without malice, though having been twice poked by that arrow certainly made him malicious. Momo, however, only sighed. "I don't want credit for anything, Manzo," he answered, "but if I leave it at the inn's door without comment, how are we to know if his lordship received it safely? And how will we ensure the return of our wagon?"

Since he was doing all the pulling, his own clothes already stained with unsightly sweat, Manzo finally did let a little of the spite he was feeling escape his mouth.

"Maybe Lord Okubo will hire you," he said. "Maybe he'll understand that you want to work your way out of one shitty business and into another. The future is bright for smart young men like you, Momo. Just smile and keep bowing, smile and keep bowing. That's as sure a path to the upper reaches of society as this one is to the inn's door."

He glared at Momo as he spoke but Momo was lost in the glory that his own imagination provided, and didn't hear a word his brother said, let alone his sarcasm. Oh, it was true, he would be heralded! Embraced by Lord Okubo, appreciated by the other family members, finally recognized for all of his fine qualities!

"I will knock and introduce myself, that's what I'll do," he said. "But I'll only stay a minute. I will present his son's head to him in the name of our father and bring back the wagon once the head is taken inside. I have even prepared a small speech I will make, but I will not take a reward. No reward is best, don't you think? Or maybe a small cup of saké, a little refreshing tea. I might even write my name down for them, so they'll know how to find me later on."

They had successfully escaped from the environs of their own village by then and were working the wagon along a rarely used valley path, struggling over hillocks and around rabbit holes, so they wouldn't have to pass through other hamlets on their way. It had already grown slightly dark, and though it wasn't raining yet, the bellies of the clouds above them were sagging.

The father had been listening to his sons and, with each exchange between them, accelerated his worry, quickly coming to the realization that, indeed, they were doing the wrong thing. They should have called the authorities immediately, before even opening the pickle jar, and he should have been the one to see how obvious a decision that was! Oh, what had made him act so boldly? What had made him think that a young lord's head, balanced precariously upon a shit wagon, bore a sense of regal passage? He had forgotten by then the way Einosuke's head had seemed to run from their shed as if it had legs . . . the way it turned and looked back at them.

"You may return what we are bringing and listen to the grieving lord," he finally told his younger son. "But Manzo will go with you and you will both come back as soon as politeness allows. Be humble, Son, don't be brazen. Represent us well. And do not speak at all unless you are asked a direct and unavoidable question."

He spoke as he always did, quietly and with measured tones, but his heart was full of dread. When Momo heard his words, however, he could not contain himself.

"Oh don't you worry, Father, I will!" he pledged. "I will represent us in the best possible manner. You'll see! And I swear it won't take long! Lord Okubo will be happy, I bet. Happy and appreciative! Oh yes he will, Father. To see his son again like this will surely bring his wounded heart joy!"

He didn't mind Manzo going with him because he believed he could make his brother stay back when the time came, far enough away to give him independence, yet close enough to hear the speech he had been practicing, and thus be able to tell their father how grand it was. He touched the hat that covered Einosuke's head and whispered, "Do not worry, sir, I am taking you home!"

Not long after that they entered a low grove of marshy pines where the ground was so soft that keeping the wagon level took all of their attention and they grew quiet for a while. Manzo pulled with all his strength, and their father pushed from the back, while Momo stayed with Einosuke's head, making sure it didn't roll off.

When they finally got the wagon on solid ground again it was easier than they expected it would be to get where they were going. So Momo began insisting that they slow way down, that they set a more funereal pace.

He didn't want to run into his new life quickly like this, but go into it with the proper decorum.

47. | *Knowable People*

THE INNKEEPER AND HIS WIFE had been up since dawn for several days running, as they always were when preparing for a visit from the Okubo family, and had grown so exhausted that when Keiki explained to them that Lord Okubo had mistaken him for the innkeeper and asked that a runner be sent to Ueno, putting off the meeting for a couple of hours, they not only thanked Keiki, laughing demurely, but began a long conversation with him about the difficulties of running an inn, about what could go wrong, and how pleasurable it was when things went right.

Keiki had brought young Ichiro with him when approaching the innkeeper—he had done so at Kyuzo's urging, to keep Ichiro away from Keiko while she was grieving—and both men were surprised to discover that it was an enjoyable thing, hearing about the inside workings of such a lovely inn as this one. Keiki liked it because he knew he had a great deal to learn about commerce if he was ever going to be an effective leader, and Ichiro remembered his father's parting words to him, that he should ensure his future by finding some sort of trade.

So since they had time on their hands before the beginning of the evening's troubles, and since neither of them were formally grieving, they decided to use that time not only to learn about inns, but also to help with the preparations. Keiki joined the innkeeper's wife while she lectured the maids, adding comments that made the maids blush, while Ichiro walked the halls behind the innkeeper as he checked to see that everything, everywhere, was in order. Keiki was good at talking to maids, his touch lightly humorous, while Ichiro truly did find the industry of the thing, the busyness of it, to be the perfect antidote to his last few months of self-doubt, worry, and unemployment. He found himself thinking that this was work with honor in it, work that would allow a man to sleep soundly at the end of the day, rather than stare at his empty palm before his face.

When the four of them paused under an archway on whose cross-beam hung the innkeeper's father's old samurai sword, Keiki told the man that he had been right to opt for commerce, giving up the warrior life some decade earlier, and though Ichiro agreed wholeheartedly, he also told the innkeeper that it was a fine-looking sword. Both Keiki and Ichiro knew that others might think it insensitive of them to enjoy these simple pleasures when the Okubo family was filled with wretchedness and rage, but in fact each man's character was such that he was not well equipped for moroseness. Both had faces that turned more easily into smiles than frowns, and personalities that wanted to get on with things.

"Having Lord Okubo and his family visit us is an honor that will be considerably diminished if there is a fight tonight," the innkeeper's wife chanced saying. She had wanted to say it to Lord Okubo himself but, of course, could not. And so as she grew more comfortable with him, she said it to young Ichiro. Neither she nor her husband were quite sure who Ichiro was, but assumed, correctly, that his rank was low.

The inn was composed of two right-angled sections, with elegant rooms upstairs, with balconies overlooking either the meandering Ino-zawa River or the garden where Lord Okubo and Kyuzo had defeated the crows. The inn's ground floor rooms were smaller, some, like those given to the Americans and O-bata, even cramped, but their great advantage was a closeness to the inn's best attraction: its *sen-nin furo,* its one-thousand-person bath.

"People laughed when we first built our bath," the innkeeper told both young men, "but they aren't laughing now."

They were standing in the bath's antechamber, and while he spoke his wife straightened the rows of straw clothing baskets, enlisting Keiki's assistance as she rearranged the stones and counterbalances of their modern new body-weight scale. And, indeed, the bath itself was larger and more elegant than any even Keiki had encountered before, almost as wide as the inn, with two long rectangular pools separated by a line of thick cedar logs. There was an outside section as well, surrounded by bamboo trees, stone Buddhas, lilies and chrysanthemums, all of it located above the largest confluence of hot springs on the entire peninsula. It was their masterpiece, this outside section, but the innkeeper and his wife were stopped from showing it to Keiki and Ichiro by the fact that the inside section was not empty, as they had expected it would be. Both of the foreigners sat in the tub near the anteroom door, bobbing like Ezo monkeys, with O-bata next to Ned and Kyuzo floating on his back, occasionally spouting water into the air like a whale.

For O-bata and Ned this was not the first time they had been in the bath together—due to the nearness of their room and the rigor of their recent activity they had bathed twice already—but it was the first time for Ace, who, embarrassed by such communal nudity, had submerged himself on the tub's far side without first washing. Ace's head rode above the water like Einosuke's did on that honey-bucket wagon, and in a certain way he was as out of things as Einosuke, too, as disconnected. He touched his face and looked at the others. His hand had been so constantly drawn to the spot where Fumiko's fingers had branded him that his cheek had become a little sore. At first he'd been perplexed by what she'd done, thinking he had run across some truly alien custom, but he had also been moved by an upsurge of feeling, a groundswell of emotion such as he'd never known before, and it unbalanced him as surely as if she'd struck him with a sword. He had looked for her that evening back in Odawara, to see if she might let it happen again, but had found her prone on the castle's floor, her body bent around such abject suffering that at first he'd thought she regretted what had happened between them. He hadn't shown himself, he'd only hidden and watched her, his desire welling up, until the others returned from procuring Ned's nose and he learned of her husband's murder.

Since then Ace had come to believe he was tied to Fumiko, anchored to her as surely as the American fleet was now anchored in Shimoda by something that had resided in both of them *before* he had come to Japan. Yet all he could do now was sit in his room or float in this tub, hindered as clearly as if she'd come to him and told him in English, by the knowledge that if he tried to go to her and declare himself, she would no longer welcome him at all.

When Keiki clapped his hands, delighted to have found them in the bath, and immediately sat down, and stuck his feet in the tub, Ace looked at him keenly, wondering if anyone connected to the family could possibly know of his feelings for Fumiko. Keiki, however, was staring directly at Ned.

"I hope you remember that we have met before," he said. "At that time, too, we were bathing. You gave me your wonderful mouth organ, your 'harmonium,' or whatever it's called, and I want you to know that I learned to play a tune or two before I left Edo. Maybe when this trouble passes you can give me a lesson. I would like that very much indeed. Great friendships have been based on less, you know."

Keiki smiled. He remembered how Ned's long nose had terrified him, giving the impression of a giant standing rat. But even so he was sorry to see that the ruined face he looked at now held little of its previous offense. It looked, in fact, like the face of a desecrated owl.

For his part, Ned understood that Keiki was trying to be friendly, and so he smiled back and said, "Guess you noticed I had me an accident." He'd been holding his prosthesis up in front of him and tried to lower it, to show Keiki what had happened. But O-bata stayed his hand. "No, you mustn't do that," she said. "Not everyone is as pleased with your wounds as I am just yet."

"What a half-baked idea a stick nose is," Keiki told Ichiro. "It not only doesn't make him look whole again, but it takes away the use of a hand!" He made sure to keep his eyes on Ned. "I heard about your misfortune and want you to know that my father and I feel a personal responsibility," he said. "Japan has far too many rogues these days, but we will see that justice is brought to those who did that to you. This very night, I hope."

He spread his hands out and tried to remember just how long it had been since he and his father had looked down upon these same two men, from the spy room of that geisha house. Three weeks? Four? Back then, though they had truly been appalled by Lord Abe's plan, they had thought of the Americans as mere curiosities, exotic to look at to be sure, but more like a couple of rare birds than men with natures and personalities. Yet when meeting Ned in his father's courtyard, and again now, with the damage that had been done to him so hideous to behold, Ned and the other man, too, suddenly seemed like people who were knowable. Something was cracking inside Keiki, and he smiled again. Foreigners were knowable people! He looked at Ichiro, and then at Kyuzo, but it was the other American who looked back at him. He sat slightly higher in the tub, and spoke in a quiet voice.

"A problem I've had all my life is that I've often affixed importance to something only to find out later I was wrong," he said. "I've looked for too much weight in things, wanted to give too much promise to a chance meeting, or a word heard out of context . . . or a touch. But I've never been able to rid myself of the idea that a man's life ought to mean something, and that its meaning would come clear to him if he remained steadfast in his waiting, if he was patient and could listen well enough for God's plan . . ."

Ace stopped. He didn't want to talk about God's plan, he wanted to talk about Fumiko. He wanted to ask what it meant in Japan for a woman to walk into the forest with a man, for a woman to look at him, and touch him, and speak to his heart. Still, they were all staring at him like they knew he wasn't quite done, so he added, "I thought this visit to Japan might mean something in my life, but I guess I was wrong."

The Japanese were all gripped by a fair amount of sadness. Kyuzo was so sure he had understood the sentiment behind Ace's words that it occurred to him that in speech, as with music, there was meaning in sound alone, and Ichiro, similarly, was thinking that melancholy was a universal trait. The innkeeper and his wife were miffed at having lost time alone with Keiki and Ichiro, and they were sad, too, but for a different reason; they knew they'd have to drain and scrub their tub once the foreigners were gone. Keiki alone would have spoken to Ace, if only to try out his theory that foreigners were knowable, but Ned croaked out another bit of gibberish, before he could think of something to say.

"Well, shoot, Ace," he said, "ain't you the unlucky one, though?"

This time his stick nose slipped down a notch or two, until everyone could clearly see the hole in his face. Even those who had seen it before turned away.

"I know it ain't exactly pretty," Ned said. "But you all listen to me. I've had mirrors at my disposal these past few days, so I know what I'm up against better'n anyone. Ace here always says that a man will know what his life's supposed to accomplish if he sits around listening for God to announce it to him, but I gotta tell you, that ain't true. A man's got to bear what burdens he gets. He can cry if he wants to yet in the end he better just keep on gettin' up every morning, since he ain't got no other choice. And if God's involved in what happened to me at all then

I figure I owe him a great big thank you, for though he took away my good looks he gave me somethin' better at the same time. He got my nose, I got O-bata, and so far as I'm concerned it's a fair exchange."

He hugged O-bata, to demonstrate what he was saying, and once again they all thought they had understood him. Ichiro and Kyuzo, who'd been there when he lost his nose, believed he was beseeching them to avenge him against their enemies that night, while Keiki believed with equal firmness that he was saying his nose was a small price to pay if the intricacies of the treaty between Japan and America could be worked out smoothly from then on.

And even Ace was more taken with watching Ned's lips and the various abstract expressions that the stick nose gave his face than with actually listening to Ned. In one way Ned looked to him like the pieces of a jigsaw puzzle, nose and mouth and eyes floating in various proximities to each other, while in another it seemed like Ned was removing, layer by intricate layer, a series of complicated masks, much like taking off his minstrel paint. It was strange, but the more Ace watched the weird configurations before him, the more he began to think of them as representations of himself instead of Ned. Whenever they had removed their stage makeup it had always been Ned who had quickly returned to himself, while Ace, no matter how hard he scrubbed his face, was always, always, still in disguise. He was the jigsaw puzzle, not the man who sat before him with a stick nose in front of his face. He was the man of a thousand faces—his father's, his music teacher's, Colonel Morgan's, Buford Holden's, as well as those of the myriad other characters he had created. And during those short periods of time when he hadn't had a stage to stand upon he had simply waited, taking other men's ideas as his own and gazing out to sea, whether on shipboard or at home with no water visible for miles. Until last week, that is, until Fumiko took him into the forest and touched his face.

So Ace brought as much contrivance to hearing Ned speak as the others did, and as with the others, he thought his own contrivance was profound.

48. | *Not Selling Chestnuts*

"I am Momo of Shimoda, come with salvaged plunder, to honor the Okubo family and the dead. I do it in the name of my father and brother and without the hope or desire of a reward."

Now that he had said his speech out loud it didn't sound so good to him anymore, and he looked at Manzo, to see what his brother thought. A fog had descended over the mountains and those pregnant clouds had opened up, yesterday's storm come back again, but there was noise in the air, too; the sounds of fireworks and the general clamor of celebration floating up the river from the harbor. The American fleet had come ashore. Oh it was a terrible thing to have to miss if Lord Okubo didn't offer him a job!

"If you want to know the truth I don't like 'salvaged plunder' very much," said Manzo. "A human head is what it is, right? So I think you should just say 'head' and be done with it. And I don't think you should go turning down a reward that's not been offered, Momo. If it was me I would say, 'Hello, sir, I'm bringing back your son's head.' That's all. Or if I was talkin' to the widow I'd say, 'Madam, I am bringing back your husband's head,' or to the brother I would say . . . But you get the picture, right? Keep it simple. And if you happen to meet his daughters first don't say anything at all."

It had taken them two long hours to creep along the darkened pathways, and they were stopped again, sitting and waiting for the appropriate moment to approach the inn, nervous and peering through the fog. The river was on their right, lined with a series of fish stalls and bars. Momo had insisted that they turn off the main road, where their father now waited for them, well before they reached the inn, go about halfway toward the river and far enough forward to be opposite the inn's main door. If he ruined this, if he wasn't timely or correct in his approach, if he failed to get Lord Okubo to see his valor . . . Well, a chance like this would simply never come again.

"I am Momo of Shimoda, come with salvaged plunder . . ."

Now that Manzo had criticized "salvaged plunder" Momo wanted to rethink his entire speech. He would not say "head" no matter what, he wasn't a hopeless bumpkin like his brother, but "salvaged plunder" truly did seem a little unclear, a little crude, even, he had to admit it now. But it was hard to think of anything to put in its place.

It was also hard to see much of anything from where they stood, but when he glanced at their gussied-up wagon now, it bothered him even more than the clumsiness of his speech, for it looked like nothing so much as one of those winter contraptions commonly used by roving tradesmen for roasting and selling chestnuts. The hat on Einosuke's head even resembled the ventilating hood at the top of a stovepipe, not dignified like they'd intended it to be, but garish and foolish at the same time. Oh, why hadn't he seen it before? He knew that his father had intended this contraption to honor Einosuke, but the more he thought about it the more it seemed likely that Lord Okubo might be offended by their mode of transporting this most essential part of his son back to him—before he had a chance to make any speech at all. What if they chased him away? What if they took out their swords and cut him up?

"I am Momo of Shimoda, come with ——, to honor the Okubo family and the dead."

Come with what? What could he say instead of "salvaged plunder"? And how could he avoid the awful possibility that they might think he was roasting and selling chestnuts himself? Oh, nothing sounded good anymore!

"I am Momo of Shimoda, a simple shit man, not selling chestnuts but returning something you have lost . . ."

He walked away from his brother until he could see neither the inn nor the fish stalls by the river, but external darkness did not give way to internal light, and his words still tripped over each other. It was strange because words had always before been Momo's ally, and for the first time since escaping the murderers that morning he got a sense of foreboding, as if an impure heart were clogging the words in his throat.

Oh, silence was the best! Speeches were no good to anyone at a time like this, his father had been right! He should simply push the wagon up to the inn and leave it there for them to find.

But how, then, would they ever get their wagon back?

All these questions! All this trouble! And no one save his brother, on whose opinion he could rely.

49. *Outraged Periods and Exclamation Points*

JUST INSIDE THE INN'S ENTRANCE stood a complex of three banquet rooms, the inn's best innovation, next to the bath. The first two rooms could be opened, as they were tonight, to form a large enough space for tables to be placed together for large dining parties, and the third room, smaller and more elegant than the others, was primarily meant for clandestine liaisons. It could be reached from the main hallway, but there was also a special panel leading to it from the back, perfect, the innkeeper liked to joke, for narrow escapes.

Lord Okubo had ordered places set in the smaller room for the women, so they could hide and listen to whatever might take place, and in the larger rooms a huge flower arrangement sat within the *tokunoma,* a simple three-branch combination, but with the middle branch springing halfway to the ceiling, making everyone in the inn feel that it, like the day they were all experiencing, was entirely too long.

But even with the longest of days, evening finally comes, and as this one fell to its dinner hour Tsune came down from upstairs, to join the others. She wore a black kimono with the slightest pattern of dark brown lines upon it, her face unpowdered and her eyes set solemnly for the night. Fumiko and Masako and Keiko awaited her in the hall. "Has Manjiro not returned yet from his prayers?" she asked. "Someone still needs to wake his father."

When no one replied she took Keiko's arm and looked with her niece toward the darkest end of the hall, where Keiki and Kyuzo, O-bata and Ichiro and the two Americans, were just then coming from the bath. When Kyuzo bowed toward Tsune, neck and shoulders loose within his kimono, Ace tried to follow his lead, smiling at Fumiko. Beneath the stairway Tsune had just descended was the passage that led to the smaller banquet room that Lord Okubo had ordered prepared for the women, and when they finally did see Manjiro, walking back from his meditation at the inn's shrine, Fumiko hurried all the women that way, not even looking toward Ace.

"Quickly now," she said. "O-bata, that means you, too. Let's go in and leave the men alone."

Tsune wanted a word with Keiki, one last chance to plead with him, to ask him to intervene concerning Manjiro's postbattle intention to kill himself, and she would have taken a final moment of communion with Kyuzo, too, to assure him of her love. When she saw her nieces hesitate, however, she first helped her sister guide them toward the hallway, and when she tried to retreat again, Fumiko would not let her pass.

"There is no more time for anything," she told her younger sister. "Do not invest yourself further, Tsune, let the men be men."

Whether or not it was a scolding, Tsune knew that to disobey her sister now would reorder everything between them. And so she turned and allowed herself to be herded behind O-bata, into that clandestine room.

When the women were gone from the hallway Manjiro, who had waited in the garden, came inside. He looked at Keiki for a moment, and at the other ready warriors by his side, and then he turned and spoke to the Americans.

"My life has been dedicated to knowing you," he said in English. "I took all my recent actions, full of mistakes as they were, only in order to return you safely to the ships from which you came. I thought I acted honorably, but I lost my way . . ."

He had more to say, words he had practiced at the shrine. He wanted to tell them that neither he nor his father had ever really intended to use them as pawns, that that had only been a ruse, something written in his father's letter to Ueno, to make him want to bring Einosuke's murderers to the inn this very night. He wanted to tell them that he knew without question that the subtleties of spirit which resided in all good men, resided in both of them, that he had seen it in Ace when first receiving the chocolates, and in Ned in his recent and most stunning bravery, the dignified way in which he confronted his injury. He had even planned on slipping into metaphor for a moment, saying he had "brought them onto a path he thought he knew well, but led them into a great unknown forest"—but in fact he thought better of it, for the good quality of the English he had used thus far gave him an extra reason to grieve, in the sudden understanding that when he finally put a blade to his belly, all those unending hours of study would spill out.

So though he would have plunged ahead heedlessly in earlier days, to make himself clear through constant explanation, now he only bowed, turning his mind to the other question he had prayed about at the shrine: not whether to kill himself, but whether or not to go back upstairs and wake his father.

He would not. He would let his father sleep and awaken to an accomplished fate.

The innkeeper's wife had been playing her *koto* in the larger banquet rooms this last little while, sitting beneath that mammoth flower arrangement, but when everyone heard what could only be Ueno's arrival at the inn's front door she stopped. And a few seconds later the innkeeper came to tell them that their guests had arrived.

"I will end it quickly and alone," Manjiro told the others, "so be ready to move out of the way."

His plan, he thought, was simple. He would kill Einosuke's murderers as soon as they were made known to him, kill Ueno, too, if he got the chance, then run back to the shrine and kill himself. He believed that by acting alone he would absolve his father, and when his father finally awoke to find everything done, coerce him into carrying on. Kyuzo and Ichiro were to fend off any soldiers that might intervene, but otherwise were under orders not to act at all.

The door was shaking when they walked toward it, the impatience of their visitor evident in its rattle.

"Hello?" Ueno called. "It's raining out here. Someone open up!"

They were simple words, really, however plaintively spoken, but a strong sense of Einosuke came to Manjiro when he heard them, a renewed knowledge of how his brother, though always bemoaning Manjiro's free and scholarly life, had in truth protected him, taking the mundane family duties upon himself. He felt sorry that he could offer only this, the death of his killers, when he should have thanked Einosuke, shown him greater deference when he was alive!

"You do it," he told the innkeeper. "Open the door quickly and get out of the way." He let his breath settle deep in his abdomen, and stood there waiting.

For the innkeeper, however, though Manjiro's orders were certainly clear enough, there was a problem in complying, for he didn't feel he could be duplicitous and welcome someone to his inn at the same time. He didn't like it, he would never have sided with Ueno under normal circumstances, but an innkeeper's responsibilities to his guests were as unambiguous as a samurai's to his lord, so neither could he bring himself to commit a direct betrayal. It simply went against the innkeeper's code.

He looked briefly at Kyuzo and Ichiro, feeling sure from his walk around the inn with them that they would understand, and then, though he did open the door, he did not get out of the way.

"Good evening, sir," he said. "How many will be joining Lord Okubo's representatives in our banquet room tonight?"

"Joining them?" barked Ueno. "I don't intend to join anyone. I want to make this exchange and go. Why would anyone want to continue this pathetic charade?"

That *Ueno* had wanted to continue it, had been unable to quit his mad scheme, even after Lord Abe's censure, was what Lord Okubo had relied on in his note.

As much as it blocked Manjiro's view of his sworn enemy, the innkeeper's body blocked Ueno's view, also, so he didn't know anyone else had heard his rude comments until Manjiro said, "A charade is not pathetic, sir, if it achieves its end. Was that not the central lesson of those paragraphs your disgraced Lord Abe liked so much?"

The innkeeper tried to move then, since his goal had been to inhibit violence, not communication, but in his irritation with Manjiro's words—"disgraced" and Lord Abe's name in the same sentence!—Ueno took his short sword out of its scabbard and prodded the innkeeper with it. He hadn't meant to do it, he'd intended, in fact, to pull the entire scabbard from his belt, only giving the innkeeper a humiliating nudge, but his sword's proper scabbard had been ruined in the trout stream that morning and the one he'd borrowed from his aide was too large. As a result he pulled out the sword itself and poked a three-inch hole in the innkeeper's side. It was as wide and deep a cut as a short sword could make. So much for the omen of the trout.

The innkeeper didn't yell. At first, in fact, he only looked around behind him in surprise. But then he sat down on the top step of his entryway and said very quietly, "There is likely to be a mess here soon. Someone get my wife."

It was a restrained and dignified response, very much in keeping with that innkeeper's code but punctuated, as he'd predicted, by drops of blood that plopped upon the floor around him like outraged periods and exclamation points.

"My poor sir," said Keiki, quickly coming forward, and then to Ueno he said, "Stand back away from him, fool, look what you have done! Can't you even knock on someone's door without causing grievous insult?!"

"You again!" Ueno hissed. "The impudent and untried heir! Don't you know when to shut up?"

A fight between Ueno and Keiki, of all people, was most unacceptable to Manjiro. He would do the cutting if cutting was to be done. But when the innkeeper slumped against the nearest wall and Ichiro came over with his wife, the idea of anyone fighting just then had to be put off, unacceptable or not. Tsune ran from the secret women's room with towels, and O-bata came too, and grabbed a big bottle of saké, bringing it over as a cleansing agent.

Manjiro was at a loss, staring first at the innkeeper's wound, then at the tip of Ueno's short sword, while the wounded man's wife held her husband's head against her breasts. "There really is a lot of blood here," she said. "Someone better get the doctor, he's just a couple of doors down the street."

Most of the others had come forward by then, too, to see what they might do to help. "It don't look like he's in pain," Ned said, "just like me with my nose," but when Tsune pulled her pen knife from her *obi* and slit open the innkeeper's kimono, everyone was shocked by what she revealed. The wound was far worse than they'd expected, a deep and yawning thing that opened and shut like the blood-filled mouth of a landed fish, each time the innkeeper took a breath.

When his wife saw the extent of her husband's injury she turned to Ueno and said, "Do me a favor, sir, and leave our inn right now." Her husband's inherent dignity, it seemed, had been somehow transferred to her.

There was, after all, only one man standing behind Ueno, not the three Manjiro had expected, so though he still touched his sword he couldn't bring himself to use it yet, not with the innkeeper sorely wounded and without first finding all of Einosuke's murderers, plus his missing head. It would have been easy to kill Ueno, though, for when he bent to examine the wound he had inflicted, his neck and chest were exposed.

It was an impossible moment for Manjiro, everyone in motion now and all his sense of drama depleted, but when Tsune got the innkeeper to his feet again there was really nothing he could do but forget his own agenda for a while and help carry the poor man back inside, however unwieldy his heart was in his chest.

"Let's lay him on the banquet table," said his wife. "Someone clear it off."

Fumiko pushed the food out of the way, while Keiki got a cushion and placed it under the innkeeper's head. Keiko had come out by then, too, and tried to help by keeping the blood in check with towels. But it leaked out to cover her hands, and flowed down her forearms to drip onto the tatami from her elbows.

"What about the doctor," the innkeeper's wife said again, "has anyone gone for him yet?"

Ichiro had left a moment earlier, but not for the doctor. Rather, he had gone to fetch the innkeeper's father's ancient samurai sword, pulling it from that crossbeam down the hall. He brought it back and laid it next to the wounded man's face, thinking it might remind him of his family's long tradition and give him strength. He told the innkeeper's wife, "I will get the doctor now," then he pushed his way past Ueno, utterly unrecognized as one of the men he had hired by number, and nearly knocking him down.

When he righted himself again Ueno looked at Manjiro and fairly yelled, "This was an accidental stabbing, you know that! It was nothing more than a problem with a borrowed and overlarge scabbard! Damn it anyway, I didn't come here to stab your stupid innkeeper. I've got your brother's killers at the river and I've kept my men there, too, as a sign of good faith. I see you have the barbarians here, so we could effect our exchange right now. Two killers for two musicians, what do you say?"

It was another mistake, but he saw it too late.

"Our laborers said there were three murderers," Manjiro said, "and the only barbarian in the room just now is your own unworthy self."

Ueno opened his mouth to answer but the innkeeper surprised everyone just then by suddenly sitting back up. "I've got a good mind to report you to the authorities!" he said.

Unfortunately, however, he had lost his sense of direction and was facing Keiki instead of Ueno. He took hold of Keiki's sleeve and, with a great deal of effort, pulled himself to his feet again.

"Stop this now, sir, and rest," said Keiki. "Until the doctor gets here to plug up that wound you must not exert yourself."

But the innkeeper had looked back down at the table and let his eyes linger on that which Ichiro had brought him, his father's old samurai sword. And with the second surprise of unusual quickness, he picked it up and wheeled around again to charge, with unerring accuracy this time, on a true death trip toward Ueno. There was no scabbard on the sword, and its blade was honed.

"Stop!" screamed Manjiro, and Fumiko pulled her daughters out of the way, but it was Kyuzo who successfully intervened. He jumped onto the top of the banquet table, slid across the spilt blood and saké, and knocked the innkeeper far enough off course that his sword not only missed its target, but pierced that long middle stem of the flower arrangement. And when he swung the sword a second time the flower came with it, lightly slapping Ueno's face.

Ueno pulled his other sword out then, and thrust it into the innkeeper's throat, neatly severing his jugular vein and flipping him back onto the table at the same time. The innkeeper's body flopped like a fish and his eyes darted everywhere, then settled on the ceiling, where he could detect a bit of dust that he wished he could tell his wife about. He couldn't speak, however, for blood pulsed out of his mouth with quickly diminishing power, to the last few beats of his heart.

"Ohhh!" wailed his wife, and while the others locked their eyes on this newest recent horror, Ueno escaped from the inn.

Two men gave chase, Ichiro, who had just then come back with the doctor, and Kyuzo. But when they got outside both Ueno and the man who had accompanied him were gone.

50. *It's a Poor Life Anyway*

THE BARS OVER BY THE RIVER had initially been chosen only as a convenient waiting place for those few of Ueno's troops who had stuck with him, but an error in timing had caused them to arrive too early and by the time the trouble started at the inn's front door, most of them were drunk, and procrastinating about carrying out the horrid orders Ueno had given them before he had approached the inn—to slit the two prisoners' throats!

These troops were old and young, fat and thin, tall and short. One or two were like Ichiro, still true samurai, though they'd lived at the edges of poverty for decades, and one or two others were petty thieves, finding trouble wherever they went and occasionally spending time in various jails. They all had swords, for that had been the single precondition of Ueno's lottery, and all of those who accompanied him tonight had been at the waterfront that morning, to take part in the capture of the villains. There were no actual geisha with them as they waited, but there were women, sifted down through the hierarchy of Japanese nightlife to its lowest level, some of them drunk, others still oddly dignified, as if their lives had been decided by lottery as well.

Each of the river bars had a burning torch in front of it, and tied to stakes between two of them, rain-soaked and stinking and awaiting their fate, stood Numbers 75 and 111. They had been left alone for nearly an hour when three of their guards burst from a nearby bar with three drunk women in their wake. Their intention was to taunt the captives, to strut in front of them and jeer before finally following Ueno's instructions and putting their swords to their throats, but one of the women had a jar of cheap liquor with her and when the older captive saw it he opened his mouth, begging like a baby bird. She danced up to him, poured his mouth full, then danced back again to pull her filthy kimono apart, exposing herself.

"You won't see the likes of this again," she cackled, and the younger captive said, "Thank God for that, at least."

That made the three guards laugh and share their drinks with both the prisoners, telling the women to go back inside for more.

"It's a poor life anyway," one of the guards said, "and you're well out of it. I wouldn't trade places with you, don't get me wrong, but that's what I'll think when my time comes."

The younger captive had remained stealthy throughout the long day, looking for ways to escape, but the older one pleaded, "How about just forgetting it then, brother, how about letting us go?"—a remark that doubly infuriated his colleague because the identifying placards still hung on the wrong necks. He wore 75, while the old fool beside him wore 111. It irked him that people might think it was he who had spoken such pitiful words, mocking him for them after his death.

"Change these awful placards," he demanded. "Give me back my name!"

He strained against his ropes, jumping up and down along his stake. While some of the guards laughed at him, however, the irony of his words began to filter through the drunkenness of others, and when the women came back with stools as well as liquor, they all sat down around the prisoners, their swords across their laps, to think about their lives.

Until, that is, they began to hear a voice coming out of the dark.

"I am Momo of Shimoda. Do not worry, I am not selling chestnuts. I have come in order to return something you have lost . . ."

That is all it took for these guards to stand up from their stools again, to glance at each other and smile. Introspection, it seemed, unlike cheap liquor, was a commodity most easily spent.

"There's a man with a name you can have," one of the guards told the younger captive, "'Momo of Shimoda'! How would you like to die with that name tied around your neck?"

The guards took the prisoners from their stakes, told them to be silent if they wanted to stay alive for another half hour, then stepped into the darkness on tiptoe, not to injure anyone yet, but to take pleasure where they could find it, striking terror into the hearts of peasants, just as they used to do in the old days, when things were so much better.

It was a small pleasure, to be sure, but a real one, and so very un-Japanese. It wasn't in the code of samurai or in the code of innkeepers either.

51. | *Alas, We Are Defeated*

MANJIRO UNDERSTOOD the weaknesses of their position—that they would have been better off, if they hadn't had the women to worry about, by simply chasing Ueno into the dark to fight—but he gave his orders as if their position were strong. He told Ned to stay near Kyuzo, so he might not be injured a second time, kept Ace securely by his side, and asked Keiki to stand over nearest the inn's main door with Ichiro.

They waited that way for only a minute, each man seeking order in his mind, when, quite like Ueno's men a few seconds before them, they began to hear a voice from the dark.

"I am Momo of Shimoda! Not selling chestnuts!!!!"

This time, though, the voice was harried and coming toward them fast, another shouting voice by its side. *"Oh, help us, please good sirs! The ghosts of those drowned in the river are trying to strike us down!"*

When the two brothers appeared out of the fog they at first seemed to do so slowly, and at odds with their harrowing sound. In the next instant, however, they were upon the inn's defenders so quickly that it seemed like ordinary time had sped up. Momo came first, high-stepping along barefooted, as he had that morning at the shore. He flew straight into Ned, knocking his prosthesis in the air and himself into the mud, while Manzo, who was right behind his brother, easily cleaved the space between Ichiro and Keiki, shot up through the inn's open door and sped down the once immaculate hall. Their father's best wagon came next, only an instant behind them and still bearing those Buddhist flags and various country flowers. It turned sideways briefly, as if it were going to capsize, righted itself and flew among the scattering defenders like that American train gone off its track. It skidded through the mud on wildly spinning wheels, slammed against the inn's front step, then turned into a mad catapult from previous centuries and sent its ghastly cargo down the hallway after Manzo.

"Oh, ghosts of those drowned in the river!"

Manzo was still screaming when he dove onto the floor just a half a second before that shameful rocket screeched over them, its own mouth wide again, skimmed around the corner and was gone.

There was no culminating explosion, though a rumbling noise did seem to follow it, like low and timid thunder from an appalled and terrified audience of gods.

———

UENO'S EXHAUSTED SOLDIERS came out of the darkness to sway in front of the inn in shocked surprise, their laughs purged from their bellies by the unexpected success of the trick they had played. To push a wagon after the terrified peasants who owned it had seemed the height of comic relief to them, and even now they had trouble suppressing slight smiles. Their soberer colleagues, following behind them with the prisoners, had met Ueno and his aide on the path, so all were gathered in the rainy clearing by the time the inn's defenders regained themselves.

There were seven defenders, counting Ace and Ned, and counting Momo, who had climbed from the mud in a fury and got his samurai bow and his single old arrow from the wagon just as his brother staggered back up the hall. And there were twelve recently sobered soldiers with Ueno. The women had come outside, too, but pressed themselves against the building, and the two bereft prisoners were on their knees in the middle of everything, hands still tied behind them with hemp rope.

This is how the stage was set for Lord Okubo's reappearance at the inn's front door. Maybe Einosuke's ghost had visited him, coaxing him from slumber, or maybe it had truly been the ghosts of those drowned in the river, or perhaps it had only been a dream he had had, but something had awakened him a few minutes earlier and he'd risen and dressed and wondered what was going on with everyone below. It had been dark in his room and dark in the corridors that surrounded it and dark on the narrow back stairway which he descended with caution, but with a calm and rested heart.

"Manjiro? Fumiko?" he called. "Why was I allowed to sleep for so long?"

He asked his question without reproach, even though on the inn's first floor, too, no one was waiting to greet him, to tell him what had happened thus far. He knew he should have taken less of Kyuzo's sleeping powders—he had known it in the garden before he took them—but the idea of seceding from the world had so appealed to him that, in a certain way, he had hoped not to awaken at all.

When he first saw Einosuke's head in the hallway Lord Okubo believed it was an animal, some wounded forest creature come in through the side door, and he feared it might bite him if he tried to pass it by. He spoke to it once, saying, "Get away!" but when it neither ran nor prepared to attack him, he took an unlit torch from its place by the bath and shook it as if it were his sword. And then he had a memory he hadn't had in years, of his first son, Toshiro, and Einosuke, too, stomping through the woods behind his castle, in search of mushrooms one late autumn day. Einosuke, only about six at the time, had come across a *tanuki,* a badger, who would also neither run nor get off the path. He had said "Get away!" then, too, much as his father did now, until the badger grew tired of him and departed.

"I will emulate you now, Einosuke," muttered his father, "so if you are watching from the grave you will be proud."

But the instant he stepped forward with his unlit torch he knew it wasn't a badger in the hallway. And as gently as he'd once taught all of his sons to brush twigs aside when searching for mushrooms, he knelt to sweep the hair away from Einosuke's missing yet bottomless eyes. There were scratches on Einosuke's cheeks and a bloodless rift in his forehead, and the straight white line of his teeth with his tongue sticking out.

"Oh wretched life that sends a father such a message," said a voice in Lord Okubo's head, but he quieted the voice with all of his will and, with all of his strength, wrapped his fist around Einosuke's somehow still combed hair and lifted his head from the floor, letting it swing from his hand as he walked.

That is how he presented himself to the weary gathering outside.

Ace saw him first and whispered, "Ah, Diogenes," and when Manjiro looked where he pointed, and beheld what his father carried, he ran toward Fumiko and his nieces, giving up, for yet another moment, the firmest resolve he had ever known, in order to spare them the sight. Ace looked toward Fumiko, too, but stayed where he was.

Lord Okubo, in turn, brought Einosuke's head to his chest and held his left palm out in front of him, obscuring the view of everyone else. He wanted to find a seat of honor for it, like the one Momo and Manzo's father had intended the wagon to provide, and when he couldn't easily find something better he climbed upon that wrecked wagon itself, placed the head in his lap, and covered it entirely with his robe. His own head hung down so his face wasn't visible, but his legs were there for everyone to see, bowed and naked, as pale as the quality of all human life.

"It is the price one pays to live in this world," he said. "I hope things will be better in the next one."

No one knew how to act anymore, not even Ueno. At first he thought to simply leave with his troops, fading back into the fog. And then he thought to step silently forward and slit the throats of the prisoners himself, before they could find their voices and tell the truth about what had happened at the seashore that day. He felt an unwanted pity for Lord Okubo, miserable upon that wagon, contempt for Manjiro, cowering up against the wall with his women, and finally a distilled and focused hatred of himself, for disorder was at his heart's cold center now and disorder was what he thought he'd cast out of it, many years ago when he'd first left home, and time and time again thereafter.

It was such a distressing moment for him that he might have stayed that way, caught in the web of his uncertainty, had Kyuzo not read his mind and spoken.

"There is order in battle, sir," he said, "and I think we should try to retrieve a little of it before we die."

He had been watching only Ueno all this time, and was standing in the center of everything with his sword out.

Fumiko was still in Manjiro's arms, her daughters well behind them now, but when Tsune heard her lover's words, and saw Ueno turn toward him, his ugly lips pursed, she moved away from the rest of her family, came out from under the eave of the inn, and stepped toward Kyuzo, really floating toward him, as if on a stage built for only the two of them. She said quite softly, "With frozen water that tastes painfully bitter, a sewer rat relieves in vain his parched throat."

In the history of life itself, no expression of love had ever been so strange.

Kyuzo smiled, briefly considering that if he had Tsune to live for he might not fight Ueno after all. He could feel his arthritic knees and oft-sprung toenail, but he also remembered what his father's ghost had told him at that small Buddhist temple behind Lord Tokugawa's lodge. *"In the rain near Nijo Castle, under the falling wisteria."* So he did not think he would die here, for though there was certainly rain, it was a month too soon for wisteria and Kyoto was a great distance off.

Without anyone moving very much, the two men found themselves inside a newly formed circle, with everyone who composed it, save Manjiro, content to let whatever happened now be final. The innkeeper's widow was once again watching from the doorway, her hands tightly holding one of Ichiro's arms, and Lord Okubo peeked up from his perch atop the wagon, like a senile old god lowered down from the heavens on ropes.

With an impertinent wiggle of his hips Kyuzo let Ueno know that he could attack first, if he wished, but it did not, as he hoped it would, make Ueno angry. Rather, he accepted the offer as if it were due his higher rank, and ran at Kyuzo fast, to slash his blade under the older man's arms. It did not come close to working. Kyuzo simply paused until the last possible second, then parried with an ease and grace that everyone watching had to admire.

But to everyone's surprise, as well, he did not immediately strike his own blade home. Instead, he let Ueno turn to face him one more time. It worried Ichiro to see such a thing, for he was beginning to understand the value of economy.

Ueno's second charge was even less effective than his first, and when Kyuzo stepped aside again, dancing out of his way like a matador, Ueno came face-to-face with Momo, the frightened little shit man, who, in order to try to compensate for his own disastrous entry, had been trailing the action with his bow and arrow, pretending that he would be allowed to fight next, to take on the winner, just as he always did at home.

Ueno stopped and smiled at Momo, muddy in his purloined samurai clothes, then laughed at an idea that came to him, perching upon the wires that strung his mind together like the body of a legless crow. He pointed his sword at Momo's chest, and utterly ignoring Kyuzo for a moment, turned to speak to Manjiro. "Behold the third murderer of Einosuke," he shouted, "the slothful and defeated spirit who dispatched your elder brother with his sword!"

"Huh?" said Momo, but Manjiro stepped away from his place by his nieces and sister-in-law, walking between the fighters toward Momo. To be easily fooled is a common symptom of grief gone crazy, though it is not so commonly recognized as such.

"Were you on the beach that day, *ronin?*" he shouted.

"*Ronin?* Who, me? I am Momo of Shimoda, not selling chest-nuts!"

Even in his terror Momo was pleased to be mistaken for a samurai, *ronin* or not. But an unfortunate by-product of that pleasure was that he did not in the least remember that he still had his bow up and was pointing his decrepit arrow at Manjiro, whose sword was loosed from its scabbard by then and swinging between Momo and the other two captives. "All three killers are before us now!" he shouted. "And I will dispatch them, one at a time!"

"Who, me? Who, me?" said Momo.

Kyuzo, however, smiled at him, held up his hands, and began walking toward him, for he not only understood that this was wrong, but also that Momo's growing panic would soon move from his heart and mouth to his fingers, and he would momentarily release his arrow. Lord Okubo saw it too and said, "Uh, oh," just as Kyuzo dove toward Manjiro, shoving him out of the way. So when Momo did, in fact, release his arrow, it missed Manjiro entirely but came into perfect contact with Kyuzo's forehead, as if that were its target in the first place. It planted itself deeply, like a foreign flag into Japanese soil, erasing the worry lines that furrowed Kyuzo's brow, cutting through his current thoughts of saving the life of his lover's fiancé, and embedding itself in the center of his brain. Since it was a particularly sharp arrow, lovingly honed by Momo each evening, it pruned Kyuzo's memories of his childhood in Kyoto and his years of happy study with his father, and pushed up against his cache of Zen koan and poems. His love for Tsune disappeared beside his recent theories on the wind and intransigence, and he forgot his anxiety over Ichiro's defection as easily as he might have were it an errant and unnoticed cicada, singing in a tree at night.

There was one set of memories, though, one set of impulses, that the arrow could not have purged had it exploded in Kyuzo's brain like a bomb, and those were the ones that defined his skill as a fighter. He did hesitate, for his vision flew from him and his hearing went off in a roar, but his arms and legs changed direction in an instant, away from their original trajectory, and he plunged his sword into Ueno's chest, easily piercing his heart.

"MURDER!" Tsune screamed, falling beneath Kyuzo's falling body, and when Momo slumped beside them both, shaking and shitting and howling, Manzo fell on top of him, lest Manjiro still not understand the mistake he had made and try to take his brother's life. "He has come with salvaged plunder," he cried, "to honor the Okubo family and the dead!"

Ichiro and Keiki came fast after that, joining Manjiro at the center of the clearing with their swords up, but by then Ueno's soldiers had put theirs back into scabbards that fit them, or simply laid them on the ground, too stunned to act, or too tired, or not enough compelled by loyalty.

And a second later they disappeared into the fog and the dark.

"'How dead the world is, how bleak this day,'" Keiki whispered, but the eyes of all the others were on Lord Okubo as he climbed down off the wagon, placed his son's head on the seat he'd just vacated, leaned past Manzo, and put a hand on Momo's shoulder. "Thank you young man," he said, "I appreciate the sentiment. No one has honored our family in a good long time."

Some of the men went to their women after that, as men always seem to do when battle is done; Ned to O-bata, his muddy prosthesis back in front of him, and Ichiro, though far more circumspectly, to the general vicinity of Keiko. Keiki turned toward Tsune, who was like a sister to him, while Manjiro walked to the damaged wagon, removed the upper garment he was wearing, and placed it over his beloved brother's head.

"Good-bye, dear Einosuke," he said. "Remember me to our ancestors. Tell them I am coming, but not now."

He, too, went to Tsune then. Her hands were drenched in Kyuzo's blood, but her eyes were steady as she watched him come.

"Alas, I have survived," he said.

"Alas, we are defeated," she replied.

Ace, in the meantime, walked directly over to Fumiko and looked into her eyes. A line that had been plaguing him from the essay he was always reading, the one he had quoted to her in the woods, *"Accept the place the divine providence has found for you . . ."* was in truth followed by the words, "*. . . the society of your contemporaries, the connection of events.*" And though he had dismissed it entirely in the bath, he understood that the society of her contemporaries was what she needed right then. And by extension, of course, what she didn't need was him.

That was all. Einosuke's true murderer lay dead before them—Numbers 75 and 111 soon spewed the real story out—and the rain started coming down in sheets again.

As the evening turned to night, however, after less than an hour had passed, some of them went back inside to eat, others to sleep, while still others removed their bloody clothing and sank into the inn's miraculous bath. Fumiko took Junichiro there, when he awoke, yawning, as if nothing at all had happened. Keiko and Masako followed them, and eventually even Lord Okubo. They bathed by themselves, as families often tended to do, in that beautiful outside section of the bath, directly over a hot springs that came to warm them from the center of the earth.

Afterword

BUT IF, IN LESS THAN AN HOUR, they could eat and sleep and bathe, think what the coming days and weeks and months could do.

Lord Okubo was so moved by Manzo's words on behalf of his brother that he went with them the next morning to meet their father, not only in order to praise his sons, but to offer to pay for the repairs to their wagon. And when he returned to the inn he ordered the innkeeper's corpse removed to the garden, in preparation for his funeral pyre. It had been a bad business, and he wondered at his surprising optimism. He continued to believe it had something to do with the omen of the crows, but more to do with the incredible sleep he had enjoyed. So though he still mourned Einosuke, would never forget such a good and filial son, he could not help wishing he'd had a chance to properly thank Kyuzo, too, for he finally understood that Kyuzo was the real "Kambei" in their midst, the last of the great samurai warriors. He intended to have Kyuzo's ashes interred at the inn as well, but Tsune insisted that he send them to Kyoto. *"In the rain near Nijo Castle, under the falling wisteria"* had not, after all, been a call to self-destruction, but directions to the family burial site.

By the time Kyuzo's ashes got there the wisteria were in full bloom, and rain, at that time of year, was common.

———

ONE MIGHT THINK that Commodore Perry would have worried over the fact that while two minstrels left him only one came back, but in truth he hardly noticed, for on the day of Ace's return, April 24, 1854, two Japanese stowaways were discovered on board the fleet ship *Mississippi,* and he had to decide whether or not to honor their requests for political asylum. And a few days later, when a sailor by the name of G. W. Parish plunged to his death from the top of a mast, he never gave the minstrels another thought. He was simply too busy, and, like Keiki and Ichiro, it was not in his makeup to think about the past.

For a time after the American departure Ned and O-bata stayed in Shimoda. They were married in a Buddhist ceremony at Ryosenji Temple, near that monk's tomato garden, and she bore him two children in eighteen months. A few years later, when peasants were finally allowed surnames, they took the name "Maki," and had five more children who gained musical reputations, first locally, then throughout the land. One of Ned's great-grandchildren, in fact, immigrated to California in the 1920s, where he had a son who came back to Japan before World War II, with an American jazz band. That, however, is another story.

And for the rest, as well, life was indelibly altered. Ichiro went to work for the innkeeper's widow, quitting the samurai life and, some years later, allowing himself to be adopted by her. He hung his sword on that crossbeam, next to the innkeeper's. He still loved Keiko, and sometimes went to Edo to court her, but Keiko declined to take him as a lover. She stayed single for a decade after her father's death—eschewing even dancing—until continuing to do so began to hinder Masako's chances to find a good match. And then she married without complaint, to someone chosen for her, after careful investigation, by her mother and her Uncle Manjiro.

Momo and Manzo, in the meantime, formed the Shimoda Marine Waste Company, and thrived.

ALL OF THIS OCCURRED, or began to occur, within days of Commodore Perry's departure, but what happened to Manjiro and Tsune and Fumiko, and to Ace Bledsoe, as well, took longer.

Immediately after he left Japan Ace grew reclusive again, for when he'd agreed so readily to come ashore he'd been sure that this would be his story, and it wasn't. He gave up music much like Keiko gave up dance, and returned to his father's Pennsylvania farm. Ace had never met John Brown, but he'd read about him, and by early 1857 began frequenting abolitionist meetings where Brown's name came up. He didn't speak at those meetings, or otherwise involve himself, until one morning when he found two runaway slave girls sleeping in his barn. He knelt to watch them—the nearest one lovely, the farther one not—and by the time they awoke and clung to each other he had decided to offer his help. A month later he did it again, this time for an entire family, and by the beginning of 1858 he had finally found his passion, the authentic society of his contemporaries. He didn't worry, this time, about whether or not it was the truly portentous story of his life, perhaps because it was.

In Edo, during those same years, Manjiro was busy learning Einosuke's old job, as his father's representative to the Great Council. At first he had difficulty outliving his reputation—to some he would always be a troublemaker, to others a hero named Kambei—but Lord Abe, whose censure had been temporary, needed his language skills and praised him publicly once or twice, and soon talk of what had happened began to die down. He lived in the remodeled Edo house with Fumiko and Keiko and Junichiro, though Masako had found her own life's path by then, and spent most of her time at her master's studio, carving Noh masks. She had first gotten the idea from seeing Ned's nose.

Lord Okubo went to Edo frequently, and when it became clear to him that a match between Manjiro and Tsune was no longer favored by Lord Tokugawa, or even by the principals themselves, he began, ever so slyly, to encourage a union between Manjiro and Fumiko. Such an idea distressed them both at first, but by about the time Ace joined John Brown's army, crossing the Mason-Dixon line to occupy the United States Armory at Harper's Ferry, they came to terms with it.

Manjiro and Fumiko were married on October 17, 1859, five and a half years after Einosuke's death and the very day that Ace emptied his rifle into the American militia, and died. Fumiko thought of him that day, briefly wondering what had happened to him. She thought of Einosuke, too, of course, but the match she had hoped to find as a girl, the man she had hoped to marry, that kindred spirit, that *jibun no ki no atta hito,* slept beside her on her futon that night, and for every night thereafter for the rest of her life.

Tsune never married but stayed near Keiki, advising him as his star began to rise. She took lovers often, never Keiki himself, and never again Manjiro, but always older men, like Kyuzo. She seemed able to visit the Edo house with the same ease of spirit she had always had, an impunity at which the others marveled. She was a good sister to Fumiko, a welcome sister-in-law to Manjiro, and an excellent aunt, not only to Einosuke's three children, but to the two new babies that arrived.

And when Keiki finally did fulfill his father's greatest wish, by being adopted into a hereditary family and becoming the last Japanese Shogun, Tsune, for a time, was the most powerful woman in all of Japan.

That was not for another decade, though, and in the intervening years she visited the inn in Shimoda each April, to walk in the garden and mourn Kyuzo. It was easier and more appropriate than going to Kyoto.

Both the inn and the bath are still there today, by the way, in the heart of Rendaiji Village, a forty-five-minute walk up the Inozawa River from the bay.

Acknowledgments

I AM INDEBTED TO the Japan-United States Friendship Commission and the National Endowment for the Arts, as well as to the Japan Foundation, for generous support during more than a decade of work on this novel. Support from the University of Nevada, Las Vegas Sabbatical Committee and the Center for Advanced Research provided much-needed time for research and writing.

I want to thank my wife, Virginia Wiley, for her belief in me and her willingness to give me honest appraisals of my work at every turn, for more than three decades now. I also want to thank my agent, Gail Hochman, for her unending support of this novel, her willingness to read and reread too many drafts to count, and her tenacity on my behalf. Thanks, also, to my friends, Charles and Keiko DeWolf, Tatsuji and Mineko Suzuki, Fumi Yoshimura, and Ayako Hara, for their help and kindness during my many sojourns to Japan.

Readers of this book will find references and small quotes from two films by Akira Kurosawa: *Shichinen no Samurai* (*The Seven Samurai*) and *Ikiru* (*To Live*); as well as from the eleventh-century novel, *Genji Monogatari* (*Tale of Genji*) and from the poetry of Bashō. Shakespeare and Ralph Waldo Emerson also peek through the curtains once in a while. In addition, the book is intended as a prequel to my 1986 novel, *Soldiers in Hiding*, which is referenced, in sly ways, here and there throughout the work.

A few historical figures appear in the book, and speak words that I put in their mouths—Commodore Perry, Lord Abe, Lord Okubo, Lord Tokugawa, Keiki—but their acts and those of the characters I made up are entirely fictional, so if they're turning in their graves over what I made them say, I apologize.

Excerpts from the novel appeared, in altered form, in the *Kyoto Review*, and the "Whitman Sampler" chapter was published in a beautiful fine arts edition by the Perishable Press.

FICTION   Wiley, Richard.
Wiley
           Commodore Perry's
           minstrel show.